A LIFE ALOFT

A LIFE ALOFT

FROM MONTANA ROOTS TO PAN AM WINGS

JACK W. BURKE

Glide Path Press
Hurstwood, Washington

CONTENTS

For my wife, Scotty, who put up with me for seventy years.

My folks always told me that if I got interested in a girl, be sure to get to know her mother. Genes are very important, and they were right. Scotty's mother, Nonie, was a perfect person, and Scotty was just like her; for my daughter Shannon and son Shawn; and for Captain Ralph Savory, our Chief Pilot of the Alaska Division of Pan Am, a great pilot and manager. He kept the division operating for twenty years after the FAA wanted to close it.

"I've had a great life; I really have. And I've been lucky—just awful lucky—in everything I've done."

—Jack W. Burke

INTRODUCTION

BORN in 1922 on an eastern Montana homestead, Jack Burke gazed skyward almost from the time he could walk. Working on the family ranch from dawn till dusk, unloading forty-ton boxcars and minding his dad's grain elevator instilled in Jack the enduring values of hard work, independence and accountability from an early age. Having already shouldered a man-sized share of responsibility, he thought nothing of making his first solo flight at fourteen.

By sixteen, Jack was flying for local companies, and by eighteen he was already instructing and well into an extraordinary aviation career that would span seventy-five years—distinguished by military service in three wars and over 40,000 hours of flight time—with no signs of ending anytime soon.

Jack's life story—as unfurled here in his own words and with his characteristic aplomb, humor and humility—has truly been one of "firsts," in both his revered Montana homeland and distant skies over many continents. He was, quite possibly, the first, if not the only, person ever to teach *geese* how to fly. He was likely the first ranch kid ever to have a steer, a deer, a collie *and* two pigs as pets. And he was no doubt the first thirteen-year-old to not only *own* a Model T, but to wrap it in an "airplane" body and drive it, unchaperoned, 300 miles to Yellowstone Park.

Jack's "life aloft" has been filled with many firsts as well. Whether hopping ranch kids in a Piper J-5, hunting coyotes from a "ski-plane," flying the bush in a single-engine, eight-passenger plane in Alaska, piloting the massive flying boats across the perilous North Atlantic in the dark days of World War Two, braving the fog-shrouded Aleutians or the "hellish winds" and ice on the "white-knuckle"

Whitehorse-to-Juneau run, pioneering four-engine passenger flights
to the far north, helping propel Pan Am and the world into the jet
age aboard the durable Boeing 707, or traversing the globe in the
majestic 747, the crown jewel in Pan Am's gleaming fleet—Jack was
always, it seems, "in the right place at the right time" to be part of
the next great leap in aviation, even though he was often barely old
enough to meet the minimum age requirements.

But Jack's youth never stopped him from channeling his one
true passion, flying, into a vibrant forty-year career with Pan Am, a
company that at one time had as much, if not more, international
clout than the U.S. government, risked everything on the 707—and
again on the 747—to help the fledgling jet age get off the ground,
and provided a degree of style and elegance in passenger service and
comfort that commercial aviation will never see again. And Jack was
part and parcel of it all.

Did I say that *flying* was Jack's one true passion? It may be,
professionally—or his "hobby," as he likes to call it—but the one
true love of Jack's life is Scotty, his wife of more than sixty years
who, sadly, succumbed to cancer in 2007. High school sweethearts,
married young and with a touch of wanderlust, they enjoyed many
fine years seeing the world on Jack's wings before finally settling
down and starting a family.

"They never had an argument," proclaim their children, Shannon
and Shawn, who urged Jack to write down his stories. The result is
this book, and the many funny, exciting and poignant treasures it
holds. In it you will meet the legendary characters Jack flew and
rubbed shoulders with, from Rodeo Champ "Cowboy" Bob Askin,
eccentric fishing baron Nick Bez, and the great aviator and pioneer
himself, Charles Lindbergh, to "battle-ready" Mrs. Burkheimer, the
Beatles and many more.

You will share Jack's "best day ever with Pan Am," January
31st, 1968—the first day of Vietnam's bloody Tet Offensive—
when he dove 5,000 feet in a 707 through shredded skies onto
the runway of besieged Saigon airport, bringing over 200 stranded

Vietnamese—many of them children—to safety. "Any of our pilots could have done it," he modestly says. But on that day, he was the only one who did.

Despite his exemplary service record and lofty credentials, Jack Burke remains refreshingly down-to-earth, humble "as the day is long," and true to his Montana roots. "It's been a good life," he reflects from his Hurstwood, Washington home. And much of it has been memorably captured in the words, pictures and pages that follow.

So ease your seat back, slip your shoes off, get comfortable and "stand by" to be entertained, enlightened and enamored with the life adventure of a man who rose from modest Montana beginnings to aviation's loftiest realms. Jack's unique stories, memories and insights offer not only an "insider's" view from the flight deck, a raft of entertaining characters and adventures, and vivid, moving portraits of a vanished era. They will, more importantly, acquaint you with one of the finest gentlemen you will ever meet—and, naturally, provide a smooth landing as well.

Charles Ganong
August, 2010

CHAPTER 1

AT HOME ON THE RANGE

Montana Roots

MY father, John "JC" Burke, was born on August 14, 1883 in Oxford Junction, Iowa, to Clarence and Sarah Burke. The family moved by covered wagon to a ranch in the Red River Valley near Erie, North Dakota, south of Bismarck, when my dad was a year old. They farmed there for several years.

My dad married Catherine Warner in October, 1910 in Fargo, North Dakota. They soon moved to Ryegate, Montana, where they filed for a homestead. Later they moved to Lavina, about forty miles north of Billings, and Ismay, Montana, where my dad homesteaded, raised white faces—cattle—and managed the Columbia grain elevators.

Lavina wasn't much more than a general store and a post office. I was born on my folks' homestead there, although I always said I was born in Ismay. I have two older sisters, Margaret and Catherine, both deceased. I'm the baby of the family.

The area where we eventually lived—near Ismay, Montana—looks a lot like the Bonanza show on television: pine hills, fine land for winter grazing. This was about forty miles out of Miles City, Montana. My dad also homesteaded there as a cattle rancher.

My dad was a great guy. He always had that market card from Minneapolis in his shirt pocket. Prior to homesteading, he pitched major league baseball for the club that became the Minneapolis Twins. He pitched for them for two or three years, and then his arm went out. That's when he came out to Montana to homestead.

Under the terms of the Homestead Act, each qualified applicant received a quarter section of land. A section is six hundred and forty acres. Whenever there was a depression, in a dry year, my dad bought up rangeland to add to his 160-acre homestead. He ended up with ten sections—6,400 acres—for which he paid a dollar an acre.

My dad, John "JC" Burke, was a "good little Irishman."
That Stetson hat was the only one he ever wore.
He'd buy a new one about every five years.

Go West, Young Man

It wasn't "all work and no play" on the homestead. My dad had heard so much about Oregon that he thought we should go out and see it. So he bought a new Model T, cloth top. He paid $380 for it, brand new.

I was less than a year old, in diapers. One of my sisters was two years older than me; the other was five years older, maybe six to eight. Can you imagine taking three kids like that—with a rack on the back, a tent and all the camping gear—driving and spending a whole month, going out to the coast and Portland?

We camped all the way. We would get a campground where they had a shower, or we would find a creek or a lake. We spent a whole month going and coming. But even in those days, there was a lot of traffic. My dad had always been back here on the ranch country. "I think there's too many people out here," he said.

Name That Town

I was about six months old when the folks moved to Ismay. My dad ran a grain elevator—which was only busy in the fall and spring—and got another ranch in Ismay. It was a nice spot: we had a creek running through it; and if there was any rain at all, we always had a nice meadow that we could irrigate. It was nice living; it was different.

You could buy grazing land with good, wild timothy grass on it. It was better than hay, and loaded with protein—good for the cows. You could buy that land for a dollar an acre. So my dad would buy acreage.

Ismay was an incorporated little town of about 2,000, south of Miles City. Ismay got its name like this: the superintendent, the big boss who was building the Milwaukee Railroad through there, had two daughters. His family was moving along with him. One of the daughters was named Isabelle, and one was Maybelle, I think it was. So he put those two names together and formed *Ismay.*

Ismay was a real busy little town. It had a big, wide main street. Cars parked angled-in at the curb on both sides, and all the way down the middle. The main street was only three blocks long. At each intersection was a great big concrete block with a big flagpole on it. On a Saturday night, you could hardly find a place to park there.

All the ranchers would come in to do their weekly shopping and go to the dance. We had a great big general store. They sold machinery and everything, and there was a great big banquet and dance hall upstairs. They would always have music on Saturday night.

At one time, Ismay, a main shipping point to the big livestock yards in the Midwest, was one of the busiest towns in the area. The old highway went through there. But eventually the town dried up, because they ran the new highway just five miles out of Ismay. And the old highway, Highway 10, went right through Miles City.

The houses in Ismay started to get vacant, and they had just built the new school—a nice, big, brick school. The town was just dwindling down to nothing. A few years ago, Ismay had declined to a population of about ten people.

Two years old on the ranch in Ismay, Montana.

Looking for a coyote with my cork gun. I would find plenty later on (Chapter 3).

Break an Egg

As a child, I would do things that I shouldn't. Occasionally my sisters, Kate and Marg, would take after me with brooms. I scurried for the nearest refuge—usually underneath the bed. Those beds sat up fairly high, so there was room enough to hide beneath them.

But my sisters would get on either side of the bed and poke at me with their brooms. It didn't take long for them to thump me good. But they wouldn't chase me outside, so I would run up to my dad's elevator, two blocks away.

My mother, who was heavyset, was going to bake an angel food cake one day for somebody's birthday, and she sent me up to the store to get a couple dozen eggs. I had a great big tricycle with a big wheel. It was just like a bicycle, but it was a tricycle. "Now, don't take that trike up there," my mother said. It was only two or three blocks. "You'll drop those eggs for sure."

Well, when she wasn't looking, I took the trike and headed for the store in Ismay. We didn't live too far from town. Sure enough, I dropped those eggs on the way home. And I had to tell Mom. They were in a sack and they were all broken.

She just couldn't stand it when all those eggs were broken. So she got out the fly-swatter and started chasing me around the outside of the house. I went around the house about four times. Finally, she started laughing. She sat down in the swing, and I sat down there with her, and she started laughing. That's the closest I ever came to being spanked.

My mother always gave me the word for something. And she was pretty fast, for her size. She always won the races at the picnics. She couldn't catch me, though.

I lost my mother when she was just fifty-two. She had a tumor, compounded by high blood pressure. In those days they just used gas to put them to sleep. They tried three times to put her to sleep so they could take that tumor out, because they knew it was malignant.

But the least bit of gas would elevate her blood pressure. "She'll have a stroke if we give her any more gas," the doctor said. So they tried to get her weight down; she was always heavy. She was never sick or anything until she got stomach cancer. She must have weighed around two hundred pounds. When she died, she was less than a hundred pounds.

She was in the hospital for about six months. My dad had no insurance; he just paid for it from what he saved at the mill. He ran an awful good business. It was amazing because the ranchers all trusted him so much.

Goose Down

One of my first and best friends in Ismay, Charles Redman, lived on a ranch not far away. I spent a lot of time at his house. He was an only child, and there were lots of things we could do.

His folks were great people. His mother had a real sense of humor. She raised geese, which she would bring in and sell at Thanksgiving and Christmas. She was proud of her geese because they always rated number one.

I suppose you could say that my career as a flight instructor started on the Redman's ranch. I was always getting something to fly out there. The geese would hop around the barnyard, flapping their wings and trying to fly. They were young geese, but they were all feathered out. So I said to Chuck one time, "I think those guys could fly if they could just get a take-off."

About two miles away rose a big hill. It sloped on three sides, but was almost vertical on one—about a three-hundred-foot drop. "You know, your mom's in there busy canning," I said slyly to Chuck. She had been picking peas and beans, and was in the kitchen canning. "I'll betcha we could get the dog and drive those geese up that hill." The hill was behind the house, not where she was looking out.

So we did. We herded those geese up there. They were pretty tired by the time they got to the top, so we let them rest. We were lucky, I explained to Charles, because a headwind was blowing over the cliff, and that would give the geese some updraft.

We lined the geese all up and got the dog to chase them off the cliff. The geese really started flopping and squawking, but they appeared to be thinking. They lost about a hundred feet in altitude before they finally got organized.

The Redman's house had two bedrooms upstairs and a steep roof. Below was a slanting porch that was all screened in, off the kitchen. Jetta, Charles' mother, was in the kitchen, busy canning the garden peas and beans she picked. That's why Charles and I thought we could get the dog and those geese up around the back of the house without her seeing us.

Suddenly a KER-THUMP from up on the roof startled her. As she opened the door to go outside and investigate, an exhausted goose slid off the roof.

That night at their supper she was telling her husband, "You know, there was a crazy goose got on the roof, and I don't know how it got on there. But I went out and this goose fell right off at my feet. It just shook its head a little bit and away it went, to where the other geese were.

"How do you think that goose got on the roof?" she wondered aloud.

Winfield, Charles' father, said, "I don't know how he got on that roof. He *couldn't* get on that roof." Charles and I were sitting there, just about busting.

We didn't tell Charles' mother about our part in the episode for a long time, because when she took her geese in to the market, she got docked; a bunch of them had bent breastbones. And the geese that didn't hit the roof thought they were landing in the water. They put their feet out, and then they would just roll.

Finally, about three years later, Mrs. Redman got the word back from somewhere. She was telling us about that goose. She was laughing about it, though, because she really did have a good sense of humor.

And those geese, they liked flying! "Squawk! Squawk! Squawk!" It was a mile or so from that butte down to the barnyard. They headed for the barnyard and they all landed there. Of course, I would have gotten into trouble if Jetta had seen her geese flying overhead.

We had a good life; we really did. Charles Redman's two sons-in-law took the ranches over. He and his wife bought a little house in Miles City. She has cancer, but she's doing okay with the chemo.

But Charlie—we never called him 'Chuck;' it was always Charles. His mother called him Charles. We sure had a lot of fun out there. I used to spend a lot of time with him because we were the same age. It's funny because he came just about to the top of my shoulder. But when we started high school, he started growing. And by the time he was a senior, he was six foot. Now he's a head taller than I am.

The Redmans are awfully nice people; they really are. But I've never been able to get them to Seattle. They travel a lot because they love to square dance. They go to Canada and different places. But I don't think he's ever even been to Spokane. He won't have anything to do with the big cities. I've tried to get him out here to go sailing with us on the little sailboats.

Anything That Flies

I was always near anything that flew. In those days, we would see an airplane go over the ranch maybe once a month. I would run as far as I could to watch that airplane. Most of these were World War I models that they had bought in surplus.

I knew what I wanted to do from the time I was five years old. I had a big, wide swing. I was building model airplanes, so I built a cockpit on that swing. And I put a propeller on it, so when my sisters pushed me, that propeller would spin around.

Back then, we were always building big kites, and trying to hang on to the tail. We would put a loop in the tail so we could put our feet in and sit in it. But we never, ever got in the air.

We also built parachutes out of heavy tissue paper. We put a pin in it and just bent it, and the wind would blow it right up the line. And we would put some knots before we got to the kite. Then we would get chickens that were about half grown—just starting to get feathers—and put them on the parachute.

They would go up there and hit the knot in the string. Down they would come, just as nice as could be. It never hurt the chickens. They were beginning to get little feathers.

I built one parachute for myself. We had a fairly high garage. I jumped off the garage, and of course it didn't have a chance to open. I sprained my ankle.

Trick or Treat

As kids we had other kinds of fun in Ismay. On Halloween, the bigger kids—the high school kids—would always upset the outhouses. Everybody had an outhouse; there were no inside toilets.

The pranksters would get a good cinch on their horse, throw a rope around the top of the outhouse, give it a pull and over it would go. They really wouldn't hurt it; they would just have to set it back up. But it was upset.

They had an itty bitty constable in Ismay; a little guy about five-foot-two, overweight. He thought he was the FBI, so the kids kind of had it in for him. They cornered him on Halloween and dropped him up in the jail. That was about the worst thing I ever saw them do.

A Dollar a Day

I worked on our ranch in Ismay. We would work for two hours in the morning, then come in and have a great big steak and egg breakfast. We would go out and work until lunch, and come in and have lunch. Then we would come in about dark and have another meal. You know, that was a twelve-hour day, and we got a dollar a day.

That was during the Depression, of course, and you were glad to have *any* kind of a job. When I got to comparing my Pan Am salary with that dollar-a-day, I figured that I was Rockefeller, you know. You just couldn't believe the difference.

We were driving the truck and the tractors out there at eight, nine, ten years old. We had two teams of the real nice Clydesdale horses, and they were just as tame as they could be. I would go out and feed them, and hook them to the sleigh.

Putting up hay on the ranch.

I thought I was having a great time, you know, getting my dollar a day. I would get to go to town—Miles City—about every two weeks.

Ismay had two general stores. The drugstore had a great big fountain. It was the only fountain in town, and the only ice cream. Of course I had some school buddies in town. We would get a nickel apiece—you could get a big milkshake for fifteen cents.

We went to the drugstore, where the big, fat pharmacist—a nice guy—saw the three of us come in. We each laid our nickel up on the counter for one big milkshake. And he got that big tin shaker and filled it right to the top. So when he got all through, we had three real nice, big tall mugs of milkshake—for a nickel apiece.

We didn't think we were poor, because everybody was in the same fix, you know. And there were two years of drought where we didn't have very much hay, and we had to cut all the river-bottom stuff that we could find to get the cattle through the winter.

But nobody was looking for a government hand-out, you know. Finally, in the third year, it started to rain, so we knew we were going to get some feed, but the cattle were getting down on weight. And there was no market for the cattle. Finally the government would buy any piece of stock for twenty dollars.

So here we were selling those big two- and three-year-old steers—you know, they would make a thousand pounds of hamburger—for twenty dollars apiece.

Deer Friend

My dad found a little buck, a little deer. I guess his mother had been shot during the hunting season. We brought the little buck in, nursed him with a bottle and got him to grow up.

We had a great big collie dog. I guess that deer figured that he was a collie dog, too, because he went every place the Collie dog did. And, of course, he would try to get in the house—only to have trouble getting his horns through the door.

That little buck would follow that darned dog everywhere it went. I would go out and load the sleigh with hay with a pitchfork, and he would get right up on the hayrack with the dog. And would you believe that one of them would run ahead of the horses on each side—the dog on one side and the deer on the other!

We had that deer for six or seven years. My mother made a big red jacket for him. In the fall we put it on him so that everybody could see that he was a pet. And he lived right there, just like he was part of the family.

He never left the ranch; he was there all the time. Eventually he just disappeared—although I suppose somebody did shoot him.

Tony

My dad had this bull—he had bought a registered, white-faced bull, when it was about a year old—his name was Tony. And that Tony was just a pet. A great big bull, you know—he was a beautiful animal.

Two or three kids would get on him. He didn't move very fast, but he walked around with us on his back. And he had big long horns. Those horns all kind of grow up, like the horns that you see on the Brahmans in the rodeos.

With a prized bull like that, you put a lead ball—about the size of a tennis ball, and they have a set screw in them—on the end of their horn, and tighten the screw down to hold it there. It makes the horn droop, rather than go up.

You see a lot of these bulls where the horns go out and bend down—well, they've had these weights on there. That makes them a lot prettier, you know; they don't look like they've come from Texas.

But during that third year of the Depression—with no hay or anything—there was no market for them. And my dad paid a lot of money for Tony when he was just a year old. But he finally found a rancher who came in to the elevator. The rancher had a couple of creeks that he used for irrigation. My dad was telling him about Tony. "Have you got any hay?" my dad asked.

The rancher said that he did. "Well, would you like Tony?" my dad asked him. "Because we're not selling him for hamburger." So we gave Tony away to a neighbor, and he lasted there for quite a few years.

Dog Eat Dog

There was this bar in Ismay. The fellow who owned it was named McNamara. He had one of those bulldogs with the jaw that sticks out; it was a good-sized bulldog. McNamara was a nice enough guy, but he was the type who would kind of like to see his dog lick somebody else's dog.

All the dogs would cross the street and go down the other side— because if they were on his sidewalk, that bulldog would go out and kill quite a few dogs. He was a miserable son of a gun.

The depot agent moved in, and he had a Saint Bernard. "Now, don't walk down in front of the south side there," my dad told him, "because the owner's bulldog is always there. He'll just bust right out and challenge anybody."

"Okay," the depot agent said, "I'll walk down the other side of the street."

The first time the agent went up to get the mail, he was walking down the far side of the street. And the bulldog either smelled him or heard him or something, and went running across the street after that big Saint Bernard. The owner of the Saint Bernard just stopped. And the Saint Bernard just stopped, set his feet and stared at this bulldog running across the street at him.

That Saint Bernard was so big that when the bulldog lunged for his throat, it just opened its mouth and the bulldog's whole head went in. And that Saint Bernard just shook him and shook him. Finally, the Saint Bernard let him down, and that bulldog had really been shaken.

The bulldog's owner said that that was the only time his dog had ever been beaten in a fight. He came over, finally got his dog back on its feet and watched it stagger back to the bar. The bulldog wasn't hurt anywhere. The Saint Bernard hadn't bit him, just put his head in its mouth.

From that time on, that bulldog still came down with the bar owner every day to the bar, but it never went out after another dog. Everybody knew that the bulldog had had its lesson.

Those, of course, were the kinds of stories that went around a small town like Ismay. There were a lot of stories like that—and they lived and live on.

Moving On

We lived in Ismay for nine years, until Dad got the chance to sell the ranch and buy two grain elevators and a mill right in Miles City, about forty miles away. The two elevators sat right together, and were joined at the top.

My dad sold all of his rangeland around Ismay—except the home section—when we moved to Miles City. But, since he would have an elevator and feed mill there, he would still be dealing with all the ranchers, and be able to keep in touch with them on a weekly, if not daily, basis.

CHAPTER 2

MILES CITY MEMORIES

Cleared for Takeoff

WHEN I was ten years old, my dad sold most of his rangeland near Ismay and we moved to Miles City, Montana, where he bought a grain elevator and feed mill. He still had a partner in the cattle business, George Griffith, on the home section of our ranch on Cabin Creek. The move didn't bother my dad's grain business any, because it was still a short haul for the wheat ranchers.

In Miles City, my dad actually had two elevators, with a catwalk in between them. There was a man-lift in it. They had weights on the other end, so that you just barely had to touch it and up you went. I went up that man-lift, took my rubber-band airplanes and wound them up. Boy, they really sailed from up there.

I made a lot of balsa wood airplanes: Stinson Reliants, Orion SDs—all powered by rubber bands. So I went up there with my model airplanes and flew them off the catwalk. I couldn't have been much more than ten years old.

South of the elevators, just a block from the school, was a big area that hadn't been developed at all. I watched my airplanes fly out there. Then I went down the man-lift and got them, or I'd have a buddy out there.

I went up that man-lift by myself, and got out there on that walkway between the two grain elevators. That walkway moved a little, because it wasn't anchored to either side. It was made to move in the wind.

My dad let me go up there. I had an awful lot of liberty, but I never got into any trouble.

My dad never, ever spanked me once. But if there was something he wanted me to straighten up on, those little eyes would just twinkle. And, boy, I knew he was talking. He wouldn't raise his voice; it was just the look.

My dad's elevator and feed mill in Miles City, Montana. I launched my model airplanes from the catwalk between the two elevators.

Feeding time at the ranch. We had about 200 head of cattle.

Helping Hand

My dad was a great guy. Everybody called him JC; he didn't have a middle name. He had some relatives named Cooney, so he said, "I'll just take that 'C' for an initial."

Those ranchers really depended on him. Because you would get a few dry years: no hay; and you can't buy hay to feed a bunch of cattle. Some of them couldn't pay their feed bill for three years. He never said a word.

Even now I find out some of the wonderful things he did. These ranch kids—two brothers, a few years older than me—were just out of high school when their mom and dad were killed in a car crash. Of course, they inherited the ranch.

There had been a drought, and the brothers didn't have any money. They hadn't raised any wheat, and didn't have any hay for the cattle. So they had *nothin'*.

The boys came into the bank to borrow money to buy seed, and gasoline for the tractors. But, since they were still teenagers, the bank wouldn't lend them any money. They went out to the wholesale oil, which always drove around the ranch in a big truck. They had a big tank on the end. They wouldn't give the brothers credit, so the two of them came down to my dad's elevator to talk to him. They didn't come down to get any money; they just came down to tell him that they thought they were going to have to sell the ranch.

"We can't do a thing," they said. "We haven't got the money to buy the seed for the wheat, or gasoline for the tractors." And they asked if my dad had heard of anybody that wanted to buy a ranch.

My dad had a fairly good-sized office there, with some old leather chairs and a davenport. So the ranchers hung out there. There was a big, pot-bellied stove with a gas burner in it. My dad knew the mother and father, and he knew these boys from the time they grew up. And they were honest as the day is long.

Their ranch was about half cattle and half wheat. Dad asked them, "Would you like to keep the ranch if you had the money?"

They said they would. So Dad called First National and said, "This is JC. Give 'em credit for whatever they want." And my dad told the brothers, "If you're gonna plant a lot of wheat, why, I've got seed here; you can have all you want. And plan on getting some more cattle."

Then he called the oil distributor and said, "Anything the boys want, why, give 'em the gas and just put it on the elevator's tab. If they have a crop this fall, they'll pay ya; and if they don't, I'll pay ya."

I didn't know that Dad had done that for those two boys until after he had passed away. They cornered me out at the Range Riders Museum one time. "Did you know what your dad did for us?" My dad didn't talk much, but he was sure deep.

My dad liked the ranchers. "If you get the word of a rancher," he said, "you don't have to worry about putting it in writing." And he sure proved it. I never realized how many ranchers he had saved. But when I go home now to some of those dinners at the Range Riders Museum, there's always some rancher—and usually some rancher's son—who comes up to me and says, "We've sure grown into a nice, big ranch out there. And we'd a lost it all if it wasn't for JC."

But Dad never said anything; none of us in the family ever knew what he was doing. He never bragged about anything. Nobody even knew that he pitched ball until he got to coaching the Little League.

He could sure throw. We had a nice, interesting loop; down the river and up and around at night. We would take a drive in our new 1929 Chevrolet. Dad got off early one night. He closed up if he didn't have any more truckers coming in to dump wheat.

We always stopped at the drugstore; it was the only place that had ice cream. We would all get a big ice cream cone. Then we would take this drive around, down the river, and see some deer and things. Then we would go up on the flat, look at the cows and come back in. It was about an hour's drive.

One night we pulled up on the flat and Mom said, "Dad, there's a big fat skunk standing on the edge of the road down there."

"Oh, yeah?" he said, stopping the car. It was a dirt road. He walked along the side and got a great big clod. The mud had been thrown out there and hardened just like a baseball. We drove on down. This skunk was used to cars going by, so it didn't run off into the bushes; it was still standing there.

Dad got out real quiet like, and stepped out in front of the car. That darned skunk was a good sixty feet away. When the skunk saw Dad walk out it stood up, and Dad hit it right in the head. It killed it right there; it didn't even have time to squirt any smell.

At fair time we went out to where they threw the baseballs. They would have to finally ask Dad, "You know, we're gonna go broke if you throw many more baseballs."

"Okay," he would say, "I got all the kids a big doll." He practiced all the time, and he played ball with me all the time.

My mom and dad—and half of our cat.

My dad and mom were real buddies. When Mom passed away, he rented out the house and moved in with my sister for several years.

When her daughter became a teenager, he felt he was kind of in the way there. He went back to his house and lived there by himself for several years, although he had lots of friends who dropped in.

His neighbor and her husband had an upstairs with an apartment. Their daughter had grown up and moved away, so they talked my dad into moving up to the apartment and being there with him, so he wasn't by himself. They had been friends with him and my mother. My older sister lived just half a block away.

It finally got to where he had to go to the rest home. They had a real nice one. One of the brothers who Dad had helped to keep their ranch finally decided that they wanted to sell it. So they sold their ranch, and he came in to manage the rest home.

My sister talked to him and said that Grandpa was getting up into his nineties, and that we would like to have him out there. But she didn't know if she could talk him into going. And the manager said, "Well, you know, we've got this corner room down here that looks right over this alfalfa field that they hay all the time, with beautiful sunsets. That's gonna be vacant here shortly," because whoever was in there was about ready to call it a day.

Sure enough, he saved it for him. And Dad enjoyed it out there.

Ranch Kids

Miles City had 10,000 to 12,000 people when we moved there in 1932. My dad operated the International Elevator until his retirement in 1949. Miles City was mainly a cattle town. There was a big sales yard there. Fortunately for the town's residents and visitors, there was nothing to smell. There was no packing or anything.

The town had a fantastic Junior Legion baseball team. They won the national championship several times. The school principal had played pro ball. He and my dad coached the team. I enjoyed baseball—but I enjoyed airplanes better.

The high school was called Custer County High School. It was a big school for a town that size, because so many of the ranch kids came in. They didn't have any buses to bring the kids to school. The state pays the ranchers so much per mile, based on their distance from the school.

Half a dozen ranchers who were good friends would get a group of families, and they would come in and buy or rent a big, two-story house in town. One of the mothers would come in and sit for a week, and then another mother would come in and take care of the kids.

Those ranch kids were real nice people; they just were. They weren't rowdies or anything. They never gave us any trouble. Never in school. They were used to working like beavers on the ranch, you know: getting up at five in the morning and working two hours before breakfast.

And they were tough in the wrestling classes—because they were muscley, you know. I knew most of their parents, because of my dad's two elevators and mill.

Me, my dad and his dog Tottie.

Yellowstone Adventure

In those days, Montana didn't have driver's licenses, speed limits or insurance. Nobody asked you your age. At five-foot-eight and a half, I was the biggest kid in the eighth grade graduation. I was the same height when I graduated from high school.

One of my best friends, Charles Redman, had a ranch next to ours. He only came up to my shoulder in junior high school, then he started growing. Now he's over six feet tall. He was a good basketball player. It's funny to see him now, compared to when he was just up to my shoulder.

Anyway, my dad bought me my first car, for eighth-grade graduation. I was thirteen. He asked what I wanted for my graduation present. I said that my friend, Allen Eslinger, had a nice Model T Ford. "Didn't he roll it over?" my dad asked.

"Yeah, he rolled it over," I said. It was a four-door, a 1925. He just scrunched it, broke all the glass out of it. "But it's a good chassis and a good engine, and it's got a retro gear," I said. So, real quick-like, I asked Allen what he was going to sell it for.

"Twelve dollars and a half," he said.

"Sold," I said. So I said, "I'm gonna get that." I went over to the elevator and told my dad that I knew what I wanted for graduation: a gift that was going to cost twelve dollars and a half. "Is that within the limit?" I asked.

"You bet," he said. So that was my graduation present.

My 1925 Model T Ford, my 8th-grade graduation gift. It cost
$12.50. I put a Bug body and a pickup body on it.

My 1925 Model T, "Lulu" (left), and
Doug Randall's 1923 Model T, "Lucy."

I took the old body off and built a Bug body on it. It had a seat
for two and a cockpit in the back. But there was no place for your
feet back there; they had to come down and go on the rear axle.

Our folks let us take that thing to Yellowstone Park, three

hundred miles away. It was a hundred and fifty miles to Billings, and then a hundred and fifty to the park. The three of us—Doug Randall, Cliff Boutelle and me—were all the same age, thirteen or fourteen. We got a tent and all our fishing gear, slapped it on the back end and drove that Model T.

"Don't go all the way to Billings tonight," Dad said. "Just go up to Forsyth; that's forty miles. Camp out; don't drive all night. You can go on up to the park tomorrow during the day."

Well, we didn't pay any attention, of course. Once we got started, we never stopped. We drove all night. We went to Billings, gassed up and went right on to Cody, Wyoming. We got into Cody about five or six o'clock in the morning.

Meanwhile, it had started raining on us. And Cliff, who was sitting in the back cockpit, had fallen asleep—his legs hanging down, and all that cold water splashing him! Poor Cliff couldn't get out of the cockpit. We had to lift him out, get him into the gas station and let him sit by the stove.

To get to the Cody Entrance on the east side of Yellowstone Park, you had to go up Sylvan Pass, a long climb. It was the middle of the afternoon, and getting hot. By the time we got to the top of the pass, we should have stopped and cooled the car off. But the old Ford had boiled before, so we just kept going.

By the time we headed down toward Fishing Bridge, we could hear the rods rattling. I wasn't alarmed, though; I had had to change a connecting rod before. We stopped and shut the car off and let it cool. I took the pan off. This time, however, not only were the rods shot; the main bearings were, too.

We limped into Fishing Bridge. I knew we couldn't drive the car back to Miles City like that. There was one service station there, and the manager didn't do any maintenance work. "I don't think you could find any Model T parts anywhere, anyway," he said.

So we were concerned then about how we were going to get back to Miles City. I had a four-piece dance band, and the following weekend we had a job on Saturday night at one of the places out on the edge of town. I said, "Well, we're gonna have to get back."

1925 Ford Model T, ready to head for Yellowstone Park, 300 miles away. Doug Randall, Cliff Boutelle and I were all fifteen years old. Montana had no driver's license and no speed limit.

As luck would have it, we met two college boys—brothers— who were working for the Greyhound Bus Company. We told them about our car. "How much will three tickets back to Miles City cost us?" we asked.

"We can get a discount on them," they said, adding: "How about us just trading you three tickets for that car?" So we got the three tickets and rode the bus home. But not before we spent a week in Yellowstone Park, fishing and having a lot of fun.

Unfortunately, my brother-in-law had lent me two nice tires off of his four-wheel trailer to put on the back of the Model T, and of course they were still on it. Needless to say, he was rather unhappy with me when I returned home to Miles City with no car—and no tires!

Well, later that summer I got a phone call, about eight or nine o'clock at night. It was from those two brothers, who were returning to the university in Minneapolis. "We're down here in the camp-grounds," they said, "and it looks like we knocked the rod bearings out of the Model T again."

So, one of the brothers said, "Would you like to buy your car back?"

"Oh, sure," I said. "How much you want for it?"

"Ten dollars."

"Good," I said. "I've got five and I'll borrow five from my mother." So I got my eighth-grade graduation present back—it was only gone about two months.

I was getting ready to overhaul those bearings, up in my dad's mill, where there was a shed that we could put the car under. There was also a fine mechanic there, Chuck Walters. All the big trucks stopped there.

I told Chuck I was going to have to change those rods and main bearings. "You've changed the rods an awful lot," he said. "You've been putting them in too tight. Just hook onto your Model T with your dad's Oldsmobile and pull it over here to the garage. You get it all apart and I'll show you how to put those bearings in."

So he put a rod bearing in and tightened it up. If you couldn't tap it back and forth on the shaft with the wooden handle on the hammer, it was too tight. Then you would have to put some shims in it. So Chuck checked us out. That car ran for a long time, once we got those new bearings in the way the expert told us to.

My Model T Ford at the ranch of my friend, Charles Redman, June 1937. "Just a little memento," wrote his mother, Jetta, on the back, "of some of your happy days. The boys—Berry Glen, Charles Redman and Jack Burke—with Jack's first car."

Mischief on Main Street

The muffler, however, finally went to pot. So we just went out to the junkyard and got a muffler that we could slip on the tailpipe. We would go down Main Street in Miles City. The kids always drove around at night, like they still do in Renton.

We would drive down Main Street, turn the switch off and coast as far as we could. Then we would turn the switch on. Coasting, it was sucking gas in the carburetor. And we would turn that thing on and it would go, VARROOOOOOOOM!

The muffler would land in the middle of Main Street, stopping all the cars behind us. But we weren't hurting anybody. Everybody would laugh.

We got a "charge" out of that car in another way. The Model T had a coil—not a battery—and coils have a lot of zip. So I wired that coil to the frame of the car. Then I dropped a chain down, as a ground.

Although there are a lot of pine hills around it, Miles City is level, right in town. People never put their brakes on. They might put their car in gear, but never put the brake on. So we would park behind somebody, and, if possible, push him up to the next car, so two cars were bumper to bumper.

We dropped that chain down and waited for people to come out to get in their car. Of course they would grab the handle of the car and—zap! We just let them get shocked a couple of times. Then we pulled the chain up, because they would walk around to see what the heck was wrong with their car.

We did things like that, but we didn't damage anything. There was a little dry coulee at the edge of town, though, where we had a little fun, now and then, with local law enforcement officials. Just inside the city limits, we called it "the dip."

With that Model T, and those old cars, you could go down through the dip. But we didn't chase one another around town. The police would stop you right away if you were caught doing that, or playing ditch'em. We wouldn't agitate a new policeman too much, but we would follow one another, and he would figure, "Those guys are gonna be playing ditch'em."

So we would go out to the dip and go down through it, and the new cop in town would be right behind us. And nothing would come out but dust. Bumpers would be hung up on both ends, and all four wheels of the police car would be up in the air.

So the red-faced rookie would talk us into giving him a ride back into town to get a wrecker. We did some crazy things, but we didn't damage or wreck anything. We would help people fix things, if they were broken.

We had a full life back there.

That Model T lasted two or three years. I took the bug body off and made a pickup out of it. Dad gave me $10 per 100 pounds for delivering from the mill. There were a lot of people at the edge of town who had chickens and whatnot.

Pleasant Street

We had a neighbor down the street who owned the Miles City Mercantile, which had the beer franchise for all of eastern Montana. The Mercantile was about a block long; it was a big spread. They had groceries and everything there.

My buddy Doug Randall, who was the same age as me, drove one of their big beer trucks every summer. His dad, who was a doctor, had a ranch out of town, where my buddy decided to go to work instead.

So he told the owner, Mr. Jacobson, that he was going to be on the ranch that summer, but that I might be available. "Jack's driven trucks and stuff out on the ranch," he told him.

So Doug called me and said, "Would you like to drive that beer truck this summer?"

"Well, that sure beats working on the railroad," I said. The summer before, I had worked cleaning out the old boxcars. I sprayed them inside with yellow paint, a preservative. I could only spray one end before I got so dizzy that I would have to go outside. I had a mask, but I would have to sit outside in the fresh air awhile before spraying the other end. "Boy, I'd much rather drive that beer truck."

So I called Mr. Jacobson. "Doug has already called me," he said. "If you're still available, I'll call the Chevrolet garage tomorrow and tell them you'll be there to pick up the new truck." He didn't ask me my age or anything.

So they hired me. For three summers I drove a beer truck in and around Miles City, which had a renowned red light district. One block off of Main Street was a street called, fittingly, Pleasant Street. There was a lake at the end of the town, and the Main Street Bridge went over it.

On one side of the lake they had swimming. They always had

instructors and lifeguards there in the summer. On the other side were boats. The madams—there were three of them—built nice, two-story houses on the end of that lake.

I delivered beer there. They bought their beer in a small case that had six "picnics" in it. My buddies always checked when they saw me around town delivering to other places:

"When are you going to Pleasant Street?" they would ask.

"Well, I'll be going down there about 4:30 this afternoon."

"Okay, we'll go with ya."

There was no air conditioning in those days, of course. The girls would lie around on the davenports, covered with only a thin sheet. And four or five of us high school kids, each with a little box, would come marching in.

"This is great," we thought. But those girls knew what we were up to. It was sure a kick, though. I did that for three summers.

One of my good buddies had a sister who was the nurse at the clinic. Even though the girls came in once a month to get checked, she kept telling us: "They've usually got some kind of bugs, you know. So, whatever you do, don't go in there."

So we didn't. It was a kick.

I drove the Mercantile truck on beer delivery runs in Miles
City for three summers, from 1937 to 1939, while I was in high
school. I was fourteen years old when I started, and a Teamster.

Corky, my Scotty dog, was my "copilot."

Jazz Mobile

As I've said, I had the Model T for a long time. Later, while still in high school, I got a big old 1929 Buick, which I used to transport our jazz band around.

I played the trumpet, and very poorly. I didn't like the trumpet; it was bleary, you know. I never played a piece without half a dozen mutes; I would always put the mute in. I just didn't have the music in me, but I could read all the music. I could kind of jam.

But these guys—now Arlan Sarff with that sax—he had two saxes and a clarinet. And Barbara Berg could play the organ or piano or anything. I couldn't join in with that pair at all, but I booked all of our gigs.

The dancers would come up and say, "Do you know this piece?"

And Barbara would say, "Well, I don't really know it—but can you hum me a couple bars, or whistle a couple bars?"

Two bars were all it would take. She would just start right in and play it beautifully. She earned her living as a musician from then on. She went down to San Francisco and was in one of the big night clubs down there, playing the organ.

Shortly after Barbara picked up the requested melody, Arlan would be playing that sax and clarinet just as well. And Walter Brockman was our drummer. He had a nice set of drums, and did a good job.

What I had mostly was the Buick, and I booked the bands. In that ranch country, they have a lot of clubhouses, gathering halls and community centers. They have a dance about every other Saturday night. So they kept us busy. In fact, we went all the way to Macy's Hall in Broadus, which was eighty miles. We went up there for New Year's Eve every year.

We got paid five dollars apiece, and five dollars for the car. On New Year's Eve we got ten dollars apiece. We would play from 7:00 p.m. until 11:00 p.m. Then we would stop the music, and we would have the supper waltz. All of the gals would bring a box lunch for two people. At 11:30 we would stop the music, and they would have supper. And they had fresh coffee made, and usually desserts.

And the fellow who wanted to have a particular lunch would dance with that lady on the supper waltz, and then they would go have the box lunch together. She might be his neighbor's wife, or whatever. But they all were good, friendly cowboys. We had thirty minutes for lunch; then we played until 1:00 a.m. We got paid that five dollars for that.

Of course, there was a bunch of those younger cowboys who never wanted to quit at one o'clock. So the fellow who owned the hall in Broadus would always tell them, "Well, I can get the band to stay longer: I'll just put my hat up there on the stage, and you guys can toss in whatever you want. I think they'll play just as long as you guys can stay on the floor."

And we would; we would play until three or four o'clock in the morning. And we would get more money in the *hat* than we got from the owner. We were doing that when we were teenagers; we were in high school.

I learned to play the trumpet in grade school, when we lived in Ismay. I could play the trumpet when we moved to Miles City. I wish my dad had given me a saxophone instead. The fellow who owned the drugstore about a block from my dad's elevator practiced over there with his saxophone all the time. And my dad said, "I can hear Ayers over there bluttin' and bluttin' on that thing. It sounds like a cow that's stuck in the mud. Boy—we sure wouldn't want a saxophone around here!"

So that's how I came to play the trumpet. I could do all right on marches and band music. But our group didn't have music; we had all orchestrations. Barbara and Arlan didn't need any music.

I met them through the school band, and we played together all through high school and two years in community college. They knew I had the car. Most people didn't have an old '29 Buick that would go like that, and that we could put the drum on top. I did real well with that car.

Arlan married the principal's daughter. They still send us a card and make a phone call every Christmas. They're still together. She got married and had two or three boys, and her husband had a real good job in Kansas. But he was killed in a light airplane in a snowstorm. He had a business where he traveled a lot.

Her name was Zona Gail Denton, and Arlan Sarff lost his wife with cancer. We had a yearly reunion with our 1940 class, and both of them had lost their mates several years before this particular reunion. Well, they got together at that reunion and got married; they've been married fifteen years now.

Minding the Store

From the time I was little, my dad trusted me to "mind the store" while he was away. Maybe that's why I didn't think anything of flying solo at fourteen; I figured I was almost grown up. He was a great dad.

My dad used to go back to see his mother in New Rockford, North Dakota, about once every two months. He could take the train on Saturday afternoon, spend Sunday and come back on Monday.

My dad had a younger brother who was a railroad conductor. He was a bachelor; he never did get married. In fact, he lived with my grandmother as long as she was alive.

My dad just had one employee at the elevator, and he didn't do any of the paperwork at all. He handled the warehouse, deliveries and other chores. So, all the time I was in high school, I would go over and stay there while my dad was away. I also got out of school at 2:15, because I sneaked out of that last period for four years, and went over to my dad's mill to unload cotton cake.

My dad closed the elevator at six, then went out and coached baseball. We had a tester for wheat. If it weighed up a lot, it was nice and dry, so they got a higher grade for it. So I would also do that. I would make a sample, weigh it up and put it on their ticket.

We had an air ramp that would raise the four wheels of the truck up and just dump the wheat into the pit. Then we sent it to any of the bins that we wanted from down there. Dad just let me do that.

So the people would come in with a truckload of wheat. I would have to ask them whether it was *winter* wheat or *spring* wheat. My dad could just reach up and *feel* it, and tell what it was.

But I asked them. Then, of course, I wasn't bonded, so I couldn't write them a check. But I dumped their wheat and gave them a storage ticket. When my dad came back, he gave them a call and wanted to know if they wanted a check put in their account in the bank.

Lots of times, when the local ranchers retired, they turned their ranches over to the sons, and just bought a little house in town. Then they came down to the elevator, because that's where the ranchers all congregated. So their buddies came in, and they sat there all afternoon.

My dad had a big pot-bellied stove that was natural gas. There were two old davenports and two old leather chairs—big chairs— that were almost always full. Those ranchers were great people. When Dad was gone, some rancher would call and say, "Oh, Jackie, I need some feed for my cows. Will ya order me a boxcar full of cotton cow cake—forty ton? And also a boxcar full of timothy hay."

"Fine," I'd say. "Did you want me to get Brantley Landis' truck to haul it out when it gets here?"

"Yeah, just have Brantley bring it out." No price, no *nothin'*. When my dad came back, I'd say, "Well, George ordered these two boxcars full of *stuff*." And I put them in. I had the address in Minneapolis where the order was from. And they said they'd be out in a few days.

And Dad would say, "Have Brantley Landis bring them out when they get here." No money changing hands; not a thing, you know.

My dad and mom with their new Oldsmobile in 1936.

I was always doing something that I liked. Of course, I didn't like unloading those forty-ton boxcars, filled with hundred-pound bags of cotton cake. I got three dollars for that whole boxcar. It took me two afternoons and evenings to unload. I went over as soon as I got out of school, and I worked until suppertime.

A lot of cotton cake was shipped by boxcar to my dad's mill and elevator. Cotton cake is very high protein. It just takes just a couple of those cubes in the local hay or grass to get a cow through the winter. They take the cotton seed off of cotton balls, process that, bake it and grind it up into a great big sheet.

One of the sheets is about an inch thick and one is a half-inch thick. It dries out and they crush that. The higher one comes out in cubes. They call that cattle cake; the smaller ones are sheep cake.

Cotton cake is miserable to handle because it's hard stuff. It's in a burlap bag, forty ton to a boxcar. We had a ramp out of the boxcar into the warehouse. We had two-wheel trucks, and we put four or five bags on a truck. We took the bags into the warehouse and dumped them so they laid at an angle.

If we had a lot of room in the warehouse, we wouldn't stack the bags; we just broke them five-high. But if we started running out of room in the warehouse, we made those five bags into steps and carried the stuff up to where there were maybe two bags up there. And that was really work.

When my dad closed up, we went home and had dinner. Then I came back down and worked until 9:00 or so. If you didn't get it done in two days, or if the railroad car was there more than forty-eight hours, they charged you demurrage. That's why I had to work until 9:00 or 10:00 at night.

I rode my bicycle or drove my Model T down. When Dad got a load of gas to come down for that big engine that ran the hammer mill, he always set a five-gallon can out for them to fill, too. That would be for my Model T.

It seemed like we went through a depression every four or five years. I learned a lot from my dad. He didn't bad-time me about not pursuing baseball, even though he had me throwing and catching the ball from the time I was a little kid.

Pig Tale

Dad was up at the bank, and I was there by myself when this rancher friend came in. He had a truckload of pigs that he had taken out to the sales yard. And he had these two little sucking pigs that they wouldn't take. "They're gonna have to have a month on the bottle; we can't have 'em out here."

So he thought that maybe his neighbor would take them, but he didn't know. "Do you know anybody who'd like 'em?"

"Well, I'd like 'em," I said.

"Well, would your dad let you have 'em?" he asked.

"I don't know," I said.

"Where are you gonna keep 'em?"

"Well we've got this big warehouse," I said, "that's head-high underneath. One end that's used for storage is concrete, and the rest of it is just all dirt." It was a big building. "They could live down there, couldn't they?"

"Oh, yeah," he said. The rancher stayed there. I waited for him. He said, "Your dad will be back shortly.

When Dad came back from the bank, I told him, "Say, I have something here I'd sure like to keep—these two little pigs that Bill's gonna give to me. They won't take 'em in the sales yard. They have to use a bottle for several weeks yet."

"Well, what would ya *do* with them?" my dad wanted to know. "You know you can't have a pig in town." That was before the little fat pigs got popular. These were big pigs; but they were just little yet.

"Well, I looked underneath the warehouse," I said, "and there's a lot of room down there. There's a nice end; it's all concrete, with a concrete floor. You could put some straw in there, and they've got all this dirt to run around."

"You know, you're not gonna smell 'em," the rancher chimed in, "that's for sure. The pig is the cleanest animal we have on the ranch; they will only go in one place. As far away as they can get—that's where they go. If you put some straw down there where the concrete is, they won't be down at this end at all; they'll be way in the back."

He was right; that's what they did. And I would go twice a day—or my sister Kate, if I couldn't make it—and feed them with the bottle. It only took about a week, because Dad had a bunch of formulas there. He had a big hammer mill that could grind anything. He had formulas for pig feed, baby chick feed or whatever. So I mixed up a bunch of that stuff and ground it in the hammer mill. And I would go over and just dump some of it out of one of the bins, and put it in this hammer mill.

One Sunday morning I got a phone call from Boutelle's Garage, just across Main Street from the large Presbyterian Church. They told me my two pet pigs had gotten out and followed the people to the front doors of the church, and laid down in the warm sun in front of the double front-entry doors.

The church-goers couldn't get around the pigs, so they all went down to the side door. As soon as I got to the church, the pigs got up to meet me, and they followed me across Main Street to their home under the warehouse at my dad's feed mill.

One of our good customers at the feed mill raised pigs at his farm in the Yellowstone Valley. I called him; he came in and picked the pigs up and paid me for them. I split the money with my sister Kate, who had helped feed them with the bottles. We took our money and went Christmas shopping. The farmer had the pigs for a long time. I would go out to see them, and they always seemed to know me.

Pee Wee

We ground up a lot of corn on the cob at the mill. Corn is too rich to feed an animal, and the cob gives it the fiber. There was a kid named Pee Wee Anderson whose folks had a ranch in the Yellowstone River Valley. They had a lot of irrigated land, and always had a lot of corn.

Pee Wee had an old, beat up truck. After school he went out, picked corn and filled that truck. Then, when he came in to school the next morning, he backed his truck in to the big, open cellar at the mill and dumped his load of corn. Elevators then took it wherever it needed to go.

When Dad came down, he ran the corn through the hammer mill. You didn't have to handle it much: just direct it to the hammer mill; then the hammer mill would blow it right back out into Pee Wee's truck, all ground up. That was fantastic feed for the cattle.

Every morning, Pee Wee had another truckload of ears of corn that he had picked by hand, and Dad ground it up for him—and he wouldn't charge Pee Wee anything. Pretty soon, here comes Pee Wee with a pretty good-looking truck. Then he put an oil tank on that truck, and started delivering gas and oil to some of the ranchers.

First thing we know, Pee Wee had a great big ten-wheeler, and he was hauling gas from the refinery in Billings down to some of the independent gas stations.

Pee Wee graduated from high school a year ahead of me. He was a little guy—about 5'5"—but he was sure a businessman and a worker. His dad had a standing $100 bet that nobody could top sugar beets faster than Pee Wee. He won every time.

Pee Wee ended up a millionaire. Great big warehouse; a big shop: Anderson Truckshop & Truckstop. All the truckers with the big ten-wheelers came in to have them tuned and to buy their tires. Then Pee Wee got into drilling. He got a big rig and was drilling deep; he hit some oil.

They decided to remove the big old iron bridge that went north over the Yellowstone River, but couldn't get anybody to bid on it. One of the county commissioners told Pee Wee, "You know, we can't get anyone to bid on tearing down that bridge, and they want to put a new concrete bridge next to it."

"I'll do it," Pee Wee said. He had a crane and tore that old bridge down. He always had a bunch of helpers, but he was right in there, too. When he died, he was a multi-millionaire. He put in a nice swimming pool for the kids at the city park.

And he started out with that corncob grinding.

Memory like an Elephant

Miss S. was the only senior English teacher at Custer County High School for about forty years. She was fantastic, and she was real interesting. She had a sense of humor; a dry sense of humor. Everybody was scared to death of her, though, because you had to pass that first half-year of English or you weren't going to graduate; you were going to come back.

Many of the kids worried about it so badly that as soon as they got their grades for the first half—and they showed that they had passed it—they went ahead and switched to public speaking. That's what my sister did; she was two years older than me. And that would really make Miss S. mad.

And I *know* that she remembered that; she just had a mind like an elephant. She could remember everybody's name. And she knew my sister Kate. She made a comment or two about whether I was going to drop English.

Well then my buddy, Doug Randall, and I both had Model Ts. Doug's older brother was about three years ahead of him. He was a straight-A student in everything, and ended up being one of the top surgeons at the Mayo Clinic. Their dad was a doctor.

So Barney, Doug's older brother, went right through the medicine. Then, when his dad retired, he came back to Miles City and took over his dad's business. People came from all over to have him operate on them. His dad wasn't a surgeon; he specialized in heart and pneumonia medicine. They were a great family, and they lived just two houses from us.

I spent a lot of time with Doug. We worked on our Model Ts together. We also went out and got cottontails. They taste just like pheasant; they're really tasty. But occasionally they'll have this tularemia that rabbits get. Humans can absorb it, and it gives them a kind of sleeping sickness.

We used a .22, and just shot them in the head. That way we wouldn't lose any of the good meat. Then we just dropped the cottontails in a burlap bag. Doug's dad said, "Don't get any of the blood or anything on your hands, you know."

When Doug's dad came home from work that night, we had the cottontails out in the garage. He just went out and gave a little zip on each piece of skin. If a rabbit had tularemia, it had little blisters underneath the skin. So, if they had any of those at all, we just threw them in the garbage.

When we were seniors, Doug got elected chairman of the student body. He handled all the events and assemblies. I was elected senior class president. So we got together real often—and with Miss S., the English teacher, because she had all seniors.

Doug Randall on his family's ranch on the Powder River near Broadus, Montana, in the summer of 1939. Very close friends, we graduated from Custer High School in 1940—and both had Model T Fords.

Miss S. had a lot of good ideas, about activities and ways the senior class could make money. So we got real friendly with her. And I just couldn't believe, after the first six weeks, when they were splitting the smart ones from the dumb ones, that Doug got put on the "smart" side—because of his older brother—and I got put on the "dumb" side—because of my older sister.

Son of a gun—I couldn't believe it. I had run errands for her, up to the bank and around town, because I was one of the few kids who had a car—an old car. I just couldn't believe it. When I finished wrestling class that afternoon, Archie Davis—a friend of mine from the reform school—was in there showering from football. He was one who had enough "good" coupons that he could come to Custer for school.

I said, "By garsh, Archie, would you believe that the English teacher divided the class. The ones that had 88 or more for an average were on the smart side. I was on the dumb side, with the ones who are going to have to come in tomorrow and take my test—my six-month test."

We had only had one written test for the whole six weeks. And I had received just as good a grade as Doug had. I got to thinking about it, you know: Boy, if she keeps pushing this sister thing, and public speaking, why, I could end up taking this class over again.

"Well, I tell ya what *I'd* do if it was me," Archie said. The janitors had all moved up to the second floor. Well, I didn't want to go trying to get one of them to come down there, because I didn't think they would open the door anyway.

So I told Archie, "Garsh, you know, the janitors are all gone here, so I guess we'll have to skip it."

"Oh," he said, "you wanted to get in, did ya?"

"Yeah."

"Oh, just a minute," he said. He ran into the locker room and got a wire hanger. And quick as a key, you know, he opened that door. "Now, what was it that you wanted?" he said.

"Look in the top desk drawer there," I said, "because I saw her always take that out, to check the kids' names in her grade book." Sure enough, there was everybody's name—and not a grade behind *anybody's*. No grades; just attendance.

And so we quick-like shut things up and got out, and he locked it right up with that hanger. On the way out to the reform school, he said, "You know, you don't have to take my advice, but if it was me, with no grades in that book, I wouldn't come to school tomorrow. I'd go up and practice your maneuvers at the airport, and get some flyin' in. Because if she sees you around there, she might wonder—you know: *Did* she exempt me, or *didn't* she exempt me?

"If she doesn't see you," he said, "why—I bet it'll work out." Well, I figured he knew a lot more about this than I did, so the next day I went to the airport, and didn't get in Miss S's sight at all. Sure enough, when the report cards came out about two days later, I had an 88 on mine. So she thought she had exempted me.

So then, I told Doug, "You know, I've never, ever babied a teacher. But I tell ya, it's going to be awful easy this year, as long as we're both seniors, and we're dealing with her quite a lot, to get to be buddies.

"You know," I said, "she goes clear up to the end of Main Street—five blocks. She walks up to the apartment house. Well, the first day we get some snow, I'm going to bring the old Buick"—my old 1929 Buick I had for the band; we had a four-piece band, with a rack on top for the drums—"I'm gonna bring the old Buick.

"And I'd like to have you sit in the front seat, and we'll pull up on the curb out there. We won't pull up close to where the door is until we see her coming. And then, when we do, we'll just pull up, and you can get out and ask her if she wouldn't like to have a ride home, rather than walking in this snow—we're going up Main Street anyway."

Boy, she was willing. And Doug jumped out, opened the door and hopped in the back seat just like a footman. We took her up to the end of Main Street and parked in front of her apartment house. Doug got out, got her brief case and walked up to the door with her.

"Boy," I told Doug, "you earned a gold star today. You didn't even *have* to do it, because you got a 92 on your report card. And I'll betcha Barney"—Doug's older brother; his name was Warren, but his nickname was Barney—"would get a kick out of this," because we were riding through on *his* straight-As.

Sure enough, we never had another exam. The next six weeks, I got over with the smart ones, and we both got 98 on our report cards—and I got 98 the rest of the year. It was really funny because we were doing a lot of work with her, and for her, for the senior class. And she came up with some good ideas to make money on.

When Scotty got to be a senior, she was sure that Miss S. would shoot her down. That was because Scotty's two brothers—who rode one horse to school and were in the same grade—both dropped senior English at the same time, something Miss S. was unlikely to forget.

Scotty said she would rather take English than public speaking, because Scotty was always kind of shy. She said she didn't want to take public speaking. "Well, as long as we're giving Miss S. a ride home," I said, "you'll be in good shape." So she was.

It turned out well, because we ended up to be real friends with Miss S. She and Scotty hit it off real well.

When Scotty came to senior class, I had the little Plymouth one-seater. We pulled up in front of the door, and I got out and opened the door. Scotty wasn't very big, and neither was Miss S. She had a wide bottom, but that was all. There was a lot of room for her in there.

And I told her, "You know, Scotty and I always stop and get a milkshake at the Penguin Shop. Would you like a vanilla, chocolate or strawberry? That's all he has."

"Oh, I'd like a strawberry," she said. So we stopped and got a milkshake, but we didn't park there because all the kids came from high school right by there. So we sat out in the car and drank our milkshakes.

Miss S. gave us some good senior advice. "You know," she said, "you and Scotty have been going together here steady this year. You're a senior and she's only a sophomore. I don't think it's too good for you young teenagers to go steady like that.

"Everybody has a different personality. You can learn a lot, you know, from the different personalities. Just a thought, you know."

We didn't think much about it, and never took her advice. But we parted as real friends. I always sent her a Christmas card, and she sent a Christmas card. When I started flying around the world, I'd go around the world once a month, and I'd send her a postcard from a different country—from Iraq and India and different places. Every month I'd send her one postcard. And she would write a nice long letter to Scotty and me.

Then she retired and went to Iowa, and moved in with her sister in a retirement home. I don't know how much longer they lived—

but a long time—because I kept sending her postcards every month, for several years.

Finally, I got a note from the retirement home that she had passed away. But we got a letter every month from her, and always a nice Christmas card. I don't think she had any other relatives; she never mentioned any. No nieces or nephews. If she did, she wasn't talking about them. So Scotty and I figured she must be all by herself.

Scotty and I talked a lot over the years, when Christmas would come, wondering what Miss S. was doing.

Flight Plan

In high school they offered a Technical & Industrial (T&I) class. We had six periods in the school day. The sixth period was the T&I. They had a class the hour before; then, for sixth period, the T&I students would all go downtown, where they had jobs.

They worked at JC Penney's for twenty-five cents an hour or something, until the store closed. The stores usually all closed at six o'clock in those days.

So a bunch of those kids would leave school at sixth period. And my dad always had something for me to do over at the mill. He gave me money for gasoline for the car. I always got signed up for a study hall for that last sixth period. But only in the office, and I never registered. So I was never absent from anything.

Mr. Denton was the principal. He was the one who let me skip the last period and go to the airport. He could see me going out with the T&I students, and he knew that I was supposed to be in the study hall. I did that for four years. Mr. Denton knew I was not taking T&I, but he never, ever stopped me.

If Dad didn't have anything for me to do at the mill, then I would go up to the airport and clean the terminal or the toilets or something. But I went out with those T&I kids, so everybody thought I was one of them—except those that knew me.

Mr. Denton was a fine principal. He was also the baseball coach.

He, too, played pro baseball. He and my dad coached the Junior Legion team in Miles City. He never told my dad when I was skipping all those baseball practices and going out to the airport. He was really great, just a great guy.

My 1932 Plymouth and my Scotty dog, Corky. We got two of those dogs; they were brothers. My sister's was always chunky. So she named hers Porky and mine was Corky.

Mr. Denton coached the baseball team from the time school was out until dinnertime. Then Dad would coach from dinnertime until seven or eight o'clock. I skipped Mr. Denton's early practice because I was always at the airport. Needless to say, my dad thought that perhaps I wasn't improving as a baseball player as fast as I should be. It wasn't just because I was only getting half the training, but finally he found out about it.

So he had a long talk with me. "You know," he said, "the chances of ever getting into pro ball are nil. And if you do—your arm goes out in two years, anyway. But I won't bother your flying, if you'll promise me you'll go to college."

"Yeah," I said. "I'll make sure I go to college."

So we talked about it, and we talked to my mom about it. She said, "Oh, why don't you take pre-med."

"Whatever you guys want," I said, "because I'm gonna just be flying."

CHAPTER 3

SPROUTING WINGS

Living at the Airport

SOON after we moved to Miles City, I started "living at the airport." I just couldn't get up to that airport fast enough. I was up there riding my bicycle. Every evening after school I would go up to the airport, and the east-bound airplane would be going through.

The Miles City Airport was just a grass field with a small terminal. The terminal was a nice building, but it wasn't very big. I don't think it burned when the hangar did. They had the radio at one end of it, and the counter and the tickets and all that stuff. It was modern-looking, and the airplanes taxied right up in the front of it on the airport side. There was lots of room for cars parking behind.

Northwest Airlines came through twice a day—one east- and one west-bound flight. They had the old single-engine Hamiltons that carried eight people. Made of roof-like corrugated metal, they were a big airplane for a single-engine.

The airport had only one employee—Bun Lindberg, the Northwest Airlines Station Manager. Bun did the whole thing: gassed the airplanes when they came in, everything. But he didn't like cleaning the place.

So he said, "You know, Jack, if you're going to be up here all the time, I could sure use your help. But I can't pay you. I don't make enough money to split it. And as long as we only have two trips in here, Northwest won't give me another helper. But I got a deal for you.

"I got this little Aeronca C-3," he said. "It's got a three-cylinder engine, thirty-six horsepower, and burns three gallons of gas an hour. I'll teach you to fly it if you'll come up and help me with that east-bound airplane, and then keep the terminal clean. Come up on the weekend and clean it. You'll have to scrub the floors because there's dust in here. And you've got to really clean the bathrooms and everything, because that's one of the things the airline really checks when they come by."

Mark Etchart in front of the old hangar at the Miles City Airport, next to the CAA weather station. The hangar burned down in December, 1942.

So I learned how to scrub the toilets out, and didn't get any pay at all. But, true to his word, Bun started teaching me to fly, and he soloed me when I was fourteen. You weren't supposed to solo until you were sixteen. You could get a private license when you were sixteen. But Bun didn't wait. You were supposed to have eight hours. I think I had five or six; seven at the most. And he soloed me.

Then Bun just let me use the airplane to build up my time. So it worked out great. That's how I got to fly. I would be up there every night after school, helping Bun. I took wrestling, so a few days I couldn't get up there in time.

Bun talked the airplanes in. There was no range station or anything there. Nothing. But he could hear them flying over. If you were in some clouds, Bun would tell you, "You're right overhead. If you turn east now, you can come right down over the Yellowstone River." He would talk them in, many times through a lot of clouds.

Luckily, there weren't any big mountains there, just what we called the pine hills, which were about three or four thousand feet high. But Bun would make sure the pilots were over the valley when they were starting down.

Bun wasn't even an instructor. But at that time there was only one CAA inspector, based in Billings, and he covered all four states: Montana, Idaho, North and South Dakota. So we never saw him.

Bun was a real nice guy to work with. He finally got transferred to San Francisco. He was station manager there for a long time.

CAA Weather Station, Miles City Airport. It was the only building at the airport for a long time. It sent out teletype every 30 minutes. The old hangar is to the left.

From Student To Teacher

My dad was easy-going, but he wasn't very impressed with aviators. He had a couple of friends he went bird hunting with who were pilots. They were just working around the airport, gassing airplanes and hopping passengers on fair day. He said there was just no way to make a living in the aviation business.

And there wasn't, then, before the war; there was no aviation. So I made my dad a promise that I would go to college if he would sign the necessary papers. He had to sign everything for me because I was so young.

But he did—no problem. The only thing I needed money for was flight instructors, and not a lot. So if I wasn't getting enough forty-ton boxcars to unload for three dollars, I would borrow some money from him. I paid him all back my first month's pay.

I registered for CPT when it started, but could not get in because I was too young. I took the primary class at Etchart-Markle Flying School in Miles City as soon as I was old enough.

I got my private license right away from that school, as soon as it was set up. Gene Etchart, a good friend of mine from Glasgow, Montana, and a good instructor himself, owned the school. His partner in the flying school, Orval Markle, also from Glasgow, gave me almost all of my training. He was an excellent instructor.

So I obtained my private license, and was building most of my time with that little Aeronca C-3. You had to get two hundred hours for a commercial license, so I was building my time up for that. And I got acquainted with a lot of good people.

I wasn't old enough to teach. You had to be eighteen to get a commercial and an instructor's rating. I went to work for George Askin's well drilling company, because he was a good friend. Building time flying for George enabled me to obtain my commercial license and instructor rating as soon as I was old enough.

My pal George Askin and I. George was like a father to me. He
was also a good well-driller, an excellent shot and a great friend.
We had many good times and laughs together. I taught George
to fly, so when I went teaching for the air force he did his own
flying, and never had an accident.

I got my commercial and instructor's rating when I was eighteen—you had to be eighteen. The only inspector for the four states
was based in Billings. I made an appointment with him about a
month before my birthday. I asked him if I could get both the
instructor's and commercial on the same flight.

"Well," he said, "we never do that. But as long as you've been so eager, I want to do it on your eighteenth birthday. So come on up."

Cliff Boutelle, who accompanied me on my Yellowstone adventure, also went with me to Billings the night before I had my flight test for my commercial and instructor's rating. I let him fly the airplane—George Askin's three-place, dual control Super Cub—all the way up, to get used to it. George let me fly the airplane all the time, to football games and wherever.

Cliff would go on to join the air force, which cooperated with hometown recruits real well. If the air force had a program in that town, the cadets could stay right there. They had their first forty hours at the community college, then the flying school gave them their first forty flight hours. So Cliff joined the air force, went to college and got into the 40-hour flight training.

Anyway, after arriving in Billings, we caught a ride downtown and stayed at the Northern Hotel. It was the biggest hotel in Billings, six or eight stories. When we walked into the lobby—only in Montana—here was Cliff White. Cliff owned a large motel and restaurant in Miles City, where he was the Standard Oil distributor. He bought a new Cadillac from Cliff Boutelle's dad, Prescott, every year. So he came over to see what we were doing in Billings.

"Well, garsh, Cliff," I said, "we're up here to get me a flight test tomorrow. I'm trying to get my commercial and instructor's rating."

"Oh that's great," he said. "What are you gonna do *tonight?*"

"Well, nothing," I said. "We're just gonna get a good night's sleep."

"Well," he said, "there's a good restaurant right up on the bluff, overlooking the city. The food's not expensive—and here's the keys." He dropped the keys in my pocket. His brand new Cadillac was just a few months old, and you could not replace it.

"Oh, no, no, no, Cliff," I said. "I don't want that Cadillac. Because if I ding that, Prescott can't get you another one until they start building 'em." So I put the keys back in *his* shirt pocket.

We chatted some more, and he said, "That restaurant is good. I go up there a lot, but I have already eaten." He put the keys in Cliff Boutelle's pocket.

"Well, I should give these back to you," Cliff said, "but we'll drive just to the restaurant and back to the parking lot. I think we can do that without dinging it." He drove, and we went up there and had dinner.

We knew Cliff White from going up to his restaurant and seeing him at the airport, because he was always up there flying. He had been flying for twenty years, but had never gotten any licenses. He finally decided to get an instructor's rating. He was awfully old, I thought; he must have been forty-five or fifty. And they were talking about drafting him.

But to give a couple of eighteen-year-old kids the only car you've got, and you can't get another one—well, that's the way these people are over there.

Next morning—my eighteenth birthday—I took both my commercial and instructor's rating together, and got my commercial license and my instructor's rating. I felt just like Lindbergh, now that I had those two licenses. I made the takeoff in the Super Cub; the wind was such that we could take off right from the ramp. As soon as I got it in the air, Cliff flew us back to Miles City. We got an awful wind right on the tail.

The wind was blowing so strong in Miles City that Northwest didn't land; it went on to Billings. We circled and made sure we rousted some people out of the coffee shop and hangar. They were standing out there on the ramp, wondering what we were going to do.

We just made an approach right square into the wind, enough so that we could land and taxi it, right up almost to the ramp in front of the hangar. So we didn't have to turn; we couldn't turn. And we kept the tail up because we thought it would blow over; it was that windy.

Cliff didn't want to make the landing, and I didn't want him to; he had never soloed before. So we landed, kept the tail up and taxied in slow to give these people time to come out. So they came out, running along and holding the wings and tail down. We made it to the hangar okay.

The Etchart Flying School in Miles City had promised me an instructor's job as soon as I got my rating. I called Pat Burke, who ran the flying school, and told her that I had just got my commercial and instructor's rating. "Can you come to work at eight tomorrow morning?" she asked.

"I sure can," I said. And, sure enough, I went to work for them the next day as a flight instructor for $500 a month—a lot of money in those days.

But there just weren't instructors. Everyone else was working in a gas station for a dollar a day. I hopped passengers all the time at fair time.

Instructing air force cadets in Miles City the day after receiving my instructor's rating. Eighteen years old—plus one day.

Both Mark and Gene Etchart went to work for the air force as instructors in California. I had given Mark dual, and I got him ready for his commercial and instructor's rating. They turned the flight school at Miles City over to Pat Burke—no relation of mine.

Pat had taken their course and had a private license; she was a good pilot. And she was a bookkeeper. She ran a tight ship; she did a nice job. She had to deal with the government on those contracts, and with the college.

When World War II started, the air force realized that they didn't have enough instructors or airplanes to teach all the pilots they needed. So they gave contracts to the colleges and universities to give these cadets their first forty hours of paperwork and ground school. Then the flying school gave them forty hours of flight time.

The four flight instructors at Etchart Flying School in 1942 at Miles City—Hart, Burke, Bennet and Ingersoll—pose with our excellent office manager (who was also a pilot) Pat Burke Gudmundson. I'm second from left. Etchart Flying Service was owned by Gene and Elaine Etchart and Orval Markle, both excellent flight instructors.

So there was a flight school at every one of these colleges and universities. We had a fine community college there—Custer

College. They got a contract, and the air force started shipping them in. Five students at a time for each instructor, and we had four instructors. So the air force would ship us twenty students, and we would give them their first forty hours.

Most of the guys—not so many of the military—that I had as students went into the air force, so they wouldn't have to be on a ship or in the walking army. But, other than that, anybody that really wants to fly can do like I did. And there's a lot of them.

I worked my way through college, teaching flying. I went two years at Custer Community College in Miles City, Montana, and I was instructing there. I flew from seven in the morning until noon, and by the time I had lunch I would be over at the college by one in the afternoon.

My first class of air force cadets, 1942. From left are
Cliff Boutelle, Orlando Vittorie, Clarence Worrall and myself.
(A Flying Start into the Big Sky, Pat Gudmundson,
Gene Etchart and Orval Markle, 1998.)

I always had a dean who was interested in airplanes. Never worried about me sleeping in class, because I didn't learn anything. You couldn't do that now, because you have to have a four-point grade average to get into med school. But in those days, during the

Depression, we had empty seats in every class, because kids just didn't have the money to go to school.

I graduated from Custer Community College with a two-year, Associate of Arts degree.

Cliff Notes

Cliff Boutelle went to the owner of the flight school and said that he would like to have me as an instructor, because we were friends. So, sure enough, Cliff was the first student I soloed. He didn't need much time, because I had let him fly when I was training.

He would come out and 'sandbag' for me. You had to have somebody in that back seat, or a couple of big sacks of sand, because the center of gravity is altogether different in those little airplanes with a person in the back. If you do spins, it would spin faster with somebody in the back, so you wanted to have somebody there when you were practicing.

So Cliff spent a lot of time sandbagging for me. Then he soloed. And they said we had to give them eight hours of dual; the navy had that requirement. So I had given him eight hours, and he could fly the airplane like a dart.

It must have been in September. It had drizzled a little, and it was cool. And that's just when those little airplanes get carburetor ice. When the air goes into the carburetor, it expands it; then it cools, so it will form ice in the carburetor. So you have a carburetor heater, which shuts that air out and brings some by the manifold.

On every approach, you pull the carburetor heat on. We were through practicing landings, and went back for him to take off. So of course we had the carburetor heat off. Another trainer was way out on a long final, and we didn't want to hurry Cliff up for his first solo takeoff. So we sat there and visited and just talked about stuff.

The trainer took forever to get in, while Cliff's plane was sitting there idling in that damp air, and just about freezing. It picked up some carburetor ice. And of course I never thought about turning the carburetor heater on, getting ready for takeoff. You never used it because it cut your power down. I never thought about it at all.

So here's Cliff's first takeoff by himself. And just about the time he gets over the end of the runway, it quit cold. Just like you turned the gas off. So I *knew* it was carburetor ice.

We always gave them emergency practice on takeoffs. We would pull the engine back, just to make sure they wouldn't try to turn to come back. There's a lot more drag in a turn. A lot of instructor's didn't drive that in. People would get killed because if the engine cut out they would turn around and be short, and wouldn't get back on the runway. Or they may not have been killed, but they dinged up a lot of airplanes.

So we really drove it into them: never turn around for the airport, even if you've got some altitude, because you're going to be landing with a tailwind. Pick a spot in front of you, thirty to forty-five degrees off, and put it in.

Anyway, Cliff just went over the fence, and he must have had three hundred feet or so, and putt-putt-putt. I looked up and that prop was stopped. The wheat field there had been plowed, but there was a strip on the side of it where they had let the grass grow. Well, Cliff just turned right over there and made a perfect landing on that grass.

I got in the car and drove over. "Cliff," I said, "I'm sorry this happened; this was my fault. With us sitting there talking, we should have had that carburetor heat on. Of course, you've been trained never to use carburetor heat on takeoff because it reduces your power. And I knew better; I should have had the heat on all the time we were standing there. No ice ever would have formed.

"But you sure did a good job, and that was your first landing solo. Do you want to fly it back to the airport?"

"No," he said. "I'll drive your car back." So he drove the car back. I had a little '36 Plymouth.

The plane started right up because it had been sitting there, the engine was warm and it thawed the ice out. So I flew it back, pulled it up to the ramp and said, "Well, you might just as well finish your hour of flying, Cliff."

"Yeah," he said, "I'll do it, now that I'm back here on the airport." So he went out and did a lot of practicing. He was really a good student. When he got out of the air force, he went to college in Boulder. He liked writing; he was going to work for the newspaper. He went a couple of years there, then his dad talked him into coming back.

He didn't like the garage. But they had a nice garage, a good shop and the Cadillac and Pontiac franchise. Cliff hung in there. His dad finally died; I think he was close to a hundred. Cliff just sold the garage a few years ago.

By George

Bob Askin, who had a ranch near us in Ismay and would go on to become a world champion cowboy, had a brother named George, who also had a ranch. Their father was a driller. He drilled deep-flowing wells for water for the cattle, and a lot of gas wells. He had one of those old *chug-chug* drills that couldn't really get down to the oil.

George, Bob's older brother, took over the drilling, and he got some rotary rigs. George was very close to our family. He gave my dad—well it *was* a nice trailer. He had this four-wheel trailer that he put drill rods on, and for a while he bought a new Chrysler every year. He would wear it out, and then he went to Pontiac. And he was driving Pontiacs for the last ten years.

He told my dad that he heard a bunch of clanking, looked back and the drill rods and wheels were flying. So he got one of the trucks and hauled it back in. He gave my dad the trailer. He made it into a nice two-wheel trailer to take camping.

George moved up to Miles City a year or two after we did. George drilled oil and gas wells all over the eastern part of Montana,

and into the Dakotas. He had three rotary rigs in his drilling operation. They were nice because two men could handle them; they
were all automatic. The old drills, that *boom-boom* stuff—they just
pounded a hole. But these were nice.

One day I was on my way to the airport. George was sitting on
the curb at the machine shop. I stopped and said, "George, would
you like to go for an airplane ride?"

"Jackie," he said, "I'd love to, but I've got two rigs broke down
out on Sunday Creek. It's not very far out—only about thirty or
forty miles—but there was a cloudburst out there last night and it
washed the bridge out. Now I'm gonna have to drive two hundred
miles to get to it."

"Well, can we land out there somewhere?" I asked.

"Yes," he said, "there's an alfalfa field right next to where we're
drilling. You could land on the edge of it where there's no plowing."

"Well, let's get the part and we'll go," I said. We could hardly
both fit in that little C-3. George wasn't too big—only five-foot-ten
or so—but he had broad shoulders. We barely got up with the two
of us in it, because George was pretty heavy as well.

We got off okay, and went out and landed. As soon as we did,
George took the part and went over to the rig and made sure they
were getting it fixed. Soon a pickup truck full of kids arrived. I asked
them if they would like a ride to go over their ranch.

I told George, "Just let me know when you got the rigs fixed
and are ready to head back. I'm gonna hop these kids and let 'em see
their ranch from the air." So they would get in and I would fly them
over their ranch, come back and get another one. Finally I got that
pickup load of kids all hopped. About that time George would be
through, so we headed back to town.

Every time we went out I would do that. I bet I gave every kid
in eastern Montana an airplane ride.

George was impressed as well. "You know, this works real good,"
he said. "It only took us half an hour to come out here," even though

that little C-3 would only go about sixty or seventy miles an hour. "Can you buy me an airplane?"

"Oh, sure, George," I said. "I can get you an airplane. I was up to Billings a couple of weeks ago, and they were rebuilding a nice one there."

"Well, it's gotta carry three people," he said, "because the drillers have to come in and spend Saturday night. We take them back out on Sunday." They all spent Saturday night down on Pleasant Street.

That's all he said about it. I didn't know what the airplane, a Piper J-5, was going to sell for, or anything. We were having supper that night, and my mom said, "George Askin wants to talk to you on the phone."

"Jackie, did you buy that airplane yet?" George asked.

"George, you're serious!" I said.

"Oh, yeah. Buy it! Can you go up on the bus tomorrow?"

"Yeah," I said.

"Well, I gotta go to Baker, the other direction, to meet with some bankers. So go up and get it. Stop by the office. Helen will take care of you."

So I stopped by the office and Helen handed me three blank checks with just GF Askin Drilling signed on them. "Gosh, Helen, why do I need *three* checks?" I asked.

Helen said: "Well, George said for the airplane and maybe some parts, or maybe with the weather you might get stuck and need a hotel. He said to give you three checks."

George had a lot of money. He hit a lot of oil wells. He would have a bid on the group that wanted an oil well. And if he got down to the depth that they had agreed on, and he didn't hit oil, the investors usually were out of money.

So George would say, "Well, I'll go ahead and finish it. And if we hit oil, I can get a fourth of it." So George, the oldest of five brothers, was well-to-do. He always had money from well-drilling, so he would help out the other brothers in a pinch.

I went up to Billings and they checked me out in the airplane, which sat a lot higher than the little C-3 that I had been flying. I made half a dozen landings, went inside and the agent said, "Okay, I'll get you the title."

I gave him a check. I believe it was for $6,500—a lot of money during the Depression. I graduated from high school in 1940, and this was three years before that.

I flew the airplane down to Miles City and called George, who was back in town. He really liked that airplane. From then on, I didn't have to fly that little C-3. I just flew this one. And George told me, "Now, don't ever let me find you buying any gas for this. Just put it on the bill."

The summer of 1942, flying for well-driller G.F. Askin in this Piper three-passenger, taking parts to the oil well rig. We landed in many fields like this near the rigs. The local ranch kids always showed up by the truckload, each wanting an airplane ride. I always obliged them.

The closest I ever came to an accident was when I was flying for George Askin and almost hit the trees. I was sixteen, flying for George after school. I had just gotten my private pilot's license, and didn't have a lot of experience. It was a Saturday, and George was drilling for oil about thirty miles west of Billings, close to the river.

They were having trouble up there, so we got up fairly early that

morning and flew up. There was a row of high hills, and they were
drilling right at the foot of those. The ground sloped out; it was a
nice alfalfa field. It was early in the spring and the alfalfa wasn't tall.

There was an airport at a little town about five miles away, but
they were going to have to come over and get us. There was a nice
strong wind blowing. The field sloped a little bit toward the creek,
which was lined with birch trees. They weren't very tall; maybe
fifteen or twenty feet.

"I can slip down the edge of the mountains and land right
there," I told George. "There's plenty of room, as long as we have
this wind. We'll try to keep an eye on it. If that wind starts to go
down, I'll take off by myself, go in and land at the little airport.
They can bring you over when you get through here." That wind
just kept right on blowing.

When the sun came out in the afternoon and it warmed up,
the wind shut off just like that. The little disturbance, or whatever
it was, had passed on through, because it was a nice, warm sunny
day—and getting warmer by the minute.

I went over to the rig. "George," I said, "if I don't get that
airplane out of here before it gets any warmer—because we've lost
almost all our wind—we're gonna have to spend the night here."

"Why don't you go ahead and take it over to the little airport by
yourself?" George said.

"Fine," I said. "But without that wind, it's gonna be nip and
tuck. Why don't you come out and help me, and we'll pull the tail
right back to the fence. Maybe you can hold the tail while I run it
up to takeoff power. I want to have full power when I take the brakes
off, but the brakes wouldn't hold it with takeoff power."

"Oh, I can hold it!" George said. So he laid down underneath
the tail, and dug his heels in a little bit. He got a hold of the tail
wheel, and there he was, lying on his back. I ran the engine up to
takeoff power, and it was running good; full bore. I thought George
would let go. But he didn't; he hung on to it.

I finally had to open the door and shout, "Hey, George: let go!"

He was a powerful guy; he had big, wide shoulders. He was about 5'10", but he could hold that airplane to takeoff power. As soon as he let go, it jumped and away it went, heading down there.

I thought I was going to be okay. I was about two-thirds of the way down, and I figured I could ground-loop it before the trees if I had to. I had this all planned out. I let the tail come up, and it didn't want to stand up very much; there wasn't enough wind yet. If you tried to lift it off, the elevators would go down, and they work as a drag.

I didn't want to waste any speed, so I just let the stick go to neutral. The elevators ferried out flat to where they weren't holding me back any. But I just wasn't picking up speed like I would have liked to. I figured I could get it off the ground, though, because we had unloaded everything in it. It was just me.

I wasn't going to put any more drag on those elevators until I was right there. So I waited until I got right up close to the creek where the trees were. I slammed the elevator back and the tail hit the ground and put me in the air. I was just hanging in the air.

I thought I heard the wheels go through the tops of the trees; I wasn't sure. Anyway, I couldn't hold altitude. There was also a hayfield on the other side; the creek just ran through the middle of it. I let it go on down and hit the hayfield. By that time I had picked up enough speed and got a nice bounce; then I could stay in the air.

But I'm sure those wheels went through the tops of those trees, because I heard something. But I was so darned busy figuring out whether I was going to get over them. That's the closest I ever got to dinging an airplane. If it did get into the trees, it was just the wheels, because there were no marks on the wings or anything.

I went on over to the little airfield. Later on, George had one of the drillers bring him over with all the stuff we had taken out of the airplane. There was a nice little field over there; it was a little blacktop, one runway. So we put everything in.

"I didn't think you were gonna get over those trees," George said. "Did your wheels go through 'em?"

I said, "George, I thought that I heard them, but I was so busy trying to keep it in the air that I wouldn't bet on it; I don't know."

"Well," he said, "from here, it looked like your wheels went through the top of the trees. I'm sure glad I wasn't in there; we'd a never made it."

"George," I said, "we'd a never *tried* it." George was not that big, but he weighed about two hundred pounds. He was all muscle; he was a great guy. And that's the closest we ever came to scratching an airplane. It sure made an impression on me: Make sure you always have an out.

That was a great life with old George. You couldn't stir him. He rode some rodeo, too; not much. But he was a tough guy; he was a real cowboy.

Ten Dollars a Nose

I flew afternoons and weekends for George Askin Drilling Company for a full year or longer. It didn't take long to get my 200 hours, especially with our latest pursuit: George was a good trap shooter; he loved to shoot. I could fly. So hunting coyotes from the air seemed like a good way to combine our skills in a profitable way.

I would call the shop every night when I got out of school to see if there were any parts that needed to be delivered. George was running two, sometimes three of those rotary rigs. They could operate those rigs with just two men, because they weren't like the old hammer rigs.

When George and I got to thinking about hunting coyotes, I said, "Well, you know, you've got to get a waiver from the government to hunt coyotes, because you're shooting out of the airplane." They didn't mind you flying low, but you had to get a permit to fire out of an airplane. And they didn't give many of those.

I was only a teenager. Harold Price was the main coyote hunter in Miles City. He and another older fellow had been hunting coyotes a long time. He took me out a couple of times to show me how he operated.

Harold didn't have a gunner. He did his own shooting. He had a little Y welded onto the airplane, and he would lay his gun in that. He would fly it with one hand and shoot with the other. Many of those coyote hunters shot a propeller off, or otherwise dinged a lot of airplanes that way, because they would get to looking at the coyote.

So I asked this "veteran"—he was middle-aged, maybe forty—I said, "Do you think I could get a waiver?"

"How old are ya?" he wanted to know.

"Sixteen," I said.

"There's no need of you applyin' for a waiver or a permit to hunt coyotes," the old-timer said. "The inspector up in Billings has been there quite a long time, and he knows ya. And he knows all about this coyote hunting.

"I wouldn't even apply, because you're gonna get turned down. He's gonna have to turn you down. Wait till there's a new inspector." They rotated inspectors every two or three years.

"We'll get a new inspector in here who doesn't know anything about coyote hunting," he said. "Just call him on the phone, so you don't have anything to fill out, and he doesn't see how young you are. That way, if you're not there in person, he can't ask you a lot of questions."

So Lynam Choat, an ex-CAA Inspector, called me one day and said, "Hey, they got a new inspector up in Billings. Give him a call. Give him a song-and-dance story that you're losin' all your calves. The coyotes are killin' all your calves, and you'd like to have a waiver to shoot them out of the airplane."

I had gotten my private pilot's license in Billings. Nobody else hunting coyotes at the time had a private license; they all had commercial. But this new inspector had come in from the deep south; somewhere where there were no coyotes. He didn't know anything about coyotes.

By golly, I just talked to him on the phone and said, "Our calves are all gettin' killed by these darned coyotes. We tried trappin' them, but they're too darned smart for that." They *are* smart.

Coyotes can be vicious, too: they'll jump a calf, slit its throat, keep right on going and chase another calf down. They won't even eat it; many times they won't even come back to it. Coyotes are just like little wolves—and they're not very little. Some of those coyotes are *big*.

"Well," the inspector said, "I should be able to just send you the waiver. You can sign it and send my copy back." Sure enough, he sent me a waiver. I don't know if he looked on my other licenses and saw that I was born in 1922, and it just didn't ring—because I was only fifteen or sixteen.

So George and I would fly out to one of his rigs, he would work on it and we would hunt coyotes on the way back. I hunted them every winter. I *still* hunt them when I go back to Montana. We lease our home section of the old homestead to the next-door rancher. He has a Super Cub, and we can use that.

George Askin, my good friend,
employer and coyote-hunting partner.

That first winter, though, it took a while to get our timing down. The first time we went out, George had a box of shells. Even though he was a crack marksman, George shot about ten shells and never even *scared* a coyote. "You know," he said, "I'm doing something wrong. Let's go back to the airport, put a can out in the snow and see where the BBs are going."

So we went back in, put an old five-gallon can out on the airport grounds and made some passes by that. Well, the first pass we made, George took a shot and a puff of snow came up ahead of the can. George was leading the can like you would normally lead a running coyote, and the shot was going way out ahead. You always lead a coyote because they run like heck.

We went by again, this time with George trailing the can. From then on, every one of his shots hit the can. We had solved the mystery: When we were in the airplane, we were going twice as fast as the coyotes, and the shells were landing ahead of them. So George had to *trail* the coyotes with the shotgun in order to hit them. Neither one of us had thought of it.

From then on, if George shot eight shells—always trailing the coyotes, rather than leading them—he almost always got eight coyotes.

I asked him, "Now, George, when we get out there, would it be better if I slowed down?"

"No, no," he said. "Keep your speed up; just go the same speed."

I said, "Well, I like that better, because I like to have a little speed, and not stall out."

So I would fly parts out to George's drilling rigs. If there was some snow on the ground, and George wasn't busy, he would go with me. We would take the parts out and get the rig running. Then, on the way back, we would hunt coyotes.

George was a fantastic shot. He sat in the back seat of the airplane and slid the window down. He had an old twelve-gauge, single-shot shotgun. We loaded our own shotgun shells with BBs. George would put his arm and the gun out the window. He couldn't move the gun far enough aft to shoot off a strut, or far enough forward to hit a propeller.

George didn't have to move the gun much, because all I had to do was to get the airplane where it was supposed to be: right on the ground. We couldn't shoot from higher up, because running coyotes were just specks from above. We had to fly at the same height as the coyotes. I tried to fly off to the side, so the coyote wouldn't be watching us and turn.

We had skis on the bottom of the plane, and we pulled the nose of the skis up a little higher than normal. Every once in a while we would hear the heel of the ski touching the snow. We would be right down there at coyote height, and you could feel the heel of that ski scraping the snow. So you knew you were down; but it didn't hurt, because you had a ski.

We liked to hunt when there was a little snow on the ground, because we could see the coyotes. Coyotes usually aren't by themselves; they travel in packs of three to six. We would just catch the farthest one that was getting away—get him and then the others. We would get three, four, five coyotes right in one spot. If they were close together, we would land in among them.

We had a rope with a clamp on it, and a loop on the other end; and a seamless bag that fleas couldn't escape. My dad had those good seamless bags around the mill, for alfalfa seeds. I would get the bag and the rope out and hook them on the ski and open up the loop. By that time George had dragged the coyote up to it.

We would each take a back leg of the coyote, run the knife down and pull the hide off. The coyotes were often hot and sweaty, and the hides would slip right off. George and I would each walk, and the hide would go up around the head. Then George would skin around the ears and cut the nose off.

By the time George had the coyote skinned around the head and the nose off, I had the sack over there, the rope off its feet and was ready to dump the hide in the bag. Then we would go and get another one. We only saved the hides in winter; they weren't worth anything in the summer.

In the summer, lots of times we wouldn't even stop to skin it. We would just saw off the nose. We got a $10 bounty for each one. For a long time, the Cattlemen's Association paid the bounty; then the government began paying it.

So you just turned the nose in and got ten dollars apiece. And we had the pelts. I had built some one-by-twos that I used for stretchers. When I got back to town I would take my pelts up to the attic of a shop that George had, put them on a stretcher and hang them up.

We just let them dry there for the winter. Then, when the fur buyer came around in the spring, he would bid for them all. Usually I had four or five hundred—and they would pretty well put me through college.

George wouldn't take anything. He wouldn't even let me buy any gas to practice in the airplane. Of course, he had more money than he could count.

If there was a heavy snow, the coyotes would hole up. The next day they would all be out hunting. One afternoon we got twelve coyotes, coming in from the rig.

I carried a little .22 pistol. Occasionally I would drag a coyote that wasn't quite dead over to the airplane. George just had the shotgun. He said there was no time to shoot more than once—and we would just get into trouble if we tried.

Lots of times George would shoot eight times and get eight coyotes. We would stop and skin each one we shot. If it was real cold, we wouldn't turn the engine off; we would let it idle. George would drag the coyote up close to the airplane. I got the stuff out to put on his feet and stretch him out. We never took over ten minutes for a stop.

One morning there had been a big snow the day and night before, and it cleared off into a nice, sunny day. Of course, the coyotes hole up when it's storming. Well, they were all out in this one big field. There were five of them, so we just took the outside one, and went around and started shooting the coyotes as they were running. And we got all five of them.

The pilots up north in Alaska, they talk about wolves. But they get one wolf once in a great while. They don't get eight of them a day like we did.

Anyway, I landed right in among the coyotes, so we wouldn't have to haul them. Some of them are pretty big; we just dragged them. One coyote was a little farther out. So George said, "Well, I'll go get that one out there." It was not too close to us, but George was a strong, husky guy. He threw the big coyote over his neck, holding it by the feet, and began walking back to the plane.

Well, I was getting ready to skin them. I had a little loop with a clamp on it, and I would hook that on to the ski. Then I would hook the loop on their hind feet and skin them. Well, here comes George with two coyotes, one over each shoulder.

George had not shaved for a couple days. By the time he got to the airplane, those fleas on the coyotes had realized that the animals were dead, but that George was alive—and they all moved into his beard. George jumped around and yelled, "Oh my God! I'm gettin' eaten up by the fleas!"

George wasn't making any headway at all in killing them, so we had to drop everything. "I gotta get to a barber!" he howled. We weren't far from the little town of Baker. George knew the barber there, so he went in right away.

"Wash those fleas and shave me please!" he pleaded with the barber. So they shaved all that stuff off and gave him a good shower and got the fleas off him. But he still had red spots all over his face where they had shaved him.

Despite the fleas and other hazards, we usually got five or six hundred coyotes a season, which helped me pay for college, or take a girlfriend to the show or dancing.

Hunting coyotes with George Askin in southeastern Montana.
We got $10 a nose for each one. If George didn't kill one with
the shotgun, I would get out and finish it off with my .22 pistol.
In winter I wore a tight suit that the fleas couldn't penetrate.
George—and his beard—weren't so lucky one time.

You wouldn't know George Askin was a multi-millionaire. He loved shooting those coyotes. He was a character; he was such a gentleman. He was just great; he was like another dad to me. He let me use that airplane anytime I wanted. We never scratched the airplane.

One older friend who hunted coyotes, Lynum Choate, had taken me out to give me some pointers. He did well. The one time he did crash an airplane, however, it wasn't his flying that did him in. This old coyote was sharp, and he wouldn't get out in the open and run.

There was a great big fir tree out there, and as soon as he saw the airplane, he scampered over beneath the fir tree. Lynum couldn't get a shot at him at all. And it bothered him so bad—and of course he kind of lost his temper—he decided he was going to *get* that coyote. And here it was under the fir tree.

So Lynum came up and put the plane into a slip so that he could shoot out. He got the coyote; but he didn't straighten out fast enough and he went right into that tree. That plane just sat out there like a big hawk, and it only poked some holes in the bottom fabric.

Lynum had to get a crane to go in and pick his plane out of the tree and get it out. They patched the fabric. Lynum was really embarrassed about the pictures of that thing sitting up in that tree.

Lynum could really fly; he flew right up until he was about eighty. He was out there spraying the golf course for mosquitoes. A lot of big trees. He would just get right down there and go through the trees. He didn't have enough room to go through flat, so he would cock it up.

Lynum never had an accident. Landing in that tree was the only time he ever dinged a plane. He was an excellent pilot. They even talked him into being an FAA inspector for awhile. They sent him to Pittsburgh. He was there for a year, then he came back to Montana.

Scotty and I went out to dinner with Lynum and his wife. It was a Saturday night. He said, "Have you ever done any spraying, Jack?"

"No," I said, "I really haven't. I've seen you go through that golf course, and I don't think I'd like to go down through those trees."

"Well, I've got a real good job tomorrow," he said. "A rancher wants me to come out and spray the sage brush on his grazing land. The darned sage brush is taking over the wild hay that the cattle like." Lynum had two sprayer planes; they were real nice, came from the factory and were made for spraying. You sat up high, over the engine; you could really see. There was a big tank behind you.

"You know," Lynum said, "we could use both airplanes, and we could go out there and have some fun spraying." I looked at Scotty. She didn't look very pleased, but didn't say anything.

Lynum picked me up the next day. We went up and fueled both airplanes. He had a flagman. Lynum said, "He's gonna stand down at the end, and I'm gonna fly right for him. Then he's gonna move over for the next pass. What you want to do is just fly behind me, and do what I do. When you see me dump my tank, you can dump yours."

Those planes have a lot of power. Lynum came up to the end of the field, and instead of putting a lot of power on and working the engine, he just reached down and pulled half flap. I just watched what he did, and we had a lot of fun spraying several sections. It was rolling land; no mountains, no trees or telephone poles—nothing.

Sage brush spreads out, and no grass will grow underneath it. One mouthful of wild timothy is better than a barrelful of hay for the animals. It grows during droughts. If they didn't have any of that in Montana, my dad would ship in a few carloads. Usually he would get alfalfa, though.

That was fun; it was the only spraying I ever did. Lynum died in his sleep. He was eighty-something.

Chain Gang

We fished on Fort Peck Lake, near Glasgow, Montana, which freezes over nicely in the winter. Fort Peck Lake is a big lake. That water goes down the Missouri River and all the way to the Mississippi. We used to go up there and land, two or three of us in small airplanes. On this particular trip there were three airplanes, and six of us altogether.

Horace Dale, who owned Dale's Jewelers in Miles City, loved to fish. But he had never fished through the ice in Fort Peck Lake. So I told Horace that we were going to go up, and that he had better go with me. So he did.

We landed on the lake. It doesn't have much snow on it; the wind blows it off pretty well. We went out and chopped a hole in the ice. The fishing was good. When we got ready to go, Horace said, "Well, I'll go over and help you put the chains on."

I said, "Horace, we don't need any chains."

Fishing on frozen Fort Peck Lake near Glasgow, Montana. We landed on the thick ice, cut a hole in it and had good luck fishing. My friend asked if we would put chains on the plane to get off.

"This is ice," he said. "How can we get off of here on this slippery ice, if we don't have chains?"

"That thing in front," I said, "is what gets us off. That *propeller.* We don't need chains. There's no traction on those wheels; those are just brakes."

"Well," Horace said, "we better puts chains on, in case we need to use the brakes."

"I don't have any chains," I said. I had a terrible time getting him in the airplane, because I didn't have chains on those wheels. But I finally did. And he always wanted to go back to Fort Peck to go fishing.

Firefighter

Scotty and I were watching a movie one night in Miles City when a rancher came in and paged me. There was a forest fire and a prairie fire blazing outside of town, and they couldn't find out how to get in to fight it. There wasn't a moon out. It was blacker than heck that night, but it was clear. So they paged me and I went out, and here was Bruce Orcutt, one of dad's good friends and customers.

Bruce was not a rancher; he was a lawyer—I think it was Chicago. And he just got to where he couldn't stand any more of that. He had made a lot of money, so he came out and bought a real nice ranch. He had registered white-faces, Herefords.

We went out there quite often. Dad would go out and hunt pheasant. Anyway, Bruce came in to the theater, and Scotty and I were about in the middle of this movie. But it was nice and dark outside. "Jackie," he said, "do you think it's too dark to fly out to the ranch? We got this darn fire goin' in the pine hills out there.

"So far the wind hasn't come up," he said. "But if it does, it's gonna raise heck with our grazing land. And we can't get to it. The ranchers are all gathered around there, and they can't find out how to get in to it. I told them I'd come in and see if I could find ya."

"Sure," I said, "we can go. I'll give Scotty the keys, and she can just go on home when the movie's over. When we come back in, why, you can run me out to her house in your pickup."

So I got things all arranged, and we headed out to the ranch. We didn't have to go very far until we could see this big glare in the sky. We went in and circled it once, and Bruce spotted a couple of places they could get up on a ridge and drive in.

Bruce had a large, white canvas bag, a rock and a tablet. He drew the other ranchers a map on how to get in to fight the fire.

There was a regular highway. It was not a big one, but it went from Miles City out to Broadus; there was a little traffic on it. They were going to have two of the ranchers park their pickups with their lights on, facing one another.

We were going to drop down, and Bruce would throw the bag out right between the lights. So that's what we did; he just pushed it right out of the door of the airplane. Well, we got it right there in the middle of the highway, and we could see them picking up the stuff. So then we came back to town.

Sure enough, they had found a couple of places, based on Bruce's instructions, and went in and put the fire out before it spread to the grass. Bruce had sketched a real good map of where to get the rural fire-fighting equipment in to put out the blaze. It didn't take him long to draw it. He had the ring of the fire, and the location of it. Then all he had to do was draw the routes to get in to it.

Bruce was well known in that area. All the ranchers thought he was really going to waste his money, being a lawyer and never having been on a ranch.

Buzz Bomb

The Redmans—you remember my friend Charles—had a super rancher's outhouse. It was a three-holer, if I remember, because it was pretty big. It was just out behind the house, maybe a couple hundred feet. There was a creek that ran by in front of it, and on down by the barnyard. There was always something going on down in that creek—ducks or geese or something.

We could come in over the ridge, take the power off and go all the way down without making a sound. Well, George and I came in one day, and before we got up to the outhouse, I said, "Hey, George—that door's open." It was a nice warm day.

"I'll bet you Jetta's in there," I said. So we really throttled right back to nothing, and went on over and got closer to the outhouse. The door was open and she was sitting in the outhouse. So I gunned it—"RMMMMMBPH! RMMMMMBPH!"—and she jumped up and didn't know what to do. Of course we went on.

Shawn, my son, says, "Oh, yeah, tell that one."

But Shannon, my daughter, says, "No, I don't think you'd better put *that* in there."

That was really a kick. Jetta always fixed nice lunches for us—they all did—because they wanted us to hunt the coyotes to get them out of their area. That was Charles Redman's mother. His father's name was Winfield. He could really play a fiddle.

Charles can fiddle, too, but he won't. He's just kind of bashful. But that was really a kick with Jetta. I told George, "I think we should skip lunch here today. We'll go on over to the next ranch, because they want us to hunt coyotes there, too."

Dropping in on Dubois

George was pretty much the father of the whole group. He took over his dad's drilling, then hired the rest of them. George was a great guy. I always kind of felt like I had two fathers. My dad was just a great guy: real down-to-earth and easy to talk to. George was the same way.

He always let me make up my mind on the airplane. If the weather was a little bad, I would say, "George, I think we can hack this weather. But the forecast says it's gonna get a little worse."

And he would say, "Jackie, I think I'd better just jump in my

Chrysler and take off." He never pushed at all, ever. I finally taught him to fly. When I left, he hired another person, but didn't have very good luck with him. He cracked up two airplanes the first year.

The next time I went home, I said, "George, wouldn't you like to learn to fly yourself? You're conservative, and you haven't had very good luck with the person who took over from me." The pilot was an acquaintance of mine, and he was an excellent pilot. He could do most anything with the airplane, but he didn't use good judgment.

Because he was so at home in the airplane, and could do everything with it, he felt that he could always go and get through. His name was George, too; George Stockhill. He never had a problem flying, except when he caused it himself.

One warm afternoon he was flying back to Miles City, but the wind was blowing the other way. He took off, made a turn and thought, "I'll salute 'em on the way back." So he dove down to the well rig with a lot of speed. When he tried to pull the plane up, it didn't pull up; it just pushed right on through that thin air.

It hit the ground—KER-WUMP!—got up on the nose and spun. George Askin was in the back seat; he got bruised a little bit. Well, they couldn't find George Stockhill; they looked around and he wasn't anywhere. Finally, they saw two feet sticking out of the bottom of the airplane.

Those airplanes have a thin plywood floor, and Stockhill's legs and feet had gone right through that plywood. They had to chop him out of there. He broke both legs. But it didn't change him; he did something else like that. He wrecked another airplane, completely wiped it out.

Anyway, George Stockhill's uncle, Larry Stockhill—who was only a year or two older than him—was also a pilot. Luckily for us, he was a mechanic as well. We went down on the train to Boise. We had bought three planes: two for the flying school, to replace those burned up in the hangar fire, and one for George Askin.

The Miles City hangar after the fire in December 1942, which destroyed all five or six of our training airplanes.

We took the train to Boise to get these airplanes to replace those burned up in the hangar fire.

I was flying the plane for George Askin. George and Larry Stockhill followed me in their airplanes on the way back, because I was the only one with a map.

During the first part of the war, you couldn't get any maps. I had to take the maps from the flying school when the hangar burned down—or wherever I could find a map. This was about 1941. World War II had started, but the Air Force hadn't gotten really revved up yet. It was just about the first year of the schools.

I had to be eighteen to get in the school and get a commercial license. I finished up the course at the school; it was just a forty-hour course. I already had a lot of flight time, so I zipped right through it.

Anyway, that country was rugged—the Montana mountains—that we had to fly over. We thought we were going to be able to make it through okay. But once we left Idaho Falls, it just began to snow and snow and snow—and we still had to get through the pass.

We couldn't go over the pass with those airplanes. We got up there and it was blocked solid. So we turned around and came back. We thought it was just a front going through. Rather than going clear back to Idaho Falls, there was an alternate airport in Dubois, Idaho, just before the pass. They built it because the pass had a lot of weather problems.

Over in southeastern Montana, wild timothy grew for the cattle. We never mowed it or anything; we just left it for winter forage. It would grow to about eight inches.

When we came back, I flew over the strip. I could see about three or four inches of the wild timothy sticking up through the snow. "Well, that will be okay to land in"—or so I thought.

Having hunted coyotes, I learned that you can never judge how deep the snow is from the air—especially on an airport, because there's nothing there. If you had a post out there that was marked or something, maybe you could gauge the depth.

Anyway, it looked to me like there was not too much snow. So I came in and landed. Hunting coyotes in the snow, I always landed with the tail wheel first.

Well, as soon as the tail wheel hit, it dug right into the snow. I had to use full throttle to keep the airplane from going over. But I stopped in a couple hundred feet with full throttle on. I knew that the snow up there was different, because it's close to the mountains. And there was about a foot and a half of snow there.

At least a foot and a half. Because when I got out of the airplane, I went right in above my knee, and I couldn't get up. I was in the snow, trying to get up, and I heard this CRACK! CRACK! as the two other airplanes came in and landed—or attempted to land—right alongside me.

But George and Larry Stockhill hadn't been coyote hunting.

They just made a normal landing; and the instant those wheels hit, they were over on their back. It was my fault, it really was. We should have gone back to Idaho Falls, where they plowed the snow all the time. They had plowed this place earlier. It looked like it was freshly plowed, but it wasn't.

This was right after Christmas, and we would be there until just after New Year's getting parts. This was during the war. Things were tough; airplanes were like cars. Larry had an A&E license, and had worked for the fixed-base operator in Kalispell. So he got him on the phone and said, "I need two new propellers and a new carburetor. If you can't get me a new one, get me ones that are good."

Finally they rounded up the parts and sent them down by Greyhound. Larry put them on. But it took us a week to get them, put them on and get out of there.

George and Larry Stockhill and I hit some deep snow in Dubois, Idaho. They both flipped over. In 75 years of flying, I have never scratched an airplane, had a violation or failed a flight test. I've had lots of good luck.

Larry Stockhill installing a new prop on airplane in Dubois, Idaho. Little did we know that we would be "pressed" into duty on the basketball court. But those townspeople really treated us well.

So we were there in Dubois—a little town of about two hundred; a little Mormon town. They invited us to come over and practice basketball with the team a lot. They were getting ready for the big game. But the other town wasn't able to make it; there was just too much snow. So they gave us a couple of substitutes. Then Larry, George and I played the high school team. It was a kick, you know, in the gym.

Both George and Larry were taller than me. I was five-foot-eight and a half, and they were more like five-foot-ten. They were taller than the high school kids, and neither of them smoked. That's why they did so well the first half. We were a point or two ahead by halftime.

But after the half, it was obvious that the high school team was in much better health than we were. Those high school kids will run you up and down the floor. They beat us by about ten points.

Then they invited us to come to the New Year's Eve celebration at the church. They had a big dinner and music. The Mormons really took care of us. I had never been around them before, but they sure were a friendly bunch.

They really took us in. It must have been something having two airplanes on their back—and the pilots right there who did the trick!

As I've said, George Stockhill didn't seem to have much caution. He handled the airplane so well that he just went. He wiped out two airplanes flying for George Askin. As soon as I taught George Askin to fly, George Stockhill went to Missoula. He did real well. He and a dentist got into mutual funds.

They bought a nice airplane, a four-seater. The dentist moved to Las Vegas. George's wife was a lot like Scotty, a real nice ranch girl. They had a boy and a girl, a few years apart, who were teenagers at the time. They were going to go down to Los Angeles for the Rose Bowl game. They went a couple of days early, and spent it with his dentist friend in Vegas.

George hadn't flown into Los Angeles. The weather there can be clear, but they don't have any visibility, with all that smog. Instead of leaving early in the afternoon, George waited until evening. By the time he got to L.A., it was dark, and smog shrouded the city.

So George was just flying right along on top of the freeway, because that's where all the cars were, going from L.A. to Vegas. He didn't have an instrument rating. He was flying just off to the right side of the freeway, with all of the lights leading him into L.A. And there was a little knoll there, off to the side of the freeway.

He hit the top of that knoll and killed all four of them, New Year's Eve. It was just another misjudgment of George's. He should have started out early in the day, when it was clear. By evening it really gets smoggy in L.A.

It was zero visibility, that's what George got into. And he had to fly just a hundred to two hundred feet above the freeway. He was off to the right of it, so he was looking out the left window, flying along, and here were all these cars and lights.

All at once, WHOMP! He hit this little knoll. It was only a couple of hundred feet high. He hit the top of it and just wrapped his plane up in a ball. Killed all four of them. He wouldn't have had that problem at all if he had been coming in at noon.

Larry eventually went into business in Kalispell, at the airport. He was spraying and had a bad accident. He hit a tree or a power line, had a fire and got burned pretty badly. But he got out of it, and flew again.

Anyway, everybody in Dubois thought that he and Larry didn't know what they were doing—because *I* didn't go over on my back. I didn't flip over, of course, because I dragged the tail in like I was hunting coyotes—and didn't know for sure if I was going to hit a little drift or something.

We were in Dubois a day or two after New Year's Eve. So we were there for almost a week, just waiting to get the parts down and have Larry put them on. They had bent the wing strut on one of the planes, and we couldn't get a new strut for it. The wing strut holds the whole airplane when you're flying in those little ones.

The bolts fastening the wing strut to the fuselage are just a base bolt. But this strut had a lot of bend in it. So we took it off, and had a nice flat spot on the hangar floor. We flattened it out completely flat, so it was plumb straight.

The wing struts are not very big. On small airplanes, they're only about four or five inches, and run right out close to the tip of the wing. But we got it straightened on the floor. Larry got a piece of angle iron and welded it onto the leading edge of each strut. It was a little heavy, but it was really strong. He flew the plane back to the flight school in Montana, where they got a new strut for it.

So it was quite a week. We really got to like those Mormons. They were nice, friendly people, and made it really comfortable for us. They had a little two-story hotel there, maybe eight rooms on each floor. We were upstairs, and they had a restaurant in the hotel.

And, of course, we were kind of odd characters, just dropping in like that—on our backs!

Butte and Beyond

When the hangar burned down in Miles City—along with all our airplanes—and the school was forced to close for awhile, I transferred to Butte to finish out the year. Johnny Fox was an old, old-time pilot. He owned Fox Flying Service there. His younger brother, Wayne Fox, instructed with me there at Fox Flying Service. I instructed CPT and attended the School of Mines Engineering School there. It was a math school.

When the war ended, Wayne went with a group that put on air shows. He had done aerobatics close to the ground. He was going right by the grandstand, upside down, when the engine quit on him. He went in—just ZZZHIK!—upside down and got killed. He was just a couple years older than I was.

Johnny Fox flew for an air show, too. His act was to fly through a hangar. He had a building that was mostly cardboard, but it looked like a hangar. And he would come down and fly right through it— with the doors closed.

He did that for several years before the war started, because he couldn't make a living up there; there weren't enough students or anything. My dad was right, you know, about pilots not being able to make a living. And Butte had its ups and downs; it all depended on what the mines were doing.

I went up to Butte in the wintertime and boy, it was cold. We flew down to twenty below—and no heat in the back seat for the instructor. They had a great big old pot-bellied stove in there, and a gas burner in it. Sometimes they would have to help me out of the back of that airplane. I would stagger in and stand around that pot-bellied stove until I thawed out—then go out for another hour.

I went over to the University of Montana in Missoula for a year, to finish up over there. The dean in Missoula was a private pilot, and really easy to work with. I flew from seven o'clock in the morning until noon, then went to school from one o'clock on in the afternoon and evenings. Sometimes I would be at college until 9:00 at night.

Johnny Fox in Butte, Montana

I also had two years of med school. I was taking the fewest number of courses you could carry, because I didn't really want to have anything to do with medicine. It was just that my folks thought it was a good idea.

I was one quarter short of having the pre-med, four-year course. But I hadn't learned anything. I did manage to take a lot of college courses, though, because I was going summer and winter.

When I called Pan Am, they wanted four years of college and a hundred hours—and I had three times as much as they needed. They said they would much rather have the extra flight time than that one quarter of college.

CHAPTER 4

SCOTTY

Meals on Wheels

SCOTTY'S father, Jesse H. Trafton, was born in Nepponset, Massachusetts on March 1, 1889, to Jesse A. and Millicent Connell Trafton. The family moved to Reedville, New York, where the father was a civil engineer on the New York, New Haven & Hartford Railroad. After the father passed away in 1898, Jesse, his mother and brother moved to Prince Edward Island, Canada.

Jesse came to his uncle Henry Connell's in Fallon, Montana in 1905. He worked as a chore boy, sheepherder and mail carrier near Marsh, Montana. In 1906 Jesse went to work for the Milwaukee Railroad as a machinist. They were having trouble with the steam engine. They had a little steam engine back on his farm, so he went down and fixed the steam engine for them and they hired him as the pile driver.

Jesse's mother cooked for the work crews. After a stint building dams and railroad depots, Jesse returned to Prince Edward Island and married Elizabeth Hazel (Nonie) Cotton on December 18, 1912.

The newlyweds returned to Miles City on December 25, 1912, where Jesse again went to work for Milwaukee, running the railroad's pumping plant on the Yellowstone River. The couple lived in a house near the water tanks—a little homestead, cattle ranch, where the railroad was being built through—not too far from where my folks homesteaded.

Jesse would go to work on Monday morning. He had his own little putt-putt car that he could put on the railroad tracks and come back down to the ranch for Saturday afternoon and Sunday.

One day Jesse brought the boss back with him. The boss wanted to see his homestead, and wanted to meet Nonie, who was a fantastic cook. She fixed him a dinner that he hadn't had in a long time. The boss said, "Do you like to cook?"

"Oh yeah," she said.

Scotty's mother, "Nonie," and her two brothers, Les and Sherman, on their ranch, ready to feed the stock.

"Well," he said, "wouldn't you like to come to work for the Milwaukee? It would be a lot easier for you to cook for just the crew—in this cook car. There's a lot of room; it's a big cook car. You're here with these three little kids—and the cows, and the rattlesnakes. And your children have to ride a horse across the river to go to school."

Scotty's two brothers, Sherman and Leslie, were a year apart. We called Sherman 'Sherm' and Leslie 'Les.' Sherm was about four years older than Scotty, and Les was a year older than Sherm. They were great guys.

Because they rode to school on a horse from the homestead across a creek, Nonie didn't want them on separate horses. She held Leslie back a year, so the two of them rode the same horse, and were in the same grade.

"It would be a lot easier if you would just come run our cook car," Jesse's boss persisted.

"Yeah, it really would," Nonie said.

"Well, I'd like to hire you," he said. "We've got a real nice dining car, with a kitchen at the end. We'll just bring in another car and attach it. It will be your apartment, the kids' apartment. It would be a lot more room than the little house you have on the homestead."

Scotty's mother, Nonie, cook for the Milwaukee Railroad, provided "meals on wheels" for the crews. March, 1920. (*Home on the Range—Recipes and Stories from Montana*, Mary Haughian, 1981.)

So that's what they did. They got a foreman to come and take care of the place, and Nonie cooked. She went all the way to Miles City, or beyond Miles City. It took them a long time to build the railroad line and bridges. Then, when the railroad got in to Miles

City, Jesse and Nonie bought a little house, so that the kids could go to school there, and Nonie gave up cooking for the railroad.

A Piece of History

After they got the railroad built, Jesse worked as a steamfitter in Miles City, where they had a big roundhouse. Then he got laid off, just as the government was getting rid of Fort Keogh, which lies about two miles west of Miles City. They turned Fort Keogh into a research station for cattle and horses. The Traftons lived out there for about ten years.

Fort Keogh is a very historic place. Situated at the confluence of the Tongue and Yellowstone Rivers, it offered access for boats bringing supplies from the east up the Yellowstone River. A paddle-wheeler came up the Mississippi River, then up the Missouri to the Yellowstone River and on up to Miles City. It couldn't go any farther because the rapids got too bad.

The order for the creation of the fort was signed in August, 1876, two months after Colonel George Custer's defeat at the Battle of the Little Big Horn. The fort was named for one of Custer's adjutants, Myles Keogh, an Irish-born career soldier who was also killed in the battle. Keogh's horse, Commanche, was found walking around the battlefield after the clash. Commanche was nursed to health, and became a legend as the "sole survivor" of the battle from Custer's regiment.

The Army's main goal at Fort Keogh was to bring the Indians in the region under control and onto reservations. General Nelson A. Miles commanded the post. He was well respected, by both his troops and the Indians whom he befriended with promises of fair treatment and a better life.

Fort Keogh had several acres of parade grounds, and a place where they worked the horses out. They built large duplexes for the officers, with two stories and two front doors. Those great big buildings were nice. Every room had a fireplace in it. Scotty and her family lived in one of those houses.

During the Depression, when the railroad laid off many workers, Jesse's work at Fort Keogh was able to sustain the family for nine years. There was a lot of farming at Fort Keogh, and raising hay for the horses and cows. They had a lot of machinery and equipment out there, and Jesse kept a lot of it running.

Officer's home at Fort Keogh, two miles west of Miles City. Scotty's family lived in this house for several years. Two families lived in each one.

A Good Little Irishman

The Milwaukee Railroad shop finally built back up again, and they called Jesse back in. He worked on and off for the railroad for the next 30 years, as a pile driver, pipefitter and bridge builder.

Jesse had a sense of humor. An Oriental fellow helped him as a machinist, and they were good friends. This Japanese guy was telling Grandpa Jesse, "Boy, I got some of this new soap—it floats! It's Ivory soap and it floats!" He was telling him all about it.

Jesse got into his locker and got this bar of soap out. He took it in and pushed some bearings in it. When they got ready to wash up, his helper was going to show him. "Just watch this soap," he said as he tossed it in the tub. But down it sank—glug, glug, glug.

"I thought you told me it floated," Jesse said.

"Well it *did* float," his helper said.

Jesse was always doing something like that.

Jesse was also the lone Republican in the whole machine shop. Like most unions, it was really democrat. There were a couple of them that Jesse really had a lot of fun arguing with, telling them about the problems that the democrats were having.

But he had a sense of humor; he never got riled up at all. He, too, was a good little Irishman; he was a kick. If some old Irish-type jig music came on the radio or TV, he would jump up and do that Irish jig. He was something else.

Jesse and Nonie moved to Eagles Manor in December, 1975. They lived there for eight years until Nonie's health deteriorated, and she moved to the Custer County Rest Home. She passed away on November 15, 1985. The couple enjoyed almost seventy-three years together.

Jesse Trafton lived to be more than a hundred years old, celebrating that landmark birthday at a family reunion on March 5, 1989. We all went back for his 100th birthday.

Scotty's folks, Jesse and Elizabeth "Nonie" Trafton, on the Wall of Fame, Range Riders Museum, Miles City, Montana.

All Scotch

Alma Millicent "Scotty" Trafton was born on her parents' homestead in eastern Montana. She hated her given names—Alma and Millicent—because they were "hand-me-downs" from her grandmothers. I didn't know her, at first, in high school, because she was two years behind me. I was a senior, and we had the ground floor. But I saw this cute, kind of bashful girl walking by my locker every day.

I would check her out, and just say "hi" as she walked by. I didn't have a clue who she was. She was a doll. I thought she was the cutest gal in town. And she was; she really was.

Scotty came to school on the "Toonerville Trolley" from Fort Keogh. Back in those days, they didn't have buses running in. Fort Keogh had its own Toonerville Trolley, a Ford Model T pickup that they built into a bus.

Anyway, I was teaching Sherm, Scotty's older brother, to fly. One Sunday we were up at the airport flying. We got through early, and there was no one else to teach. "Why don't you come on out and eat with us," he said. "Mom was fixin' a turkey when I left."

"Gosh, that sounds good," I said. I didn't know that she was his sister.

So I went out to his house. There she was in the kitchen, whipping cream for the pumpkin pie. "I'd like to have you meet my sister," Sherm said. "This is Alma."

"You know, I didn't realize that Alma was your sister," I said. "She's been walking by my locker every morning and afternoon, goin' to the Toonerville Trolley." She knew my locker number, because a time or two she just stopped. I didn't know who she was, but I always admired her.

She was just finishing up the whipped cream, filling a bowl with it and putting it in the refrigerator. I noticed she left a lot of whipped cream in the beater, and was cleaning it out with her finger.

"Sherm," I said, "you've always told me that you guys are Scotch and Irish. But I don't think you're Irish. By the looks of that whipped cream that your sister saved out"—and she was over there licking it out with her finger—"I think she's all *Scotch*.

"You know, I think you should change her name. I think we ought to call her *Scotty*."

"Gee," she said. "I'd like that. That's better than Alma or Millicent. I don't know why my folks named me after my grandmothers. One was Alma and one was Millicent. Those are my two names—and I don't like either one of 'em. I like Scotty."

So it was Scotty from then on. And it didn't take any time at all for the word to get around the high school—and that was a big high school. Custer County is the largest county in the state, and Miles City is the county seat. It was the only high school in the county.

After I had met Scotty at her house and had dinner with her family, she was coming by my locker one afternoon from school—we got out at 3:15—heading for the Toonerville Trolley. She stopped by my locker for a minute.

"You know," she said, "I sure hate to get on that bus. We've got a whole bunch of new sewing equipment in the Home Ec class. They're getting it unboxed, and the class is going to stay there until six o'clock and learn how this new equipment works. And I gotta get on that darned Toonerville Trolley."

"Just a minute," I said. "Let me run in to the gym here, and I'll call my dad to see if he has anything I have to do over at the elevator. I can take you home at six o'clock. My airport work will be done by then."

Dad didn't have anything for me, so I said, "I'll go out and tell Sherm—he's in the bus—that I'll bring you home around six, so that you can get in on all that new equipment."

From then on, if there was anything special going on, I would tell Scotty to be sure and stop at my locker, and I would call my dad.

So I started going with Scotty when I was a senior in high school and she was a sophomore. The next year, when she was a junior, she got elected to the Usher's Club. It was kind of the elite club of the girls; they all liked it. They had uniforms and ushered the school plays. The class elected them, kind of like electing an officer. Scotty was elected junior representative.

At Custer High School, we had a dance every other Friday night in the gym. There was a bowling alley downtown. Downstairs they had a little bar called the College Inn, where they made hamburgers and sold soft drinks. It was open every night except Sunday. There was nickelodeon music there all the time. Scotty and I went dancing several nights a week. It was a lot of fun.

One Foot on the Ground

Scotty didn't like little airplanes. But her mother, Nonie, did; she just loved them. If you're training with a small tandem airplane, it really changes the performance of the airplane if you don't have anybody in the back seat. So we had a big sandbag that we would put in there.

Nonie would go up with me. I would practice rolls, spins, loops and all of the other maneuvers that we had to do to get our license—and Nonie just thought it was great. I took Nonie up in the plane all the time. I would go out and get her and use her for a sandbag.

Grandpa Jesse rode horses, but he didn't want to have anything to do with an airplane. "Anytime that you can give me a ride and I can keep one foot on the ground," he said, "I'll go."

We lived out near Seward Park, close to Boeing Field, and I did a lot of instructing for Pan Am anyway. If there was any major service at all on an airplane, you had to flight test it. They had changed the propellers on this DC-3, so we had to take it up.

They called me on a Sunday afternoon and said, "Gee, we didn't think we were going to get through this until tomorrow. Are you busy this afternoon?"

"Well, no," I said.

They said, "We need to take it up and feather both engines and make sure the propellers are working."

"Good," I said. "I've got my in-laws here; I'll bring them along." So I took Nonie and Jesse, and I noticed that Jesse grabbed the Sunday paper as he got in the back seat and rode down to Boeing Field. We parked where we could look out at the runway.

"Now Jesse," I said, "I realize that you didn't want to fly with me in the small airplanes—especially if I was practicing maneuvers. But here we have an airliner, and it's gonna be *just us* up there on this beautiful day. We'll go up and circle Mount Rainier as we do this."

Jesse looked over at me and said, "Can I keep one foot on the ground?"

"Well, you've gotta have a long leg for that, Grandpa," I said. Do you think we could get him out of that car? No, sir. He sat there and read the Sunday paper, and the three of us went. We had one mechanic who acted as copilot and wanted to feather the engines and test the props.

So we went up, circled Mount Rainier and went up and down Lake Washington for about two hours with our own DC-3. When we got back, Grandpa was still reading the newspaper. He never did get in the airplane.

Seeing the World

Scotty and I got married my first year in college. We were together seventy years. Nobody in Seattle ever knew her by any other name. Our first few years married we spent a lot of time in Montana. We lived in Seattle. We were operating out of Boeing Field then; SeaTac hadn't been built yet. It was nice, and Seattle was good.

When we first came out to Seattle, the war was on, and you couldn't find a place to live anywhere. Pan Am's Ground School manager was married to the daughter of a woman named Mrs. Burkheimer, who had a nice home just north of the University of Washington.

We went up to see her, and she was happy to see us. "You can stay right here with me for as long as you want," she said.

"Oh, no; we can't impose like that," we said. But she liked to have people around, because three or four of her sons had been drafted. So we stayed there for a month or two.

Then I made an arrangement with another pilot and his wife to rent an apartment up at the Ambassador Hotel, just a block and a half off Broadway. It was about a ten-story building.

He was getting transferred to San Francisco, but he didn't know for how long. "I'll just tell them that I'm going down on temporary duty," he said, "and that you're gonna hold it for me." So that's what he did.

He was still in San Francisco when Scotty and I got transferred to New York. I was twenty-one, and Scotty and I got married just a little before that. We lived in that Ambassador for about a year, in one of those apartments where the bed unfolded out of the wall and covered the whole living room. It wasn't very big, but we really enjoyed it out here. The old apartment is still there; they've made it into condos.

A photo from our wedding.

Our wedding photo.

Scotty and I on the locks at "The Thumb," Yellowstone Lake. My
sister Kate went with us on a week-long trip.

We went to New York and enjoyed six or eight months there.
But the war had started and you couldn't get gas to go anywhere,
except to the airport to work. We lucked out again there: we got a
row house out on Long Island. But it had to be within the circle of
the gas coupons.

There was a couple who were transferred to Miami, and they
didn't want any children in the house. So they rented that for us.
And a brick row house—you can't get through from the front yard
to the back yard without going through your basement; they're all
attached.

It was a nice little house with two bedrooms, and a good-sized
basement with a garage in it. So we were there until we figured we
had had enough of New York.

Our first apartment, the Ambassador, two blocks west of
Broadway in Seattle. Scotty could walk to a nearby theater and
go to a show every day while I was up in Kodiak, Alaska.

Our rental house near Flushing on Long Island, New York.

As the war was winding down, they started building more apartments and houses in the Seattle area. They built some nice, two-bedroom houses off old Highway 99 where you started to pull up out of the valley from south Seattle. You had to be a veteran to buy or rent one, though. They preferred that you buy one. But we didn't; we rented one.

It was a nice two-bedroom house with hardwood floors. The only thing was that they had an unfinished basement with a coal furnace—you couldn't get gas or anything—so they dumped coal in the coal room. We had to keep the fire pot in that darned thing, and it would scare Scotty to death.

I would be out on an Alaska trip or something, and she had to go down there at night. She had to turn on all kinds of lights, go down in the basement and fire that thing up. If you didn't keep the flame open—if you just threw coal on it—it would kind of smother itself down, then build up gas and blow.

Sometimes it would blow the door open; it didn't ever shoot sparks out. But Scotty would be sound asleep in the middle of the night and hear this BOOM! That would scare her to death.

We stayed there until they built some nice little townhouses close to Seward Park on Lake Washington, just over the hill to Boeing Field. So we got one of those; that was when we bought the little flatty sailboat. We kept it in a little boat harbor at Seward Park, just up around the corner. You could moor your boat there for $10 a month, and we would bring it home in the wintertime.

So we stayed there, and we were happy there. We had a garage, and they were just one story. You had to be a veteran to get in there, too. So we had a lot of friends about our age.

We were married so young—I was twenty-one and she was not quite twenty yet. We didn't want any children, so she was taking the pill—it was just new. After ten years, she had really seen the world. There were no airline miles or coupons or anything—so there were always empty seats in First Class. And Pan Always put the employees in First Class. The only thing was, you had to wear a sport coat and tie in First Class. So Scotty went First Class all the times she went with me. She would just stay in my hotel room.

After ten years, we were having dinner in Honolulu under the palm trees, dancing to that good music, when she said, "I think I've made up my mind: I've loafed long enough. This has been a fantastic ten years. I think we should start a family."

Starting a Family

We had a neighbor right next to us in Gregory Heights, a doctor who delivered babies. He and his wife had three daughters, and they wanted a boy. They were talking about adopting, so she talked about adopting with Scotty. They kind of decided between the two of them that that would be the way to go.

We didn't have any children, so we went to the doctor and he gave us physicals. He said that all he would have to do is give us some hormones, to get things livened up again from the pill.

Scotty wasn't very fond of hormones. She just wanted one child; she didn't want eight. "Well, how about adopting?" the doctor said.

"Scotty, it's up to you," I said, "whatever you do; because it's gonna really change your life."

"Well, we'll talk it over," she said. So we talked it over. "If we don't have any luck within a month or two," she said, "we can consider adopting." And that's what she told our neighbor.

About two months later, his wife came over and said, "You know, Fred just told me that that young couple he was so impressed with, her husband was killed on a motorcycle." The wife had a little beauty parlor, was pregnant and worried about having a child, and didn't know what to do.

Fred said that he would be happy to take the child—especially if it was a boy, and she wanted to adopt it out—and thought his neighbor would take a girl. So, give it some thought.

So, she gave it some thought. She decided she would adopt it out. We figured, if we don't have one—get started on one here before that happens—well, we got a girl, anyway.

Well, as luck would have it, the doctor's wife came over about a month before this girl was supposed to have her child and said, "I had to tell Fred this morning that I'm pregnant again. Gee, I hope we don't have another girl. But you can have the baby—boy or girl."

Well, it did happen to be a girl. We just went down to the doctor's office and picked her up when she was three days old. We went to the Washington Children's Home a year later. We wanted a boy, and we adopted a boy. They turned out so well that we never did worry that we didn't have any genes there.

She Ran the Show

Scotty was really a cute gal. She was just barely five-foot-two. Always had a smile on her face. We bought an eighteen-foot sailboat before we had the kids. We kept it on Lake Washington for the first summer. I think we left it moored there most of the time. We brought it home in the wintertime to paint and maintain it.

Scotty didn't want that boat at all, because she couldn't swim. So I taught her to dog paddle. But she and our neighbor decided to take swimming lessons from the Highline Pool. The first thing the instructors did was have them get in the pool, face-down, getting their hair all wet and everything.

They came home and said, "Our hair's all mussed up! We're never going back there. No way!" But she finally did learn to swim. And, once she did, she really did like that boat. She sailed it a lot.

That little flatty was a class boat. You could race it, but we never did. They're worth a little bit more if they're a class boat. I think I paid two or three hundred dollars for it.

Our flatty on Lake Washington near Seward Park.

Mary and Glenn Crone and Scotty on the flatty.

Scotty on our eighteen-foot sailboat on Lake Washington.

We spent many enjoyable hours aboard our sailboat
on Lake Washington.

After she learned to swim, Scotty loved to sail.

Scotty got a tumor—a breast tumor; just a little one, like a marble—and they took it out. They said this is one of those tumors you don't mess with. We don't have anything to kill it. We feed it chemo and it grows; it thinks that's great. And they said that sometimes it's fairly dormant, and that they had more luck by not doing a thing.

Scotty did fine for two and a half years. She has a lot of roses around the house, and she came in one evening and said, "My arm is hurting. I think I've been out pruning the roses too much."

The next morning she couldn't get out of bed; her arm was paralyzed. So I took her in and she had several x-rays taken. The tumor had blown out and gone to the top of her lung and the bottom of her heart. She lasted two weeks. . . . She's such a doll.

My folks always told me that if you get serious about a girl, make sure you get well acquainted with her mother. Because those genes are strong. And Scotty was just exactly like her mother. Just a doll. We never had an argument, seventy years.

We were out eating, the kids and I, recently, and they said, "You know, we never heard you and mom argue about anything."

And I said, "Well, she was so sharp. She ran the show here completely when I was gone." I went around the world for ten years, every month—an eight-day trip. I handled the real estate we had, and she handled everything else: the house, the kids, the bills, the schools, everything. She did a great job with the kids.

The Burkes: Jack, Scotty, Shawn and Shannon.

Scotty and I in front of Scotty's pretty roses at our present house
in Hurstwood, Washington.

Scotty and Shannon in front of Scotty's flowers
on our backyard patio.

Shawn, Scotty and I on New Year's Eve at our Hurstwood,
Washington home. We had many New Year's Eve gatherings
in our rec room.

Scotty making homemade ice cream.

Scotty looking out from her "office," where she took care of
all the paperwork and "ran the show." Everyone who went by
would stop, wave and talk to her.

Scotty and I enjoying a Pan Am cruise.

CHAPTER 5

PAN AM: THE EARLY YEARS

A Bunch of Cowboys

ONE of my sisters was the reason that I went with Pan Am. The younger one—she was two years older than me. Her husband, Haley Kirkpatrick, was an engineer with the Army Corps of Engineers. He got transferred to Panama, where they were enlarging the locks. They were there for two years.

Of course, all of my friends went to work for Northwest; I never considered anything else. My sister Kate—her name was Catherine, but everybody called her Kate—started writing me. The whole letter was about Pan Am, because the Clippers were coming into Panama every day.

Eventually I would fly the 707s to Panama, and then on to the next stop down there in the mountains. Anyway, Kate said, "Boy, every time I hear that Clipper, I go out and watch them come in and land and take off. They change crews here. That crew gets off in those nice dark blue or black uniforms—navy uniforms—and march ashore two by two, on every arrival and departure. It's really impressive.

"But those Northwest guys," she said, "are a bunch of *cowboys*." She told me to be sure and go with Pan Am, as soon as I was old enough. So she was the one who talked me into flying for Pan Am. Of course, I was watching Pan Am on the newsreels, because they were always on the newsreels with something. So I knew Pan Am, but only by the newsreels.

My sister Kate was two years older than me. When she and her husband were living in Panama, she called me about once a week to tell me to "be sure and go with Pan Am."

Class Reunion

When I was nineteen, Pan American Airways sent out information to the colleges. I called and asked if they had heaters in their airplanes. They thought that was pretty funny. They laughed and said, "Yeah, we've got heaters, all right. How come you're asking that question?"

"Well, I'm instructing here at Butte," I said, "flying an open airplane. I sit in the back seat, and there's no heat. The other day it was twenty below."

"Oh," they said, "I see why you're asking that question." They said I could come out to Seattle to take their exams. Most of the people I worked with had a real sense of humor; they really did. Most of the operations managers and the dispatchers—they were all just real nice people.

I came out when I was nineteen, but Pan Am wouldn't hire me. They said I had more than enough flight time, but I was short one year of college, and that they really liked to have people who were at least twenty-one. They couldn't push the age limit down to nineteen, they said.

They hired my buddy, Del Daly, who was twenty, and just going to be twenty-one. About a year later, he called me and said they had a new operations manager, and that he hadn't told him my age. I was going to be twenty within a month or two.

"I told him that I thought you had four years of college," Del said. I was all but just a quarter short. "But I told him you had about 300 hours," he said. You needed to have 100 hours to get to commercial. "As soon as you get finished with that bunch of cadets, come on out," he said.

So I came out to Seattle with the owners of the Miles City Airport, the Etcharts. Markie Etchart was younger; he was my age. We got in this little Taylor Craft and flew out. They wouldn't let us come to the coast; we didn't have the right radio gear, because the war had started. You had to have that ID and everything.

We left the plane at Wenatchee and took the bus over to Seattle. That bus depot was right where it is now—still by the Vance Hotel. So we went across the street and stayed in the Vance Hotel. Markie and I caught the bus to Boeing Field the next morning, went down and took exams all day.

They were going to have one more day of written exams, and then the third day to take your physical. We finished the second day of written exams; Mark and I both passed them. When we went back to the hotel, there was a message for Mark. His father had passed away with a heart attack.

"I gotta go home," he said. His other two older brothers were in California, teaching for the air force. So Markie got on Northwest that evening and went back home to Glasgow, Montana. He stayed there with his mother until he could get things organized, and one of the other brothers could get back. He didn't come back to Pan Am; he just went in the navy as an instructor.

The Etcharts had half of McCone County—a big county—and one of the biggest ranches in Montana. As soon as the war was over, all of the boys went back to the ranch. There was enough work there for all of them.

Markie ran for state senator—as a Republican. I think it was the first time they had ever elected a Republican from McCone County. He was up in Helena for several terms. But he's gone now, too. Gene is still alive. He was the oldest brother. They've got a couple of airplanes on the ranch. They're awfully nice people.

I had to fib about my age with Pan Am. Actually I didn't *lie*, but I tried to blur it. I finally had to tell them that I was born in 1922. At first they thought they couldn't hire me. Then they found out I could go up and fly the bush in Alaska. I flew it for a year until I was twenty-one.

Pan Am didn't ask for my birth certificate. They did say, "Have you ever worked where there was seniority?"

"No," I said, "I really haven't. I've been driving a beer truck every summer, but that's just a summer job." I drove that beer truck three summers, when I was fifteen, sixteen and seventeen.

So the Operations Manager said, "Let's get you started on seniority, because that's everything in the airline. You bid your base, you bid your airplanes, you bid your schedules, routes and everything."

"Well, that's great," I said. I was instructing for the navy, and had to go back and finish with my five cadets. So I said that I wouldn't be available for a couple of weeks, at least.

"That's fine," they said, "but we'll start your seniority now. I don't know what to call you. I'm just gonna call you a student pilot,

and I'll pay ya $150 a month just to keep ya." They wanted some-
body with college, and I just had one quarter left of pre-med. I never
really learned anything in those classes. During the war they had a
lot of empty seats, and you didn't have to wait to get in.

I stayed with Pan Am and moved in with Delmar Daly, who
began his flying in Miles City, and A.J. Anderson. Both had
been CPT students and instructors for Johnson Flying Service in
Missoula. They were renting a large, two-story house off Madison
Street, east of downtown Seattle. A Boeing test pilot was also living
with them. They had an extra room, so Del said, "Come on out;
we've got a room for you."

The four Flight School instructors at Miles City Airport: Bennett,
Ingersoll, Hart and Burke. We all came with Pan Am from
Etchart Flying School. Here we are at Boeing Field in Seattle.

When I returned to Miles City on my first vacation, I stopped in
Helena and helped Lynn Ingersoll finish up his CPT students, then
took him back to Seattle to join the rest of us at Pan Am.

The entire instructor group from Etchart Flying School in Miles City was reunited at Boeing Field in Seattle. Spencer Hart also came with Pan Am, and Harry Bennett was just across Boeing Field as a test pilot for Boeing.

Planes used by Pan Am for instrument training for the company's Pacific-Alaska Division during World War Two. Pan Am leased the Perry Vocational-Technical Institute in Yakima; there was no local training on the Coast during the war. I got my instrument rating in the twin Beech craft at Yakima.

I got my instrument rating from Pan Am about 1942, in a twin-engine Beech craft. Over at the airport in Yakima is a big building called the Perry Institute. They were working with the college's aviation program.

Pan American leased that building during the war, and they used their link trainers and the Beech craft for our instrument ratings, because so many pilots didn't have instrument ratings. So Pan Am was giving us all an instrument rating.

Guide Dogs

I always had a problem with my age. I was a year or two too young for every position that was open. Pan Am needed First Officers to fly the Boeing 314 flying boats on the North Atlantic, based in New York, but you had to be twenty-one to fly international.

Alaska was then a territory and not considered international. The Chief Pilot from Fairbanks came down to Seattle and Ralph Savory called me in to meet him. "I know Jack looks young," Ralph said, "but he has a lot of flight time, most of it in Montana in the mountains and snow—hunting coyotes and instructing air force cadets. Do you think passengers will ride with him?"

"His passengers will be drunken miners and Eskimos," the Chief Pilot said, "and they won't give a damn how young he is."

Pan Am was using single-engine, 8-passenger Fairchild Pilgrims for the Pacific-Alaska bush mail routes. The pilot sat up behind the engine all by himself; you couldn't get in the cabin. We used skis a lot, because we often landed in rough grass fields. We kept the skis on as long as we could, because they made for a smoother landing.

When Pan Am bought the dog team mail routes, they hired the dog team owners and had them check the mail stop and keep us from killing ourselves. We had no radio beams or voice radio, just Morse code.

The dog team driver that was assigned to me had been carrying the mail from Fairbanks to Nome with his dogs for about ten years and really did know the country, so I never headed up a canyon without Freddy's approval.

I always had my dog team driver sitting up with me in the front seat. When I was going down the Yukon and had to cut through the mountains to go over to the Arctic Ocean and up to Nome, I never cut through that mountain range without him up there. He would just stick his head up there, and with the plane being level, he could see.

"I think this next one goes through," I would say.

"No, Jackie; this not the one. *Two* more," he would say. Because they all looked big; they all looked alike in the Yukon. Then you would go in and they got narrower and narrower; so narrow that you couldn't turn around. And we didn't have instruments, so if it was snowing you couldn't climb out.

One pilot didn't have any passengers, and the dog team driver was stretched out on the floor, sleeping. The pilot didn't wake him up; he was going to go right on through. He ended up augured in on the end of the pass; piled it up. But they got out. So they lost a few airplanes in those mountains. But I never turned in there without my dog team driver giving me the nod.

Those Pilgrims were fun to fly, though. They were not very fast; their top cruising speed was only about ninety mph. But they sure could pack a load. They had a great big flying wing on them; a lot of lift. You could slow those Pilgrims right down to forty mph.

It wasn't long before we got DC-3s on the mail runs and had some radio ranges and even voice radios.

Pan Am's bush airplane before the DC-3s. Built in 1929, the Fairchild Pilgrim had a 575-horsepower Pratt & Whitney engine and carried eight passengers.

Air Raid

Mrs. Burkheimer had a big, beautiful, two-story brick home, two blocks north of the University of Washington, right on the main street. She had four sons who went in the service. Her daughter married the manager of our ground school.

The daughter came out and was talking to us. "You know, Mom is awfully lonesome with all of the boys in the service," she said. "Why don't some of you guys go out. She's got a big house; she can handle eight. She wouldn't charge you anything at all; two to a room."

So eight of us Pan Am pilots—single guys—went out there. Mrs. Burkheimer's—"Mrs. B's"—husband was the contractor who built Edmund Meany Hotel. They got a divorce, and she got that hotel.

She was great. The eight of us lived there for about a year. She was an air-raid warden for the area. When you came in her big front doors, there was an entry. And the master bedroom was off of that entry, with big glass swinging doors. She always stayed in there reading at night, with the light on.

As we came in, she would yell at us, "Where did you go tonight?" And we would stop and talk to her. She had a bucket of sand and a helmet on the first landing as you went upstairs. She didn't allow any beer-drinking or anything there.

This one guy from Texas was kind of a character; he went out and drank beer with the guys. He came home one night and Mrs. B was still awake, reading. So he was afraid to go in the front door, because she would see him, and that he had been out drinking beer.

So "Tex" went down the side of the house to his room. He tossed some pebbles up to hit the window and wake up his partner in there. But the pebbles didn't wake him up until the last one, and Tex didn't know it. The hose was right there at his feet. So he got the hose out and pointed it right up on the window. He turned it on full bore just as his roommate opened the window.

His startled roommate, doused with cold water, shouted, "Damn you, Tex! You can just sleep on the grass," and slammed the window down.

Well, Tex decided to go around and climb up the drainpipes on the back porch. There was a window off of that to a bathroom that they usually left open. So Tex figured he would climb up there and get in that window.

Tex got about halfway up the drainpipe when it let loose. It all crashed to the ground, covering Tex with debris and making an awful racket. The noise woke us all up. I came out and looked around at the front door. Mrs. B was already there. She had her robe and helmet on, and she had the bucket of sand.

"I think we're bein' bombed!" she said.

The Texan's roommate came out. "Naw, it's just that damn Tex," he said. We went around back and, sure enough, Tex was lying there with the drainpipe remnants all over him. So we helped him up and put him in the house. But, boy, Mrs. B was right there with her helmet and bucket of sand.

Mrs. Burkheimer—without her helmet and bucket of sand—and I outside the house where I roomed with seven other young Pan Am pilots.

A.J. Anderson (left), myself and Del Daly (right) outside of the house we rented off Madison Street, east of downtown Seattle. From there I moved to Mrs. B's.

Yellow Icicle

Scotty and I flew to Miles City in an open-cockpit, Fairchild PT-19 training plane, excellent for aerobatics. Scotty came back to Seattle later with her folks in their car. A friend asked me if I was going via Great Falls. I told him I could, so he went with me to pick up a new car there.

It was a cold, rainy fall day, so he was wearing galoshes to keep his feet dry. We had a good breakfast at the airport, and I noticed that Mr. Keinest drank a lot of coffee. We were only about an hour out on a three-hour flight to Great Falls when he said he had to go to the bathroom. I told him we couldn't land this airplane in a rough field, so maybe he should take off his galoshes and relieve himself in those. We could dump them out when we landed.

He accepted that solution and filled his rubbers; but, shortly after that, we ran into a little turbulence and it all spilled onto the plywood floor of the airplane and ran back to the tail section. When we taxied to the gas pumps in Great Falls, two guys came out to gas us. They stood by the tail laughing, so I stuck my head out of the open cockpit and asked what was so funny. They told me to get out, come back and see.

A long yellow icicle was frozen to the underside of the fuselage, just ahead of the tail wheel. It was cold enough that it was not thawing a bit. The manager got his camera out and took some pictures of the big yellow icicle, enlarged one of them and put it on his office bulletin board.

Several months later I stopped for gas, and the picture was still on the bulletin board. The manager said there had been more discussion about that picture than anything they had ever had on the board, so it was going to stay there.

Poncho & Cisco

One of the eight guys I lived with, his dad had a ten-cent store in Oakland, California. His mother died when he was born, so he didn't know anything but his dad. They lived above the store. So he was in the store all the time. And so was Warren; Warren was down there with his dad.

We came home from the show one night at Christmastime. We had this great big Christmas tree, all decorated with lights on. It was late—eleven o'clock and the lights were still on. So my room-mate and I stopped in there, and here was Warren—we called him Poncho—sitting in this big easy chair, feet up on the footstool, just gazing at the Christmas tree.

"My gosh, Ponch, how come you're not in bed?" I said.

"This is the first Christmas tree I've ever had in my life," he said. We had just decorated it that day. "My dad always had some of those little plug-in ones down in the store. But I've never had a real live Christmas tree before, and I sure like the smell of this."

I gave Poncho a route check back from Kodiak in the DC-3 to Ketchikan, and then down the coast to Seattle. He was like George Stockhill: he was an excellent pilot, but he used poor judgment. He never did scratch an airplane, though.

Seeing as how I was a buddy and check pilot, he trusted me. "Jack," he said, "why don't you go up and look at the weather and sign my name on the clearance."

"I'll do that," I said. He was having breakfast. I went up and stopped at Weather. They showed me this—it was the Jet Stream, but they didn't know it then—120 mph wind straight from Kodiak to Seattle.

"With that kind of wind," they said, "your DC-3 will go twice as fast as normal. There's no reason why you have to cross the Gulf to Ketchikan and down."

"That's true," I said, "but we don't have a certificate." You have to have a certificate for all those routes before you can fly them.

"Well, I guess that's right," I said. I shouldn't have mentioned it, but I went down and had a roll and a cup of coffee while Ponch finished his breakfast.

There were Poncho-Cisco jokes. We called him Poncho—and he wasn't fat—and me Cisco, because I was always bailing him out. He would go down for the six month's check and take my manuals, because they were all up to date.

Anyway, I said, "By gosh, Ponch: look at this wind. It's right on the tail; straight from Kodiak to Seattle. We could make that nonstop with the DC-3 with 620 gallons of gas."

"Could we?" he said.

"Oh, yeah," I said, "but we can't make it legally because we don't have a certificate. We've got to go across the Gulf to Ketchikan."

We got in the airplane. We had radio operators because we didn't have any voice radio, just code. The operator had the map, because he got bearings from other stations. Poncho turned around to him and said, "Would you draw me a line direct from Kodiak to Seattle?"

"Oh, what for?"

"Well, just see what the heading would be," Poncho said.

The radio operator drew a line on the map. "Here's what the heading would be," he said.

I had flown the plane up, so Poncho was flying it back. As soon as we got in the air, he turned to this heading, direct to Seattle. "What have you got on your mind, Ponch?" I asked.

"We're goin' direct to Seattle," he said. "We've got enough gas with all this wind."

"We have, but it's not legal," I said. "We don't have a certificate to fly this route."

"Oh, what about a certificate?" he said—and there he goes. And he comes to the first position that we're supposed to reach going across the Gulf, to Annette Island-Ketchikan.

"Well, we're not over here," I said. Of course, nobody knew it, because there was no radar in those days.

"Just give 'em that position," Ponch said. "That'll satisfy them for awhile." There were about four positions across the Gulf, and we gave them every one.

"Poncho, you'd better start thinking," I said, "because after this next position, the next one is Annette Island, and we're gonna be way out here in the middle of the Pacific Ocean."

"Oh," he said, "what should we do?"

"Well, you got yourself into this fix," I said.

"What would *you* do?" he said.

"I'd just request a re-clearance," I said, "that we picked up a tail-wind and request a re-clearance from our present position to Seattle, because we're practically at Ketchikan." So that's what we did, and they cleared us direct to Seattle. Of course, that would have put us coming right down the Coast, and we were way out over the ocean. So we didn't make any positions.

Finally we came in over Port Hardy at the end of Vancouver Island. We reported over Vancouver, and about that time we should have just been leaving Annette Island. And here we are, an hour and a half from Seattle. I got an airways clearance down the airways to Seattle, and we went right on in to Seattle.

When we talked to Pan Am radio, the dispatcher said, "Where in hell have you guys been? These positions don't seem to jibe."

"We'll tell you about it later," I said. "We'll be in within an hour."

"My God," he said, "you didn't leave Kodiak that long ago. What have you been doing?"

"We've been having 120 knot winds right on the tail," I said.

"Well, the Chief Pilot and Check Pilot have been over here about three times wondering where you guys were."

"You tell them we're in good shape," I said. "We'll be landing shortly."

So he told them, and he called us back and said, "Now, they're waiting for you in the Chief Pilot's office." This was now about three o'clock in the afternoon. "And they want you over there as soon as you land," the dispatcher added.

So we landed, and old Poncho grabbed his coat and headed the other direction. We had the car parked down by the hangar. "Where are you going?" I said. "We're supposed to go to the Chief Pilot's office."

"Well, we're not going to talk to him *today*," Ponch said. "They'd be unhappy with us. Let's go to the sailboat. We'll change clothes, then we'll go have dinner." Ponch had a real nice sailboat by the University. You could sleep on it and everything. So that's what we did.

After we had dinner, we went home to Mrs. B's. "Where have you guys been?" she asked. "I've been getting calls all day from Pan Am wondering where you are." I told her what we had done. "Oh, no," she said.

"Well, that was Warren's leg," I said. "He was flyin' it. I had nothin' to do with it; he signed the clearance."

"Well, they called me here about eight or nine o'clock tonight," she said. "You weren't home yet, so they said to give them a call first thing in the morning."

So, first thing in the morning, Ponch woke up and said, "Let's go have breakfast."

"Well don't you want to call the Chief Pilot?" I said.

"Oh, they haven't had long enough to think this over yet," he said. And he was right. We went and had breakfast, and we didn't get to the Chief Pilot's office until about noon. And here were the Chief Pilot and Check Pilot with this map with a line drawn from Kodiak direct to Seattle.

They were talking about it; we had knocked about three hours off the flight. And it was just like Poncho said: "Give 'em enough time and they won't be mad anymore." And they were talking about getting a certificate to fly that route if there was a plus so-much on the wind.

But they said, "By the way, you guys shouldn't have been doing that."

"Well, you know," Poncho said, "the airplane is made to go in a straight line, as fast as you can go. You don't find 120-knot winds giving you help all the way like this. I figured everything would be all right. It was all my idea; Jack didn't have anything to do with it. He flew it up, but I was flyin' it back."

"Well, we're going to apply for a certificate now to go direct from Kodiak to Seattle with the DC-3, if there's a plus so-much wind," they said. And that always happened: Every time Ponch got into a fix like that, he would get out of it. I don't think he ever had a violation filed against him. I know he never scratched an airplane.

I was giving Ponch a route check from Fairbanks to Seattle and Seattle was fogged in. But at that time, if you had an ILS approach and a radar following, they had what they called the look-see.

Now, we had a 200-foot minimum that we could come down to. Then, if you didn't break out at 200 feet, you had to go to your alternate. So we were coming down from Fairbanks, and Ponch was checking the weather. "That darned Seattle's been fogged in," he said, "and this time of night it's not gonna change."

"Well yes, it's too bad we don't have 200 feet," I said, "because with ILS and radar following"—they had radar in the tower there—"why, we'd be legal."

Well, we got to Seattle, and Ponch never even thought about an alternate. Portland was our alternate. "Ask for an approach, would ya," he said.

"Okay," I said. I told Seattle that we would like an approach, and that we had an ILS with radar following. That way you could go down and take a look. So Ponch went down and, coming up on 200 feet, we didn't see a thing but fog. Well, he just kept on going. He was right on the glide slope; he was right where he was supposed to be, and we weren't seeing anything but fog.

Finally we started to see some lights at the end of the runway. So he just went in and landed. And we're right there, not going to any alternate or anything, saving time and money. So I said to Ponch, "What exactly does that look-see privilege mean?"

"Oh," he said, "you look till you see it."

"Well, not really," I said. "You shouldn't go beyond your minimum."

"Oh, well we saw some lights," he said. And do you know Ponch *never* went to an alternate, he never got a violation filed against him, and he must have saved the company a million dollars. But he just lucked out every time. He was something else. He's still alive, too; he's older than I am.

Lockheed Loadstar in Whitehorse, Yukon Territory, used for Seattle-to-Alaska passenger service, 1942-1945. It was fun to fly, but the engines were right next to you—and they were noisy. It had a high-speed wing and wouldn't hold much ice.

Coin Toss

Pan Am sent me to Fairbanks, Alaska. I flew single-engine, eight-passenger Fairchild Pilgrims to Nome.

Later I flew the old twin-engine DC-3, which carried twenty-one passengers and one stewardess, from Whitehorse, in the Yukon Territory, across the 10,000-foot Alaska mountain range. We flew "down in the weather" much of the time, contending with turbulence, ice and an unpressurized airplane. We would go over Gustavus for the approach, where we let down for Juneau, and then fly underneath the clouds to Juneau.

It was only an hour-and-a-half flight; two hours at the most, a little over two hundred miles. We were out an hour, and we were still over those darned mountains. So we thought maybe we were past them. We were getting ice, and we kept putting power on, power on. We had to hold at 11,000 feet or we were down in those peaks.

You can only draw takeoff power for about five minutes; it heats the cylinders too much. If you draw it longer, the engines get hot. Rated power was the most you could draw continually. So I was at rated power, and we were losing about a hundred feet a minute, just hoping that we were going by those 10,000-foot peaks.

But you were over that mountain range for about half an hour. And this was before anybody knew what the Jet Stream was. Years ago, we didn't know anything about that Jet Stream; they hadn't plotted it for any length of time. We just knew that we got hellish winds sometimes. But that Jet Stream is there.

We would leave Whitehorse, and the only way we could tell what our speed was—or just *what* we were doing; whether we were making headway—was by tuning into Whitehorse with one radio, and putting the lowest volume we could on it.

Then we would tune Juneau in ahead, and put that volume right down to where we could just barely hear them. One in each ear. You knew you were making headway toward the one that was gaining in strength. And the one behind you would be fading out.

All we could do was turn the volume down on both of them, and hope that Gustavus was building—because we were getting closer. They put up an old loop range—low frequency; a lot of static—and all it did was send out signals. On one side was an "N", and on the other side was an "A".

An "A" is dot-dash, and an "N" is dash-dot. When those two merged together, they formed the beam. You always used to hear about the pilots being "on the beam." Well, that's what they were doing.

That "A" and that "N" squashed together and just had a hum. If you went off to the right, you would start hearing the "A". If you went off to the left, you would start hearing the "N". That's how you stayed on the beam, and that's all we had.

I've sat up there over that mountain range, drawing rated power, getting no change in the volume on either station—so I knew I wasn't moving. It meant we were just sitting there. The headwinds were over a hundred knots.

When it was clean—no ice or anything on it—the DC-3 only went about 160. But if ice built up on it, it would slow down to where you just weren't moving.

You didn't have any idea where you were along the route. You just knew that you were making headway. And you wondered, "Gee, whiz: should I turn around and go back to Whitehorse with a tail-wind—or are we almost there?"

Every time, I debated it with the copilot and radio operator. We didn't have voice; just code. I'd always discuss it with them, saying, "You know, it's a toss of the coin—because we don't know how far we are."

The beam let you know you were on the airways, but you had nothing to tell you where along the airways you were, past the mountain range or still over it. We would occasionally have a 100 mph headwind, but no way to know it until you got to the radio station putting out the beam.

Now we know these strong winds as the Jet Stream, and use them to plan our flight plan route. I have had a Jet Stream of 140 mph most of the way from Tokyo to Los Angeles, that reduced the flight time from nine hours to seven hours.

You can stay in the Jet Stream by watching your temperature. If it starts to warm up, you are getting to the south of the stream. If it gets colder, you are getting to its north side.

Now they also have DME—Distance Measuring. All the FAA radio ranges have it. You just tune that in and the dial counts down.

If it's 200 miles ahead of you and you're going to it, the dial counts down: 199 . . . 198 . . . 197.

But then, you just had to make a decision: Are you gonna turn around, and hope to catch that wind all the way back to Whitehorse, or are you gonna stick it out and make it. The problem was that we would build up ice on the airplane, and it would get to where you just couldn't hold your altitude.

You'd have rated power on, and you would be descending about a hundred feet a minute—just barely descending. And you weren't going ahead very fast.

We went quite a little ways. And about the time we were discussing this real good, well, we would spot a big blue hole in the clouds, look down and see some water. And there was Lynn Canal, running right in to Juneau. We would go down through that hole and there the water was. And even with that cold water up there, it was enough warmer that the ice would melt off.

Juneau didn't have any approaches, nothing, for navigation. Gustavus was about forty miles west of Juneau. They built a nice airport over there, mainly so the military would have an alternate.

We went to Gustavus and made the approach. We then could go down over the water, underneath the weather, and fly the forty miles into Juneau visual, from island to island. But it could be miserable.

You know how it is when you're driving through a lot of snow and you can't see anything ahead. So we would have to get right down on the deck. We had a sliding side window; sometimes we had to slide it back and peek out.

We would get down there and fly along the coast, two or three hundred feet above the water. The pilot kept an eye on the shoreline, while the copilot looked across to see when he could pick up another island across this particular body of water. It wasn't far, but as soon as he could see across, we headed across.

If we started across and it fogged or snowed in on us, we would turn right around and go back to Gustavus. We usually went back and held for awhile, then tried it again. If it didn't open up, and we had a load of passengers, we took them back down to Annette Island and Ketchikan.

They had a bunch of nice Quonset huts there for the military during the war, which they built into motel-type units.

So I never did turn around from Whitehorse to Juneau, but I sure debated it a lot of times. But, you know, there was nothing you could have done. The only flying book I ever really enjoyed was *God Is My Copilot*. And boy, I tell you, I used Him a lot. It seemed like every time I got in a jackpot like that, I had that Copilot.

There was a group of air force R-40 DC-3s that left Kodiak to go to Whitehorse. There were five of them in the squadron. They never found any of them until spring. They got across those mountains, and they iced up. They didn't know whether they should turn around or keep going.

They didn't luck out like I did. They went right into them.

"First You Get the Money"

Everybody in Alaska knows Nick Bez. He came over to the U.S. from Croatia. He spoke very little English. He arrived in New York with little, if any, money, and rode the freight trains to Seattle.

Nick wanted to go to Alaska. He got acquainted with some people here in Seattle. He went down to some of the canneries. He said he was going to go to Alaska and open up some canneries. I played cards with him quite a lot. We just played penny-ante poker there on Annette Island.

Nick would go up to Juneau and rent an old boat, the biggest outboard he could afford. And he would buy some booze. The natives were the only ones who could have fish traps. They had their fish traps fairly close to the shore, in the water; then they would put a net out into the water.

The salmon swam along, close to the shore, because there's more food there; then they come to this net, go down the net and get in the fish trap. That's how the natives made their money. They had their traps all along the shore; you could see them when we flew over.

Here would be this little hut floating out in the water on some logs at the end of the net. And there would be one of the natives in it. The next day a larger native boat would come out and pick up the fish in the fish traps. Nick figured that there were so many restrictions on the non-natives that he wasn't going to battle the natives.

So he would get a case of booze and come out, and give the guy who was sitting in this hut at the end of that net a bottle of booze, so he could take some fish out of his trap. He would stop at two or three of those places and fill his boat with fish, then go in and sell those fish.

Everybody in Seattle knew Nick because he started West Coast Airlines. His son wanted to be a purser on an airline, so Nick bought DC-3s and started West Coast Airlines, and his son managed it. His son did a good job. They turned into a pretty good-sized airline; they covered the whole western part of the U.S.

Nick would take these fish back in and sell them. First thing you know he's got a nice big boat; and he would go out and fill up this big boat with fish. He made enough money to build some canneries. He became the largest canner in Alaska. But he was a kick because he liked to play penny-ante poker.

We sat there at Annette Island sometimes for two or three days before we could get into Juneau. The DC-3 also made the milk run from there to Fairbanks. Lots of times the milk run would get turned around back to Annette, and even the Fairbanks businessmen would be there. That's where I got acquainted with so many of them.

Fairbanks was a little town at that time, until the army built it up. It only had a couple thousand people. We would have a hot poker game; I think we had a maximum of 25 cents.

Nick was a real kick. I got to know him well, because I let him ride up in the cockpit. They weren't strict in those days. I would have him up there when the weather was not too good going into

Juneau, and just let him know so he could see what we were up to, having to turn around and come back to Annette Island.

President Truman came out. Nick had a big cruiser at that time, and he took Truman up to Alaska to fish. I think Truman spent about a week with him. After that happened, I was playing penny-ante poker with Nick there at Annette Island. "Boy, it's kind of impressive to get to where you can take the President of the United States fishing," I said.

"No," Nick said, "first you get the money—*then* you take 'em fishing."

Nick spoke broken English, but I was around him enough so that I could understand him. He did have a thick accent. I liked Nick; he was just what he was. He never changed. He was a wheel in Alaska. He never wore fancy suits. He usually wore what we called the Alaska Tuxedo. Black Bear made them; right down here on Rainier Avenue was a Black Bear factory. It was a medium-gray pants and an Eisenhower jacket, made out of heavy corduroy. It was a real good-looking outfit. And they were warm. They were lined.

Most of the people like Nick Bez, that's what they wore, because it was an easy little jacket, and the corduroy pants were heavy and held a press—and they didn't care if they *didn't* hold a press. I had an Alaska Tuxedo.

"The Regular"

I had these real good friends, the Krize brothers. There were five boys, all from northern Minnesota, where it's cold. One of them, the oldest brother, was a school teacher and a musician. He was a good musician; he could really play the guitar.

As soon as the war started, there were a lot of businessmen—and just normal people who owned homes in Fairbanks—who wanted out of there, because the Japanese had already bombed Attu and those places, and they were sure that they were going to get to Fairbanks.

So, many Fairbanks residents and businesses just sold out for practically nothing and came south, and there was no market. The oldest Krize brother had some money from being a school teacher and a musician, and he went to Fairbanks and bought half the city—houses, a restaurant, small hotel, big nightclub, a bar or two.

The Krizes had never owned a bar or anything, but he had the other four brothers all come up. They did well in Fairbanks. They had a clothing store called Top O' the World Clothing. It had these Alaska Tuxedos. So any time I wanted any clothes, I would drop in and they would give me the clothes for cost, because I brought them fruit and watermelon from down here on my trips. I got to be real well acquainted with them, especially the one who owned Top O' the World Clothing.

I used to go out and have dinner with him and his family. He had a real nice wife who could sure cook. His son was tall and big; he was the star of the basketball team. When they came to Seattle, I would pick them up and they would stay here. Scotty just thought they were great because they were down-to-earth people from northern Minnesota. And no put-on about anybody.

The brothers all had fairly common names. I still get Christmas cards from Rudy Krize, or from his wife. One of the brothers ran the night club, one ran the restaurant; they had the nicest restaurant in town. What he put up was good.

The restaurant had a real nice cocktail lounge upstairs called the Flame Room. I would eat downstairs, and then go upstairs and talk to Hank, the bartender—and another one of the brothers. That was when they made this drink with orange juice—a screwdriver.

They had a real good Nickelodeon up there with good records on it. So I told the crew who had dinner with me that I was going to go up and visit Louie, one of the brothers, upstairs. "Come on up and join me if you want," I said. "You'll be in for some good music."

All five brothers were musicians; they could all play guitars. And if they had a guitar up there they would play and sing for us. Some of the crew members and stewardesses would come up. I knew the bartender real well, and he knew that I didn't drink alcohol, because it just made me sleepy. So I told him, "I'll just take the regular—that's orange juice with nothing in it." Looking at it, you can't tell the difference.

The crew members would come up and be listening to some music, to the guitars and singing. It was a real show, because these guys were *good*. Rudy made his living teaching music in high school. So the crew all ordered drinks, and I would just tell Hank, "Well, I'll have the regular." So they brought me my orange juice, and made sure I got the one with no alcohol.

We got well acquainted with one of the stewardesses who had a room close to our house over on Three Tree Point. She and Scotty got to be real good friends. She was also a nurse. One day she was telling Scotty, "We sure had fun up in the Flame Room. The guys all got their guitars out and sang for us, and we had a wine or two."

The crew never drank much because they were going to fly the next morning. She told Scotty, "I've never seen anybody who could hold his liquor like Jack. He can drink two or three of those screwdrivers; they never affect him." They never did know what Hank was fixing me.

Scotty finally told her, "You know, Jack doesn't drink at all, except a glass of wine occasionally, because it puts him to sleep. Can you keep that a secret?" She said yes, and she did. She was a good nurse, and a good stewardess. On the DC-3 we only had one for the twenty-one people.

If we got into some choppy turbulence, the tail would wag, and the stewardess would get ill back there. We didn't have electric ovens or anything. They made some pots that they could plug into twelve-volt batteries just to keep things hot.

Pan Am had all of its own kitchens, and they would make some of the tastiest shrimp or chicken dishes in these pots. The girls would plug them in as soon as we took off, to keep them hot. When they got through serving the passengers their coffee and roll, or whatever they wanted, and it was time for lunch, they would get this pot out and dish it up. They would come up to the cockpit and say, "Jack, are we ever gonna get out of this turbulence? It's just about enough to make me sick back there, dishing up all this food."

Our copilots were just as well trained as we were; they had flown the route a lot. So I would say, "Take my seat, and I'll take my coat off and just go back in my shirtsleeves and finish serving the people."

So I went back. She would have it half served, and I would finish dishing the things up. There were always people I knew on board. Somebody would get up and come deliver, and I would just be dishing the stuff up back there. And we would get them all served.

When they got through, somebody would start picking things up. Everybody was part of the crew. It was just a fun trip; it was just like getting out on a vacation, to be with all these people.

People from up north also thought that Crown Royal—the smooth whiskey in a blue velvet bag with a gold tie on top—was something else. So I used to pick that up in Whitehorse. The station manager would buy it at a discount and bring it out. Some of my friends from Canada had been up there; I would give them one of those.

That Crown Royal smelled better than the beer I used to haul empty kegs back on. You couldn't do what I did now. They wouldn't let a fifteen-year-old drive that beer truck, and go to the red light district with that beer. And it wasn't that many years ago; it's not like I'm a hundred and fifty.

And then it was so nice to have someone like my dad who trusted me when he bought me that car when I was thirteen. And for three different families to let each of their boys take off in that Model T and go three hundred miles to Yellowstone Park for a week. You could no more do that now with a fourteen-year-old; you would be worried to death. Those were the good old years.

Lift Off

We only had one stewardess on the DC-3. We made the milk run: Whitehorse – Juneau – Ketchikan – Seattle. She was engaged to an Air Force pilot. We went up on the DC-3 and made all the stops, spent the night and came back down the next day. It took us a little over eight hours flying.

We had radio operators then, because we didn't have any voice radio. We had radio operators to get us weather and other information with Morse code. With the three people, we could fly over eight hours.

We would get into Fairbanks, Joyce would call her husband-to-be and they would go out for dinner and dancing. The Pan Am Traffic counter was on the main floor of the hotel, and we had the whole second floor for all the Pan Am crews. I always stopped by there because I knew all the people in the Traffic Department. I knew half the passengers I was carrying back and forth, so I wanted to see who we had.

Well, this particular day we had no passengers between Fairbanks and Whitehorse, a three-hour flight. When Joyce came out to get in the cab, she said, "Oh, I got a shower, but it didn't help much. We were dancin' all night, and I'm really beat." She was a cute blonde gal, a good stewardess.

"Well, by gosh, you picked the right day," I said. "I checked with the Traffic Department and we've got no passengers from Fairbanks to Whitehorse. We'll just make a bed for ya." We flew out over the water, so we had life rafts back by the galley.

"You won't even need to go upstairs to talk to Traffic," I said, "because we've got no passengers. You can start your nap right now."

So we did. The copilot and I fixed her a bed. Boy, she was all tucked in. We went up to Dispatch, got the clearance, came out and she was sound asleep.

In the three hours to Whitehorse, it doesn't bother your ears going up, but it does coming down—the pressure on them. She was sound asleep back there. "We're gonna have to wake her up," I said to the copilot, "because we're at 8,000 feet. We're gonna descend, and it'll rupture her eardrums."

The DC-3 wasn't that long: just 21 seats; two seats along one side and one on the other. We could see her back there. "You know," I said, "I'll bet I can raise her off that life raft, put her on the carpet and not wake her up." It was nice and smooth that day, but there were a few cumulous clouds. If you get under one of those, they do have quite a riser. The air is drawn up; that's what made the cloud.

Well, we were so busy deciding how we could get Joyce on the floor that we never even thought about the radio operator, who had gone back to use the lavatory. They just had those old honey buckets. And, of course, it was nice and clean, because they service them overnight. We didn't even miss him.

Anyway, we pulled the airplane up a little bit, kind of like a roller coaster, and pushed it down, put a little rudder on it. We looked back and here's Joyce right in the aisle. She woke up, shook her head and never got up, she was so sleepy.

Well, about that time, the lavatory door swung open. And there's only one lavatory door on the airplane. Out he comes. Boy, was he mad. "My God," he says, "what's happening?"

"Gee, you know, we didn't go underneath that cloud," I said. "We went around it. And I didn't think we were gonna get *that* kind of a lift out of it."

"Is *that* what happened?" he said. "It pushed me right up against the ceiling. And here all this stuff was coming out all over me. Just look at my uniform!"

"Well," I said, "we've got these good Pan Am coveralls here. You can go on to Seattle in them." If we got to an alternate airport where there were no people, they always had some gas there in 50-gallon drums. We had these coveralls so we could pump some more gas in to get us to where we were going.

So our radio operator went the rest of the way to Seattle in those white coveralls. It was a couple of years before he found out what happened. He thought it was funny then, but he sure didn't at the time.

Weather or Not

We finally got pressurized airplanes and could cruise at 25,000 feet, out of most of the weather and icing. The icing is at its worst between 30 and 35 degrees F. At colder temperatures, the moisture is mainly dry snow that doesn't stick to the airplane like the wet snow.

I flew the DC-4 prop airplane to Fairbanks. It took us eight hours to get there with all the stops. We stopped at Annette Island for Ketchikan, because they didn't have an airport then. Then to Juneau, Whitehorse in the Yukon Territory and Fairbanks.

Of course, with Daylight Savings Time—and then it never got dark up there in Fairbanks, in the summertime—they had a baseball game at midnight, without any lights. There was two hours' difference in time, so I would get in there about four o'clock in the afternoon.

Two or three of the mechanics would be there waiting to get soloed, or for some instrument dual. They had bought wrecked airplanes and rebuilt them. It seemed like every mechanic up there had an airplane that somebody had busted up. Of course, they had bought them for little or nothing.

So they had the airplanes themselves, and only had to buy the gas, because they didn't have to have an instructor. I think there was only one instructor in Fairbanks at the time, and no instrument instructors. Of course, the one instructor was expensive—and busy.

So I would stay right out there at the airport until eight or nine o'clock at night. I never charged anybody for lessons. A lot of them just couldn't afford instructors, especially the mechanics who had built their own airplane. My price was right.

My friend Johnny Amundsen learned how to fly, and flew his own little airplane. Both of his boys learned how to fly as well. Johnny got a job with Alaska Coastal, flying single-engine float planes out of Ketchikan. So he flew in a lot of nasty weather up there.

Ketchikan didn't have an airport. The airport for Ketchikan was on Annette Island. That "Bridge to Nowhere" that they had so much ballyhoo about—well, that was really a wise move.

Ellis Airlines and Alaska Coastal flew these little amphibious, twin-engine Grummans that carried six or eight people. The "Grumman Goose," we called them. They flew from Ketchikan to Petersburg to Juneau, and got in there when we did. We were flying from Seattle to Annette Island and Juneau. And then we had lunch there with them.

They took off ahead of us and came back down to Petersburg and Ketchikan, then loaded up the passengers for Annette Island, just a ten-minute hop. But often there was nasty weather, wind and cross-winds. And that airplane was miserable in a cross-wind, because the engines sat way up on top of the wing. It was top-heavy.

So they took off in the water over Ketchikan, dropped the gear and came over and landed on Annette Island. They made Annette Island just for the Coast Guard.

They flew that "Grumman Goose" in and out of Annette Island. The Coast Guard used the same airplanes. They weren't flying, but Ellis was hauling the passengers back and forth. And Johnny flew up there. He went to work for Pan American from there.

The two commercial carriers from Ketchikan flew in the nastiest weather. And they landed over there at Annette Island in a cross-wind. It was a real handful. But they never wrecked one.

It was a lot of fun, though; it really was. But occasionally you were sweating a little bit. Because there was nothing you could do about it, you know.

"Hi, Jackie!"

I have another madam story. We took the airplane from Seattle up to Fairbanks for ten days and flew to Nome and back every other night. I knew so many people up there. We called it a Nome Row. One of those nights we would go down the Kuskokwim Mountains to Bethel with DC-3s. I was about twenty years old then. I couldn't fly international; you had to be twenty-one to fly international.

I was flying commercial planes for Pan Am. Eventually I took a leave of absence and went in the navy. Anyway, the air force had decided they were going to close down the red light district in Fairbanks. It was just one little street, about a block and a half long. You couldn't drive a car down it. The girls sat there in their windows.

Well, the girls had this good Irish lawyer. He was just a clown; he was really a kick. Sometimes he had to vacate a little early in the afternoon because he'd had a few too many sips. But he was really good.

On the days we weren't flying to Nome, the copilot and I went into the courthouse and watched the proceedings. The madams who owned some of this property—there were six of them—sat in the front row, and we sat in the bench right behind them.

The copilot and I were talking, of course. He was calling me Jack, and I was calling him Bill. Pretty soon, the half-dozen madams were calling me 'Jackie' and the copilot 'Billie.' We didn't know their names, but they sure knew ours. The next thing you know, they were turning around, telling us about their business, stories about this girl and that girl, and what their lawyer was saying.

Well, their lawyer successfully argued to the judge that simply admitting you did something was not enough to incriminate; somebody also had to *see* it. You had to have a witness. So they had to throw out the whole case against the madams.

Well, I was flying south on a milk run that went to Whitehorse, Juneau, Ketchikan and Seattle with the DC-3. It was three hours to Whitehorse. I had to go back and use the lavatory—just a honey bucket in the back of that DC-3.

I had a full load of passengers. Half of them were businessmen whom I knew; they went back and forth all the time. Well, I opened the cockpit door and here were four of these madams, sitting about a third of the way back.

As soon as they saw me, they started yelling, "Hi, Jackie! Hi, Jackie!" Everyone on board was looking around. And, of course, all of those Fairbanks passengers knew who they were. Well, I backed into the cockpit and held it until I got to Whitehorse.

One of my friends up there was a Chevrolet dealer. We would trade cards. Every time I saw him, if he was across the street or wherever, he would yell: "Hi, Jackie! Hi, Jackie!" A lot of funny things like that happened up there.

"First" Things First

I called my good friend Hap Holdrup—he was a dispatcher and a station manager—who has a lot of Pan Am books and records. I said, "Hap, do you have any idea when Pan Am flew the first passenger trip to Alaska?"

Pan Am's first passenger flight to Alaska was in 1938, he said. They brought four-engine, S-42 Sikorsky Seaplanes up from Miami. They flew the survey flights to Ketchikan and Juneau, and just landed there in the water. The planes didn't have wheels on them; they were all boat. They had been using them in the Caribbean and down into South America.

They got the survey flights all taken care of. The next year, in June of 1939, Pan Am started the first airline passenger service to Ketchikan and Juneau with the S-42s. The trip to Ketchikan cost $75; it was a five-hour flight. The flight from Seattle to Juneau was about seven hours, and a $95 flight.

They flew the S-42s until they built an airport on Annette Island, about five miles from Ketchikan. They couldn't build one in Ketchikan because there's nothing flat over there. They had a seaplane service—Alaska Coastal and Ellis; there were two of them—that went back and forth. They flew the little twin-engine

Grumman Gooses that carried about six people. They would bring the passengers over to us at Annette Island.

Juneau finally got their airport built, so then we started DC-3s in there. We were flying DC-3s both places, and getting fed with Alaska Coastal and Ellis from Ketchikan to Annette Island. Annette Island was a military base; it still is a Coast Guard base. They keep a couple of Grummans there.

Pan Am used the little Fairchild Pilgrim single-engine, eight-passenger planes up in the interior of Alaska, not on the coast. When we finally started flying the DC-3s, we had life rafts back by the galley. The rule was that if you got an hour away from land, you had to have life rafts. But we didn't worry about the water up in the Fairbanks area.

We flew out to Nome with the eight-passenger planes, and then down to Bethel, down the Kuskaquim River, but there was no water that we had to cross. When we flew to Nome, we went over the mountain range to Moses Point; then we could go up around the coast—the Arctic Ocean—to Nome, or we could go straight across just a little ridge.

A lot of the fellows did that. I did it some in the summertime, but not in the winter. Because up there around Nome they don't have any trees or anything, and the little bushes are all covered with snow. You could get a snowy day—low clouds, snowing and snow on the ground—and not be able to tell where that ridge was, or where the clouds were. They all merged together. It was a whiteout.

We lost one of our airplanes there with a load of passengers on it. He was just going across there, saving half an hour. He just flew into the top of that little rise; killed them all. But I would go around the point; it took about thirty minutes longer. But you were right out on the coast, all the way around. If you had a problem, you could land, even in the wintertime.

When the salt water started freezing and getting the wind, it would blow big hunks of ice up along the coast. But if you just got behind the ice a little ways, you could land on the beach. But I never had to land up there; I always lucked out. You could fly when it was pretty nasty around the coast. No matter how hard it was snowing, those big cakes of ice would really make the coast distinguishable.

Crew of first DC-4 passenger trip to Alaska. Chief Pilot Ralph Savory (left), myself (second from left) and rest of crew preparing for first four-engine passenger service between Seattle and Fairbanks. Courtesy Pan Am.

So you just flew along—and all those big cakes of ice were on the coast—and went right to Nome. We didn't have any radio ranges, no voice; we just had the Morse code. You were out there on your own.

Finally they extended the runways a little bit so that we operated with the DC-4s. The DC-4 was the first four-engine passenger plane to make regularly scheduled flights to Alaska. Pan Am's Chief Pilot, Ralph Savory, and I were on the crew that made the inaugural flight. The mayor of Fairbanks and other dignitaries were on that first DC-4 flight to Fairbanks.

Up to that time, Pan Am—and everybody else—was just flying twin-engine, 21-passenger DC-3s, with no pressurization and limited altitude. It was quite a change to go to a four-engine airplane, although the DC-4 was not pressurized, either.

Ralph flew the first airliner with wheels, a Stratocruiser, on the ice at the South Pole. And he and I went on the first around-the-world charter trip, with Philco. I got to do a lot of "first" things with Ralph, because most of the pilots didn't have instructor's ratings—and didn't want to instruct, anyway.

I liked instructing; I enjoyed working with new pilots. So Ralph was always calling on me if a copilot was having trouble with landings or something. I would take them out. I always lived fairly close to the airport, so I was always right there, ready to go.

Ralph was just fantastic. He could fly each of Pan Am's airplanes better than the pilots who flew them on a regular basis. He was really down to earth. He had been a bush pilot, had his own business in Alaska hauling the mail, when Pan Am first bought those routes. He was really a prince of a guy, raised on a ranch in Nevada. We had a lot in common.

He just had one daughter, and he always wanted a son. He kind of adopted me, and let me do things that none of the other pilots did. I know some of the other pilots thought that I was getting special treatment. When we would get some new equipment at one of the other bases, the pilots would bid out. "Jack," he would tell me, "don't bid it; we're gonna have some new stuff here, too."

Ralph bought a ranch out in Enumclaw, because he was raised on a cattle ranch, not far from Reno. He ran over fifty head of cattle out there; one of the mechanics was helping him.

I also got well acquainted with the Wien brothers. Merrill Wien, their son, came to work for Pan Am, because he wanted to get some of the four-engine flying on the DC-4s we had then, and instrument flying. Neither of the Wien brothers had an instrument rating, because there were no radio ranges or anything for them to use. They finally started building them—mainly for the military.

The Wiens bought a real nice new Cessna, with all of the modern instruments in it. "I've never instructed," Merrill said. "I can help them because I've got an instrument rating. But I can't sign them off or anything. Could you help us?"

"Sure," I said. "I'm up there soloing all those mechanics all the time. I'll just catch your dad and your uncle and get 'em checked out on instruments." I couldn't give ratings; you had to be an FAA inspector for that. But I gave them enough training; and then Merrill gave them a lot, because he had an instrument rating.

We got them both instrument rated, so that they could at least pull up on top, and get out of the ice.

My flying in Alaska was really great. Going to Fairbanks was just like going to Miles City, because Fairbanks wasn't as big as Miles City when I started up there. We were right at home. We had a nice dining room out at the Elks in town there. We went over there quite often for dinner. And you would know everybody there.

That's why I stayed up in Alaska so long. I enjoyed the flying, except for Whitehorse-to-Juneau. We needed all the help we could get in conditions like that. And we always got it—too many times to just be luck. That was the only time I was concerned about any of the flying in Alaska.

The Aleutian weather—you always had a range that you could fly into Dutch Harbor or someplace on. You knew where you were;

you knew you were out over the water. That was the only area I was concerned about: getting caught up over Chilkoot Pass.

My dad, John "JC" Burke and I. Dad finally "forgave" me for skipping baseball practice after I proved I could make a living as a pilot—and took him on a scenic tour of Alaska.

Getting ready to depart for Alaska with my dad.

My dad and crew in Fairbanks, Alaska. Dad flew all around Alaska
with me for ten days on a Douglas four-engine DC-4.

Blow Torch

When they brought the jets in, it just completely revolutionized the whole aviation industry. They're such fantastic machines. All those problems that the prop-planes had with ice were gone. The fan blades in the jet engine don't build up with ice like the old propellers.

We used to get ice on the props, and they would get out of balance and shake the engine out there. We had so much ice up north with that DC-3, because we always flew down in the icy range—8,000 to 10,000 feet. That first winter we flew them, we had so much ice coming off, banging into the side of the fuselage, that it was denting the aluminum.

The centrifugal force flung so much ice off the props that Pan Am had to put a piece of stainless steel—about a foot-and-a-half wide, the full length of the fuselage—up and down, opposite the propellers on both sides, because the ice was poking holes in the aluminum fuselage.

Of course, those airplanes weren't pressurized, so that didn't make any difference. But when we got the jet, there was so much power that we would go right through the ice range. Most people figure the higher you get, the colder it gets—and, of course, the more ice you're going to get.

Well, it's not that way. You get the most ice right around freezing—right around 32 degrees F—because it's damp enough that it will stick. But if you go on up another 5,000 feet, it gets enough cold enough that it's just dry snow blowing off of stuff.

So with the jet, you just bust right on through it to 35,000 or 40,000 feet, up on top of the weather, so fast that you don't put any ice on. If you have to get down to where you have to hold to come in in a pattern, or if you need anti-ice, all you have to do is turn the heat on and it drains hot air off of those engines and right onto the leading edge of the wing.

With the old prop airplanes, they had a rubber boot that went the full length of the wing. They had five tubes in there, and they would blow up—alternate—so that would ripple. The ice would build up on that, and then we would turn the boots on, and they would ripple it and ice would break off.

Well, then there would be pieces of ice that would stay. First thing you know, there was more ice building up over the pieces. Now you had the boots in there working; but the ice was out here, not even getting touched.

So it was a handful; it really was. We had alcohol that we spread it with. We had a little rubber boot with grooves on it on the leading edge of each propeller. It had centrifugal force. We turned the alcohol on—I think we had twenty gallons—and there was a slinger ring up there, and it ran down the propellers. It had a little gauge so you could measure the number of quarts that you were going to put out.

You turned it on, and you saved your alcohol. It started with a quart, maybe, and it drained right out there. There was a little tube right at the hub of the prop. It just sprayed it out, then it ran down that rubber boot on the leading edge of the prop.

That system did get us out of trouble, because if you got too much ice out there, the props got rough and lost their air foil. They wouldn't be pulling you, either. The props are just like a wing. So you could get augered in with just prop ice.

You ran the RPM up fast and that threw some of it off. And the ice flew off—BANG! BANG!—hitting the fuselage in big chunks. It was different.

But now with the jets there's none of that. Those jet engines are so dependable; you just don't plan on anything happening to them. They're really nothing but a blow torch. They have some accessories on them, of course. Instead of a carburetor they have a fuel controller. And, of course, the generators and other equipment are on there.

It was crazy, because as a captain you got $620 a month for flying the DC-3 down in all that weather. And then they would build your salary on your productivity.

So you would get a jet that was four times as heavy, and four times as fast, and it was really productive. Then they came through with this wild pay scale on the 707. We just couldn't believe it. In fact, we told the company that we would take the bottom scale that any of the airlines settled on.

Well, at United Airlines the employees got control of the airline, and they doubled their 747 pay. They were getting $150,000 a year, and they went to $300,000, if you can imagine. But then, of course, in just one year they were bankrupt.

But you sit there with all this equipment—automatic pilot and navigation connected to the pilot—and watch things work. No ice, no mechanical problems. The only things that you ever have to change on it are the generators and the fuel controller—stuff that was connected to it.

And we got quieter engines all the time—they had the fan in the front, you know. It would push the air in to the compressor—it was shooting fuel in it—and then it would blast out the rear end.

You were getting about one-fourth of your thrust out of these fans in the front, but three-fourths of it out the tail—from the jet blast. Well, they were noisy, those first ones; they really whined. So they re-engineered the whole engine; Pratt & Whitney was the first to do it. They doubled the size of the fans. That way you were getting three-fourths of your thrust by the fans pulling you, and just one-fourth out the tail—and a lot less noise.

You don't know where that jet can go from here, other than supersonic. And they haven't found any way to quiet down that supersonic boom. When the British and the French were flying that supersonic across the ocean, they had to slow down below the speed of sound when they approached the coast near New York. There was this BOOM-BOOM-BOOM-BOOM all the way across.

It's been a fantastic occupation to have been in through such a change. The changes come in stages. They make a development, then they take time, bring you through school and give you the proper training. Right to the last day, I flew the 747.

I learned to fly in that little Aeronca, thirty-six horsepower. You pushed that throttle up and it just started creeping down the runway, but it wouldn't push you back in the seat. Every time I pushed the power up on that jet—they're over 50,000 horsepower per engine; there's four of them, 200,000 horsepower—I'd think, "Boy, this is sure different than thirty-six horsepower engines." Because it pushed you right back in the seat.

But you can see why, I think it was last year, the U.S. airlines went all year without a fatality. The feeder airlines have a little more trouble, because they're back down there with props. Most of them are turbo props, so they do have a jet engine. But they still have the props to worry about.

When I started flying, you could not get life insurance; they just wouldn't write it to you. Now there's no extra charge for pilot's insurance.

Navy Blues

I never wore my uniform coat in the airplane. I just had a dark nylon jacket, and it was more comfortable, anyway. And getting off in Alaska, I never even put my coat on. Those early uniforms for Pan American—we didn't have any stripes on our coat.

We didn't have anything, really. The reason for that was that Pan American was really navy when it started out—flying boats and stuff. So they just went to the navy store and bought navy uniforms—the navy blues.

We had a double-breasted uniform—real dark blue, or black. We wore those as a uniform with Pan Am with no stripes—and no gold on the bill of our caps, like the other airlines—because we were going around the world. And some of those trips would take two or three weeks in the flying boats.

They were always inviting us—some of the political functions, city council meetings and such—to talk about flying around the world. The company always wanted us to be dressed up as well as the other people were. So we just put our uniform on, and our black tie, and we could go to the best formals.

We didn't have any stripes on our uniforms or gold on our caps until the jets. All the time we were flying the prop airplanes, we just had that navy uniform.

In uniform, with my 1936 Plymouth.

Finally, the company got to be so international, and wanted to be identified, that they went to the four stripes. It was a couple of years later before we got gold on the hat. I wore an old cap without any gold braid on it for five years after the new hats came out. The Chief Pilot saw it sitting on the counter down here and ordered me a new one.

We didn't have a big enough suitcase to carry a bunch of sports coats. So we just had that navy blue uniform, and we went to the best dinner they wanted. The airline had classes for us when we went down for our six-month check. We spent one day being a diplomat, training in what we could talk about—and what we couldn't talk about—on our trips to foreign lands.

Big Wheels

There aren't many occupations or airlines that had as many international operations as Pan Am. It got to where Pan American had stations all around the world. I had so many passengers tell me they couldn't get their passports stamped or renewed or something, and they were afraid they weren't going to get out of a particular station.

So they just went over to Pan American. Our people had the stamp, and fixed them up just like the Customs. So Pan Am was almost another Customs office. We never went anywhere to cash a check or anything except to Pan Am. And if Pan Am wasn't giving us the best in exchange, they knew which bank in town was. They sent us over to that bank to get our money exchanged.

Pan Am was fantastic; it really was. Almost all of those mail routes that we got into South America, Pan Am got on its own. The CAB would try to negotiate with foreign countries, and not make any headway at all. We couldn't get the State Department on the ball, either. So a couple of the Pan Am wheels would go down and negotiate the permits, sign the mail permits and everything—and not ever get to the government until after we had the permit.

Juan Trippe, Pan Am's founder and president, and Andrew Priester, the company's head engineer, would make a trip down there. I don't know how exactly they would do it, but they always came back with a certificate.

Trippe was the politician and businessman. Priester was a German fellow. He and Juan Trippe really saw eye to eye. Priester was a fantastic engineer, ran Pan Am's maintenance department and chose all of the airplanes purchased by the company.

I know the State Department said that, "You Pan Am guys can

do better than we can." Because the Pan Am wheels could take the people they were negotiating with out for a good dinner and night on the town. And they did; they did a fantastic job.

Pan Am was all international; we didn't have any domestic routes until deregulation came in. But we were very political, and had a real good connection with an ambassador—I think he was based in New England. He was a close friend of Juan Trippe. Then he became a senator.

He had a real 'in' with the State Department, and would help us any time we needed a new route to compete with the foreign carriers. They were all government-owned—British Airways, Japan Airlines—and didn't care if they made any money or not.

We were trying to make money, and they would increase our mail rate if we started to lose money on a particular route. So he helped us a lot getting these routes. Pan Am tried to keep it quiet, but they didn't. Because this senator was right there working for us in Washington, D.C. all the time.

And, of course, everybody did. Senator Magnuson's family from here in Washington state had the most stock of any single family in Northwest Airlines. When Northwest wanted to go to Tokyo, Magnuson just went back to Washington and got them the route.

Pan Am was the only international airline in the U.S. until after World War Two. The reason they did that was because we were competing with all those foreign carriers that were state-subsidized or government-owned. So they felt Pan Am could at least break even if we didn't have U.S. competition, because the other domestics would feed us.

Then when they started giving all the rest of the domestic carriers international routes, Pan Am didn't have any domestic routes. We didn't have any until deregulation, and it went well. Pan Am would have been a great airline if the management could have just lived; they were all about five years older than I was. I had to retire at sixty, and they went to age seventy.

When they retired, the Board of Directors decided to go to

Harvard and hire the whiz kids. They came right out and said, "This new management's gonna make a profit every quarter." Well, no airline made a profit in the wintertime. But we did. They sold routes and sold airplanes and sold bases. Pretty soon there was nothing left to sell, and Pan Am just had to close up. All those whiz kids from Harvard.

But in its heyday, Pan Am had a lot happening. The company was like General Motors; it was like several small companies. Seattle was head of the Pacific-Alaska Division, and we flew Honolulu, Alaska and London. We only had about forty crews here.

San Francisco was head of the Pacific Division, and they covered all of the Pacific, as well as our round-the-world flights. Over a hundred crews were always stationed there. Our base in Texas flew the west side of South America. They were like Seattle; they only had about forty crews.

Miami flew the South Atlantic and South America. Miami was big because that was where Pan Am started. They started flying to the Caribbean Islands in airplanes with pontoons. They finally got some small flying boats. New York got to be the largest because it covered all of Europe.

Pan Am was like a big family; it really was. The New York crews were different; most of them were New Yorkers. They put a little bit of value on rank. We never did out here; it just didn't make any difference. When I was flying with regular copilots, like to Fairbanks, I would fly it up. Then I would change seats; I would get in the copilot's seat, and he would fly it back.

When the stewardesses came up there, they didn't even know who was captain. Most of the time, I was younger than the copilot. I always told them that, if anybody called me "Captain," I'd prefer "Jack." We didn't have any titles on the ranch.

Pilots could bid from division to division. First of all, you bid the base—and you knew what routes they were flying. Once you got there, if you had enough seniority, you just made one bid where you wanted to go. They put out new bids every two months.

At first, you could fly eighty-five hours a month. Then it became eighty, then seventy-five—because they found out that the pilots were getting fatigued. The last ten years of my career, I just bid one line, because I was at the top of the seniority list.

I bid a lot of the round-the-worlds just because they were interesting. It was fun to start with, but over time you could see the world slipping, and then it got to where we didn't trust certain countries.

Aloha

Pan Am was the only airline flying to Honolulu for the first year or two. We only had one trip a weekend; nobody else wanted it. There wasn't that much traffic. But when we finally got the traffic built up, Northwest wanted it, and Magnuson got it for them right away.

That's when we got competition out there. Before that, we just had the one trip on the weekend. We left here from Seattle on Saturday. We went out, and there would be a crew that had been there all week in Honolulu. They brought the airplane back on Sunday. So, if you wanted to go out to Honolulu, you had to go out on Saturday and come back on Sunday.

Of course, the fellow who brought the Sunday airplane out would stay there all week—five days until the next Saturday. Scotty and I didn't have any children, and we had just gotten married. We would spend practically the whole winter in the Moana Hotel.

We would go out on Saturday and stay in the Moana on Saturday night. I would leave, and Scotty would stay right there in my room. And I'd come back to bring the airplane back to Seattle. Then I went back out, and would just be gone the one night. So we spent at least half the month out there.

This is why I always said I've never had a job; I got paid for my hobby—and for having a real good vacation, too. Yes, it was a fantastic life.

Charter Members

My buddy, Ralph Savory, died on January 18, 2010. He was Pan Am's Chief Pilot; such a great guy. He turned one hundred years old in October. He had his birthday and got his new five-year driver's license. He was just as healthy and sharp as he could be. But he fell and hit his head, and only lasted about a week.

Ralph put together a twenty-eight day charter for Philco that went around the world. They had to have two crews. As soon as the word got out that the Seattle crews were going to get it, his phone never quit ringing. He finally had to turn it off. It was a small base—about 40 crews—and word got around fast. Everybody was calling and wanting to go.

I was in Montana hunting Coyotes and helping this one fellow get an instrument rating, so I didn't call. I didn't even know there was going to be a charter. We had flown over to Boise, Idaho. His wife knew where he always ate over there.

We were having lunch. They said, "Is there a Jack at this table? You've got a call from Seattle." It was Ralph.

"I hate to bother your coyote hunting over there," he said, "but there's something I wanted to ask you. We have an extra airplane and crews available, and Philco wants a 28-day charter around the world. We're gonna take a DC-6. We'll be running over eight hours on some of the legs, so we're gonna have to have two crews.

"I just wondered if maybe you'd like to go," he said. "You're the only one who hasn't called me. If you want to go, there'll be two crews. I've already picked my copilot and flight engineer. Who do you want?"

"Oh, boy," I said, "I think you're wasting your money for a phone call. But yeah, I got an idea for a copilot and a flight engineer. The copilot has just transferred back from London; he'd been flying to Europe. He knows the airways over there. He ought to be handy.

"And the engineer is an Austrian professional skier. He and his brother came over here and made some movies in California, and bought the operation at Squaw Valley. Then he got his engineer's license, came to work for Pan Am and wanted to fly around the world.

"He can speak half a dozen different languages," I said, "so he can speak anybody's language. And he's got a real sense of humor. So we've got to have Freddy on board, too."

Freddy was one of these guys that went full-bore all the time. He was funny. He had real short legs. "You know, I sit tall—but I stand short," he always said.

"So those would be my first picks," I told Ralph.

"Well, you've got some good ones," Ralph said. "That First Officer's good at telling jokes and entertaining passengers." So we went around the world with the two crews on a four-engine DC-6, the most reliable reciprocating prop airplane that was flying.

We had about sixty Philco people: half executives and half store owners. It was fun; it was a kick. We had a great big Texan on the trip, a store owner. He couldn't stand those darned bulls sleeping in all the intersections. They have these traffic 'wheels' in Texas where you drive in, go around and go out. And those darned bulls would get out there, enjoying that nice, warm asphalt and just bog down all the traffic. And they would never make them move, because this was old Uncle George, you know.

So there they were, they were going around the blocks. And they would get up and lie down on the sidewalk. Well, this big Texan—one was lying on the sidewalk in front of his store, and he wanted to go into it. Well, he went up and kicked the bull—and it got up and kicked *him*. He was walking around with a crutch for the rest of the trip. It didn't break his leg—but it really bruised it.

Raising Hob

Pan Am transferred me from Alaska to New York. Scotty and I got married three or four months before we went back there. She was two years younger than I was. She was nineteen and I was just twenty-one.

We had a little 1936 Plymouth with re-capped tires. That's what you had to get by with; you couldn't get a tire. There was a fifty-five mile speed limit. Because of those tires, we never went over the speed limit. It was in the summer and it was hot.

But we never blew out one of those tires. When we got to Miles City, going to New York, I told Scotty, "We're just going to spend a couple of weeks here at home. We're gonna call Pan Am and tell 'em we blew out a tire, and that we're waiting for a tire." So that's all we did.

We got to New York in the middle of the afternoon, and pulled into the Pan Am parking lot at the terminal. Before I could get out of the car, this big, crazy, red-headed pilot, Ted Alderson, practically mauled us.

Ted was a rower at the University of Washington. You might have seen his brother's name in the paper—Tom Alderson. He was the number-one lawyer, had a lot of cases before the Supreme Court. "Ah, that damn brother of mine," Ted would joke, "he doesn't know anything. All he knows how to do is talk."

Ted coached the freshman crew team when he was on the varsity. They went to Poughkeepsie and won both varsity and freshman. He was kind of a star out there, but he was a character. He was working for a furniture store, in a four-story building. They had a freight elevator. He stepped out and the elevator wasn't there. He fell and hit the cement with his hands, breaking both of them.

Ted wanted to go in the navy when Keith Petricks and I took a leave and went in the navy. But he couldn't pass the physical, because of his fingers. So he didn't get in, but he was trying to get out of New York. He was a character.

We drove in that parking lot and I hadn't gotten out of the car when he spotted me. Down he came: "Jack! Scotty! Don't get out of the car! Just start it up and head right on back! This is a helluva place."

"I can't do that, Ted," I said. "I've been transferred. I've gotta at least check *in*."

"No, no, no, no!" he said. "Tell 'em you couldn't get here. You can't go up to that Chief Pilot's office lookin' like you do." I had a summer sports shirt on.

"I went up there with a sports shirt on," he said. "And the first thing Miss McGoldrick told me, after she had checked me in, was: 'Now, sir, don't you *ever* come to the Chief Pilot's office again without a coat and tie.'"

Miss McGoldrick was, in effect, the Chief Pilot. She had been the secretary there for a hundred years. The Chief Pilot was a real nice, easy-going guy, and he just let her run the place.

"Really?" Ted said. So he went right down to a men's clothing store and bought the loudest shirt he could find, with stripes all the way around it. He kept that in his car. Whenever he went to the Chief Pilot's office, if he had a coat and tie on he would take them off, leave them in the car and put this on.

Ted raised so much hob around there that they transferred him back to Seattle. They didn't even have a vacancy here, but they made one for him. He came back to Seattle.

"If you chip away at 'em long enough," he said, "you can win." He was a kick.

Enough of New York

That was our first time to New York; we had never been back east at all. And we lucked out. When we went to New York, you couldn't find a house or an apartment anywhere. So when we transferred there, Pan American really took good care of everybody. They took us out to the Forest Hills Tennis Club; it was the fanciest place on Long Island. Scotty and I lived there for two months, with Pan Am paying the bill.

No air conditioning, though. I went down for breakfast—this was in July or August. Hot, humid. The maitre d' was standing in the doorway. I had a white shirt on. "Would you like a jacket and a tie?" he said. "We have one hanging here." He was wearing one, of course.

"A jacket and a tie?" I said. Perspiration was just running off my face. I said, "We're gonna go across the street to eat." So we never did eat in there, ever. But it was really a nice place; it was first class.

We lived there for two months. They had a circle around the airport. You had to be within that circle or you couldn't get gas-rationing coupons. So we went as far out on Long Island as we could go. We looked and looked, and couldn't find anything.

One day this pilot who had a couple of kids called me. "We found a real nice little row house," he said. You know, they built them on the whole block. You had to go through the house to get to your back yard. He said, "There's one down here. Kind of a stuffy couple have it, but they're being transferred to Florida.

"They want to rent it," he said. "But they want to rent it to somebody who doesn't have any children."

I called them and said that it was just two adults, and that we didn't smoke or drink. "Come on out," he said. So we went out. It was a good-sized place, with two bedrooms, a living room, dining room, kitchen and basement. There was a garage in the basement, and you could walk right through to get to your back yard.

So we got that, and were there all the time. There was a little grocery just around the corner. A nice old guy and his wife ran it. We bought everything there. It was funny because they had doughnuts—powdered sugar and chocolate. The package of choco-late-covered doughnuts was five cents more than the powdered sugar doughnuts.

Well, Scotty and I didn't like the chocolate-covered doughnuts, so we always got the powdered-sugar ones. I would set the stuff up on the counter, go get something else and set it there. When I came back, that package of powdered-sugar doughnuts was always turned over. The package was the same except for the top.

And the store owner charged me an extra nickel—all the time

we were there. I think we spent about eight months there before I went in the navy. I told Scotty, "I'm not gonna say a word until I leave. But I'll just see how long he'll go through all that trouble to watch me, not wanting me to see it." And he turned that darned package over every time.

For the eight months we were there, he turned it over. Finally, when we got ready to leave, I said, "You know, I guess we're not gonna see you anymore. We're getting transferred."

"Oh," he said, "I thought you were going down to visit every weekend or so."

"No, no," I said. "This is not Washington, D.C. This is Washington *state*."

"Where's Washington state?" He didn't know there *was* a Washington state.

"It's the very far end of this country," I said. "As far as you can go without going in the Pacific Ocean." I was kidding with him. "By the way," I said, "we don't like chocolate doughnuts." And that's all I said. I didn't tell him about all the times I had watched him turn that package over.

A lot of those easterners were just obnoxious. You would have to stand in line to get your meat coupons, and they could get mean. I was happy that I had been raised on a cattle ranch and didn't care for meat anymore. I had eaten it three times a day.

But, overall, we really enjoyed New York. Our neighbors in the row houses were nice and friendly. "Well, what did you do today?" they would ask.

"Well, we went over to the Statue of Liberty."

"We gotta do that, you know. We've lived here all our lives, and we've never been to the Statue of Liberty."

We saw everything in the eight months we were there. We went to the zoo; they had a fantastic zoo there. We would go to the movies—during the war, no less—for a dollar, and then sit there and hear a big band on the stage for an hour afterwards. All for that one dollar.

I was flying a navy airplane, the Boeing 314 flying boat, which Pan Am had owned, but I was a civilian. We couldn't get transferred back to Seattle. They really needed us on the East Coast, and I hated to leave, because the Chief Pilot was a real nice guy. But, finally, we had had enough of New York.

Then the navy said, "We'll swear you right in as an officer, and send you wherever you want to go."

"Have you got a spot in Seattle?" I asked.

"Yes," they said. "We've got Sand Point, right out there on the north end of Lake Washington. It's a base, and you've got an instructor's rating. You can teach there."

We liked Seattle because we had been here before.

CHAPTER 6

THREE WARS

Flying Boats

I flew for seventy years: forty years with Pan Am, and the navy and air force in between. Because Pan Am had routes, airports and service around the world—and the military didn't have enough equipment or pilots—Pan Am had an agreement with the air force that the air force could have a third of Pan Am's airplanes and flight crews. If necessary, maybe more. So they just leased them from Pan Am. It was kind of an odd arrangement.

I served in three wars altogether. In World War II, I was sent from Alaska, where I was flying Fairchild Pilgrims for Pan Am, to New York, to copilot on Boeing 314 flying boats. My pay went from $450 a month to $620. Eventually I would get sworn in the navy and return to Alaska.

I stayed in the navy; then, during the Korean and Vietnam Wars, the air force got a hold of me. I stayed in the reserves. I received four physicals a year: two from Pan Am and two from the government. A copilot only has to have one from the government a year, but a captain has to have two.

Anyway, as I had my twenty-first birthday, they sent Keith Petrick, Roy Wise and I to New York to go to navigation school and learn to take star fixes with a sextant. We got our navigator's license to fly as First Officers on the flying boats.

The flying boats were in a class by themselves. As airplane travel—and the desire to fly across the oceans—increased during the 1930s, Pan Am sought a long-range, four-engine flying boat. Boeing responded with the Model 314, dubbed the "Clipper" in honor of the legendary sailing ships of old.

The flying boat was grand, I tell you; it was the most deluxe thing flying. It was quite an airplane; it was way ahead of its time. When it first took to the skies—and seas—a year or two before the war, the Clipper was the largest civil aircraft in service. With a nose resembling that of a modern 747, it was the "jumbo" airplane of its era. It had a range of 3,500 miles, and made the first scheduled trans-Atlantic flight on June 28, 1939.

Everything Boeing builds, they can be proud of. With Pan Am's airplanes, about ten of the company's design and mechanical engineers would come right out and live in Seattle for a couple of years while Boeing was developing an airplane.

Later, for the 747, Pan Am was the only airline which ordered or bought any of the first twenty-five produced. Pan Am worked with Boeing, which incorporated a lot of suggestions and equipment needed for international flying. So Boeing and Pan Am were real good friends.

Anyway, Boeing built just twelve 314s, all between 1938 and 1941. At the outbreak of World War II, the Clippers were pressed into service to carry personnel, equipment and materials across the oceans. They made many key flights during the course of the war, and carried several VIPs—"Very Important Passengers"—including Franklin Roosevelt and Winston Churchill.

In fact, the first flight that President Franklin Roosevelt ever made to a foreign base was in a flying boat. He went over to Casablanca, Morocco in January, 1943 to meet with Winston Churchill and French leaders to plan the Allies' European strategy in World War Two. He wanted a Pan American flying boat, so they rigged three of them up—two of them for backups.

One of them was all fixed up for President Roosevelt. They went down to South America; I think they went to Rio. Then they went across the Atlantic to Africa. It was a lot shorter and safer that way, rather than going across the North Atlantic and being out there all that time over water. They figured there was less chance of a problem, having a shorter water flight.

The other two boats flew along behind them—just making sure that if they had an engine problem or whatever, they would have a backup airplane for him.

So the flying boats took Roosevelt over to the Casablanca Conference, and brought him back. That was the first time that a president had ever flown from the United States to Europe on an airplane for a meeting. He had always gone by ship before; gone by navy ship. Roosevelt celebrated his birthday in the flying boat's dining room on the return trip.

So Pan Am was responsible for a lot of aviation "firsts," because up to that time, we were the only U.S. international flyer. The reason they did that was to keep Pan Am competitive. We didn't have any domestic routes. About the only route we had that wasn't international was the Alaska sector—Seattle to Alaska. And, of course, Alaska was a Territory at the time.

Going Along like Lindbergh

Only the best and most experienced flight crews were assigned to the Boeing 314 flying boats. Since Pan Am's pilots and crews had a lot of experience flying the Clippers in extreme long-distance, over-water flights, the company's pilots and navigators continued serving as flight crew during the war.

Critical to the Clippers' success on their military missions was the proficiency of their civilian Pan Am flight crews. Experienced and highly skilled at long-distance, over-water flight operations and navigation, they also received rigorous training in dead reckoning, timed turns, judging drift from sea currents, and astral and radio navigation.

The navy purchased all of Pan Am's Flying Boats; I think we had eight. The others carried passengers. The navy said they would return the flying boats at the end of the war. So they were operating them. They had taken all of the seats out of a couple of the 314s, which were hauling just special cargo. Given the military designation C-98, few other aircraft of that time could meet the wartime requirements for load and distance.

We had to go through navigation school, because the flying boats navigated just with the stars and the sun. It was all celestial navigation. We went through a two-month school and got a navigation license. We had a sextant that we could shoot the stars and the sun with.

For the wind, we opened up a little trapdoor back in the tail, went back there and shot out a bomb. When it hit the water, the water ignited it, and it would come alive and smoke. We would get the sextant on the bomb, and see what the wind was doing. Then we would have the pilot make a ninety-degree turn so we could get another fix on the smoke bomb. That way you could figure out what the wind was.

At night, the smoke bomb lit up. As soon as it hit the water, it blew up and burned, for maybe half an hour. So at night we could get a fix on it, and that's how we figured the wind. In the daytime you could see the smoke. There was no radar, there were no ships out there—there was *nothing* to report anything, you know. We were just out there going along like Lindbergh.

Full-scale replica of the Boeing 314 flying boat, including cockpit and navigator's station. I flew the "Clipper" from New York to London (and later Ireland) during World War Two. Photos courtesy Foynes Flying Boat Museum, Ireland.

"Yes Sir, No Sir"

Flying boat pilots were members of a select group. For one thing, it cost a lot of money to qualify all of us in it. Of course, coming from Alaska, we were a very informal bunch. But a few of the older captains who had been in the navy and had come with Pan American were really staunchy old guys.

The first training flight we had in the boat was right there in Flushing Bay. There was this little pip squeak captain who thought he was running the airlines. He was just an instructor, but he had assumed that he was the manager of the training department.

We were finishing up our navigation class. They called us and said they were running a training flight, and to come on over and see how the boat worked. So the person he was giving some landings to came down and checked us out on the bow line.

You had this door that you opened, and then you had this light line with a four-pronged hook. You would just throw that out, and that would hook the big line. Then you would pull the big line in. You put the big line on a post.

And, of course, they had an intercom. We had never seen an intercom—we just had radios on most of our planes up in Alaska. "Why, when you get this hooked on, just get on this intercom and say, 'It's on the buoy,'" the instructor said.

This other pilot was my age, too—we were young—and he had been born and raised in Juneau. His dad was a government inspector up there; he checked passengers when they came in. When we landed, he ended up with the hook.

We were headed for this buoy. He was going fast; he was going right for the buoy. And he didn't tell us that he was going to go by it and come back. Keith was standing there with that hook, watching this buoy come up. "Jack," he said, "we're going too fast to catch that thing."

"Well, it's no different than roping a calf," I said. "And I've done an awful lot of that. Let me have the hook." So he gave me the hook, and I spun it and threw it way out ahead of the boat and got the big line. We put it on the post. And the darned boat just about upset, because they didn't have wingtip floats. It had those sponsons that were on the fuselage.

The instructor was going to go down and come back, but he didn't tell us anything about it. And why he went so close to it, I don't know. But he went close enough that I was able to rope it just like a calf. We pulled it in and got the thing on the post. The boat was just about upset—it was really leaning when we hit the end of that rope.

Of course, that disturbed the little guy. So Keith got on the intercom and said, "It's on the buoy."

"It's on the buoy *what?*" said the instructor.

"I guess he didn't hear me," Keith said. "IT'S ON THE BUOY!"

"It's on the buoy WHAT?" the instructor said again. All he wanted was, "sir."

We had no idea what he was talking about, because we had never worked an intercom before; and those intercoms weren't very good, anyway. "Keith, we must not be using the right nautical terms," I said. "Tell him we've got this son-of-a-b tied up."

So Keith said into the intercom, "We've got this son-of-a-b tied up." And boy we could hear this little guy slide his seat back up overhead, and down the stairs he came.

"Where are you fellas from?" he said.

"Well," we said, "we're from Alaska. We've been flyin' the bush in Alaska."

When we got through with that sass, we didn't argue or say anything to our instructor. He lectured us all the way back to shore: "You're no longer a bush pilot . . . now you're down here with the big boat pilots, and it's 'yes sir, no sir.'" Keith and I—well, it just went right over our heads.

I spent a year in Alaska. And that's what I would have liked to have told that 'yes-sir-no-sir' guy. I'd say, "You know, we fly in Alaska visual. And there's a lot of mountains up there, a lot of weather up there. No radio; just the Morse code. No radio ranges; you had to know the country." And I would have added, "Nobody even thought about 'Yes sir, no sir.'"

But I didn't; I held my tongue and didn't say anything. But I did mention that to the Chief Pilot. I said, "You know, if he would come up there and fly the bush with us—one trip to Nome and back—I think he'd want to get back here on the boat."

And then: I just couldn't believe it. Thirty years later, I ended up giving this same instructor his last route check. And he didn't have a clue who I was. He wouldn't have a clue until he read the report, and I made a comment about, "Yes sir, Captain" and "No, sir." And, "I see that you got this son-of-a-b tied up at the terminal." He would have recognized that, I'm sure.

Anyway, Keith and I went up to the Chief Pilot—a great guy.

He was tall and skinny, raised on a farm in Iowa. He flew fighters in World War I. "We want to get a leave of absence to go in the Navy," we said.

"Oh, no," he said, "you just had your first ride in the airplane."

"Yeah—and that was enough," we said. "We got a little pip squeak out there who only wants to lecture us about not calling him 'sir' and 'yes sir' and 'no sir.' As long as we're gonna have to do that, why, we'll get some credit with the navy."

That Chief Pilot was such a nice guy. "Gosh," he said, "you know, we need ya. You finished up your navigation now, so you can go as First Officer, and you can navigate with the sextants and the stars. We really need ya.

"I'll make you a deal," he said. "If you'll stay for six months, I think you're gonna like it, and want to continue on. If not, and you still want to go in the Navy, I'll give you a personal letter from the Chief Pilot's Office that will guarantee you will accrue seniority all the time you are gone."

That was a rule the government had. But some airlines would argue about it. So he wrote us this letter, and we had it. Well, both Keith and I stayed about eight months. We had that twenty-hours-to-London route. The flying boats were slow-moving machines—although it was interesting, you know. And we used our navigation, because neither one of us had a navigator's license until then.

Pan Am flying boat crew at La Guardia preparing for a transatlantic flight. The New York-to-London trip took
20 hours—two 10-hour segments.
The Boeing Company Collection at The Museum of Flight.

Hooking the bow line of the flying boat to a buoy was
"no different than roping a calf."
The Peter M. Bowers Collection/The Museum of Flight.

Sitting Ducks

It was a kick flying the Clippers, even if the technology was somewhat primitive—especially by today's standards. We had no radio navigation. The flying boats were not pressurized, so we flew at about 6,000 to 8,000 feet. We never tried to get above 10,000 feet, because oxygen starts getting thin up there. All we had were portable masks that would come down. Sometimes we would have to get lower to get underneath the overcast.

The fuselage of the flying boat had different levels on the rooms in there. Right in the middle was a real nice dining room. It had a big oval table that seated ten passengers and a crew member.

They always had a crew member there to answer questions. And we had all-male pursers and cooks; no girls. And they would just cook up a real meal for you. They kept several of the flying boats with the passenger configuration.

The flying boats were fantastic machines. They were just slow, because of that big old hull. I flew the flying boats from Flushing Bay, New York—right next to La Guardia—to Botwood, Newfoundland. Botwood, an amphibious air base in a sheltered harbor and fog-free climate, was originally selected by Pan Am and British Imperial Airways in 1935 as a landing base for their transatlantic flying boats.

It took ten hours to get to Botwood. We would fuel, then go ten hours to London—a twenty-hour trip—and land in the Thames River. We felt safe during the first part of the war. The German fighters didn't have enough range to follow the bombers back across the English Channel. They had to turn around and go back; they were running out of gas. So we were in good shape.

But the Germans developed extended-range fighters that could make it all the way to London. Now we were sitting ducks with those great big flying boats. So right quick-like they changed it, and wouldn't let us go to London. We began terminating our flying-boat runs at Lake Neagh, a large lake just west of Belfast, Ireland. The military would unload the airplane and take all the stuff on over, because they could do it at night.

You just can't fly those boats at night, because there are logs and debris in the river. You can't see any of it, and you can't land at night—unless it's an emergency.

It wasn't but an hour shorter terminating at Lake Neagh instead of London. But it was still a long trip at about 130 knots, our cruising speed. The flying boats would go faster if you wanted to push the power up, but it wasn't economical.

We flew the flying boats with constant air speed. Usually you get up to cruise and put the power on, and as you burn fuel you lighten up and go faster. But we were burning too much fuel that way. So we used cruise control once we got up to altitude.

Belfast was a kick. And having this Irish name, I couldn't do anything wrong there. I got acquainted with a lot of the crewhands at the dock, and brought them lots of fresh fruit. During the war they didn't have anything to eat over there. They just had boiled potatoes and mutton—and that was about it.

We would go into these little restaurants, and they didn't have a menu. They would just say, "Well, did you just want tea and toast, or did you want something to eat?" If you wanted something to eat, why, they brought it; you didn't order it. They always had potatoes, which they used in a lot of ways. But usually just boiled.

Well, I would bring a whole case of oranges for these guys out on the dock. And, of course, they weren't getting any fresh fruit at all. Every trip I had a case of oranges or a couple of boxes of apples. They really appreciated that.

So they started giving me linen and table cloths that the wives had embroidered on. I would come back with those fancy things. My wife gave them to all of her relatives. They all got these hand-embroidered, linen tablecloths.

Cannonball

Scotty and I didn't like New York; so, after six months, I got a military leave of absence and went in the navy, on my own, in order to get out of New York and move back to the West Coast. I'd never been in the service before. The navy swore me in and gave me a commission as an ensign, because I was so young. When I turned twenty, they advanced me to a junior grade lieutenant.

Some of our pilots that went in—Johnny Amundsen, a check pilot in his forties—they gave him three stripes, because of his age. They just didn't waste any time. When I went into the navy, I had been instructing for Pan Am, and flying the line, so they gave me a DC-3 and put me in instructing right out here at Sand Point, on Lake Washington in Seattle.

When I went to the navy school, all they did was to give me a uniform and a handbook of rules and regulations. That was it; no training at all. They didn't even teach me how to salute. I had the braid on, so someone would salute me and I would just say, "Howdy." They got quite a kick out of that.

Of course, you could always find some guy with a few stripes who wanted to be saluted every time he turned around. As for me, I couldn't care less about rank. You look at things differently when you're raised on a ranch in Montana.

I would do instrument instruction for a month at Sand Point, then go to Kodiak, Alaska for a month and fly out the Aleutian chain with the new pilots to get them used to that stinky weather and wind.

We organized a VR-5 squadron with all airline pilots. I was flying a cargo DC-3, but the navy called it an R4-D. The aircraft had bucket seats that folded up to the sides so it could hold all cargo. Or, if they wanted passengers, they could drop them down. They were just metal seats with cushions.

With my navy crew and R4-D plane in the
Aleutian Islands in World War Two.

There were two battles up in the Aleutians where they had a higher percentage of soldiers killed than anyplace else—even the Pacific. They had two carriers—and of course no radar in those days. Always foggy and drizzly. The Japanese brought in a big bunch of troops and let them off at the shore. They went up the mountain partway and really dug in.

When the U.S. tried to land, they were just sitting ducks down there on the beach. They really lost a lot of lives there. But it wasn't that big of an operation, and they were talking about the Pacific all the time.

It would take ten days to two weeks to get the mail out the Aleutian chain, where the weather was pretty nasty. When you go through meteorology, they tell you that you can't have fog if there's a wind of more than about ten knots. Well, you can have a fifty-knot wind and still be fogged in out there, because that fog is coming from clear up in the Arctic Ocean.

So it can be nasty weather, and these young guys had just graduated from Pensacola. They hadn't flown in weather like that; they hadn't flown *nights* that much. So we formed this VR-5 Squadron, all ex-airline who were called back in.

We started a cannonball, we called it. The airplane didn't lay over. You would take it from Kodiak to Cold Bay to Dutch Harbor. You would get off, and the crew that went out the day before would take it from there on out to Adak. They would get off, and there was a crew who had gone the day before that would take it to Attu, and back to Adak, Dutch Harbor and Kodiak.

The servicemen based on the Aleutian chain really appreciated the reliable mail service we provided. They said that before we started the "cannonball" schedule, their mail took weeks to get through. Now it was coming every day.

On our overnights, the navy cooks sure fixed us good food to show their appreciation for the improved mail service. We had this VR-5 Squadron emblem on the top of our wings. They knew we were all ex-airline. And they would come out and say, "Would you like a T-bone steak tonight? We've got some hidden in the freezer."

Well, of course I said, "Give it to anybody else. I'd rather have a hot dog, 'cause I was raised on a cattle ranch and ate that three times a day." They took awfully good care of us.

I finished out World War II flying for the navy in Alaska and the Aleutian Islands.

Views of volcanoes over Alaska's Aleutian Islands
from a DC-3 in 1942.

Sherm and Les

My brother-in-law, Sherm, whom I taught to fly, graduated
at the top of his class, which meant he could pick the airplane he

wanted to fly. Well, he picked fighters. But in World War II, you couldn't be over six feet tall and fly a fighter. The cabin was too small. And he was six-foot-two.

They didn't have any spots open on the B-17, so he ended up with a B-24. Out there in the South Pacific, the B-24 was supposed to compete with the B-17. But it wouldn't go to altitude with a load. So they were using it for strafing.

Sherm was only out in the Pacific about six months. He got blown up; they blew the wing off. A missile hit him and just blew him out of the air. All of the Boeing airplanes have liners in the gas tanks.

Scotty's other brother, Les, was one of the first people drafted out of Miles City. He had a garage and had been a mechanic. He ended up in Europe, following the tanks, repairing the tanks. He didn't get hurt at all; but he said he ended up a long ways from where he thought he would be—in a stationary garage someplace.

He was out there with these two big trucks—one was a wrecker—with one of the first groups into Berlin. He returned to Miles City after the war and ran his garage.

Help Wanted

One of my good friends at Pan Am, a copilot whom I was checking out in the airplane, went over to Europe during the early years of World War II as a B-17 pilot. He was in the 8th Air Force, and a lot of them got shot down. But that Boeing B-17, you just wouldn't believe what it would take. Half the tail would be shot off and it would still get back.

He said we were having trouble because we didn't have any long-range fighters. But they were thrilled when the twin-engine P-38s came over. The P-38s had enough range to escort the bombers to their targets and back. The first mission they went on with a P-38 sitting out there on each wing, they felt a lot safer.

"We hadn't quite got to the target yet," he told me, "when an engine quit on one of our P-38 escorts. The pilot feathered the engine, and we could see that it was shut down. We all figured he would turn around and head back to England. But he just stayed right there."

The B-17s went in and dropped their bombs, and the German fighters started coming up. Then he was *sure* that the P-38 pilot would head back for London, or at least get in under the airplane where he could find some protection.

But that P-38 joined the fray and shot down the first Messerschmitt that headed up his way. Altogether, the P-38, with one engine feathered, went on to shoot down two more German fighters that day.

As soon as the bombers and fighters landed back in England, my friend, the B-17 pilot, jumped out of his plane, got in a jeep and headed over to the mystery P-38, curious to see "who in the heck was flying it." Out clambered an older, bald-headed gentleman.

"Are you an air force pilot?" my incredulous friend asked him.

"No," the mystery flyer replied. "I'm Lockheed's chief P-38 test pilot. I just came over here to see if you guys needed any help."

Korea

I flew the DC-4 when they called me in the second time—to serve in the Korean War. The only time we flew the DC-3s was in World War II, up in the Aleutians. We landed way down south in Korea. They had a big base down there, and all of the activity was up on the China border. We would just go in there—we were mostly freighters; occasionally there would be an R&R flight—get it unloaded and go. Never saw any enemy there at all. So Korea was really quiet, because we were coming in way down south.

We flew into Korea from Japan and from Guam. A lot of the freighters would go from San Francisco. There's an air force base east of San Francisco. We would fly empty over there, get loaded up, then go to Honolulu and Guam.

We had crews that would get off, and there were crews that had gone out the day before. They would get on and take it on to Korea.

Berlin

We had a crew base after the war in the eastern part of Germany, where they flew what we called the inter-German service. When the Russians blocked off the road into Berlin, we took all of our DC-4s over there. They were flying in and out of Berlin every twenty or thirty minutes, hauling in food and other goods for a year. I went over and flew a few of those trips, just to see what was going on. But I was never based in Europe.

"This Ain't No Movie"

I had flown a trip from Hong Kong to Saigon to Singapore, and was coming back to Saigon the next day. When I went out that morning, the dispatcher called from Saigon and said to be sure to put on enough fuel so that I could go right on to Hong Kong, because no transports had made it into Saigon at all.

"What's your condition there at the airport?" I asked.

"I don't think you can come in here," he said. "We haven't ever seen this much firepower. There's missiles all around the airport, and everything's blowing up in town."

People in Saigon were fleeing the city, scrambling to get on board two navy ships that were there.

The dispatcher said that the fighters had got the base clear, as long as you didn't get beyond the perimeter of the airport. They were still blasting any of the Cong out there that they saw, but couldn't control things much beyond the perimeter.

There hadn't been any multi-engine airplanes in at all, he said; only fighter-bombers. "What I'm worried about," he said, "is that I've got over 300 people here in the terminal—and we can't do anything with them. They came out thinking they could get on an airplane, you know.

"We haven't had one passenger airplane in here. We've had them go right over, because the crew didn't insist. I just suggested they go to their alternate—and they all did. You're the only one who has discussed it. If you decide, you might as well come in."

I told the stewardesses about it while we were having breakfast in Singapore. "Well, what's going to happen to those people?" they said.

"It's only a matter of time before the Cong are on the airport," I said. "And chances are, they'll just shoot them."

"Well, we can't let them do that," the crew said. "If you think it's safe, we'll go in."

So I told the dispatcher, "Yeah. If it doesn't change—if you don't have any firepower on the airport—I'll be in and we'll empty the terminal. What's the landing pattern?" I asked.

"It's just a fighter pattern," he said. "They're having them come in over the middle of the airport at 5,000 feet, drop everything, make a 180-degree turn and land—and not go beyond the perimeter. We haven't had a transport in at all—and don't expect to."

"Well," I said, "I'll talk to the tower operator when we get there."

As we neared Saigon, I talked to the controller. He said they hadn't had a shell or anything land on the airport. Those fighters had been circling the airport, blasting anything that moved.

But the tower operator said, "I don't think you can make an approach, because it's all fighters making the approach."

"Well, if the fighters can go in and out," I said, "then we certainly can. This is a 707, and I've instructed on it for several years. It'll do most anything we want it to. I can stay within the perimeter."

"Can you come over at 5,000 feet?" the tower operator asked. I said that we could.

When we began to get close, we could see the airport down there ahead of us. The copilot looked out and said, "You know, that airport's just a *spot* from 5,000 feet. How are we gonna get *on* it from here without making an approach?"

I said, "Well, if you've instructed in this for a couple of years, it's just like a Cub. We can do it with just putting everything out. There's no problem, because if we can't get down where we want to, we'll just put the power on and go on to Hong Kong. But we sure should try to get in there."

Just about over the middle of the airport, I slowed the airplane up. You have a maximum speed for dropping the gear and the flaps. So I slowed it to the gear speed and dropped the gear, then dropped the full flaps. So we had the gear and the flaps down as we came up on the airport.

When we got over the center of the airport, we pulled the speed-brake on, 10 degrees at a time. It goes up to 60 degrees; and at 60 degrees, it's just like an elevator. Over the airport I put down 10, then 20—and the airplane doesn't tip at all. We went to 30 degrees.

Now we were slow enough so that we could pull the spoilers on. The spoilers are ridges that come up on top of the wing and kill all of the lift. The attitude of the airplane doesn't change; it just goes down like an elevator. The nose doesn't go down; the plane just goes down.

We pulled all of that on and started down. Once I had a nice sink rate in it, I was looking at the runway. We were going to have to stay within the perimeter, turn and land. I could adjust the spoilers for descent rate real easy, and the passengers would never, ever know it—because it doesn't go SWOOSH.

We made a 180-degree turn, right at the end of the runway. As I came up to the end of the runway, I had the spoilers down to 10 degrees. I could see that I was going to come over the end of that runway about 2,000 feet, so I took the speed brake off and let the flaps down, put some power on and landed about 2,000 feet down the runway. But we didn't go anywhere near the end of the runway—we still had 6,000 feet of runway ahead of us.

My copilot said he couldn't believe that we got in there. I was sure happy to be flying a Boeing 707. A great airplane, it can do most anything a fighter can on approach and landing with its wing spoilers, which give it a smooth, fast descent—just like an elevator.

There was a taxiway into the terminal, and we made the middle taxiway right into the terminal. We taxied up to it—a large, solid, concrete structure. I went to go down the steps, but couldn't get down. Most of the sixty passengers were out on the steps taking movies, as dive bombers shrieked and missiles screamed overhead. "Hey folks," I said, "this ain't no movie. This is for real. I'm headed for that concrete building as fast as I can go—and I suggest you follow me."

"Oh, gosh! We'll do that!" they said. So away they came right away, and they all followed me in.

All Those Little Kids

We made it inside the terminal, but we didn't stay very long because there were so many people coming from town. There were over 300 people there—standing room only—and they didn't know what to do with them. The wife would have one little kid and the husband another, and all four of them would be crying. They couldn't go back into town; Saigon had already surrendered to the Viet Cong.

The road was blocked between the airport and town, so that nobody could get out. So there were no passengers at all, and here they had these 300 people in the terminal. They couldn't handle them in the terminal. There was nothing there except a little restaurant. No place to sleep, nothing. I thought, "My God, I'm sure glad we came in."

"How many of these do you think you can take, Jack?" the station manager asked me.

"We'll put 'em all on," I said.

"But you've only got 180 seats—and 60 passengers from Singapore," he said.

"That doesn't make any difference," I said. "We got some-place for 'em. There's an awful lot of 'em that are little," and the Vietnamese are little people anyway. And they're not heavy. "I'm not worried about the weight at all," I said, "because we're not going to even be up to gross maximum." Over half of them were little kids.

"Boy, that's just fantastic," he said. "They're sure gonna be thrilled when we announce that everybody's gonna get on. They're looking around because they know there's a lot more people than there is airplane."

When we got ready to leave Saigon, everyone followed me out. I was sitting on the left side of the airplane, so I could see the people coming out. They were just a mob. Everybody was carrying a couple of little kids. They were coming out four abreast, pushing and hurrying to get on the airplane, because they were sure that they weren't going to get everyone on.

I thought we couldn't handle all of them. There must have been over a hundred kids; I think that there were 211. Finally I could begin to see that no more of them were coming out of the terminal, but there was still a bunch in line—and they all got on.

We didn't get much gas because we were only going to Hong Kong, and didn't need the extra weight. We had 60 passengers from Singapore. That was all we had coming up; they were going to Hong Kong. The stewardess said they had very little baggage in the over-head racks, so she had them put it all under the seats, and we left all those overhead baggage bins open.

Those bins were nice; they were bigger than most baby cribs. So they were using those as bassinettes. They put the little ones up over-head, and just left the baggage containers open. And they got two or three babies in each one of those. On both sides of the airplane, those overhead baggage bins stayed open, and were full of babies.

I got to looking around and there were so many children, I wasn't going to worry about the weight. A head count wouldn't have done us any good at all; I think we ended up with 371 on board, and there were 180 seats.

Finally, the stewardess called and said, "Jack, we've got all the seats filled back here, and they're still coming. What do you want me to do now?"

"There's going to be quite a few more coming," I said. "Let the little kids sit on somebody's lap. If there are two seats full, they can hold at least two kids, maybe three. Can you bed some down back there in the galley?"

"Yes," she said, "I've got blankets."

"Well, bring some blankets up here," I said. "We have a navigation station, and we don't have navigators any more. We've got room for eight or ten up here, too. I've got a couple of seats here in the cockpit. They can sit on the floor if they need to. They've got things to hang on to. Just keep putting 'em on as long as they're coming out.

"It's going to be a short takeoff," I said. "I'm not worried about the weight, because it would take three of those little kids to weigh what an adult does. So just stuff every corner you can stuff."

We got most of them that were out, and finally we just couldn't stuff them anymore. The stewardess figured we had at least 200 kids on board, along with the hundred and sixty passengers that the airplane carried. We had to shut the cabin door, but I left the cockpit door open. Then I looked back there at all those little kids. And it really got me.

It was so nice to see such a change in them, because they were all crying as they were coming out of the terminal, they were so scared. They didn't know where they were going to go.

So we had people all over that airplane, and never a complaint from anybody. The passengers who were paying full fare from Singapore thought it was great. I never did walk back, because there were people in the aisle; but I could look back there and see that the kids were all laughing and eating cookies.

They were so happy to be on that flight. All the rest of the flights that day had gone overhead to their alternates, because they were told that they thought it would be a good idea just to clear to your alternate.

I could see out my side of the airplane toward the terminal. I think they quit coming; I think we emptied that whole terminal. The stewardess said, "I can close the door now." And away we went.

We taxied down to the end of the runway, just held the brakes and put on a lot of power, because we didn't want to go any farther out than we had to. That Boeing 707 just flew great; it wasn't overloaded at all for weight. With that takeoff power run up before we ever let the brakes off, we popped right off halfway down the runway.

We left takeoff power on, and maximum climb rate, and we were at almost 5,000 feet by the time we got to the edge of the airport. Oh, it just went like a rocket. Well, takeoff power is a lot of power. As soon as I hit 5,000 feet I pulled the power back, because I didn't want to heat the engines.

The shoulder-held rockets used by the Viet Cong were not much good above 5,000 feet. That's all they had.

We got up and got leveled off. I don't know how those flight attendants got so much stuff: cookies, cake, candy, suckers and everything. They rounded up everything in the terminal, everything the restaurant had.

I don't think any of the kids were much older than eight or ten. They came up to the cockpit, and were all smiling. They told me, "We're going Hong Kong! We're going Hong Kong! We've always wanted to see Hong Kong!"

They were really thrilled that they had gotten out of there, because their folks were crying, and they didn't know what they were going to do. They couldn't just sit there at that terminal. There's no way you can take them out in a fighter; there are no extra seats.

We went from Saigon to Hong Kong, still not knowing what was going on. When we got to Hong Kong, they put an 'extra' paper out, with big headlines: TET OFFENSIVE STARTED TODAY, SAIGON FALLS. So it was pretty much all shot up by the time we left.

It was sure nice that we got them all to Hong Kong. A lot of the

Vietnamese came to the U.S. They're the nicest people in the world; you can really depend on them.

So that's what we got into. We were the only transport that flew into Saigon the day the Tet Offensive started. And I thought, Dag-gone, I was lucky, you know, to be coming back from Singapore. One fellow I was talking to from the air force said, "I think the airport's gonna be okay until dark; but after that, I don't know how we can keep it clear all around." And it fell that night.

But I was sure happy we got all those little kids out. The Viet Cong had pretty well conquered Saigon, and were just going in and shooting everybody they saw in the streets. That was the first time they'd ever done that in Saigon.

I don't know how long the Viet Cong controlled the city, but the Americans and South Vietnamese had to get a lot more help in. They had a heck of a time chasing them out of there. I had been in and out of Saigon for two years before that, and had never had a problem, or seen anything like that. No fighting close to town. I don't remember getting back in there.

But that is the day that I'll always remember—the best day in my 40 years at Pan Am. I had some really good days with Pan Am; it was just a fantastic company to work for. Any of our Pan Am pilots could have done what we did that day, if they had been there at the right time. Once again, we were lucky to be at the right place at the right time. I have sure had my share of luck with all my 75 years of flying.

I just remember looking back at those little kids, all those little heads and feet sticking out. We got them all out of Saigon. That made our day. I felt like we had won the gold star and done our good deed for that day. It does your old heart good when you have an opportunity to do something like that.

(One of the reasons why I didn't hesitate to go into Saigon that day on such a steep landing pattern was my Pan Am training and experience instructing in "emergency descents," which were steeper than the approach into Saigon that day.

We went to San Francisco for five days twice a year for our six-month test. Until they got the fancy simulators that will do more than an airplane, we always went up to altitude—usually 25,000 or 30,000 feet—the engineer would turn off the compressors that were pressurizing the cabin and just say: "Hey, we've got decompression." You didn't wait for anything else. We just pulled the power back, pulled the speedbrake on partway till we slowed down enough to drop the gear and the flap, and just pushed it over. We would go down to 8,000 feet or below, because there's air down there.

You've only got minutes to live at 40,000 feet. If you don't get that oxygen mask on right away, the only thing that's going to keep you alive is us getting lower quickly.

I've explained this to passengers at times. And they say, "Well, I can hold my breath for several minutes."

"Well, you can't," I tell them. "You have pressure inside your body that you had while everything was pressurized. You remove all the pressure from outside you, and your breath just comes out in one big WHOOSH. So you don't have any oxygen left in your lungs, once explosive decompression takes place."

"Gee, I never thought about that," they say. That would be fine if you could hold your breath, but you can't.

In the cockpit we have a special oxygen mask. It's got a padded metal frame over it. The mask fits right to it, and it's hanging right above us. You just grab it with one hand, pull it on and you've got oxygen right now. As soon as that mask gets moved, the valve opens. You don't have to turn it on or anything.

So that's what we would do every six months. It was nice when we finally got all that in the simulator; we could do it there. That way we could go right up to 41,000 feet. It didn't take any time; you just cranked it up there. Then they would give you a decompression and you would grab that mask quick, because at 41,000 feet you're not good for a minute.

But the people don't understand the operation of jet airplanes, and how much thought and engineering they've put into them.)

Midnight Run

I got shot at a lot in Vietnam. The Cong would lie out in the rice paddies off the end of the runway and shoot at us with the biggest rifles they could get that didn't smoke. If it smoked, the air force was right out there blasting them.

There were times during the day that we just kind of hated to go into Da Nang, up north near the North Vietnamese border. Da Nang is on the water, but they always have a north wind. So you always had to land over the rice paddies. But you can take off out over the water. As soon as you got in the air, you were over the coast and going.

Although the Da Nang Air Base was, at the time, one of the world's busiest airports—in terms of number of flights per day—we had a lot of trouble there. They always had two fire engines, one on each side of the runway, ready for incoming flights.

I had an engine shot out a number of times coming into Da Nang. They would shoot the darned engine and the oil radiator would explode. Those jet engines were just a blow torch, you know, and you would catch an engine on fire. So you would come in and land and go right up to a fire engine and stop.

I was going to fly an R&R trip from Tokyo to Honolulu with a load of the veterans going down for some rest. The dispatcher called me the evening before and said, "Jack, we'd like to have you change your pattern tomorrow."

"Oh, what to?" I said.

"We'd like to have you go to Viet Nam in the morning," he said, "rather than to Honolulu."

"Well, there's got to be more to the story here," I said. "*Where* are we going in Viet Nam?"

"Da Nang," he said. Of course, I had gotten shot at in Da Nang a number of times.

"What's on the airplane?" I asked.

"Missiles."

"What happened to the other crew who were supposed to take it?" I asked.

"They all got sick," he said. "And you're the only crew in Tokyo that has enough rest."

"They all got *sick?*" I said. "They just came in from Honolulu. You don't get sick in Honolulu; you get sick in *India.*"

"Well," the dispatcher said, "the air force is running out of missiles down there. They want to get this 707 freighter in as quick as we can. So if we can get it out in the morning, then we can get it to Da Nang by noon."

"If you want to get out of here in the morning with a load of missiles to Da Nang, then *I* just got sick," I said. "No way am I making an approach down there in the middle of the day with a load of missiles. All they have to do is get one of those rifle shots to hit one of those missiles and we're *all* a missile."

"Oh, gosh," he said, "but they're running out and they need 'em bad."

"Well, I'll negotiate with ya," I said. "If you'll roll it twelve hours, so that I get out of here just before midnight, and get in down there at one or two in the morning—then I'll take it."

"Oh, great," the dispatcher said. "We'll get 'em down there, anyway. We'll go ahead and set it up."

"Well, I can't go by myself," I said. "I've got a copilot and flight engineer, so you'd better call them. I don't want to go if they don't want to. But if they'll go—okay."

So the dispatcher told them that that's what I was going to do—get into Da Nang at one or two in the morning. He must have been a pretty good salesman. "Well, if Jack will go, then we'll go," my crew said.

I always alternate every leg. I fly one and then the copilot flies one. I had flown into Tokyo, so it was his turn to fly it out.

The captain always sits in the left seat. Terminals are built so that as you pull up to the terminal, the left side of the airplane always faces the terminal. They have a steering wheel to steer the airplane on the ground on the left side, not on the right. It's different between the two seats. They don't trade seats, unless you're an instructor.

Because I had instructed a lot on the 707, and was a check pilot for the newer pilots, I always got in the copilot's seat. The copilot is senior, and they're getting close to checking out. Besides, these guys were going to be over in that left seat one day. So I would just be a good copilot in the right seat.

So this was the copilot's leg. It was up to me to operate the radio. "Well," I said, "here's what I plan to do: We know the Cong have little receivers that they can listen to the tower and the airplanes on." Short-range, visual, high frequency.

But we used long-range to give our position reports; that was an HF, long-range frequency. Some radio waves are line-of-sight, like television and the tower. But HF will go all the way around the world. You can call Seattle from Tokyo. Or New York from Tokyo.

So I said, "Well, I plan to talk to Hong Kong as we go by. I'm gonna tell him that we're gonna turn off the VHF line-of-sight tower frequency. And the lights. And as soon as we leave the coast"—it's about a hundred miles in—"we'll take the power off completely." That 707 would glide a hundred and fifty to two hundred miles— ten times as far as a light plane.

I talked to Hong Kong on the radio as we were coming up on them. I told them what we were going to do, and that I would be waiting for a call if there was any traffic. We were only a little over an hour to Da Nang. But there wasn't any traffic; it was one o'clock in the morning. He said, "If any traffic takes off in the area at all, I'll call ya."

I didn't call the tower. I didn't know how far out that signal would reach, but we suspected that the Cong had the tower frequency and were listening. We knew they didn't have the HF, however.

As we approached the coast, heading into Da Nang, I called Hong Kong on the HF. "We're at the coast," I said. "I'm doing this because I'm going to Da Nang with a load of missiles, and I don't want to wake 'em up. So once I leave the coast, we're gonna pull the power back to idle and go all the way in with the power off. No lights, and no more talking on the tower frequency. We're not talkin' to anybody, just you guys."

We didn't have to listen to the HF all the time. It had what we called a "doorbell," a little chime. You don't sit there with earphones or anything. A "ping" would alert you to pick up the microphone. They could just press a button and it would ring in the airplane.

So I said, "Just call me on the HF radio if there's some traffic, or you got something that I need to know, because I can always come back to Hong Kong."

I pulled the power off and turned the lights off. We never heard another thing, and we went all the way with the power off.

That 707 will glide farther than a Cub will. It's so heavy and so fast that it's got a lot of kinetic energy pushing it. As long as you keep it going down, it will glide a hundred and fifty miles without any problem at all. We used to cut the power north of Victoria, come in and land at Sea-Tac without ever touching the throttles again.

So we went all the way in that way. We got there about two o'clock in the morning, never making a sound. That jet was just idling. We just approached and didn't put any power on until we came over the fence. We got in there fine with that load of missiles; but I understood why that other crew got sick: they weren't about to go down to Da Nang during the day. Needless to say, they got the plane unloaded very quickly.

My Honorable Discharge Certificates from
the U.S. Air Force and Navy, covering my time served in
World War Two, Korea and Vietnam.

Chapter 7

A Pilot's Pilot

Corncob

WHEN World War II ended, I returned to Pan Am and instructed in the DC-3 until I was old enough to get my Air Transport Rating. I got to fly the latest planes soon after they came on-line, including the DC-3, DC-4, Lockheed Loadstar, DC-6, DC-7, Boeing 377 Stratocruiser, Boeing 707, and my last ten years on the 747.

Boeing has always built the strongest airplanes that fly, including the 707 and 747. They built a heavier airplane; they don't net quite as much load because of their weight. But they're good airplanes. Those Boeing guys—they know what they're doing. Boeing makes the best airplanes. They have a lot of engineers, but the reason they make the best airplanes is that they didn't build many transports until after World War II. They built all those bombers—B-17s, B-29s and B-50s. And they were really rugged.

We had our Pan Am offices at Boeing Field, right across from the factory. They were pushing those B-17s out of there—about five a day. They were really coming. And I just couldn't see how they could be building nice big airplanes like that and not have some use for a while, because there were cargo airplanes, too, being built.

A Douglas is a little more productive; you can carry more stuff on it to get the gross weight. But Boeing builds some of that gross weight right into the airplane. They just build a fantastic airplane.

I'll tell you about the Stratocruiser. That was a B-50. They put another fuselage on top of it, and they made a big fuselage. You don't usually work an airplane over and end up with much. But they did a great job. Well, when they got this all together, of course that was a lot bigger fuselage. The engines then were all fourteen-cylinder; two rows of seven. And they didn't have a fourteen-cylinder engine that had the power.

So they went to Pratt & Whitney and said, "Hey, we've got to have a bigger engine."

"Well, we can't put any more power in fourteen; we've got to have more cylinders. So we'll start engineering." Pratt & Whitney always built good engines. So, instead of using two rows of cylinders, they used four. Instead of a fourteen-cylinder engine, it was a twenty-eight-cylinder.

We called it the corncob, because they had all these cylinders. Well, of course, they had a little trouble with the back cylinders heating, so you had to watch it. You had to make the mixture richer if the back cylinders began to get hot.

They didn't have a propeller that would handle all that horsepower, either. So they went to Curtiss-Wright—they had a bigger propeller than Hamilton Standard had—and they took this propeller. The darned blade was almost a foot wide. And it was *hollow*.

They filled it with a fiberglass substance to give it strength. It was a four-bladed prop. It would handle all that horsepower—for a while. But with that centrifugal force—with those props turning all the time, and with the vibration the engine has; they all have some—it broke down that fiberglass, and it would fall to the end of one of those blades.

The first one or two, it just threw a blade off. But we had one coming back from South America, over the mountains down there. It had a propeller that jerked the whole engine off. The propeller went through the fuselage and cut it in two. The cockpit landed on one side of the mountains and the tail on the other.

Then they started inspecting the darned things. After every landing they would inspect them; they would run a vibration meter on it. These were B-50s that they tried to modify. It was almost like the B-29, just a little larger.

So they grounded them all for a while. Then, every time one landed, they put a vibration machine on it, and could tell if there was anything loose in the propeller.

Northwest bought our old Stratocruiser props. And they had several break off, too.

In the cockpit of a Boeing Stratocruiser, 1959 or 1960.

The Stratocruiser did have a lot of windows—all around by your feet. It was so roomy in the nose, that rather than squeezing stuff in, we went around the outside of the seats—between the seat and the window. We had plenty of room; that big old front end was all glass. That sure made it easy getting into Juneau in a snowstorm.

Tall Drink of Water

One of the planes lost a propeller right out over the middle of the ocean. The jets are so much more dependable than the prop airplanes. They used to have a Coast Guard ship halfway between the coast and Honolulu. They called it the Guard Ship. They had radios, weather, radar and everything. And that ship was stationed out there all the time.

This friend of mine, Dick Ogg, was also an instructor back in Missoula. His folks owned the Ogg Shoe Store. He was a big, tall guy, about six-foot-two or –three. He could not fly the DC-3, which had a post that came up with the wheel. He couldn't get the wheel back over his knees. So he had to fly the Lockheed Loadstar, because he could land that. But he was in good shape when we got the bigger airplanes.

Dick was coming back from Honolulu in the Stratocruiser. He had seniority enough to fly the DC-7c, which was faster than the old Stratocruiser. But he couldn't get the yoke back in that, either, because his knees were so high.

So he was on this old Stratocruiser. Just about the time he got to the Guard Ship, one of those props let go and jerked the whole engine off on one side. So now he had this big flat plate area, and he had to use so much power that he didn't have enough fuel to go either to the coast or back to Honolulu.

It was night. He said he had plenty of fuel to hold for two or three hours until daylight. So at daylight the Guard Ship got the little cruisers out and marked a path for him into the swells, so he wouldn't go right into them.

The Coast Guard was out there showing him where to land in the middle of the ocean. He came in and landed between those two little boats, on top of a swell, and didn't even hurt the airplane. And that old Stratocruiser just sat there.

They pulled the little boats up to the wings. Everybody got off; they never even got their feet wet. And that darned thing floated for twelve or twenty-four hours. It had burned up so much fuel that the wing was nearly empty, and was keeping the plane afloat.

The military may have had to finally come out and shoot the plane to get it to sink, because it was right in the traffic lanes. There was one in the North Atlantic that had to be sunk because it was in one of the busy sea lanes. Of course there were no lights or anything on it; it was just out there floating around. Boeing builds such good airplanes that it just wouldn't sink.

The chairman of American Motors, George Romney, who was also a private pilot, was in London listening to the TV and the radio about this thing crashing out in the middle of the ocean. Romney was real interested in Dick's ordeal—circling out there over the Pacific Ocean, waiting for it to get daylight.

Romney had to take off to fly for San Francisco before they found out whether Dick's Stratocruiser landed okay. So he asked the stewardess to have the captain keep listening to this one frequency, and let him know how they landed.

So they did. The stewardess came back to tell him that Dick's plane landed okay, and that everybody got out. After Dick made that successful ditching, Romney called him and told him to go down to the American Motors dealer in the Bay Area and pick out any car he wanted.

The only thing that Dick, being so tall, could fit into was a station wagon. The last time I talked to him, he still had that little old station wagon. They moved out of Missoula up to the lake, just out of Kalispell. "I got it up there on the lake," he said. He said it was one of the few cars he got into that he could push the seat back far enough.

Pan Am flew the Stratocruiser until the other company, Hamilton Standard, made a prop that was solid metal. I didn't fly the airplane; I stayed on the DC-6. It paid a hundred dollars less, but I wasn't about to get on one of those things and blow it up.

Hurry Sundown

Jimmy Stewart—he was another one of our pilots, two of us—we were the only ones who stayed on the DC-6. When they put the new props on it, they were fine. No vibration, nothing. So Jimmy and I both bid it, with the Stratocruiser. But by that time they had torn the simulator apart, and were making it into a 707 simulator. So we didn't have a simulator to go fly. That was just two years before the jets.

So they sent a ground school instructor up who spent four or five days with us, going through the systems—the hydraulic and electrical and everything. Ralph Savory, the Chief Pilot here, flew all the airplanes; and he flew them better than the guys who were flying them all the time.

Ralph got a Stratocruiser—we were flying it to Honolulu and on up to Alaska. He had one that was going to go to Alaska that night. So he had it for all day. He just took Jimmy and I out to Boeing Field, where we practiced landings. And it was just a big ol' Cub. It was fun to fly, but it was different.

When you took off, you would rotate it. In all the rest of the airplanes, you would get the nose up and you would climb. We would rotate it, and it would just lift off, because of that high-speed wing they had on it.

We practiced our takeoffs and landings. We stalled—we had quite a few more than we intended to—but we each had to make three night takeoffs and landings before we could get on the line. So we did. We waited until it was a legal sundown so we could put it in the book, but it wasn't even dark. We didn't turn the lights on or anything. But we each made three.

Close Call

Then we had to have a route check, en route. So I went out. Johnny Amundsen—a real senior check pilot, great guy—had been off flight for six weeks. He had had a "window sinus" operation, they call it. They open up your sinuses and drill through.

Johnny hadn't flown for over a month; but the doctor said that he had it all cauterized, and that everything was healed over and scabbed. So it was okay for him to fly.

Johnny is a good friend of mine. "As long as Jack is getting a check-out to Honolulu," he said, "why, I'll go ahead and give him the route check." Even check pilots still had to have the route check.

It was nice talking to Johnny. He was sitting there in the copilot's seat. We talked about his operation and about everything. We always had a lot in common, because I taught one of his boys to fly.

We had just reached the equi-time point, halfway across. Johnny said, "Jack, I'm going to get up and stretch. I'll take a little walk." So he got up. Suddenly, he said: "Jack! Jack!" Blood was squirting out between his fingers. Just coming out.

And there we were, halfway to Honolulu. I took pre-med, but I didn't learn anything. We had a bunk on the airplane, so I told the engineer to get Johnny in the bunk as quick as he could, and raise his head up.

I called the stewardess, the best one we had. Half an hour after takeoff she knew all the passengers. I called Mary Ellen and told her to bring the first aid kit and come up, and make sure it had a lot of gauze.

I looked in Johnny's briefcase. He had always had sinus problems. He had a big, brand new bottle of Neosynephrine, and that will shrink it. As soon as Mary Ellen came up, I said, "Just dip that gauze in the Neosynephrine." I had a new pencil that had a new eraser on it. "Pack it with that," I said.

She put that whole carton of gauze in his nose. And then he began to bleed out his tear ducts. Not a lot, but we were at 25,000 feet. According to the cabin, we were at 8,000 feet, a lot less pressure than if you were at sea level.

I called Honolulu traffic control and asked if they had any traffic underneath us on the Seattle-Honolulu leg. "No," he said, "we don't have any traffic there at all."

"Then I'd like to descend to 2,000 feet," I said. He didn't ask me why, and I didn't want to tell him. I get to thinking about this, and I realize we almost lost Johnny. I told the engineer, "I'm just going to descend a couple of hundred feet a minute to keep the speed up."

We have a "barber pole," a red line that you don't want the air speed to go over. "I'm gonna get right up under that barber pole and hold it there," I said. And boy, we were really going.

There was a DC-7c, which was about forty miles an hour faster, going from San Francisco out. He was just about even with us. And, of course, he was gaining on us. The pilot was a friend of mine. "What are you flyin', Jack?" he asked.

"We're flying a Stratocruiser," I said. He didn't ask me why we were going to go down to 2,000 feet. But we were almost abeam one another, on longitude. So he was the same distance I was. We report position on every longitude. Well, on the next one, I was ten minutes ahead of him.

"Did you say you were flying a Stratocruiser?" he asked.

"Yeah," I said. We were another ten minutes ahead of him on the next longitude.

He called back and said, "Did you say that was a Stratocruiser? They won't fly that fast."

"Well, yeah, they do," I said. "They like cold air. This is the way we fly them all the time in Alaska." So that shut him up.

The engineer just kept pushing that pressure down, and pushing it down. I think we got it down to about 2,000 feet below sea level. So there was more pressure than there would have been at sea level. And Mary Ellen—of course, she was a doll—she said, "I've got a surgeon back here who just got out of surgery. And he's got some medication to stop bleeding. I'll get it."

So she went back, got it and brought it up. I had never heard of it. Of course, I didn't know that much about medicine, anyway. So I called dispatch on the long frequency. "Will you call Johnny Amundsen's wife and ask her what the name of the doctor was who gave him his surgery?" I said. "And ask him if it's okay to use this medication.

"Johnny's got a nosebleed," I said, "and we just wondered if we could use this for him." In just a minute the dispatcher called, and he hadn't told Johnny's wife that Johnny had had a hemorrhage or anything. In fact, the dispatcher told her that *he* wanted to go in for that sinus operation.

Johnny's doctor said that they used that medicine all the time to coagulate, and to use the same two teaspoons an hour, whatever it was. So we started getting that to him.

And we had a real good engineer, one of the 'good ol' engineers. Our early engineers were all mechanics out of the shop. Then they would go to school and get an engineer's license. And they were great; they were just great.

We had a ground engineer—his name was Lindbergh—who designed this Lindbergh engine analyzer. You could put that on an engine and you could go to each cylinder, and it had a scope that you could read. I was coming out of Portland with the Stratoruiser, and was just at the top of the climb—had just pulled the power back to cruise—and that Number 4 engine started misfiring. It wasn't shooting out any flames or anything, but you could hear it going, CLICK! CLICK!

This engineer was an old senior mechanic out of the hangars. His name was Swede Rothy; he was great. I said to Swede, "Are we gonna have to dump fuel and go back into Portland?"

"Just give me a minute, Jack. Give me a minute," he said. It was the only airplane I ever flew where they had throttles and mixture controls at the engineer's station, as well as the pilot's station. He was pushing that thing around, and finally I see him reach up and push the mixture control to rich, and it smoothed right out.

And I said, "Swede, is that temporary, or do you think we can go all the way?"

"We can go all the way."

I said, "What is it?"

"Well, it's one valve that's hanging up," he said. "But as long as I keep it lubricated with extra fuel, it'll be fine all the way to Honolulu." And there we were just off the coast.

I said, "Are you sure we won't have to shut it down at equi-time point?" I had to do that one time.

"No, no, no," he said. "Don't worry about it at all."

It didn't burn that much extra gas. And because we were down lower, we *saved* fuel. On a jet you would burn a lot of fuel if you got down to those low altitudes. But with the reciprocating engine, we were in great shape.

When we got to Honolulu, it was dark. I had always been flying Douglas equipment. And you extend the landing lights and turn them on overhead. Well, I never thought about that. We turned in; it was kind of a long final. That was the fastest way to keep our speed up.

And I'm looking up here, and I've got my little pen light. So I asked the engineer, "Where in heck do they have the landing lights on this machine?"

"Oh," he said, "you're not in a Douglas; you're in a Boeing. It's right down there behind your throttles."

So I hit the switches, and the landing lights came on in plenty of time. But I think we were maybe down to 500 feet. Of course, you can land without lights. But before I got those darned landing lights on, we told the tower we wanted to taxi as fast as we could, right up the taxiway. He let us get in there as quick as we could.

And, of course, that guy from San Francisco still couldn't believe that I was an hour ahead of him when I got to Honolulu.

They had the ambulance right out there on the ramp. So we just went down the stairs. When they picked Johnny up to put him on the stretcher—just raising him up that much, he passed out.

And I tell you this story goes on: Johnny said, "Would you go to the hospital with me?"

"Yeah," I said. Well, we got about halfway to town, in this big old Cadillac ambulance. I saw this light coming out of the corner of my eye. And I fell down over Johnny's head. It was a kid in his dad's new Buick; he just got it that day. He went through an amber light and hit us broadside.

Glass flew all over everything. Well, Johnny was baldheaded. I had covered up his face, and there were shards of glass everywhere, but nothing in his eyes. His stretcher flew across and hit the attendant; broke three ribs. So they had to call for two more ambulances.

We didn't have to use the second one. It knocked us across the street and we hit the curb, but not hard enough to blow out a tire. So he took us right on in. And Pan Am had an eye, ear, nose and throat surgeon there waiting for us.

They started pumping blood into Johnny as soon as we put him in the ambulance. They were pumping blood in him all the way to the hospital. We got him into surgery. This little doctor kept walking around him, and Johnny wasn't bleeding anymore.

"Well, he took three pints of blood, but everything is okay," the doctor said. "But if you had gone another hour, he would have had brain damage."

So this little guy was walking around and around him. "You know," he said, "I'm not going to disturb that. With all that gauze and Neosynephrine and medication, you've got the bleeding stopped. I'll just let it settle down, and I'll cauterize it tomorrow when I've got a helper here."

They were cleaning glass out of him, all over him, but Johnny didn't get any in his face. I lucked out.

Johnny and I still can't talk about it; neither can his son. His son called me the other day about something. This one son is a minister. "I know how close Dad came to dying," he said. "I got tears every time I talk to you, so I'll hang up."

But you know, he's such a good friend at that. And he has these four children. I've had dinner at their place a number of times, and they've been to our place. The first time I met this one who's a minister, he was a little kid. They came to see us, and they got to stop and have lunch with us.

He was ringing the doorbell. When I got there, he was the only one at the door. That little guy. I said, "Hi!"

"My stomach tells me I'm hungry!" That's the first thing he said. Johnny's wife had gotten up there by then, and it embarrassed them. So Scotty got him something to eat before we got our fried chicken out.

But, you know, you're so close to somebody like that. And I knew how close he was, because I couldn't even feel a pulse. A guy like that, to have brain damage, would be worse than losing his life.

I never told many people that story, because Johnny was still flying. I didn't want them to know that he was within a few minutes of having brain damage, because then I thought they might start checking his physicals a lot more heavily.

That's why I never told the kids or anybody. I told the flight engineer and Mary Ellen that if they talked to the doctor, not to repeat anything. But they never did talk to the doctor. So I was the only one who knew that Johnny had lost all that blood and was right up to brain damage.

But Johnny never had a problem. And he didn't know how close he had come. I didn't tell him, and neither did the doctor. So he didn't know it until after he retired.

But it seemed like every time I got in a fix, I had a helper. That's why a lot of pilots put a lot of faith in that book, *God Is My Copilot*. Because there are times when you can't do anything.

Big Belly

When the 707 first came out, it had a real sweep-back wing, and a tendency to roll. If you tried to catch it, it just made it worse. In fact, the Boeing test pilots snapped a couple of engines off one up north, trying to get ahead of that rudder.

Our Pan Am guys did the same thing. We had an airplane that was ferrying every day from London to Paris, and then they needed it back in London. So they were using it for training on the way back and forth, because they were always short of training airplanes. And they snapped an engine off of one.

In fact, the airplane went all the way around. It rolled. Like Tex Johnson did with the 707 at the hydroplane races. That's tough on an airplane—a snap roll. A barrel roll is fine, because you fly it all the way around. And you don't have negative g's on it.

Pan Am was flying the 707 on North Atlantic routes for a year before anybody else had any, because Pan Am got the first twenty-five 707s that Boeing built. Then Douglas hired some Boeing engineers. They designed the DC-8, and they copied all they could from the Boeing 707. But they didn't give it much sweep-back in the wing, so it took more power to push that wing through the air. They got a lot less fuel mileage than Pan Am did.

Douglas also built the DC-8 fuselage fairly skinny. If you had a full load of passengers, you couldn't get all the baggage in the belly. So they would try to schedule one of their DC-8s out of New York the same time we were flying a 707. Then they could put the extra bags that they couldn't carry on the DC-8 into the 707, and Pan Am would take them over. We hardly ever filled the 707's baggage compartment. It has a big belly.

The 707 was just a better-designed airplane than the DC-8.

I was coming back from London to Seattle one day. This nice couple was sitting there in First Class, telling me what a great airplane this was. "Well, this is a Boeing airplane," I said. "They build them strong; that's what I like about them."

It turns out they worked for Douglas. "Well," I said, "you built a good ship in a short period of time. But we do carry some of your passenger and crew baggage out of New York when the DC-8 fills up in the belly, and the 707 still has room.

"We also get better gas mileage," I said, "because the wing slopes a lot more than yours. But I can't tell you how many hours I've got in Douglas airplanes. The first transport I flew was a DC-3. And I flew the DC-6 and the DC-7c. They were all fine airplanes. But Boeing does build an awfully strong airplane.

"But don't be disappointed," I said. "We like that 7c."

A Pilot's Pilot

There's no way to really know an airplane as well as the instructors, because they're doing this over and over, and it gets to be second nature. I instructed a year on the DC-3 because I wasn't old enough to fly the line. When we got the DC-4s, they checked me out in it right away and I instructed on the DC-4 until we got the other line pilots.

When we got the jets, they only had that one 707. Boeing had all its money in it, and Pan Am had all its money in it. The test pilot was a good friend of Ralph Savory's, so he would call us any time he was going to go over to Moses Lake.

"Come on down to Boeing Field and go with me," he would say. Then he would let us fly it. So we had some time in the airplane before it had ever been certificated.

That 707 was a fantastic airplane. I like it better than any of them. It's a rugged, beautiful airplane. We would come down from Fairbanks, and cut the power just north of Victoria. Go all the way in and land, never having to touch the throttles, except to put them in reverse. Make the whole approach. And we just used the flap and the landing gear to slow down; we had the throttles all the way back.

Talk about a guy who has the power all the way off and has to get someplace: That pilot who put that one in the Hudson River sure did a good job. He was special. He had an instructor's rating in gliders. They suggested that he go into New Jersey; but he said no, it's too far.

The 747 is a lot more airplane than the 707; and it's great, too.

But I wouldn't have wanted to subject it to what I did on the 707. I instructed on the 747, but not nearly as much as on the 707. The 707s are still in service, but there aren't very many of them in the U.S., because they don't get very good mileage. There are a lot of them in South America.

When they changed the engines—they had the early jet engines, and that was small fans—when they went to the big fan engine, you had to spin it up on final in case you needed some power, right at the end. They didn't spin up. So we would spin it up at about 500 feet.

I just thoroughly enjoyed every time we got new equipment. It was a thrill. I was one of the first to get on it because I kept my instructor's rating. Several times they sent me down to Boeing, and I got trained by the test pilots down there, then I could instruct the Pan Am pilots. But it was really a lot of fun.

I always enjoyed instructing. I did so much of it for Pan Am. Any time we got a new pilot, or a copilot was having trouble with landings or something, Ralph Savory, the Chief Pilot, would call me and wonder when I could work it in and take them over to Moses Lake.

For a long time, they didn't have the airplane time in San Francisco because we just used the line airplanes between schedules. We were lucky here in Seattle because for a long time we went to Fairbanks and back every night, and had the airplane all day. So I could take it to Moses Lake and have it all day. It was like having my own airline.

I flew night trips for forty years. Our Fairbanks trip left out of here at midnight. It's three hours to Fairbanks, there's an hour on the ground and then it comes back. That's why I've been doing the instructing. That airplane sits there all day, so I usually used it as a training airplane.

Pan Am was hiring after the war—mostly navy pilots, because they required college. The air force required two years of college, but they waived it. But the navy stuck with the four years of college. You know, college doesn't do you any good, but they thought it did. So did Pan Am.

So it was mostly navy pilots that we got. They would send them to me two at a time to get their ratings on the airplane, because we had a 707 sitting here during the day, and it went to Fairbanks at night. For about a year I must have had eight Blue Angels. They would come two at a time, having put in their five years with the navy. They all wanted to go with Pan Am, because it was international, and it was navy. Pan Am started out with all navy pilots.

It was really fun to work with those Blue Angels. They were true gentlemen, really sharp guys. But they had never flown a multi-engine airplane. They've been all fighters, so you have trouble getting them to hold it off. I would give them a rating. You have to have a rating from the FAA to fly the airplanes.

I was lucky to get to instruct on the Boeing 707 so much—because then you just become part of it. The only way you're going to really learn to fly an airplane is to instruct on it. You do all the maneuvers over and over, and you're going to watch students screw up. The 707 is my favorite airplane, just because of that.

I also instructed on the 747, but we didn't do that much, because we got new simulators in the last few years. The pilot never flew in a 747; he was a 707 captain. He would go through all that simulator training for the 747, never having been in the airplane. On his first trip, he had a load of passengers, but he had a check pilot in the copilot's seat.

But here he is sitting over there in that left seat. Never been in the real airplane; he's just been in the simulator. He would go out there and fly that thing just like he had been in it. That 747 simulator was so good; they could do anything with that simulator.

When we went through, we had an old 707 simulator that they had rebuilt into a 747 simulator. We had the instruments, but not all of the computers. You can make a circling approach, or any kind of approach, with the new simulators.

I got to fly with a lot of the new captains who were on their first trip. I would fly in the right seat and go around the world with them. I would be there instructing and checking, giving them a check-ride. When we finished, or when we went from London non-stop to Los Angeles, I would sign him off.

If there were a few things that you didn't like, you would check him out, but note that he should go back to the simulator and do a few more things, cross-wind landings or something.

The Japanese pilots—captains—came over and got their training from the Boeing test pilots on the 747. But the Boeing test pilots were not able to check any of them out; they just wouldn't turn them loose. They had to hire retired Pan Am and British airways captains for that 747. And those Japanese captains didn't like riding in the copilot seat, learning how to fly with one of us over there in the left seat.

You just would not believe all of the equipment, machinery and computers that are on the 747. And they all work! You hardly ever have anything that doesn't operate. If it doesn't, you just pull the circuit breaker back and forth a couple times—it's mostly all-electric—and it will kick in.

Pan Am bought the first twenty-five Boeing 747s. The photo on the previous page is one of the first "poses" over Washington's Cascade Mountains in a promotional photo shoot. I didn't know they were going to use my portrait with it. Courtesy Pan Am.

But I felt really at home in that 707, because the simulator wouldn't do what the 747 simulator did. You had to fly the airplane; the minimum was six to twenty hours in the airplane.

The Boeing test pilot called one day and wanted to get some pictures of a 747 in flight. He said we don't have an airplane down here that's big enough to put those big cameras in. "Have you got anything?"

I said, "Yes, we've got a Stratocruiser, with big exit doors over the wing—both sides. It goes to Fairbanks and back at night, and it's here all day. I can have it all day."

"Well, can you have it tomorrow?" he asked.

"Sure," I said.

"Well, we'll send some cameramen out early to get those doors out, and get their cameras mounted. Then we'll go out." He told me what he wanted to do. He wanted the Cascade Mountains as a background, and he was just going to go back and forth in front of the Cascades.

We would turn and he would go by, and we would turn and the other cameraman would get him. They took a lot of pictures.

I knew that Pan Am had pictures of all the crew, but I never told him. When he got that big picture of the 747 over the Cascades, he went to Pan Am and they opened up the file and got the picture of me that's on there. I was pretty young.

Weight and See

The 707 was the first jet that we all got checked out on. I had been instructing on the DC-6, so I was late getting to San Francisco for the training. They had already taken the Stratocruiser simulator apart, and were making it into a 707 simulator. So I didn't get any simulator training at all; they just had a paper in there. The instructors would point out the fuel system, and what you could turn; but there was nothing to turn but the pictures.

The mechanics were having a dispute with the company at the time, and this one 707 would come in from London, and they would have us scheduled for training. Well, if there was anything written up at all, the mechanics wouldn't get it fixed. I was down there for six weeks. They wanted to give us ten hours of training in the airplane, because they didn't have a 707 simulator. Then you would take your flight test with the government inspector.

Well, they were running short of airplane time, and I only got four hours in the airplane—two flights in six weeks. My instructor was a professional instructor to Pan Am; he didn't fly the line. And he was good. He said, "Jack, you've been down here for six weeks, and you've only gotten four hours of flight time. And it doesn't look like it's gonna get any better." The mechanics were still negotiating.

The airplane that came in from London was the one we took out to train. But they always found some minor maintenance item on it, and never got it ready. So, day after day I didn't do a thing. I said, "I just don't think I'm ready with just two two-hour flights."

"Oh, yeah," he said. "We can do it, all right. We can't spend another month for another couple hours. Why don't we try that type-rating test from the FAA."

"Well, I don't know how to fly that airplane," I protested.

"Oh, yes you do," he said. "It'll be okay."

Well, wouldn't you know it: I drew the worst inspector. He was an ex-Marine; big guy. Everybody was scared to death of him; he was full of questions.

Dick Ogg—the one who ditched the Stratocruiser out in the ocean, a good friend of mine; we instructed together in Missoula—got his rating before I did. I was over just loafing around at Pan Am and had lunch with him. He said, "Well, what do you have scheduled?"

"Well, *nothin'*," I said. "We don't have an airplane. But the instructor thinks that we should give the rating a try. That big Marine—everybody tells me he's a bad time."

"He was the one who gave me my oral exam," Dick said. "He spent a whole day on an oral. One of the pilots ahead of *me* said that you don't need to study the whole manual, because he thinks the weights are the important part." The empty weight, gross weight, fuel weight, landing weight, takeoff weight and on and on—there's one page of weights in the front of the manual.

"He really thinks those are the important part of that manual," Dick said. "The manual's sitting right there on the dispatch counter. All you've got to do is open it, you know, to check something. You don't need to memorize that stuff."

So I did; I memorized that page. I spent a whole day and evening. When I went over that next morning, he introduced himself. I had a little conversation with him before because he wanted to order a pickup from us with an Alaska license. And I told him we would get that for him. No sales tax or anything; just $10 for a license. So I had kind of an in.

"Gosh, I guess you're gonna be the youngest captain on the 707, huh?"

"I've been the youngest ever since I've been here," I said. "But I've sure had a lot of fun going through this new equipment. I've been instructing on all the different equipment, right from the DC-3 on."

"Well," he said, "on this 707, what do you think is important on an oral?" I opened up the manual, turned the page—"What do you think about all these weights?"

"Oh," I said, "they're *really* important. Of course, Pan Am has that manual on the dispatch counter, and it's opened to that page. But if you'd like to know those . . ." I was sure if he stopped me I would know them. Of course, I had stayed awake until about midnight that night at the hotel, just running through that page."

"Oh," he said, "why don't you tell me about these."

"Well," I said, "I'll just start right with the weight empty, and tell you each weight." There's about ten or fifteen different weights, and I went right through them. And I knew that if he stopped me anywhere, I was shot down. I'd have to start over.

"Gee," he said, "I think you consider the same thing important that I do. What about the rest of the manual—do you know it like that?"

"Yes," I said, "it's a fantastic manual. When Boeing builds an airplane, they build an airplane that can read the manual. It does what the manual says. Anytime you have a question, just open that manual and do what it says."

"Why don't we go have lunch," he said. And that was the whole oral exam. I visited with him for awhile, and we got to talking about hunting coyotes; he'd never heard anything like that before. When we finished, he said, "Well, you seem to know the airplane real well. You won't have any problem."

Lucky Like That

We finally got an airplane. No more training, but we got an airplane. They run you around the airplane: "What's this hole for? What's this do? What's that do?" I drew the same inspector for the rating ride in the airplane. He complained a little bit because I only had two flights in it. They wanted to get everybody ten hours, at least. I only had four, and I hadn't flown a jet before; I'd been flying the DC-7c, that big Douglas.

There was a strong wind blowing down through the gap in San Francisco; a north wind, colder than heck. I thought I was never going to get in that airplane. Of course, that's where all the airline traffic was—going off into the wind. There's a cross-runway that goes over to Oakland. And that airport is all on fill, so it's just like a roller coaster.

The instructor said to the inspector, "I think what we'll do is use the short runway. That way it will save us some time about getting in the traffic." That instructor was one of our best. He was so far ahead of the rest of us; he was great. He flew the China Hump during World War Two. He was also a commercial fisherman. He had a nice boat, and he had a commercial license.

So the instructor turned to the inspector and said, "If it's okay with you, as long as we're using this cross-runway, we'll request a cross-wind takeoff here, and get a cross wind and an engine cut on the same takeoff."

"Oh, yeah," he said, "that's fine, but that's a lot of wind there. Can he handle that much cross wind?"

"Oh, yeah. Oh, yeah," he said. But I had never had a cross-wind takeoff in a jet before. And I assumed that I was going to have to get a lot of rudder in to offset the cross wind.

We took off from behind the buildings. Just about the time we got to the cross-runway, we got out in the open where the wind hit us. Well, that instructor—of course, you've got an outboard engine, and the other two engines will pull you around—cut the outboard engine to offset the cross wind.

I could see him pulling the power back on the engine, but it wasn't doing anything. I was waiting to put some rudder in, and keep it straight down the runway. Usually they'll get a little of that. But we just went right straight down the runway.

I thought, "Well, this jet must not be affected by a cross wind like the other airplanes are." All he did was to offset the cross wind by pulling the power back on the outboard engine. The inspector didn't catch it. And *I* didn't catch it.

We got in the air, and the inspector said, "Why don't you go ahead and put the power back in." We were going to Sacramento to do the training over there. He tapped me on the shoulder and said, "You know, I normally don't make any comments until the flight's over. But I gotta compliment you on that takeoff. That was the smoothest engine cut I've ever seen handled, and in that cross wind."

Now I feel like Lindbergh. I had nothing to do with it; it was the instructor. Everything he did made it easy. And nobody got it. I got to thinking about it then, and realized what he had done. We went through all the maneuvers, and it went fine.

Well, when we got back, that inspector went right up to the Chief Pilot's office. "Hey, you oughta make an instructor out of

Jack. That young guy gave me the best flight test that I've had," he said. And I didn't do it; it was all the instructor!

Because everybody else had bad-timed this inspector, when he went in and talked to the Chief Pilot, the Chief Pilot made me a check pilot right away. But I do like to fly, and any time they would call me I'd be there.

So I've been lucky like that. Because a cross wind affected that jet just like all the others, because it had a big tail. And I got out on the line and I thought, "My gosh, this thing doesn't fly like it did when I was on my flight test."

But I've been lucky. I've just been lucky at things like that, you know. They're not planned; they just happen. So it's been a fantastic life. I never felt like I should be taking the pay, really.

"Come on Up"

Alaska's sure got mountains; there are a lot of them in the Alaska Coastal Range. Mt. Fairweather is one—17,000 or 18,000 feet. We gave the passengers a real good ride in the summertime, when there were tourists and the weather was good, flying alongside the peaks and glaciers.

With the prop airplanes, we took off at Juneau, and you couldn't go up the Mendenhall Glacier right there at the airport. So we had to come down. The Juneau icecap had these glaciers. So we went from Whitehorse and cut across. If the weather was good, you could see all the glaciers.

So we came right down the Mendenhall Glacier, making turns, and the people would just go wild taking pictures, because they were looking right down into that blue ice.

Ralph Savory, Pan Am's Chief Pilot, was the one who kept our Alaska bases going. Ralph was fantastic, such a great guy. He wanted to bring DC-4 service to Alaska, when the four-engine transports became available to the airlines by the end of World War Two.

"Oh, no; you can't fly in and out of a tight spot like Juneau with four-engine airplanes," the FAA said. "They're too big for an airport with no instrument approach—just visual VFR approach." We were flying twin-engine, 21-passenger DC-3s.

So Ralph talked the company into letting him have a DC-4 for the day, rounded up some of the FAA inspectors, took them up and showed them how he could go in and out of Juneau just as well or better with a DC-4 as with a DC-3. In fact, Ralph proved that the DC-4 was actually much safer than the DC-3. So they couldn't turn him down anymore, and Ralph and I flew the first four-engine plane that went to Alaska.

The airport in Juneau is surrounded by mountains. The straits go on down, and Juneau's on the side of the mountain where they have a gold mine. We had to come in, make a turn and go back out. We flew the DC-4s in and out of Juneau for a number of years, with no problems.

When the jets came out, Ralph said we could fly them in and out of Juneau just as well, but the FAA wouldn't even go with him. They said that we couldn't do it with the jet; it was just too big and too fast to operate in and out of Juneau.

So Ralph flew the trip up to Fairbanks. We were flying nonstop to Fairbanks and back. He had some passengers, and he told them he would give them a nice view of the Mendenhall Glacier, which is right beyond the Juneau airport.

So he came down and made all of his approaches there, but never did land. He put the gear and the flaps down, made an approach and turned to the right. He had a lot of room. Then he put the climb power on and climbed right over the mountain range. And the passengers just had a ball.

Well, Ralph convinced himself that the jet would do more than the prop airplanes. So he lobbied the FAA. But the FAA said no; they looked at the maps and said that it just wouldn't fit in there. And Ralph said, "Well, it *has*, and I *fit* it in there; so come on up."

So finally some of the FAA people from Washington, D.C. came up. Ralph took them out on a nice, sunny day and did everything with a jet, and more, that you could do with a prop plane. With a jet, for example, you could climb right up the Mendenhall Glacier.

Well, the FAA officials had to admit that the Boeing 707 was even better than the DC-3 or DC-4, and were so impressed that they let Ralph go ahead and put it on the schedule. There was jet service after that to Juneau, and there still is. And we never, ever scratched an airplane.

We flew the 707 in and out of Juneau until just a few years ago, with no problems. And the Alaska passengers had their flight time cut in half from what the DC-4 prop planes took. We flew the 707 nonstop from Seattle to Fairbanks in three hours; the DC-4 took eight hours.

The Juneau Airport and Lynn Canal. My friend Ralph Savory,
Pan Am's Chief Pilot, proved to the FAA that jet service into
Juneau was not only feasible, but better than with prop planes.
Courtesy Pan Am/FAA.

There's a lot to see in and around Juneau. You can take the ferry on up to Skagway; that's only an hour's ride. You can get up there early enough in the day to take the narrow gage railroad up into the mountains, where the miners walked over the pass.

At the top is Stewart Lake. There's a "Y" there so the two trains can meet; one from Whitehorse and one from Juneau. You can get off of the one from Juneau, catch the other one and come right back down. That's a great one-day trip.

The Red Dog Saloon is on Franklin Street in Juneau. It's got sawdust on the floor, and a big round hunk of cheese on the counter. You just go by there and cut one off and leave them a quarter. Alaska's a lot like Montana; it still is.

I'm going to take the cruise ship or fly up to Juneau some day, and make a deal to get on the cruise ship and go up to Skagway and then go up to the top of Chilkoot Pass on the narrow-gauge railroad. That narrow-gauge railroad goes right up the side of the mountain. There are a lot of snow sheds on it. When they had the little steam engine, the steam would come out both ends of the snow shed, because it's just like a tunnel.

If you wanted to, you could go on over to Whitehorse and see the beginning of the Yukon. You could come back out the next day. That way you could see the head of the Yukon. There are still some old paddle-wheelers that run down the Yukon from Whitehorse. A lot of merchandise comes into Whitehorse up the AlCan now. They load those old paddle-wheelers; they go where the roads don't. They go into Dawson and some of those mining places.

Northern Exposure

I never got tired of looking at the scenery flying over Alaska. In the summertime it was beautiful, with daylight all night. The moon would be out shining on those glaciers. In the wintertime you looked down on the Northern Lights. And they were just going back and forth, all different colors.

We went over the North Pole all the time on a lot of our flights from London to Seattle. It was really a kick, because we still had the old liquid compass up there—the old magnetic compass. But we had an electronic compass, too. It's hooked to a gyro, so that it doesn't wiggle around.

But it was funny with that big old ball compass: as you approached the North Pole—twenty or thirty miles out—the thing would start turning and tipping. And it would point *down*. And when you went over the Pole, it would go round and round, then point the back way.

It was just a kick to watch that magnetic compass; you could see why it wasn't much good up there. We flew that trip some with the Stratocruiser, but mainly with the 707. But we had other good equipment and compasses. They have what they call a magnetic compass—an electronic-magnetic—which has a gyro attached to the compass, so the compass doesn't swing. It moves just like a gyro.

I used to look down at that North Pole—nothing but snow, that magnetic compass going around—and every place you went was south. It was just a kick. Some of the copilots would go to sleep up there. But I never could. If I was over the North Pole, with the compass going round and round, it was so darned interesting that I'd just sit there and look out, you know.

Lots of times, if there were Northern Lights, they would be down below us, because we would be up high. On the SP we would always be at 41,000 feet. But occasionally we would have to descend. It would get so cold outside—seventy below for several hours—that the heaters for the fuel going into the fuel controller wouldn't be hot enough.

First thing you know, we would see the fuel pressure wiggling just a little bit. Not enough to have a red light come on; we would never let it go that far. But as soon as it started wiggling, we went to a lower altitude, because it would always warm up some as we were coming down.

I enjoyed that polar flight. We would go over Greenland—which should have been named Iceland. Iceland has a lot of warm water, but Greenland is all ice. I always carried National Geographic maps, which gave the depth of those glaciers. Some of them are 10,000 and 12,000 feet deep.

They usually served dinner out of London, just about the time we got over Greenland. So I would check to make sure the weather was really clear and nice. Then I would tell the purser to just delay the dinner for thirty minutes or so, because we were coming up on Greenland.

We went across Greenland at ninety degrees. As we came up to the shore, I would make a right turn ninety degrees and fly north, and the people on the left side could get a lot of nice views and pictures.

I had just arrived in Seattle from a trip over the North Pole from London in this Boeing 747 in 1981.

Then we would make a 180-degree turn and come on back the other way, and we only took several minutes. The passengers could get good pictures out of both sides through the windows.

When we arrived in Seattle, and the passengers got out of Customs, they would come over and say, "Boy, we sure loved those pictures that we were able to take."

Around the World in Eight Days

Pan Am was fantastic, and the crew scheduling was so good. With the San Francisco and Los Angeles flights—the round-the-worlds—all of those people commuted. San Francisco had a pretty good-sized base, but people didn't like to live in the L.A. area. So about half the pilots commuted for their trips.

When they built the patterns for each month, Scheduling would make a bunch of eight- to ten-day patterns, so you only had to commute once. We would come in from that round-the-world, which got in there about six o'clock at night, and the copilot and engineer would go over to the terminal or the hangar, where we had our offices.

We had bulletins that came out every day for all the different airports. We had a big thick manual we carried, and we kept that up to date for our instrument approaches. You would be gone for a week on those round-the-worlds and there would be a whole bunch of those in your mailbox. These fellows who lived in the Bay Area would just stay at our office for a few hours and get their manuals up to date, and not get out in that traffic. The only road down there was the Bayshore Highway, and it was just bumper-to-bumper.

They would tell me, "If I go out and get on that Bayshore, it'll take me two hours." They lived twenty or thirty miles down the peninsula. They lived in Redwood City or one of those places, and they would say, "It's gonna take me two hours sitting on that Bayshore. So I'll get my manuals up to date and then get out there two hours later, and I can go home."

Well, I would just get on Western or United—or Air West; they were all flying out of San Francisco—which had a lot of flights. I bet I never waited more than twenty minutes. It was only a little more than an hour, and I would be home before they would. I enjoyed that commute, because I could read all the news up to Seattle.

I never left my car out at the airport for the whole week. For a while we just had the one car, because we didn't need two. We finally got a station wagon for Scotty. But she would take me out and drop me off. Then Dispatch would call her when I was going over and on my way; I would be landing in San Francisco in half an hour. So she would know, and I wouldn't even have to call her from San Francisco. I would just wait until I got here and call her; and she would come out.

Two flights left San Francisco every morning—Flights 1 and 2—both 707s. One went eastbound and one westbound. We would lay over at the same layover stations. If we went westbound, we would go to Honolulu, and have twenty-four hours there.

The next day another airplane would come through, and we would take it right on through to Tokyo. We would have twenty-four hours in Tokyo, go from there to Hong Kong and Bangkok, and have twenty-four hours in Bangkok.

Then we would go to Rangoon, Burma; then to Calcutta and New Delhi. We would have twenty-four hours in New Delhi, and go from there to Baghdad and Karachi, Pakistan, on to Beirut, Lebanon, and have twenty-four hours in Beirut.

We laid over twenty-four hours in all these places that we had a crew layover. They had to make these layovers to put another crew on, so they didn't run out of flight time. We would get about sixty hours' flight time. And that airplane went around the world in sixty hours, except for gassing it on the ground.

The whole trip took eight days—and it was an education. I went around the world once a month for about eight years. I bid those trips because you would fly around the world, it would be an eight-day trip and you would get sixty hours. You would only have to fly to Honolulu and back for a two-day trip, and you were through for the month.

Then Scotty and I would go over to Montana. If it was in the wintertime I would hunt coyotes.

That round-the-world flight was an interesting trip; you never knew what was going to happen. Jet fuel was ten to twenty cents a gallon. I was overnight into New Delhi, India and going to Beirut the next day. The serviceman came out and said, "I hope you got a lot of money."

"Yeah," I said.

"Well, they just raised the price of gas out here to a dollar a gallon. What do you want to do—do you want to fill it?"

I said, "I've got to put enough on it so that I can go to Beirut and then Istanbul as an alternate. So pretty well fill it." That was the 707, which carried about 40,000 gallons. The 747 carried much more than that—two tank cars full.

We figured out how much gas we needed to go to Beirut, and then on to Istanbul for the next day, without landing in Beirut—just in case they had somebody there stopping us. When I came out the next morning, here he was with his clipboard. "Well, you said you have a lot of money," he said.

"Yeah," I said, "I've got a Pan American credit card."

"Well," he said, "it's gonna cost you $40,000." So, at a dollar a gallon, I guess they put on 40,000 gallons. But that was what we went through on that round-the-world trip. Usually they were fighting their next door neighbors.

I went around the world once a month for eight years. It was an interesting trip because you never knew what was going to happen. Pan Am took a photo of every crew member. This one was taken on one of my six-month tests in San Francisco.

Silent Treatment

The Iraqi Minister of Aviation was on one of my flights. The Baghdad Airport had been giving us a lot of problems for a long time, and we were skipping Baghdad every other trip—maybe every trip. It was a daily stop for Pan Am on Flight 1. The airways went almost due east and west between Beirut, Lebanon and Tehran.

Halfway across, you would make a ninety-degree turn, then go up to Baghdad. It was only a hundred miles, but it was right up into those big, high mountains. And would you believe that they would turn off the radio range that we used to make our approach. You needed that signal because you had to stay between those mountains.

I think there must have been a few militants in there doing that, because we got along well with the locals. But it sure did surprise this gentleman. I would say he was in his fifties—old, at the time, to me. He was a nice-looking guy, and he spoke English well. He was so happy that I let him just get right up there in the jump seat before we took off. He stayed right there and watched the whole jet operation.

He had never been in the cockpit of a jet before, because the 707s were new then. So I explained it all to him, and on the way over I told him that we had been having trouble with the radio range. By the time we headed north on the start-down, someone would turn it off.

"Nobody in his right mind is going to start down among those mountains," I told him, "unless you've got a good radio range." So I would have to just pull up and go on to Tehran—then we would get a nasty letter from the State Department.

"Well," said the Minister, "we'll see what goes on today." This was in the 1950s, just after we got the 707s. Whoever was shutting off the radio range was hoping that we would just keep right on descending, hit the mountains and blow up a new jet. It was no different than an act of terrorism, because that radio would shut off just like that; just dead. Plumb dead.

The Aviation Minister was listening to us, and it was coming in loud and clear—an A&N type range. "See: that's what's been happening," I said. "I do this once a month, and it happens almost every time."

"Can you give me a radio transmitter that I can talk to Baghdad on?" he asked.

"Oh, yeah," I said. I already had one tuned in. "So I'll just put the toggle switch up there, and you can start talkin'." He called Baghdad, and was speaking in his language. I couldn't tell what he was saying, but he got loud. And the radio came right back on.

"He'll never turn that off again," the Minister said, gesturing with a finger across his throat. He no doubt realized that it was somebody that had infiltrated the communications there. He gave me all of his cards, and told me to give them to the Operations Manager in San Francisco and the Chief Pilot, and to keep a few for myself. If there was ever another problem, call *him*. There never was.

At that time Iraq was one of our allies. We were furnishing them with missiles and helicopters. The Minister had gone to Beirut to shop. Everybody went to Beirut to shop. It was like Hong Kong: fantastic shopping; lots of gold. There was a gold street about a block and a half long. It was just a real narrow street, with little shops on both sides. You could buy gold there for about half of what it cost in Hong Kong.

There was always something coming up, you know. I could see many areas of the world going socialistic and communist. In some places, they wouldn't even let us out of the cockpit.

I never had a real argument with any of the station managers or dispatchers in the Mideast, though. Pan Am always had a maintenance foreman who kept me posted on any local problems or developments, or who to talk to if he wasn't there: "You can trust him; he'll handle it."

There were always one or two real good Pan Am employees at every station. And some of those stations were nasty. I told the Operations Manager in Beirut, and also in Tehran, "If you have a pilot in here who hasn't flown this route, be sure to brief him that they might shut that transmitter off in Baghdad."

I told the new captains as I was checking them out, "Be sure and use all the information you can get from the ground, but don't depend on it completely." And I would tell them about Baghdad. "Whatever you do, if a station like that shuts off, climb out of there and go on to the next one. Don't worry about the letter from the State Department; they're all back there sitting behind nice big desks."

I tried to teach these new captains that *they* had to make the decisions on something like this.

Sandblaster

There always seemed to be a war in Beirut; the Arabs and the Jews were always fighting. I came in there one day, and I was talking to Pan Am Operations on the radio. They said, "We think you're going to have to go on." The next stop was Istanbul, Turkey.

But we laid over in Beirut. A new crew there took the plane on to Istanbul, then to Munich, Berlin and London. They would lay over in London, then fly nonstop to San Francisco.

So I asked the dispatcher in Beirut what happened. He said, "Well, last night Mideast Airlines"—they had some small twin-engine jets—"had six of their airplanes lined up here in front of the terminal." In Beirut, you had to walk in on the ramp; they didn't have the tubes.

So these planes were all lined up out there to get ready to go for the next morning. They said that two Israeli helicopters came up. One of them had a crew in it with machine guns, and they just went back and forth in front of the terminal. If anybody opened the door, they would rat-a-tat the concrete out in front.

The other helicopter had bombs on it. They put a bomb under each one of these Mideast Airlines jets—right under the middle, between the landing gear. They had them all set with timers that they could initiate.

They got all six of those jets with bombs under them, so the two helicopters took off. Once they got a little ways out of there, all six of these airplanes blew up. With the bombs being pretty well underneath the gear, the jets were all in a heap. They really ruined all of them.

The only military there usually spent most of their time at the big waterworks on the other end of town. They shared a couple of them at the airport, but that was all. The morning after these things all blew up, they moved the whole gang in from the waterworks. They had tanks and trucks—the dispatcher said he thought they had every soldier, tank and truck they had in Beirut at the airport.

The Israelis, of course, had gone home the night before in the helicopters. And the dispatcher said, "We can't get the Lebanese soldiers off the runway; they're charging back and forth out there."

You know, those Arabs get excited real easy. They were just really stirring up the airport. It had been closed all day. We got in there in the late afternoon. We were supposed to get off, and another crew get on.

I asked them what they had tried to clear the runway. "Oh, we've tried everything," they said, "and we haven't been able to get those guys off of the airport."

"Why don't I talk to the tower," I said. "Have you had any other airplanes in here?"

"Yeah—but they wouldn't let them land." They ran most of them to Istanbul, which was only about an hour away.

So I called the tower and said, "Do you have any estimate of when the airport might be opened?"

"No," he said. "We've been trying to get these guys out of here and back to their base out at the waterworks, and we can't move 'em. One of those Israelis could paddle ashore in a boat out there and blow up the whole waterworks. Because we think they're all here.

"We've counted the tanks, and we know that they've got all their tanks here."

"Well, I can make a low approach down there," I said, "and just put on a lot of power, put the gear down and put the flaps down. When it hits the flaps, it will go straight down to the ground. I can fog that in with dust down there, because this is sand, and maybe that will chase them out."

"Go ahead," he said.

So we went out and got on a long final. We got down to about a hundred feet, and got the gear and the flaps down so we could use a lot of power. We flew right down the runway, about a hundred feet off the ground. We pulled up at the far end, looked back and couldn't even see the airport; it was just a big cloud of sand.

I told the copilot: "We'll just circle out here for a while and see what's gonna happen. We don't want to go on to Istanbul, because there's no crew there who's going to be rested. It'll foul up our whole schedule, and we've got all these passengers who want to get off in Beirut."

So we just circled out there for ten or fifteen minutes, and that dust all settled. We didn't want to get the dust in our engines, either; all that sand. And there wasn't a soul on that airport; they were gone. I guess that the sand and the wind scared them out.

"They're gone," the tower finally said.

"Do you think it's okay if we come in and land?" I asked.

"Oh, yeah," they said. "There's nobody else here, just the airport people."

So we went in and landed. And the crew that was going to take the plane on was there. They got it organized, and away it went to Istanbul and on around the world. They wouldn't even take us into town in a limo. They put the crew in three armored cars and took us to the hotel.

At one time, the crews really liked Beirut. It was known as the "Miami of the Mideast." The weather was nice and warm, with beaches on the sparkling Mediterranean. Pan American owned a great big hotel there, the Phoenicia; it was a beautiful hotel. There was a big dining room downstairs, with a glassed-in swimming pool on one end and a stage full of belly dancers on the other.

There was a Holiday Inn across the street. Fighting had been taking place near there. So when they put us in the hotel, the clerk gave us a coded phone number and said, "Don't go out of your room. We don't know what's going on around here, but it's not good. We're trying to have all the guests stay in the hotel, at least overnight.

"Just call this number, and there'll be a special crew that will bring you any food you want."

So that's what we did. The next morning they had limos to take us back out. We didn't have to ride in the armored cars again. You never knew what was going to happen in Beirut, because the Israelis stirred them up often.

What's Cooking?

Every summer, Pan Am would base an airplane in Tehran. We would fly what we called the Hajj Charters. This was when all of the locals had to go down for this big get-together in Saudi Arabia, or they weren't going to get to heaven. They all had to go down for that, one time.

I tell you, we would have an airplane based out there about two months. When I flew it, it was a DC-6, and we made two trips. We carried a load down and came back, then took another load down; two a day.

On this one trip—it must have been a later trip and the passenger got hungry. The stewardess called up and said, "Hey Jack, we've got a problem back here. One of the passengers has got his hibachi set up back here in the kitchen area, and he's putting charcoal in it. He's gonna cook his hot dinner. Well, we've got dinners for 'em, but he's gonna cook his own; and I can't get my English across to him."

We had flight engineers at that time; we had a great big Swede on there as the flight engineer. So I said, "Well, I'll send the flight engineer back." I had him put on my cap with the braid on it. So he went back and told this fellow that he couldn't do that. The Swede was big enough that I was sure the man wouldn't argue with him.

So the flight engineer went back and explained to this gentleman that we couldn't have open flame back there because we had gas heaters and other things that could "blow up the airplane! BLOW UP the airplane!" The flight engineer was able to get it across to him. He poured water on the hot charcoals.

But that fellow was going to, by gosh, cook his meal back there in the airplane. The stewardess was just beside herself, calling: "You gotta get somebody back here *quick!*"

But we got that stopped. They were good passengers, only they didn't have a clue about flying. This was the first flight most of them had ever had. It was only an hour and a half to Saudi Arabia, where they went for this big gathering. There were thousands of people there. And every day, somebody would get smothered in one of these packs.

I only went out there for a week. I wanted to see what they were. Then one of the round-the-world pilots got off and stayed and I took the airplane on back. I could work my schedule real well because there was usually somebody coming up for some training or something.

It was really an education; we had nothing like that back on the ranch.

Up in the *Stuff*

At Pan Am, all of our jets had auto-landing for fog. Some of the airports have the ground equipment for auto-landings. I have made many autopilot landings in the 747 when you couldn't see a thing, especially at Los Angeles International and London, and the auto-pilot would do the whole trick. That autopilot was just fantastic in a 747. One computer was coupled to the autopilot, with two more computers monitoring the one that is coupled.

You watch all of the flight instruments just like you were making the approach yourself. It had cross-hairs on it, just like a scope in a gun. You kept them crossed. One was the descent altitude, and one was for lining up with the runway. As long as you had that crossed, you were going to hit the end of the runway.

We would fly down to a hundred feet ourselves, but the auto-pilot would come right on down and land. But you sit up so high in the 747 that, even when you land, you're still forty-five feet in the air. So you were up in the *stuff.*

But you sit there completely at ease, because it was just like you were flying it. It had a button on the top of each side of the flight control wheel. The button on the left-hand side disconnected the autopilot. The button on the right-hand side disconnected the automatic throttles.

If you didn't like the looks of anything, you could press both buttons and the airplane was all yours for a go-around if it was not in a position to land.

So you sat there with your hands on that wheel, thumbs on both buttons. You were looking at those cross-hairs, and it was just perfect. Just like here you were Lindbergh, really flying this thing. But it was the autopilot, and the other autopilot backing it up.

The autopilot used the radio glide slope—one hundred percent for the first 1,500 feet. When you got down to five hundred feet, the radio-altimeter was right to the foot. It sat there right beside the instruments, so you could see this radio-altimeter going down.

You knew that the autopilot was on the glide slope, and you felt completely at ease. If for any reason they had a burp in the glide slope, a red light would come on and say, GO AROUND.

As long as you were on the glide slope, when you got down to a hundred feet, then the computers in the autopilot began to wash out the glide slope and pick up the radio-altimeter. So the last fifty feet was just radio-altimeter; it was not the glide slope feeding it.

At fifty-two feet, the green light came on, which showed that the computer was starting your flare. That green light would come on, the throttles would start to come back and it would start this flare. You could watch that radio-altimeter, and you went from fifty . . . forty . . . thirty, and it kept flaring a little more, little more. Finally, you just barely felt the wheels touch.

There was no thump, there was no anything; it was just kind of a SWISHHHH. Then the automatic brakes would come on. You put the automatic brakes on before you started your approach, and the automatic throttles.

So at fifty-two feet you would have this green light and the throttles would start back. The airplane would start to flare, and it would flare right out flat and go right on that runway. No thump at all, just PSHHHHHHWISHHHHHHH.

Then the automatic brakes came on, and all we had to do was reverse the thrust. The throttles had already been closed by the automatic landing. But we would reach up ahead of the throttles where another set of buttons were connected to the other throttles. Those were the reversers. You pulled those four reversers back. That's the only thing we did on the landing: just reverse them.

We pulled them back, then got on the brakes, too—just to override them in case the brakes would go off, or anything. But we would just let those automatic brakes stop it.

You stopped out there on the runway, and would be sitting forty-five feet in the air. You were up in that darn smog, and all you could see were one or two lights in the center of the runway. You were looking right down over the middle at them.

The tower would call you and say, "Clipper, you're clear to make a left at the next taxiway."

And we would say, "Tower—we don't *see* any taxiway. We don't see a thing; you're gonna have to vector us in."

They had ground radar in L.A. and London, and the places where we got a lot of fog. And they would say, "Well, okay: you're coming up on the left taxiway, so start a left turn. Turn a little more. Turn a little more."

The taxiways had bright blue lights down the center. The blue lights would shine up through the fog better, because you could see this blue glare. So you would just get over until you were on the blue glare, and follow it.

They controlled those taxiway lights from the tower. If you came up to another taxiway intersection leading you into the terminal, why the tower would say, "Clipper, you've got about two hundred feet to come to this next intersection. It'll be a ninety-degree right turn on the other taxiway."

We slowed right down to almost a stop, because we were looking right down over the nose at those blue lights. And here you came up on the intersection. They had the lights on real bright, so that you would see the new taxiway. You turned ninety degrees on those blue lights and followed them. And they led you right up to the ramp.

We never parked the airplane. We stopped about two hundred feet from the terminal. They sent a mule hook out onto the nose wheel that towed us in that last two hundred feet.

When you pulled up to the terminal, all you had was that glare shining through the fog. You really couldn't see anything, but it was just lit up. The mule would pull you right up to where you would line up with the exit tubes that the passengers got out on. And you could look out and *still* not see the lights on the wing tips. It was zero-zero.

"How Would You Like Your Eggs?"

In the wintertime, I flew the Los Angeles-to-Sydney or New Zealand nonstop quite a bit, with the SP—Special Performance—747. It's a little faster than the big 747, and it's got another thousand miles of range. It left Los Angeles at six o'clock at night. I bid it a lot, and it was all-night down there.

The junior pilots, laying over in Sydney, would say, "Jack, what in heck are you doin'? You're number one on the seniority list, and here you are flying all night, when you could be flying a nice daylight trip."

"Well, I tell ya," I said, "this is about as much vacation as I can stand. You know, I can really sleep on an airplane. And I know the rest of you guys can fly just as good as I can. That's the best dinner I've had in a long time, and I had a good sleep too."

They have two nice berths on the 747, up in the cockpit: one for the pilots and one for the engineers. The berths are air conditioned; they've got music in there and reading lights. They're just really first class.

There were two engineers. With Pan Am, they didn't use two captains. They qualified all of their first officers as captains. They had the same ratings and six-month checks. So they were really great guys to have along.

So they would send one captain and two copilots. And we would split it in thirds, because it was usually twelve or thirteen hours. That 747 SP would go fifteen hours; it was a great machine.

I would tell the other two pilots, "If it's all right with you, I'd like to be in the cockpit on takeoff and landing, sleep in the middle, and you can have the other two-thirds." If we had problems on the takeoff—had to dump fuel or something, or if there was fog during the landing and we had to go to an alternate airport—I liked to be up front.

"Go ahead, Jack," they would say. "We could care less."

As soon as we taxied out, the flight attendants got the cocktail cart out. So they would be serving drinks to the passengers on our climb-out. As soon as we got climbed out, leveled off and on the pilot, there was nothing to do but watch the machines work. By the time we got to altitude—got her all set up with inertial navigation—it was a half an hour or so into the flight.

Soon they would come into the cockpit with the hors d'oeuvres, on a cart that fit through the door. She would give us each a plate. Not a paper plate, but a regular glass plate. Then she would have this great big tray of hors d'oeuvres. And they always had the fish eggs—caviar. I never eat it because it's terrible. But I always razzed the copilots.

I said: "You know, I never see you eat the fish eggs. I see you put all that onion and stuff on it, and eat that. But do you ever eat just the fish eggs?"

"Oh, no, no," they would say. "They're too *fishy.*"

But all this other stuff. So then she takes that out. Then she comes up with the salad cart. Great big bowl of salad; about six different dressings. So you have your salad. And you've got the hors d'oeuvres and the salads—so now I guess it's dinnertime.

Upstairs you had twenty-one seats in the older 747s. They had a stewardess and a purser up there, as well as a kitchen. They did their own cooking. You had five entrees to choose from in First Class, and two and sometimes three in coach.

In First Class, you always had prime rib. The prime rib would be raw when we started out. They would cook it in electric ovens. They put three of them in so that they would have well-done, medium and rare.

Other entrees were lamb chops, fish and lobster. That Lobster Thermidor, I tell you: we never heard of anything like that in Montana. They took the tail of the lobster out, cut the meat into bite-sized pieces and put it back in. And the sauce was delicious. I always ate Lobster Thermidor.

Then, after all that good dinner, it was: "Well, we've got cherries jubilee for dessert today." So up comes the cherries jubilee.

Then they would come up with an after-dinner 'nibble' tray, with cheeses, nuts, fruit and all that. By the time you finished, you could hardly get to the bunk. And I would say, "Well, you know, fellas, by the time I finish this dinner, I've flown my three hours. It's time for me to get my three-hour nap."

"I can sleep," I said, "because I came down from Seattle this morning; I commuted down to L.A. And I only got a nap over at the motel this afternoon. So I can go in there and I'll sleep."

So it was time to go to bed. I would sleep three, three and a half hours. Sure enough, pretty soon somebody's waking me up. "Jack, time for you to get up and shave and get in the cockpit."

So I'd get up, jump in and have an electric shaver just quick-like before I got in the seat.

I'd no more than sat down when up would come the stewardess saying, "Good morning, Jack. How would you like your eggs? We're getting ready to cook breakfast."

You could have French toast; you could have anything. So, by the time you eat this big breakfast, you're at top of descent and ready to go in and land. And I said, "You think that's tough duty?"

"Well, we can't sleep. We can't sleep," the other pilots would say.

"Well, when you get as old as I am," I said, "you trust the rest of the guys. Because I know that you can fly the airplane just as well or better than I can." But that was part of the life, and it was just fantastic.

That's why I considered the Los Angeles-to-Sydney flight the best trip I had. I flew this trip a lot in the winter because it was summer down south then, and Scotty would go with me for a ten-day pattern. I commuted down from Seattle in plenty of time. I had all day to come down. We all were commuters; nobody lived down in clown town.

The cover of Pan Am's in-flight menu.
Many of Pan Am's aircraft were named after famous
Clipper sailing ships of old. Courtesy Pan Am.

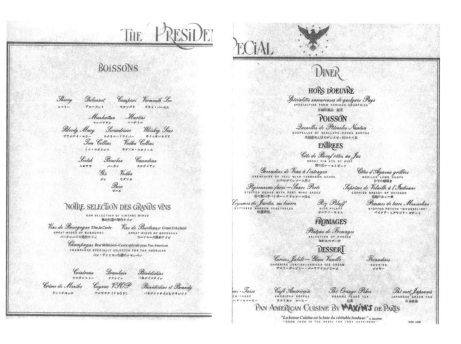

Pan Am in-flight menu. Pan Am really did go all-out to "make the going great," offering a level of style and elegance that will likely never be seen—or tasted—again. Courtesy Pan Am.

Bedtime Story

Although I liked Rome, because the food was so good and the people so friendly, New Zealand was probably one of my favorite stops.

New Zealand had good, wholesome food, because the government subsidized the dairy industry a lot. And there would be these little bottles of milk in your hotel room. They would put fresh milk in the refrigerator before you got there. And if any of their ice cream melted in your dish, it's there. It doesn't evaporate like ours.

If I couldn't live in the United States, I think I would pick New Zealand. The people are so friendly; they're really nice. I always hauled my blue bag full of peanut butter. They have the old style peanut butter with the oil on top, and they liked the homogenized and the chunky type. So I filled my blue bag every time I went to Auckland. You could tell it was heavy.

"Gee, it looks like you must have that peanut butter in that bag again," the limo driver would say.

"I got it for you guys," I said.

"Well, we'll stop at the cheese factory," the driver said. So then we would stop at the cheese factory and get this wholesale cheese. They make good cheese there. I would unload all the peanut butter in the limo for them and fill it up with cheese. I really enjoyed all the people there.

We stayed at the Intercontinental Hotel Corporation—Pan Am owned that. They owned that until they shut down. They were really nice hotels, first class. They treated us real well.

I bought jewelry there for my wife. Opal is her birthstone, and they had some nice opals in a nice little jewelry shop in the corner of the hotel. Just one guy was in there all the time, and every once in a while he would say, "I got in some good opals here." Those opals ran in a lot of nice colors, so Scotty had a good collection.

The only thing wrong with New Zealand was that the gals would make those beds so you couldn't see a wrinkle in it. They would tuck everything in so that you couldn't get in the darned thing. It was like somebody short-sheeted you: you would have to get in and pull the stuff all out.

Well, we got in early one morning. The gal who was the foreman of the maids was around, and she stopped to talk to me. "You know," I said, "I'm kind of embarrassed to do this, because I know that you've been making beds a lot longer than I have. But I have short-sheeted some guys, and it seems to me that I am getting short-sheeted every time I come in to Auckland. I have a heck of a time getting into that bed."

"Well, how come?" she said.

"Look at this," I said. "You've got the sheet tucked under the bed. You've got the blankets tucked under; you've got everything tucked under. And everything is as smooth as can be up here.

"And I always tear up your bed. So when I get in, I pull all of that stuff out. I don't tuck *any* of it in under the mattress, because that's just draggin' your feet down."

"Well, I'll be darned," she said. "Let's make a bed together." So we made a bed together, and I showed her what we had in all the rest of the hotels. And she was kind of embarrassed.

"You know, you *can't* get into that bed," she said, "unless you're *short*—real short. Because you get your feet down in the end and it's dragging your toes down."

And, by golly, she said, "I'm going to check out the other girls."

I went down there about once a month. And the next time I went down, the beds were all made the way I showed her. The New Zealanders are such nice people. I don't think I would have done that in Australia, in Sydney, because they're a completely different personality.

Rough Bunch

These people were all raised right there in New Zealand. Whereas Australia was completely populated by the prisons from England. And they're kind of a rough bunch. They're nice enough people. But they're kind of rough. You get on that streetcar and they'll gad you over; that's just the way they are.

We came in to both of those places real early in the morning. And we would come in over the city. With New Zealand, they don't like to have you come in over there at five o'clock in the morning, with a jet.

But it was quicker to come in over the city and just make a turn in, rather than go on out the other way. So I would call the controller, and I would tell him, "I can make this jet so quiet, we'll pull power all the way back on all four engines if you'll let us come in over the city."

"Oh—okay," they would say. No big deal at all.

But you wouldn't think of asking an Australian that. "Well, we got traffic to control," they would grumble. It was funny.

A 747 was on a long final approach in Sydney. We had plenty of room to go in and land ahead of him. But, oh no: they've got to take care of their own airlines first. So they asked if we would drop in behind that 747 on long final and be number two.

Their airplanes have a kangaroo painted on the tail. The copilot was landing the aircraft, and I was working the radio for him. I shouldn't have said it, but I said, "A 747—now I want to get the right one. Is that the one that's out there with the *rodent* painted on the tail?"

Boy, that did it; that set him off. He was grumpy with all of us before we got to the blocks. But they've never had an accident, the Australian airline. Of course, they never fly in bad weather, either.

There was one going ahead of us one time like that in Sydney. He got down to about a thousand feet, and it was rough. "I'm going on to Melbourne," he said.

He had a whole load of people for Sydney, and he had a whole load to pick up in Melbourne and go on down. But no, they could care less, because they were owned by the government. They didn't have to make any money.

So we went in. It was rough and nasty, and there was a cross wind because the long runway that was into the wind was out of service. I was landing it that time. I told the copilot, "We might have to make a go-around. It depends on what we find down there when we hit the ground." The air gets thicker when it hits the ground.

When you come into a runway in a cross-wind, you have to come in sideways. But you can't land that way because you would knock the gear off. So, just before you land, you roll it out to put it on. It's a little tricky; you just have to do it right.

If at any time it doesn't look right, all you have to do is put the power on and go around—because you're light; you're not full of gas.

So we went in and it was rough. The stewardess asked if the turbulence was going to last all the way to the ground. "I hope not to the ground," I said. "But all the way."

"Boy, it's miserable back here," she said. There was enough ground cushion, and it had rained a little so there was a little water on the runway. And that's good, too, because the tires don't screech or anything. So we came in and, boy, we lucked out. We just made a real smoothie.

Even with the door closed, I could hear the people all clapping and whistling back there. When we went in, the dispatcher said, "Well, do you want to take off in this, Jack?"

"Oh, yeah; taking off is nothing," I said. So we got rid of our load and went on down to Melbourne and back, because we only came from Auckland.

"Well, we're gonna have a fight out there in the terminal," the dispatcher said, "because their airplane just over-headed, and didn't land. They're all sitting here waiting to go to Melbourne, and we're going to pretty well fill it with just our passengers."

The Aussies were fighting to get on, but we didn't have enough seats. We did go out of there with four hundred people on, though.

It's nothing on the takeoff. You hold the airplane on, going down the runway. You make sure that you're holding it on. Have a lot of weight on the tires, and get about twenty knots above what you normally rotate at. And lift it right off, so that you're not getting any skipping. And you can handle it as well as normal.

I'd Rather be Dancing

My relationship with the national news media actually began while I was flying in Vietnam. We were flying into Da Nang, and the Air Force had complete control of the airport. But the Viet Cong, as I've said, would lie down in the rice paddies and shoot at us on final approach, using the biggest rifles they had that wouldn't smoke. We would make a steep approach, and we always had a north wind. We could come in over the water, but there was always too much tailwind. So we always had to go over the rice paddies.

The air base usually had four fire engines—two on each side of the runway, parked there all the time. I must have had a dozen engines hit over the years. They would shoot at the engines, because Boeing has a liner in the tanks.

We were going into Da Nang one day, and the newsman that handled the West Coast—Terry Drinkwater, really a nice guy—was sitting in the jump seat behind me in this freighter. And they hit the engine right outside his window.

Of course, when that oil radiator gets hit, that jet engine is nothing but a blow torch. It's a fire right now. We had to have the engine changed. Usually we would get right up next to the fire truck, and they would put the fire out so quick; but that one burned all the accessories.

So Terry Drinkwater and I spent a week together. He was a prince of a guy, and his uncle was president of Western Airlines.

When Russian fighters shot down Korean Air Lines Flight 007 on September 1, 1983, just the other side of Japan, the *Seattle Times* called Pan Am, and asked if they had anyone here that flew that route to the Orient on the 747, with that kind of equipment and navigation gear. They gave them my name, because that's what I was doing at that time.

The *Seattle Times* called me. "Have you got any idea why that Korean Air Lines 747 drifted up over that fighter base?" they asked me. You don't like to speculate on something unless you know the answer. In this case, I felt that I did.

"Well, I know exactly why," I said. We have a flight plan, and every time you cross a longitude you put it on the flight plan. You give them that when you cross this position. The dispatch is keeping track of your speed and how you're doing. There are only ten way points in there; so, going all the way to Korea, they would have to reload. Ten won't get you there.

Or, when you leave the Alaskan coast, you can punch in 'Present

Position' and it will go all the way. No need to give a position every thirty minutes or so. Of course, you're never right on that flight plan, due to the winds and other factors.

Well, here Flight 007 had given every position off the flight plan. And you know they weren't there. So what they had to have done was to put 'Present Position' as Seoul. I guess their navigation course wasn't too good because they didn't realize that that navigation always goes a Great Circle, because that's the shortest distance.

So when you leave Alaska, a Great Circle will put you right up over that fighter base in Russia. So they had to come out and see what the heck was going on. Here the Korean Air Lines flight was 200 miles off course—200 miles north of where it should have been.

Whenever we got north of the Aleutian Islands, we always had the 200-mile radar headed toward the Russian Islands. So we made sure we were a hundred miles south of them. But that's what happened, and I told that to the *Seattle Times*.

Then CBS got the wire on their news machine. Dan Rather, their lead anchorman, called me to see what went on. I told him the same thing I told the Seattle newspaper, and I really didn't have anything more to offer.

When I couldn't help Dan Rather, Terry Drinkwater, the CBS newsman who had flown with me in Vietnam, called. "You know," he said, sounding a little flustered, "Rather jumped into this thing before you turned him down. He's hired a whole camera crew from L.A., and he's rented a 747 in Las Vegas. Boeing wouldn't rent him one. They said they didn't have one here.

"They're going over there. And he wanted you to come down tonight or tomorrow, put that flight on the computer and run the whole thing, to show them exactly how the inertial navigation worked."

"I know," I said. "Rather mentioned it to me. I told him I couldn't get away, because it was Friday, and I had an engagement." Our neighbors, we all got together on Friday and Saturday night and went over to the Elks, because they had our vintage music. *That's* what our appointment was.

I told Terry Drinkwater. "Well, you refused Dan Rather completely, didn't you?" he said.

"Well, I don't want to go down there," I admitted.

"Well," he said, "would you do it for *me?* I'm down on my knees and I'm crying. We've got all this equipment going over there; it's on its way. If you'd like to come down and spend a week on CBS," he said, trying to sweeten the deal, "bring your wife and come on down."

"That's all right," I said. "But I'll come down for you. I'll get up for the morning flight, come down and then go back that afternoon."

"Fine," he said. "I'll meet you at the bottom of the stairs with the limo, and we'll take you out to where the airplane is. We can do it and I'll bring you right back."

Western had a first-class ticket waiting for me. Terry was great to work with. He was there. We flew the whole trip, right there on the ground. You would never know it was simulated, because they were taking pictures of it, and the inertial was going around.

CBS used it on their news broadcast for several days. They were going to put it all together and have a thirty-minute tape. I don't know if they ever did. Not too long after that, Terry Drinkwater had throat cancer. He was fun to work with; he was just great.

On December 21, 1988, Pan Am Flight 103, a Boeing 747-100—the "Clipper Maid of the Seas, flying from London to New York—was blown up over Lockerbie, Scotland by a terrorist's bomb. A friend of mine was the pilot on that flight, which carried a lot of college kids coming home for Christmas. All 243 passengers and 16 crew members were killed, as well as 11 people on the ground. One hundred seventy-nine of 259 people on board were American.

John Nance, nationally known aviation expert, called on me for advice. John Nance had never flown the 747. He was a nice guy.

Very knowledgeable, he really was. I also got another call from Dan Rather. "So, I guess there was another collision here, huh?" he said. "Dan," I said, "if there was another collision, where's the other *airplane?*"

"Oh, I hadn't thought about that," he said.

"I know what happened," I said. I had talked to Pan Am. That flight started in North Africa with all the passengers, and went on to London. There were some through passengers, and they were supposed to take all of the bags off and x-ray them.

Remember when President Reagan bombed Libya? Well, that's where it came from. There were two guys that had tickets on the airplane. They didn't get on in London, but their bags stayed on it. Eventually they found out that those were the people responsible.

So the *Seattle Times* and other news media called me a number of times. Bill Marsh, the gentleman who handled our media and public relations while Pan Am was still operating here, was a good friend of the *Seattle Times*.

Pan Am Airlines is no longer in operation, however. They sold the name. Someone tried to start it up, but to no avail.

"Fly by Night" Outfit

I'm kind of a morning sleeper. I usually get up around eleven a.m. We all say that when we were on the airline it was a "Fly by Night" outfit, because Pan Am went twenty-four hours a day.

It was a great life with Pan Am; it really was. I did so many things that you couldn't do any other way, other than being right there. My thirty nine and a half years with Pan Am were wonderful, even if I did end up flying in three wars: World War II, Korea and Vietnam. Pan Am gave me a ring for flying in all three wars.

I've never heard of another pilot who put himself through college by hunting coyotes. There are not that many pilots today that have flown a 747, either, because they haven't made that many.

Pan Am bought the first twenty-five. And there are even fewer who have instructed in it. I've instructed in all of Pan Am's airplanes.

Ralph Savory, Pan Am's Chief Pilot, was a great guy to work with. When he retired—you had to quit at sixty—he asked me if I wouldn't like to go in the Chief Pilot's office. "Well, not really, Ralph," I said. "I like flying the line—flying the airplanes—and training and instructing better."

So Ralph put another good friend of his, Roy Holm, in the Chief Pilot's office. He was only in there two years. He wanted to bid the 747 when it came out. So he had to go to San Francisco, because we didn't have the 747 in Seattle then. He only had two or three years left before he was going to be sixty and have to retire. "Well, I just have to go," he said.

So they talked me into trying it for a year. "Well, I don't think I'm gonna like an office better than an airplane," I said. "I'm no Chief Pilot; I'm just a plain old pilot who likes to fly. But as long as you guys think that I should give it a try, I will. But just for a year—and only if the secretary stays," because she had been there almost as long as I had.

She was the same age as me; we both graduated from high school in 1940. Phyllis Gordon: she was from Enumclaw, just a great gal. She had been Ralph's secretary all the time, and had stayed for Roy. So I said, "If Phyllis will promise to stay here and be the Chief Pilot, why, I'll drop in. Because if Phyllis leaves, I'm leaving. And one year is all I want to agree to."

And that's exactly what I did.

I like to sleep in. If New York called and wanted something, she could give them a better answer than I could, anyway. Once in a while they would want to talk to the Chief Pilot. "Well, Jack's down the hall in a meeting," she would say. "I'll have him give you a call as soon as he gets back."

Then she would call me and tell me that she had this call from New York; they wanted to talk to me. "Okay, I'll come on down to the office," I would say. Occasionally she would give me the number, and I would call right here from the house, and not let them know. I just didn't spend much time in that office.

Phyllis did such a great job, anyway, that New York didn't even know I wasn't there most of the time. She knew that office better than anybody. She knew it so much better than New York or San Francisco. She always had the answers for them; usually they didn't even have to round up the Chief Pilot. She was a lot better Chief Pilot than I was; she took care of everything.

Phyllis still comes to our Pan Am lunches. She's the same age I am. She's a real nice gal; she's doing well. She lost her husband, but she's doing well.

As the Chief Pilot, I spent most of my time flying the short trips and instructing new pilots. San Francisco would run out of airplane time for training and they would send me a couple of new pilots, and I would take them to Moses Lake. So I flew almost as much that one year as I had on the line. After a year of that, we talked Joe Deichl into trying the office.

We had a flight that came from London to Seattle, then we took it on down to Portland that afternoon. I flew that one a lot. I would go down and have dinner at the terminal, then they would have the airplane all ready to go back out. I would bring it back to Seattle, and a crew would take it to London. So I got to fly it a lot, and just didn't spend much time in that office.

After a year, I told them that I just hated to be messing with it; I had so much more fun instructing. When we got the 747, it was fun to check the people out in that. So I've got an awful lot of flight time. I think I must have 40,000 hours from Pan Am. A lot of the time we flew a hundred hours a month in those older airplanes.

I had a nice log book that was full of a lot of my private flying back in Montana, but the hangar fire burned up everything—including my records and log books. So I never kept a separate log book from then on. Pan Am gave you a computer copy of everything you did each month. We have that.

I. UNITED STATES OF AMERICA

Department of Transportation - FEDERAL AVIATION ADMINISTRATION

THIS CERTIFIES IV. JACK WARNER BURKE
THAT   V. 13625 18TH AVENUE S.W.
517120883   SEATTLE   WA   98166

DATE OF BIRTH	HEIGHT IN.	WEIGHT	HAIR	EYES	SEX	NATIONALITY
08-07-22	68	160	BLACK	HAZEL	M	USA

X. HAS BEEN FOUND TO BE PROPERLY QUALIFIED TO EXERCISE THE PRIVILEGE

AIRLINE TRANSPORT PILOT   III. CERT. NO.   136219

RATINGS AND LIMITATIONS
AIRPLANE SINGLE & MULTIENGINE AND
DC-3 DC-4 DC-6 DC-7 B-377 B-707 B-720 B-747

III.

SIGNATURE OF HOLDER   X. John L. McLucas
DATE OF ISSUE: 03-27-76   VIII.   ADMINISTRATOR

AC FORM 8060 2 (9-75) SUPERSEDES PREVIOUS EDITION

My pilot's license, showing all the different airplanes I was qualified to fly. We didn't get a rating for the Boeing 314 flying boats
because Pan Am sold all of them to the navy at the start of
World War Two.

I. UNITED STATES OF AMERICA   III. CERTIFICATE NO.
DEPARTMENT OF TRANSPORTATION—FEDERAL AVIATION ADMINISTRATION
II. TEMPORARY AIRMAN CERTIFICATE   136219CFI

THIS CERTIFIES THAT   IV.   JACK WARNER BURKE
                       V.   13625 - 18TH AVENUE S.W.
517120883   SEATTLE WASH 98166

DATE OF BIRTH	HEIGHT IN.	WEIGHT	HAIR	EYES	SEX	NATIONALITY	VI.
08-07-22	68	156	BLACK	HAZEL	M	USA	

IX. has been found to be properly qualified and is hereby authorized in accordance with
the conditions of issuance on the reverse of this certificate to exercise the privileges of

FLIGHT INSTRUCTOR

RATINGS AND LIMITATIONS
XII.   AIRPLANES & INSTRUMENTS
        VALID ONLY WHEN ACCOMPANY BY PILOT
XIII.   CERTIFICATE NUMBER 136219 EXPIRES 06-30-75

THIS IS ☐ AN ORIGINAL ISSUANCE ☒ A REISSUANCE   DATE OF SUPERSEDED AIRMAN CERTIFICATE
OF THIS GRADE OF CERTIFICATE   08-26-71

BY DIRECTION OF THE ADMINISTRATOR   EXAMINER'S DESIGNATION NO. OR
                                      INSPECTOR'S REG. NO.
X. DATE OF ISSUANCE   X. SIGNATURE OF EXAMINER OR
                          INSPECTOR   SEA 1000
                       Duncan R. Shand   DATE DESIGNATION EXPIRED
06/22/73   DUNCAN R. SHAND   4-3-35

FAA Form 8060-4 (4-69) Supersedes Previous Edition

My Flight Instructor's Rating Certificate.

My Check Captain Certificate for Pan Am's 707s and 747s.

It was a great life, I tell you. I wouldn't change anything.

As I look back, I truly appreciate and thank the CPT program for helping me to "get paid for my hobby." It sure beat working! I disappointed my dad quite a lot because I was skipping baseball practice all the time and going up to the Miles City Airport. But when he went around the world with me, to London and Honolulu and everywhere, why, he forgave it all!

My dad also went up and spent a week with me in Alaska, flying up to the North Slope, where they were building the pipeline, and going back and forth to Nome, where we panned some gold. He always thought that was great.

He could sit right up there in the cockpit. The DC-4 had a seat for the flight engineer that pulled up between the two seats. They dropped it down and clamped it in, so the flight engineer sat between the pilot and copilot. He could reach the throttles, and do everything he needed to do from up there.

They didn't have a big flight engineer's station like they did on the Stratocruiser. We got to where we didn't use flight engineers on the DC-4, so we had that seat for Dad. He rode all around Alaska in that flight engineer's seat.

Dad also flew with me quite a little in the light airplanes, especially the Culver Cadet. That was a real machine. We had a cruise prop on it that was higher pitched, and it would go 150 mph.

And Dad always had that post card in his pocket. Every morning he would get that in the mail from Minneapolis. It had the price of the grain and all of that stuff. He was a great little Irishman.

To recap: I flew the old Fairchild Pilgrim on the Alaskan bush until I was twenty-one (1942 & 1943). Then I went to New York and flew the Boeing 314 "Flying Boat" as copilot (1944). When I came back, I flew the Lockheed Loadstar (1946) and Douglas DC-3 as captain in Alaska. I flew the first four-engine passenger flight to Alaska, the DC-4 in 1950. And I flew the last flight, when they closed the base up there.

I was based in Los Angeles. But Seattle and San Francisco had all the records. And they said that, as long as I had flown the first flight, why not fly the last one? So I flew a 747 up there. It was rather sad because we got all the company employees who were moving back, and a whole bunch of our "good ole" passengers. We were full; we had over four hundred people on that last flight.

Pan Am flew the 747 up there for about a year—but it was too big. When they decided to take the 747 off, they closed up the whole base in Fairbanks. There were a number of Pan Am people up there who were in Traffic, Dispatch and Maintenance—a lot of maintenance guys.

On my retirement trip, I went from Sydney to Auckland, New Zealand with a load of horses. You could pick any trip you wanted and take your whole family. But I had taken them around the world, so I picked this pattern; it was down in the South Pacific. It had one leg with a freighter on it; that way I could have Scotty in the cockpit with me.

We laid over in Sydney, then went down to Auckland and laid

over there. Another crew took it from there to the Coast. I had to retire at sixty. Just a year after that, they raised the retirement age to sixty-five. I would have gone just as long as I could have. I was able to pass the eye exam without glasses.

Opera House in Sydney, Australia, an eight-block walk from our hotel. We laid over in Sydney and enjoyed some fine shows here. Scotty went to Sydney often in the winter, where it was summer "down under."

Pan Am Boeing 747 cargo aircraft on the ramp in Sydney, Australia, July, 1982. Scotty flew with me to Auckland, New Zealand on my retirement trip. We were carrying a load of race horses. There was no one else on board except for two groomers, so Scotty got to sit in the cockpit with me.

Chapter 8

The Going Was Great

Nose First

THE jet airplanes have completely made the flying industry grow into almost a failsafe operation. You look at the thousands of flights made each day and for a number of years the U.S. airlines have not had a fatal accident.

The reason for the improvement is the safe jet aircraft and the excellent crew training and maintenance the Pan Am mechanics provided.

Once you signed that clearance at Dispatch, it was your airplane. And I treated it like it was my own; it was a multi-million-dollar toy. But when I signed that clearance, it was mine to get around the world. You had to know that Pan Am was putting a lot of trust in you, to give you that expensive airplane, and four or five hundred people.

You didn't have to have anybody tell you about all the passengers who were sitting behind you.

Often a passenger asks me if having all those people in the airplane makes me nervous, or concerned about the liability. I tell them that it really doesn't. If there is a big problem, I am riding in the nose of the airplane and would be the first to get there. So I sure don't want to run into a mountain, and I sure don't want to scratch the airplane. This thing is worth as much money as most corporations, and it's up here in the air flying around.

So I make sure that I am going to arrive without a serious problem, and the passengers will be right behind me on a happy landing.

We also will get the question: "Do you think pilots are overpaid?" Personally, I would have to say yes, because flying is not a job to me; it is my hobby, and it is nice to get paid for your hobby. I am sure there are many pilots who wouldn't agree with me.

I was flying a plane full of oil executives from Jakarta to Los Angeles International. One of the executives—he was kind of cocky, reading the *Wall Street Journal* upstairs in First Class—remarked that United Airlines had just signed a new contract with their 747 pilots, greatly increasing their pay.

"Skipper," he said, "have you seen this article?"

"Oh, yes," I said, "I heard that United had really gone overboard. It won't stay there, because they doubled their pay. They're getting twice as much as anybody else for flying a 747."

He asked me if I agreed with this. I told him I really didn't, because the 747 was so much fun to fly. Well, United wound up going broke; they had to restructure completely. "Anyway," he said, "do you think a pilot's worth all this money?"

"Well *I* don't personally," I said, "because flying's my hobby, and I would do this for *nothin'*. If I had enough money, I'd even buy the gas for it. I feel I'm terribly overpaid, and have been ever since I left the bush in Alaska.

"But there's two ways to look at this: If a 747 pilot screws up, and augers this thing in, everyone on the plane could buy the farm, and a $250 million airplane would be *gone*.

"But if an executive in a large corporation makes a bad mistake, their next quarter dividend would be smaller—but the whole *company* doesn't crash. So I guess what matters is the value one puts on the mistakes."

"Gee," he said, "I never thought of it that way." Most of the executives running these big corporations make more money by far than we do; and if they make a mistake, the company keeps on going.

I never got a scratch on that fancy machine. It's hard taxiing around, because there's other traffic around the airport, which is where most of the accidents happen.

I guess I am a little prejudiced because of my love for airplanes, but I do have one concern: the airplane manufacturing companies often come out with a fix that requires the airline to take the airplane out of service, and make a repair or even an engineering change.

With the FAA's approval, and a time limit date which is often too long, even up to a year or two can develop into more serious problems and even accidents. Get the politics out of these delays, and get the repairs done as soon as they are deemed necessary.

With our present recession and the airlines losing money, this problem could become larger than in the past. The problem never heals itself, and something like flexing, rust or corrosion can be serious if not corrected early. The airlines know where to look for these problems, and should correct them early before something breaks, like an explosive decompression in the fuselage—which has happened.

The fuselage is like a balloon. There is no pressure in it on the ground, but every takeoff and climb to altitude pressurize it to about eight pounds. So it stretches, then shrinks back to normal size on the descent. This happens many times a year on a short-haul airline, and should receive more attention.

'Auto' Pilot

I had this garage up in Juneau. Now that was a story, how I got into that. Prescott Boutelle's son was the first student I soloed. He was the only student I've ever soloed who had the engine quit on his first takeoff, by himself—after he had left the airport. He was just over the fence. But he landed in a grass field.

During the war, when I went home on leave, Prescott, who was the Cadillac-Pontiac dealer in Miles City, told me, "When they start building cars again, in 1945 or 1946, you can have the first car that we get in." In those days, they shipped them four in a boxcar. And I was home for Christmas. I always bid the December vacation because there was snow on the ground and we were hunting coyotes.

"Hey, I got a boxful of cars coming in while you're here," Prescott said. "Can you come help us unload them—and take your pick?" He told me what they were, and they had this Streamliner Eight. It really caught my eye. It was a four-dour, but it was streamlined. A beautiful car, black.

"Prescott, have you promised this one to anybody?" I asked.

"No," he said. "I told you all the times you came back on furlough that you'd have your pick out of the first carload. You can have it." It cost me, new, $1,865. Prescott let me have that one, when I was home for Christmas hunting coyotes; he let me have my choice out of the boxcar.

At that time, new cars were at a real premium. In order to buy a new car in Seattle, the dealers ordered them with all the junk on them; and then you had to have a good used car to trade in for a hundred dollars.

Well, on the way home, everywhere we stopped—to eat or for gas or a motel—somebody was trying to buy that car. They were offering me a thousand dollars more than I paid for it, they wanted a new car so bad.

"There's got to be a place where there are cars and no customers," I told Scotty. I thought about it and woke up that night from a dream. I woke up saying, "Nome! Nome!"

I woke Scotty up. "Are you talking in your sleep?" she asked.

"I just had a dream," I said. "I know the Harpers—Bud and Rita Harper in Nome. They've flown in and out of there a lot. And they had the whole General Motors franchise in Nome. They had all the cars: Chevy, Pontiac, Buick, Olds, Cad and GMC trucks.

"They have two ships up there in September," I said. "That's it for the whole year. And they only have a road from town to the airport. So I'll bet you they got cars."

So, as soon as I got home, I bid a Nome trip. It was a ten-day trip; we flew there every other night. I called Bud and Rita, and we were there four hours. And I said, "I'd like to go in and see ya, if you're not busy."

"Oh, come on in. I just baked a cake, because I knew that some of you crew members would be in to have cake," Rita said.

I went in and said, "You know, I got this new car from my good friend in Montana, and somebody tried to buy it all the way back. Do you have any extra cars?"

"Well, yeah," he said. "You know the military moved out of here. And I got *nothin'*, because you've got this road from here to the airport, which is only two miles. That's all the road we got. I've got eight down there in the warehouse I'm paying storage on. And I'd sure like to get rid of 'em all."

"Would you *really?*" I said. "Why don't you sign the eight titles for me, and I'll send you money for them in a week, because I'll sell them to the Pan Am people."

"Really?"

"Yeah," I said. "Keep ordering cars, cars without a bunch of stuff on 'em. Cars that you think people would like—get some two-doors and some four-doors. Just get as many as you can get. You know, everybody's on a quota now, so you get as many as you can get."

I put an ad on the bulletin board down in the hangar for these cars and the price on them. All he wanted, like mine, was the $1,860. I got rid of all those cars in less than a week, because all the traffic people parked down there by the hangar and walked by. So all the traffic people, mechanics and a few of the pilots saw it, too.

I deposited all that money in Bud's account—I didn't take any—and he and Rita came right down. "We needed to spend the weekend in Seattle, anyway," they said. "Now here's the kind of cars I've got that I can order," Bud said, "and here's what you might suggest I order. I'll just sign a bunch of titles and leave 'em here."

That's how I got in the car business. We had the whole GM line up there. It started in Nome. I was with Bud and Rita for maybe ten years, and then Bud died of a heart attack.

It used to be that, in the event of the husband's death, General

Motors let the wife take over the dealership. But now they recom-
mend that the wife sell the garage, because they usually sold it to a
friend, or some guy they had hired, and then it went to pot. In a few
years they would have nothing to sell. So they would rather say, "We'll
just sell it when it's worth a lot."

So Rita sold it and moved to Seattle. An army colonel in Alaska
bought the dealership.

The chief mechanic in Juneau was a good friend of mine. He and
his wife had the GM agency there; they had the whole GM line. She
was an accountant, and he ran the garage. That was called Conner's
Motor.

They wanted to double the size of the dealership, and put up a
new building. "Why don't you buy into the garage?" they asked me.

So they became my partners in the car dealership. The chief
mechanic handled the mechanical end of it, and she handled everything else. They were really, really nice people.

So I was in the car business in Juneau from then on. We went to
Juneau with the DC-3. It was too much time to go up and back. So
we went up and got off, and the crew would take back the one that
went up the day before. So you were up there from noon until the
next noon. So we went fishing, and it was great.

Juneau is a very small town, and all it had was a road out to the
airport. We couldn't have made it without the big Coast Guard base
there. The Coast Guard boys would start buying a car when they
arrived, paying for it. They would pick their car up in Seattle. Then,
when they left two years later, they had a car paid for and we had their
money all year.

Cars and airplanes were always my hobby. I used to hang out a
lot in the downstairs office in my home in Hurstwood, Washington.
When I was busy with the car business, that office was used mainly
for that.

We always had customers waiting for a Cadillac up to the half of
a year. So I would get a new Buick or Oldsmobile at the factory. As a
Cadillac dealer, I received a new car every year. In those days, the new

cars came out around the first of the year, between Christmas and New Year's.

In January, we would order a car so it would be ready for me at the factory. And I could ride Northwest to Detroit for nothing. On my way back east to pick up a car, Scotty and I would stop over in Miles City. She would get off there and visit her folks. I would go on to Detroit and drive the car back.

Highway 10—right out of Detroit is where it starts. I would get on Highway 10—they have those 'wheels' as you go around. The first time I was there to pick up a car, I got on that wheel and couldn't find out how to get off of it and onto Highway 10. A policeman saw that I was having trouble, pulled up behind me and blinked his lights. So I pulled over.

"Where are you trying to go?" he asked. I had an Alaska license on the car.

"I'm trying to get Highway 10 up to the ferry crossing," I said.

"Well, you just follow me," he said. "I'll lead you right to it." So we went around and he turned off, pulled over, came back and said, "This is Highway 10. Just keep right on going and you'll go right up to Ludington, and then it will take you across to Manitowoc.

"Where are you going?"

"I'm going to Montana to pick up my wife," I said, "and then back to Seattle."

"Well," he said, "can I make a suggestion? When you get into Ludington, the ferry comes in and it's there for five or six hours while we're unloading and loading. You can go on and get a berth, and pay the purser for it and tip him. Make sure that he gets your car on, and you can go to bed while they're loading, and then it's several hours across the lake. By the time you get to the other side, you'll have eight or ten hours' sleep.

"But just make sure you tip the purser, so that you don't get over there without a car."

So I did. And sure enough, I slept all the way over, and here the guy came in and woke me up. "Well, we're about ready to pull out from over here in half an hour, so I thought you might want to get your car." So I did that every time.

I got off over there around four or five o'clock in the morning, picked up Highway 10 and went into Wisconsin. As I came into this one little town, there was Joe's Diner, or whatever, run by a guy and his wife. So I would stop there and have breakfast, every time.

You could have bacon, eggs, hotcakes, toast, orange juice and the whole thing for ninety cents. So I always stopped there for breakfast, and I would drive that Pontiac—or Oldsmobile, whatever I would get in January—because we always had people waiting for the Cadillac until the middle of the year.

As part of this routine, I would spend several days in Miles City. I'd call Scheduling and say, "Hey, I'm here in Miles City. What do you need me for?"

And they would say, "Aw, take a week off." Pan Am was just unbelievable.

Then I would wait until the middle of the year and we started getting a few extra Cadillacs. I would sell my Buick, Pontiac or Oldsmobile and get a new Cadillac. I would go to the factory again— and we would get another trip to Montana.

So I went back to Detroit twice a year. In those days they charged you the full freight from Detroit to Seattle. It was about $600. Now they equalize it; all the dealers pay the same freight. Even the Detroit dealers pay freight. It's about $150—everybody pays that now, so the people on the coast don't have that $600 or $800 freight bill.

I quit going to the factory once they got the freight equalized. But I got two new cars every year. I sold that first one for more than I paid for it, because I got it for dealer's cost. Then I sold the Cadillac in September or October, for more than I paid for it, because a Cadillac stays up in price. Cadillac always filled the quota, and you would always have to wait for a Cadillac.

The only dealer that operated on a quota was Cadillac. We had Chevy, Pontiac, Buick, Olds and GMC trucks. I would drive that car until the middle of the summer. By that time we had supplied all of our customers that were waiting for a Cadillac.

You could go down and buy a Lincoln anytime. They sold only half as many Lincolns as Cadillacs. So that's how I got in the car business. I was in the car business until I retired.

With Alaska, it doesn't make any difference whether it's a Cadillac, Chevrolet, Ford or the biggest truck you can get; a license is still ten dollars. No sales tax in Alaska, either. So these people were getting an Alaska license. There weren't that many, so the state wasn't bothering them.

We also got an Alaska driver's license with the license plate. So I drove with an Alaska license for twenty years, because I paid income tax up there.

I got cars for many of the Pan Am people in Hawaii. In fact, I got Alaska cars for all the policemen in Honolulu. They buy their own car, then they get mileage for it. They just put one of those magnet lights on the top of the car. They were really sticking them for new cars in Honolulu, so it wasn't long before every policeman had an Alaska license plate. They didn't bother them.

When we lived in Seward Park, we had this one good friend, Chuck O'Brien, who lived next door. He and his wife were real nice people. Chuck was the president of Boeing's right-hand man.

Chuck was telling me one day that his boss wanted to buy a new Cadillac convertible for his wife's anniversary president. The local dealer couldn't get him one, and they were expensive. So Chuck came to me and said, "Can you get one from the garage up in Juneau?"

"Sure," I said. We never bought convertibles up there. We ordered just what he wanted. It was a fancy car, and I gave it to him practically for cost. The president called and wanted to meet me. Chuck had taken him the title and everything.

So I went down and he wanted to thank me for getting that car at such a good price—no sales tax on it or anything. "What do you drink?" he said.

"I drink diet root beer, usually," I said.

"Well, I have this case of champagne and case of scotch here that I was gonna give ya," he said.

"Well, really, that would be a waste of that good stuff if you gave it to me," I said. I couldn't drink beer after driving that beer truck. Any liquor—just a glass of wine—makes me sleepy. So I just never drank at all, except a glass of wine once in a while.

"Well, I've got something that I'll bet you won't turn down," he said. So he went and got me a nice metal statue of a 707 that's in my living room bookcase. Boeing gave those to the presidents of the airlines that they sold airplanes to. Later on he gave me a nice model of the B-52.

My 1936 Plymouth. We drove it to New York when
Pan Am transferred me there in 1942 to fly the
Boeing 314 boats to London.

Scotty and I with our first new car after World War Two, a 1946 Pontiac 8. Price: $1,860. From my friend in Miles City, Prescott Boutelle, Pontiac and Cadillac dealer.

My two-door Pontiac in front of our little townhouses near Lake Washington.

Airplanes and cars were always my hobby—and still are. I had an interest in a GM agency in Alaska for about 25 years. We had the whole General Motors Line: Pontiac, Olds, Buick, Cadillac and GM trucks. I took care of deliveries in Seattle and shipping to Alaska. This Olds is parked in front of our home on S.W. 170th, above Three Tree Point in Seattle.

I still have my 1968 Mustang, nice and shiny in our garage. The
kids learned to drive in our 1968 Camaro.

Cowboy Bob

George Askin, the oil driller who became my employer and
coyote-hunting partner, had a brother named Bob. They had a
ranch close to ours in Ismay. As a boy, Bob liked to ride the cattle,

especially the bulls. We all rode the calves and steers now and then, but nobody would ride the bulls with the big horns except Bob.

The ranchers didn't like that, because Bob was riding the fat off of their bulls! He was always in trouble because of that. But he would become one of the most respected cowboys ever, one of the top bull riders in the nation, and perhaps the greatest bronc rider of all-time.

Bob Askin was something else. He wasn't an outgoing fellow; he was fairly quiet. In those days, people didn't telephone, or have computers or anything. So it was pretty much just the rodeo and community, and of course where he lived, because he had this nice big ranch not far from ours. And he was breaking horses there all the time. Anybody who had a horse that they couldn't ride, they would bring it over and leave it with Bob.

Next time they came over, a week later, they could just put the saddle on him and take him home. We never let Bob break any horses for us, though. He was a little bit rough with a horse.

We broke our own horses. We just babied them. We got well acquainted with them, fed them apples. Finally they would let us do most anything. So we would put a saddle bag on. It was just a cinch; no weight or anything. After they got used to that, we put a saddle on, nobody on it. We never had a horse buck.

At the ranch, most of the kids broke their own horses. They just became a pet. And a horse is smart, but there are renegades in the bunch. And it was his ability to ride the renegades that made Bob Askin not only a big hero in the community, but, arguably, the "world champion cowboy" longer than anybody else.

In order to be a world champion cowboy, you have to enter all the events. Bob was not a big guy—about five-feet-eight or –ten and a hundred and sixty or seventy pounds—but he could ride. He was never injured, for about ten or fifteen years. He was rodeoing year-round, right up until he was in his late forties.

A lot of the cowboys said, "We don't know anybody who can judge a horse like Bob does." The people who really knew Bob

Askin, and rodeoed with him, said that it seemed like he could judge a horse as soon as it bucked out of the chute. He had the darned horse figured out, and was always ahead of the horse.

They said that as soon as Bob got on that horse, and it took a couple of jumps, he seemed to realize what it was going to do. There was a bunch of different horses that had never been ridden. And Bob rode every one of them.

You just never saw anybody ride like he would. Now they lean way back in the saddle. But Bob sat up just like he was sitting in a rocking chair. Bob was something else.

Rodeo legend Bob Askin won 13 straight saddle bronc riding competitions. "Bob Askin, 8 Diamonds." Circa 1925. Ralph R. Doubleday, photographer. Edith Jones Waldo Bliss Collection, Dickinson Research Center, National Cowboy & Western Heritage Museum, Oklahoma City.

Bob had some fantastic horses. For bulldogging, the horse can't come out of the chute ahead of the steer. The bull has to go out first, and get his head out. But Bob had his horses trained so that the instant the bull got its head out of the chute, Bob and his horse were right behind him.

Then Bob would bail off his horse right over the bull, grab the horns as he went over its head and just flip him. He wasn't strong enough otherwise, and they didn't make you put your feet on the ground. As long as the four feet were up, that was a "doggy."

But they finally changed bulldogging to what they called "steer wrestling." Then you had to drop down beside the steer, plant your feet on the ground and wrestle the steer down. And all the doggers got to be two- and three-hundred pound guys. So Bob retired from that event; but he was sure great.

During the height of his career, Bob competed at almost every rodeo, and nearly always won one of the cash prizes. He was the saddle bronc event winner for three years at the New York Rodeo in Madison Square Garden. He also won 1st place in Los Angeles, Chicago, Portland, Kansas City, Philadelphia, Calgary and Montreal.

During the 1920s and 1930s, all the big rodeos invited Bob to attend and compete. He had a solid reputation with both the rodeo producers and contestants. One of the movie stars, a cowboy down there, formed a rodeo. He took it to Europe. In London, where Bob was both a big money-winner and crowd favorite, he was asked to give a special performance for the Queen.

Bob rode the most notorious bucking horses of the era, including No Name and Midnight, becoming a living legend along the way. At one time he garnered 13 straight wins as a saddle bronc rider, managing to stay in the saddle on horses that many thought could never be ridden. He was no doubt the biggest winner in his day.

After spending a year traveling from rodeo to rodeo, Bob and his wife Helen bought a couple of sections of land south of Ismay on O'Fallan Creek. By the time Bob retired from rodeo riding, he and Helen and their family had a sizeable ranch.

All of us kids had a ten-dollar horse and a thousand-dollar saddle. Along with all the prize money Bob was winning, he would often get a silver-plated saddle. And he just put one of our names on it and sent it express. I got a call from the depot agent—we had to go over there for express: "Bob sent you a saddle."

So I went over to pick it up and it was a beauty. I rode with it for a long time. All of us kids around that area had a Bob Askin gift, a silver-plated saddle.

That's all he did for a living. But there weren't many rodeos during the winter, so Bob always came back to Miles City then. And it was ironic, because when Bob saw me he would say, "By gosh, it's good to see you Jack. But those damned airplanes—every time I see you, I think it's the last time."

And here he was, riding those nasty bulls, risking life and limb. He was busted up quite a bit, and finally had to quit riding. He made a lot of money, though. He traveled year-round. He was down in Dallas and he was in Chicago. The only thing was, he had trouble getting from place to place, because he wouldn't ride in an airplane!

Bob Askin was inducted into the Rodeo Riders Hall of Fame
in 1978, five years after his death. "Bob Askin." 1946, Ekalaka,
MT. DeVere Helfrich, photographer. DeVere Helfrich Rodeo
Photographs, Dickinson Research Center, National Cowboy &
Western Heritage Museum, Oklahoma City.

Most people don't know this. I haven't told anybody, but I'll tell
you:

There were two pubs in Ismay, the little town we had lived in.
They had a wide main street, and there was one pub on each side of
the street. George and I landed close to town; there was a field we
landed in. And we were walking up the main street—all four blocks
of it. We were going to have lunch.

It was summertime, and this one bar had nothing but a screen door on it. The door was open, and there were people standing there looking in the window. So George came up and looked in the window. Bob was in there, and he had had a couple too many beers. He was going around with a broken beer bottle, making people buy him beers.

Everybody was a friend of Bob's, but he would get carried away occasionally. So George went in and said, "Brother Bob, you've got to get on your horse and go home. You're not behaving right."

"No, way," Bob snorted. "I'm gonna have another beer. You're gonna get me one, George, or I'm gonna hit you with this bottle."

George was quite a bit bigger than Bob, and he was as fast as a cat. Bob took a swing at him; and as Bob spun around, George grabbed him by the back of his shirt and his belt. He was standing real close to the door, so he just threw him through the screen door.

The sidewalks were pretty wide in front of these places—about six feet. But Bob didn't even land on the sidewalk. He landed out on the gravel street—skinned up his nose a little bit. Didn't hurt him. And George walked out and said, "Now Brother Bob, get on that horse and go home." So he got on the horse and went home.

You couldn't rile George up; he had no temper at all. He was just like a big Saint Bernard; he was a great guy.

Tex Rankin

Tex Rankin was the best aerobatic pilot there was. He lived in Portland, Oregon. He had the franchise for the Seabee that came out. It was a Husky four-place built by Republic—they built one of the good fighters—but it was heavy.

It had gear on it, so it could land on a runway, and retract; and then it was a boat. It was underpowered, just because of all the stuff it had on it. Tex was taking off to demonstrate it to a customer, and just as he got in the air, the engine quit. No speed; it just went right into the river and killed him.

Tex Rankin did his stunt flying in this airplane for years. He was
killed in a four-place seaplane when the engine quit on takeoff
over the Columbia River, near Portland.

For years, Tex Rankin was one of the best stunt pilots. Tex
was the Seabee distributor of the four-place seaplane built by
Republic. It had retractable wheels, but was very under-powered.

Living Legend

Another celebrity I got to know very well was Charles Lindbergh. I spent a week with him in Fairbanks, Alaska just before I retired. I was heading up to Fairbanks one night with a load of stuff for the North Slope on a DC-4 freighter. We had our mailboxes at the end of the dispatch office. I was going through my mail when I noticed this tall fellow at the other end talking to the dispatcher. He looked familiar.

Finally the dispatcher came over and said, "Jack, have you got room for a passenger tonight on the freighter to Fairbanks?"

"Well sure," I said. "We've got the jump seat. Who is it?"

"It's Charles Lindbergh," the dispatcher said.

I kind of recognized him, because I had seen his pictures all the time. "The *real* Charles Lindbergh?" I said.

"It sure is," he said.

I couldn't believe it. "We have that lounge chair for him too, if he'd like."

If the weather was decent, one of us would get in the lounge chair right after we got the gear and flaps up, and he would sleep to Petersburg—that was halfway. You had the chair there so your feet were right behind the throttle, and if you wanted you could just wiggle his foot.

So I went down and introduced myself. "You know, this is a thrill for me," I said.

Charles Lindbergh truly was a "legend in his own time." After a half-dozen flyers before him had died in the attempt, he became the first person to fly nonstop from New York to Paris. He was just twenty-five years old when he accomplished this feat on May 20-21, 1927, flying The Spirit of St. Louis.

Overnight, Lindbergh became the first truly international celebrity, as the mass media spread the news of his historic achievement across the globe. He was awarded the nation's highest military deco-

ration, the Medal of Honor, as well as being named Time Magazine's
first Man of the Year.

Charles Lindbergh became the first person to fly nonstop from
New York to Paris, giving the international aviation industry an
overnight boost. The Museum of Flight.

Lindbergh's heroics sparked the nation's imagination and stoked
its appetite for aviation. Within a year of his flight, one in four
Americans—thirty million people—personally saw Lindbergh and
the Spirit of St. Louis on their nationwide tour. Applications for

pilot's licenses increased threefold, while the number of licensed aircraft increased fourfold. Between 1926 and 1929, U.S. airline passengers grew by 3,000%, from 5,700 to 173,000.

"After Lindbergh, suddenly everyone wanted to fly," said Elinor Smith Sullivan, 1930 Woman Aviator of the Year, "but there weren't enough planes to carry them."

I asked Lindbergh about his historic flight. The hardest part was staying awake, he said, because he didn't get any sleep before he left.

He was there on Long Island, New York, waiting for good weather. He had been up and back down, up and down. Finally he said, "It's not going to clear up today." So he stayed up. Well, it did clear up. So he went without any sleep.

But Lindbergh was no stranger to aerial adversity. He pioneered some of the first airmail routes, mainly from Kansas City to Chicago, where the weather was nasty in winter and not much better the rest of the year, with thunderstorms and tornados wreaking continual havoc.

He cracked up quite a few airplanes because the engines quit. He had to come down, but he never got hurt. When the civilian carriers turned these routes over to the U.S. Army Air Force, the military had so many crashes that they ended up giving the routes back.

Among his many positions, interests and titles, Lindbergh was a Pan Am vice president and consultant. "I've got all your books, and all your wife's books," I said to him at Dispatch in Seattle before our trip to Alaska. He and his wife surveyed all of our new flights, and wrote books on all of them.

"What are you going to Fairbanks for?" I asked. "It's forty-five below up there."

"That's why I'm going," he said. "I've had a lot of people, and a lot of meteorologists, tell me about cold weather. I've studied it, but I've never seen an airline operate in cold weather. I just want to go up and see the real thing.

"I'd like to ride up and spend the week with you," he said. I was going to be up there a week, going back and forth to Nome every other night.

I said, "Well, we only have a few trips a day in here. We've got a freighter now going up to the North Slope. But if you want cold weather, we got it; it looks like it's gonna be there all week."

The Northern Lights were beautiful that night as we looked down on them. "The Wien brothers are good friends of mine," I said. "They're original up here. They were the first bush pilots, the first to start an airline—Wien Airline—and they have a lot of flights. They're great guys. I'll take you over tomorrow and introduce you to them so they can brief you on their flights."

"What time do you get up?" Lindbergh asked me.

"Well, there's two hours' difference," I said. "We're getting in there around five in the morning, so I get up by noon, or before."

"Why don't you call me as soon as you get up?" he said. "Maybe we could go out to the airport to have lunch." So I did and we went out. I called the dispatcher and had him get us two down-filled mechanics suits and boots that they used in that weather. Then I took Lindbergh over to Wien's and introduced him to Noel and Sig. He spent the whole afternoon there.

Lindbergh didn't get out of that gear the whole week we were up there, except when we were on the airplane. And he stayed right with me. The nights we weren't flying, we ran a pretty regular schedule.

I had a Nome trip, and we had four hours in Nome on our layover. So he had to go to Nome with me. He went down to the beach in front of the hotel and did a little panning for gold. You don't often get a nugget, but he "got a little color," as the prospectors say.

While Lindbergh was with the Wien boys, I just stayed around Dispatch with the dispatcher. He had a little float plane, and I had been teaching him. It was too cold to fly that day, but Lindbergh didn't return until almost dark. We went back in, I rounded up the other two crews that were laying over from Seattle and we all went to dinner.

Of course, the other pilots were really impressed with Lindbergh, and asked him all kinds of questions. But he was very quiet and didn't talk about himself or brag. He would answer all of our questions, but wouldn't tell us about anything unless we asked him.

"You know, I heard you got to be kind of a fighter pilot over there," I prompted him, having heard about some of his exploits in World War II.

Because Lindbergh had increased the range of Pan Am's fleet by about twenty percent, Pan Am sent him to the South Pacific in 1944 as a civilian consultant. The P-38s, considered to be long-range aircraft, still had limited range, and had to turn around before the bombers they escorted reached their targets.

So Lindbergh went out to the Pacific, never having flown a P-38 before. He was checked out on the two-seater P-38, and allowed to accompany the other P-38s on their missions.

They had a radio frequency over which Lindbergh could talk with the other P-38 pilots, telling them what to do, what to watch for and to make sure they didn't burn any valves. Lindbergh would tell them, "Now, here's your head temperature, and here's what your manifold pressure should be."

This technique is similar to when a car engine 'pings' when going uphill. Airplanes have what's called a BMEP, which measures this ping. You don't want to have the BMEP too high, or else you're just pinging. But Lindbergh found out that if you just richen up the mixture, you can keep those heads cool enough so that you don't have problems with the BMEP, and it doesn't ping.

You just keep pushing the throttle up and pulling the RPM back. That really cuts down the fuel flow, if you can get that RPM back and have all the pressure you can on it. Lindbergh discovered that you could have that high pressure in the cylinder. As long as you didn't let the head temperatures get up, you wouldn't damage to the engines.

That's all he does: Just head temperatures!

Lindbergh was only in the Pacific a week, and the P-38s, using his cruise control and engine-leaning techniques, were going all the way to their targets with the bombers.

That's how Lindbergh developed Pan Am's cruise control, and had us using about one-fourth less fuel than anyone else. But, when I was flying with Pan Am, Pratt and Whitney thought we would damage the engines, so they canceled our warranties. But we never burned the valves or damaged an engine, because we did it all with head temperatures.

"Is that when you got into the dogfight?" I asked, referring to Lindbergh's stint in the Pacific.

"Oh, no," he said. "I was just flying along. I noticed a Zero go flying in front of me, and I pulled the trigger." That was about all he would say about it. But he shot down two of them.

In his six months in the Pacific in 1944, Lindbergh flew fifty combat missions, earning the respect and admiration of the military pilots with whom he flew, and making a significant contribution to the war effort.

Lindbergh was fantastic; he was always working on something. He was the sharpest person I've ever seen. He was not an engineer; he didn't even go to college, except for a year or two because his mother was a teacher.

I had a good time with him in Alaska. He was just great. It was really a lucky break for me to get a chance to spend a week with him.

Some years later I was in Pan Am's Chief Pilot's Office. Ralph Savory had retired, and I agreed to try a year in there. There was a flight that came in from London and landed in Seattle. Then it continued on to Portland, and the Portland passengers would get off. Then the trip would start in Portland, come up here and go on to London.

Just to keep my hand in it, I would fly that trip. Well, someone in the dispatch office said that Charles Lindbergh was on a flight that came in from London. He was going to Portland to do some lecturing. "Do you want to go and meet him?" they asked.

"Oh, I spent a week with him in Fairbanks," I said. "I consider him a good friend. But if you go out ahead of me, you tell him we've got a jump seat in the cockpit." This was on the 707.

When I went out, Lindbergh was sitting there in a first-class seat. "It's sure good to see you again," I said.

"Well, yeah," he said. "And it's not forty below, is it."

It was a beautiful day. I said: "Did you hear we had sunshine in Seattle and had to come see for yourself?"

"No," he said, "I got honkered into giving some lectures down at the University. So that's what we're gonna do."

Lindbergh was a real environmentalist. And Mount Rainier was just spectacular that day. Usually, if we took off to the north, we would turn left to go to Portland. But I called the controller before I left dispatch and told them that I had Charles Lindbergh on board, and that he would love to see Mount Rainier and look down the crater on top.

"Sure," the controller said. "And if you want to circle it, go ahead. We'll watch it."

"Well, we'll be just about the altitude of the mountain," I said. "Then we're going to climb on up."

Lindbergh thought that was great. He was looking down into Liberty Cap on the top of Mount Rainier. Then I climbed to 25,000 feet. A United DC-8 taxied out just ahead of us, took off and made the regular turn. At that time, almost all of the airlines were flying at 8,000 or 9,000 feet to and from Portland, because it's not very far from Seattle.

But Lindbergh, and Boeing, both said that no matter how short the flight, you should climb to the highest possible altitude, then go all the way in with the power off. That's the fastest, most fuel-efficient way.

I've gone up as high as 30,000 feet with a south headwind, then powered all the way off and descended. Of course, after we left the mountains on the flight with Charles Lindbergh, I climbed right on up to 25,000 feet. We have a distance-measuring device that will tune in Portland and just crank down the miles. It will tell you that you're a hundred miles out, ninety-nine, ninety-eight. . . . So that's what you can use for the descent.

I got just about to 25,000 feet when the mileage was right to start down. I just closed the throttles and down we went. We have what we call the "barber pole," which is the maximum speed. It is hard on the flaps if you get any more.

So I went right up to about ten knots below the barber pole. The copilot called the Portland tower to say that we were just about five miles north, and would like landing clearance. "Fine," they said. "You're number one to land. There's no traffic. There's a United behind ya."

We passed that United flight on the way down. We pulled up to the blocks. Our station manager and the dean from one of the colleges were with him, standing down on the ramp, waiting for Charles Lindbergh to arrive. And here he was looking at the fuel counters, and the total amount of fuel that we had burned, because that's when the price of gas had gone up so high.

Well, he said, you saved so many pounds of fuel on this trip over your flight plan.

All I had done, I told him, was to follow his and Boeing's pattern. That was what we all did at the Seattle base. "But none of the other airlines do it," I added. "We pass them all the time—and save fuel doing it."

Lindbergh was impressed that we were using his techniques—just one of his many contributions to modern aviation and global travel. He also pioneered and charted polar air routes, high-altitude flying techniques, and increasing range by reducing fuel consumption.

In addition, Lindbergh was a prolific and Pulitzer Prize-winning author, international explorer, inventor and environmentalist. And it seemed especially fitting for this pioneer of global aviation to visit the crew of Apollo 8 in December, 1968 on the eve of the first manned spacecraft to venture beyond earth's orbit.

Charles Lindbergh is buried on the grounds of the Palapala Ho'omau Church in Kipahulu, Maui. Scotty and I went out and found that out. I think Andrew Priester, the chief engineer, is buried there as well. It's just a little white church. The graveyard is in the front yard of the church.

About five miles of the road leading to it is not paved. And the church is beyond that. A sign there says, Four-wheel drive only beyond this point. But it wasn't that bad. We just had a rental car. We went to the church and I got a picture. There weren't very many big headstones there. Lindbergh's was just a little stone.

On it is inscribed a verse from Psalms 139:9: ". . . If I take the wings of the morning, and dwell in the uttermost parts of the sea . . ."

May 20,1927–May 20,1977

FIRST DAY OF ISSUE

Official Commemorative of the 50th Anniversary of Charles A. Lindbergh's New York to Paris Flight

TO JACK; THANKS FOR YOUR GUIDED WEEK LONG TOUR OF ALASKA IN THE 50° BELOW F. WEATHER & YOUR YOUR MEETING MY GOOD FRIENDS, THE WIEN BROOTHERS THAT ARE THE BEST .

I had the good fortune to spend a week in Alaska with this aviation pioneer and "living legend." Lindbergh "wrote the book" on flying for Pan Am and the industry.

High Roller

As I've said, I flew for George Askin's drilling company, and for J.P. Johnson. He owned the Chevrolet and Buick garage and some oil wells near Cut Bank, Montana. J.P. had a twin-engine airplane. He used to be an old-time pilot, but he didn't fly anymore. But anytime I came home, he had places he wanted me to go: up to see the oil wells, go into Great Falls and have dinner.

It was then that I was introduced to Tex Johnston, who served as a fighter pilot in the Italian Theater during World War II, and later became a test pilot for Boeing. He flew a stagger-wing Beech for Texaco out of Great Falls. They were about the fastest private airplane going; they would go 200 mph. It was a bi-plane; the bottom wing was forward of the top wing.

Tex didn't have an engineering degree; he was a natural. He was another one of those like Lindbergh, who could just put his finger on anything that the other guys couldn't figure out.

A.M. "Tex" Johnston, Chief of Flight Test for the Boeing
Company, helped bring the industry into the age of jet airliners.
The Boeing Company Collection at the Museum of Flight.

Tex Johnston was the one who barrel-rolled the 707. The engineering pilots would take the airplanes out and try to figure out

what was wrong with them. And if they couldn't do it, Tex would take the airplanes out and pick out things that they needed to fix.

Tex was doing the testing on the 707, the only one Boeing had. Both Pan Am and Boeing would have gone broke if that airplane had been cracked up, because they had all their money in it. And they did the same thing again with the 747.

Tex took the 707 over to Moses Lake to do his testing. I went over with him a couple of times. Nobody knew anything about this, except his crew. They unloaded everything off the 707, and Tex would go out and practice slow rolls. In a slow roll, you fly all the way around. You can't do a snap roll with the big ones. And Tex Johnston had that down great.

It just so happened that one of our pilots always rented the Sea Scout boat, and tied it up on the log boom on Lake Washington for the Seafair hydroplane races. We all would cook chicken and bring shrimp cocktail for the festivities.

Well, we happened to be tied up right next to Boeing's yacht. They have a beautiful cruiser. All these company bigwigs were there; you could tell by the way they were talking. We could hear them saying, "Now, Tex Johnston's gonna make a low fly-by here today with that new 707." It was the only one they had.

Well, here he comes, just right over everybody. And they were all saying, "Here it comes! Here comes our 707!" And Tex gets down close and starts that slow roll. And he had enough speed that he was able to climb it a little in the slow roll. Those guys just about fell off the boat.

They had some vice presidents over there, and they said, "Oh, no: what's happening? Is he having trouble? Is he gonna crash? My God—that's our whole business! We've got all our money in it! That crazy clown!"

"He's fired! He's fired!" one of the high mucky-mucks said, as they all moaned and groaned. "Who here can fire him?"

"Well, I can fire him," someone said. "I'll call him tonight and tell him he's fired."

"Okay, because if that airplane crashes, we're out of business. All our money's in it; so is Pan Am's."

Well, Tex went out, turned around and did it *again* on the way back. And the second roll extended over town. You are not supposed to do aerobatics over town. But Tex started the slow roll over Lake Washington, and was still going around in the roll when he went over downtown Seattle.

Pan Am's Scott Flower (left) in the cockpit of the Boeing 707, accepting the jet's logbook from Tex Johnston, Boeing's Chief of Flight Test. The 707 was the first U.S. jet airliner delivered to a commercial airline. Pan Am ordered twenty-three 707s, and began using them on transatlantic routes.
The Boeing Company Collection at the Museum of Flight.

Tex took the 707 to the airport. The Boeing execs waited for him that night. And they fired him. But the next morning they started getting calls from all the other airlines: "My God—what kind of an airplane do you have that'll do things like that? It must really be rugged."

Well, the airlines all started buying airplanes. So Boeing hired Tex back the next day. But I thought for sure those guys were going to jump off that boat the first time they saw Tex roll that irreplaceable 707.

That Beatle Gang

There's always someone interesting on the airplane. Or famous.

I flew the Beatles from London to San Francisco in August of 1964 on the first leg of their inaugural U.S. tour. I think it was the last segment of my round-the-world trip, a nonstop flight over the North Pole.

I didn't really know who the Beatles were. They were new. I had seen them on television a few times, but I didn't really have a clue who they were. I thought they were just a foursome.

I've never seen four such nice young boys. They wore suits and ties, were clean shaven and their hair was short. They were just down-to-earth types. Not loud or anything—really impressive kids. They wanted to help the stewardesses, so they were pouring coffee and serving people back there. The crew thought they were great, really nice kids.

During the flight, I went back and talked to them. They were real nice; they looked like high school kids.

As I've said, I didn't really know who they were. But before we got in at San Francisco, Dispatch called and said, "Jack, you're not going to be able to park at the terminal. This place is just mobbed."

"Well, what's up?" I said.

"It's those four passengers you've got on there," Dispatch replied. "They're all out to see 'em. So we're going to have you park over here at the hangar. We'll have the limo come over here to pick 'em up."

"How come these kids are so famous?" I asked.

"Oh," he said, "the young people just can't believe it."

"Well, I've never heard of them before," I said.

So we parked at the hangar, while nine thousand people were waiting for them at the San Francisco terminal, which was completely packed. I knew that the Beatles weren't just arriving and only going to sing in San Francisco. I thought that maybe it was something else. But I didn't wait to get a newspaper or anything. There was a Western or United Flight almost every hour from San Francisco to Seattle, and I was commuting.

I had them up in the cockpit, and I never even thought to ask about an autograph. And here my daughter was a teenager. When I went home, I said, "By gosh, Shannon, I wish you had been on the airplane with me today. We had that Beatle gang on board, really nice kids."

"Did you get their *autographs?*" she asked.

"No," I said. "Are they popular? Is their autograph good for anything? I didn't even know who they were."

"Ohhhhhh, my!" she wailed. "The Beatles' first trip to San Francisco—that autograph would have been worth a lot!"

I said, "Well, I didn't even know that they were famous until we got to San Francisco."

Needless to say, she was pretty unhappy with me for a while.

The Beatles got to be real musicians, as the world found out. They wrote some great music.

A Great Life

Because of the many interesting and exotic places we flew to, a lot of famous people traveled only on Pan Am. I met a lot of Hollywood people and celebrities on my flights. We were going from Honolulu to Sydney on the 747. It was a midnight departure, so they served a nice dinner right after takeoff. And it was a six- or seven-hour flight down there. About halfway through I decided to walk back and see what was going on.

I stepped out of the cockpit door and in the first two First-class seats were this movie star and her traveling companion. They were playing cards, and here it was three o'clock in the morning. "Why aren't you girls sleeping?" I asked.

And this movie star said, "You know, I'm a white-knuckle flyer. And I can't nap on the airplane at all."

"Boy," I said, "it's the middle of the night. You know, *I'd* like a nap. I got my seat empty up there. Why don't you go up—that's a more comfortable seat, even than this one. That costs as much as a DC-3. You can have it—just let me know before you get to Sydney."

"Don't talk like that! Don't talk like that!" she hollered. She was a kick. An elderly lady traveled with her. She had a walker, but was still making movies.

I took Will Rogers up to Fairbanks. Several real well known people. Spencer Tracy, I took him up there. He was going up fishing.

Jimmy Stewart, Spencer Tracy—they were nice guys on board. Jimmy Stewart went over to fly the B-17 during World War II. They tried to get him to instruct or something—not going over and getting *shot.* "Gonna do what all the rest of the guys do," he said. And he flew fifty missions.

I used to take a passenger, Brian Ladoon, up to Fairbanks. He lived near the ice floes on Hudson Bay, east of Churchill, Manitoba. He had several dozen dogs—Canadian Eskimos—which he valued most highly. Each dog had its own house, each with its own chain.

Brian used the dogs mostly for trapping and hunting, but he entered the dog races, too. He got acquainted with a prominent National Geographic photographer, Norbert Rosing, who flew with me up to Fairbanks on his way to visit Brian. "Be sure to let me know how it goes out there," I said as he departed.

So he did. He waited until I came back up, then went south with me. "We could not believe what happened," he said. Brian had kind of a cabin on the edge of the water, where they were sitting. That season, the polar bears, which relied on the ice floes for fishing and hunting, had not been having very good luck, because the ice had yet to form on the bay.

The fellow who lived there was afraid that the hungry bears were going to turn inland and go after his dogs. Sure enough, three big polar bears, each weighing over a thousand pounds, began lumbering up the shore. "Boy, I gotta get my rifle," Brian said, "because I'm gonna lose some dogs."

So Brian grabbed a big rifle. By the time he returned, two of the three polar bears had gone up the beach. One of them, however, approached the first dog, which had come right to the end of its chain. Brian was afraid the bear was going to eat the dog. Instead, the bear began to play with it. The dog just had a time with that bear, right up there in its face.

"By gosh," Brian said, "that bear was there for half an hour or more, and the other two bears just kind of sauntered on up the beach." Finally this crazy bear left his canine playmate and rumbled off to join the others of its kind. I couldn't believe it. I was going to hate to see him shoot those bears.

When the photographer from National Geographic got on board to come south, he said, "I've made some pictures here for you."

It's been a great life knowing and flying all these people.

Buckingham Palace

Ward Buckingham was my partner in the building on S.W. 152nd and 4th Avenue S.W. We leased the upstairs to Leavitt Brothers. The county wanted us to cut four feet off of the end of the building. At that time there was angled parking on the 4th Avenue side. I spent a whole afternoon with three guys from the county. "Well, it's a rule we gotta follow," they said.

"We're not cutting anything off of that building," I said.

"Well, if you buy parking footage within a hundred feet, that would suffice," they said.

The next morning I was going to Honolulu. One of the owners of Bartell's Drugstore and his wife were on board, riding in the front two First-class seats on the 707. After we got up and they finished dinner, I would usually go back and walk through before they put the movie on, in case anybody had any questions. The 707 was new then; nobody had them except Pan Am, which bought the first 27 Boeing made.

As I came out of the cockpit door, he stopped me and said, "Gee, we sure want to compliment you on this beautiful airplane."

"Well, this is a Boeing plane," I said. "Boeing builds them this way—and they fly just as well as they look."

We talked some more about the airplane and he said, "Where do you live?"

"I live in Burien," I said, "not too far from the airport, on top of Three Tree Point. By the way, we just bought this piece of property on the main street in Burien, at 4th and 152nd. They're moving the old house off, and we're going to put a building up.

"But I spent all yesterday afternoon with these clowns from the county. They told me I didn't have enough footage for parking; I had to cut four feet off of the west end of the building," which we hadn't yet built.

"Was that just for parking?" he asked.

"Yes, there has to be so much footage for parking, compared to the size of the building," I said.

"Yes, I understand that," he said. "What are you gonna have in there—a drugstore?"

"No," I said, "we've got Leavitt Brothers."

"Well, that new building going up across the street is a Bartell Drugstore. We have that whole half a block in front of the building." There was nothing else there. "When I get in to Honolulu I'll call my brother, who takes care of all of our legal matters, and have him call you."

So the next day I got a telephone call. He said, "My brother called from Honolulu and said to sell you ten parking spaces right up on 152nd, just across from where you're going to be building—for a dollar. I can write this up so that it will just expire in a year. The county won't even catch it."

So that's what we did. We didn't cut anything off the building, and Bartell's gave us the ten parking spaces for a dollar. They just reverted back to them after a year.

There were some stairs going down on the 4th Avenue side in the back corner, with a nice double door. The county said, "If you do that, you have to have some more parking, if you're going to have retail downstairs." We had listed it just as storage.

"Well, we don't want that, then," we said. "We'll just have it as storage." The face of the building was that poured exposed aggregate concrete—the big slabs they put up. The contractor framed that all in for the door, braced it all up for the steps to go down and everything, but didn't put any of that in. Then he just put one of those big slabs on the outside; you couldn't tell.

Here were these slabs all the way around the building; there still are, although they have painted them. The county never went in and looked up there at all. So we gave them a year, and no one from the county ever showed up. So we took that slab off and put in the doors and the stairs. And the county never bothered us.

There was a big old house on the property when we bought it. It had been there forever. It was the only structure between Ambaum and First Avenue—there was nothing there. And here was this big old house; it was vacant. There were a couple of fruit trees in the back.

We wondered about having to pay to move the darned thing. Well, the real estate person in Burien—there was only one in Burien at that time, and he was a real nice old guy—he did all our paperwork for us. "I'll take care of that house," he said. "I have a friend who moves houses, and I'm sure I can get him to move it, just for the house."

So that's what we did; he moved it someplace, and didn't charge us anything at all.

So we built a brand new building, one of the first on S.W. 152nd and the biggest in Burien at the time. Bartell's was building just ahead of us across the street, where the Dollar Store is now. That was Bartell's first drugstore out here.

We called our building Leavitt Brothers. They had a five-year lease, with a five-year option. Our real estate person who sold us the lot wrote up the lease, all one page. I went down with it and talked with the Leavitt brother who was the lawyer. It was a very simple lease, because the real estate person was not a lawyer.

So we signed it, and the next year we just made a new copy and put a new date on it and signed it; then they were in there for five years or so. We never had another lease.

The Leavitt brothers had a great big clothing store across the street from the Bon Marche downtown; it was four stories. They were just the nicest gentlemen I ever worked with. There were five of those brothers; they were all specialists. One of the brothers was a lawyer and did the negotiating. Another was a buyer, and another promoted the sales.

The factory salesman came out at the beginning and middle of the year. In the wintertime they came out with all their spring apparel to all their customers. And the factories that made all those ladies clothes went back, and they would already have an estimate set up for their production.

They always had some cancelations, so Leavitt Brothers bought everything that the different factories had when the new fashions came out. They got what the factories had not sold at a real good price.

So Leavitt Brothers got all of this good, new clothing the same time the Bon and everybody else got it—but for second-hand prices. Lee Asher, a great guy, was the store manager. Whenever they got a big shipment in from the factories, they would take all of the clothing off their hanging racks in the big back room and put the new merchandise on. He would always call Scotty and say, "Come on down; we just got a big shipment in, and we've got some good stuff here for you."

Then Scotty would pick out different outfits and they would just charge us their cost. She thought that Leavitt Brothers was the greatest place in the world.

Eventually the five brothers wanted to retire. They had been in our building for twenty or twenty-five years. They paid for the building for us in the first five years. They retired, and didn't want to lease anymore.

Our real estate person found another occupant who would lease the whole building. He wanted an option to buy within five years. We had had it long enough to know that there weren't that many people who would lease a building like that, because it was so big. So we put in the option to buy it; and by the end of the five years he bought it, and we got a fair price for it.

He had a little factory on the other side of the post office where he was making all the products for his wholesale beauty supply store. He furnished all the operators. It wasn't retail, but a lot of people did go in. He was a real nice guy.

Well, before the five years were up, he realized that he didn't need that big building. He wanted to sell or lease it, but it stayed vacant for over a year, because it was just too big for a restaurant or anything. He finally sold it, but only fairly recently, to the fellows who put the brewery in.

They had a business like that in West Seattle. They said that it was so small, but they were always full. So they bought the building from him and put in Elliott's Brew Pub.

Ward Buckingham and I were partners in this building on 152nd and 4th S.W. in Burien, Washington. Now a popular "Brew Pub," the building housed Leavitt Brothers Clothing Store for many years, as well as a shoe-repair business.

Ward Buckingham was my friend, neighbor—we both lived in Gregory Heights—and business partner. Buck didn't talk a lot, but he sure did do a lot. He was from Kalispell, Montana. We both instructed at the university there. He worked his way through the University of Montana in Missoula teaching flying, and graduated with an engineering degree.

We taught flying for Johnson Flying Service, which was known all over because they had the only school in the country for "smoke jumpers"—firefighters who parachuted in to combat forest fires. It was a large school. Johnson had a big contract with the navy; I think it was the largest. They must have had ten instructors.

Buck flew for Pan Am until the compulsory retirement age of sixty. He then went to the University of Washington and took a two-year medical course in correcting an alcohol problem. Most of the airlines would just fire a pilot who drank alcohol within the 12-hour window—a rule of which we all approved.

Pan Am had a lot of much money invested in a pilot's training: a week every six months; a month or more off of line flying to get qualified in a new airplane through ground school, simulator training and a route check. Pan Am would put any pilot who broke the 12-hour rule on a one-year medical leave. By the time the year was up, the pilot had to prove to the company that he was completely cured. Most of them did go on to retirement without another problem.

After Buck got his medical training, he spent the rest of his life educating the other airlines in the U.S. and around the world to use the Pan Am system, which has worked out very well, saved a lot of experienced pilots and a lot of money for the airlines.

Buck had a medical office in Burien, Washington, close to Sea-Tac Airport. When Buck passed away, his funeral was held in a large church in Burien. It was so full they had to open some side rooms. There were pilots there from almost every country in the world that had a pilot's crew base.

Shoe-In

The building that Buckingham and I built in Burien on S.W. 152nd had four big rooms downstairs. You could even drive in from the alley. Buck had a friend named Jim Nelson. He and his wife had a little shoe repair shop in Burien, and they wanted to expand. So he moved all of his equipment into one of those rooms downstairs. He and his wife were real doers.

Jim came to Buck and me one day and said, "You know, the elderly man who owns the big shoe repair store in the Bon Marche downtown would like to retire, but he's got an awful lot of equipment in there. He says that it costs a lot of money new, but it doesn't sell for that much used.

"He has six employees, all in wheelchairs, and he's had the shop for a long time. He would like to sell it to me, because I'll keep those handicapped employees. But he said that I don't have a hope at all of raising that kind of money."

"Well, Buck and I will go down and talk with him," I said. "We'll get his folder and take it to the accountant." So we brought it out to Ian and he said it looked real good, if we could get a decent price on any of it. "Well, we'd like to buy it," we said. "Just make us a price on it." And he made a real low price, according to what Ian thought.

So Buck and I bought it. We had Jim and his wife managing that one, too. In six months or a year, the Bon was so impressed with how things had improved that they wanted us to have a shoe repair at the Northgate store. So we didn't have to buy much equipment; we bought some good used equipment.

Then, pretty soon, the Bon wanted us over in Bellevue in the Bon Marche store there. So we got some more equipment, and we had the one in Bellevue. Then the Bon or one of the other department stores wanted us in the Tacoma Mall. So we went down there, and had these shoe repairs all over the area.

Jim and his wife were doing a fine job. She handled all the paperwork, and he managed the operation. We had handicapped employees in all the stores. That went on for a year or two, and they were just doing real well financially.

About that time, Pan Am decided to split the pilots' retirement from the other employees, because retirement age was 60 for the pilots and 65 for everybody else. You put in a percentage of your salary, and the company matched it up to 10%. Then you could put in more, which they didn't match.

Two of our pilots were accountants. They were CPAs; they were real sharp. "We'll work with the company," they said, "and keep the old retirement for what we've got in it." I get $99 a month out of that old retirement fund. "Then we're going to have a new retirement fund, so that we can put in 10% and the company will match it. We can put in as much as we want after that."

The two pilots were going to manage this, and they went into mutual funds. They just did real well, and we were all putting in more than the 10%.

We had just gotten a new increase on the pilots' retirement plan. Buck and I were having lunch one day—and I don't know whether Buck brought it up or I brought it up—and I said, "Buck, we're gonna have all the money we need out of that pilot retirement plan; it just keeps growing. And those two pilots who are managing it are CPAs and know the stock market, and it's just growing like heck. What does Jim have at the shoe repair?"

Jim was a good friend of Buck's, so Buck knew about Jim and his wife. "They don't have anything but Social Security," he said. Buck said that Jim had learned the shoe repair business when he was a kid in Minneapolis. He was delivering the morning papers, and this fellow in one little shoe repair shop invited him in to warm up. He got Jim interested in the business, and he started working there after school. So he had been in the business a long time, and of course he had no retirement except for Social Security.

I don't know whether it was Buck or it was me, but one of us said, "Well, we're not gonna need that retirement from the shoe repair business, so let's give it to Jim and his wife. So we did. We gave Jim all the shoe repair stores, all of them. We just signed them over to him; I think we sold them to him for a dollar.

They just couldn't believe it. When Buck called Jim to tell him that the shoe repair shops were all theirs now, Jim called me and said, "I just want to thank you for what you and Buck did," and couldn't talk anymore. So they were real pleased, and Buck and I felt good about giving the shops to them.

And Jim just kept those shops going. He always kept those handicapped people their. Most of them were in wheelchairs, but they had the equipment they could work with. He just did real well. And when he sold the stores just a few years ago, they retired first class.

So we were always pleased that we could help a kid who was delivering papers and repairing shoes after school like that. And he just couldn't believe that we were going to give him all those stores and all that equipment. Buck and I never regretted it, because our Pan Am retirement was always good.

Home Front

We used to live in Gregory Heights, above Three Tree Point on Southwest 170ᵗʰ Street, about three miles west of SeaTac Airport. We bought the lot in 1950 from the older couple next door. It was $2,500, and we paid $12,500 for the house. So we got into that whole thing for $15,000. We just figured we didn't want to go through another war having to rent. And it was the best buy we ever made.

Of course, it's a nice view up there. You look right down the Sound, and catch Mount Rainier also. We loved it. You know, the boats cut in close down there around Three Tree Point. You could see the guys on the deck.

Our first house in the Burien area, on S.W. 170ᵗʰ
above Three Tree Point.

My builder, Kinny Leonard, was just fantastic. He had a real nice office. One whole wall just full of pigeonholes, a plan in each one. They were all numbered, so you could see the ones that they were building and go in and check the plans.

Scotty and I wanted to build some on the golf course back in Montana. So Kinny said, "Come on in. The office is open all day. Just pick out anything you want, take it home and copy anything you want."

So we put our ideas together and got the four townhouses back there on the golf course—because of Kinny Leonard. He wouldn't let us pay for any of this stuff. It was nice because you could go in there and pick out a plan and see the number of it, and then go over and they were building it.

I just thought the world of Kinny Leonard and his dad. They were great. The brother was good, too. But he didn't work with his dad; he was on his own. He built more expensive houses in Normandy Park.

So it was great, and you just wouldn't believe it. That little house was about 1,800 square feet. It had three bedrooms, two baths, hardwood floors and a double-car garage. It had a shake roof, stone part way up and then big, hand-split cedar boards. It was really well built.

Those were good old days. And it was a kick, you know. It would snow, and I never, ever had problems getting to the airport. I could go down 170th, down to the beach. As you climb up off the beach on the far south end, it was all covered with trees. There was never any snow on the road, and I never had a pair of chains on—ever.

People were getting over there to work with chains on, and having an awful time. And I said, "Well, we just came from Three Tree Point. There's quite an 'S' hill coming out of there, but there's a whole bunch of trees over it, and it's just like a tunnel. There's no snow in there."

But 170th is a pretty good slope, and there's a lot of traffic in there now. And we had adopted two little kids. We adopted a little girl when she was three days old. And a year later we adopted a little boy who was three weeks old. And you could not keep him in the fence anywhere. He would get out on that road and they'd come down that hill. So we decided that we just had to get off 170th.

We lived there until we couldn't keep Shawn in the back yard any longer. Then we moved over here. But we kept the house on 170th and rented it to a United purser. He was a nice guy, but he couldn't even get the lawnmower started. I would have to go over there and start it for him. After a couple of years of renting it, he wanted to buy it. So we sold it to him for about $25,000—just about double what we paid for it.

That house just kept getting bigger and bigger. Somebody added on to the dining room and the kitchen into the back yard. I went over when the owners were doing that remodeling. I think they paid $150,000 for the place. They were going to do the add-on, then put it on the market for $250,000. With that view, it was just amazing.

Howie Gwynn, one of our pilots, developed Hurstwood, right above Seahurst Park. I was having lunch with him in Hong Kong, and he said, "I've got some real nice lots up there on the ridge, on 18th. I've been selling stocks and bonds to pay for this as I went. I've run out of money, except for three good stocks. I don't want to sell them, so I'm going to sell three lots on the view side of 18th, up above, on the water side."

I think he said he was going to sell them for $8,000 apiece. But those three, he wanted to get rid of them so he could blacktop the roads. So he sold them to us for half that—$4,000. As you come up on 18th, on the bend, they are all 85-foot lots, and 100 feet down the bank. But that one is 140 feet, because it's on the bend.

We lucked out on building this house, because it was a time when things were kind of quiet. It was nice to have Dick Wagner, my next-door neighbor, do the wiring. He sure did a good job of that. My dad always told me, "Don't under-build the lot." And if you got a real good lot, that will really increase the value of the house.

Scotty's flowers and my Japanese black pines that I flew from Tokyo to Seattle in the cockpit. Now about forty years old, they were much smaller—about four feet tall—then.

Scotty's roses in foreground. In background are my Japanese pine trees, pruned and shaped every fall, around September.

Snow covers our deck and the trees behind our Hurstwood,
Washington home.

A nice contrail at sunset above the Olympic Mountains and
Puget Sound, off the deck of our Hurstwood home.

Cooking T-bones on our charcoaler in the kitchen.
The kids wouldn't eat anything that wasn't cooked on it.

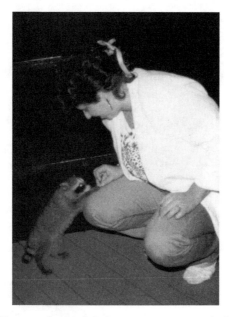

Shannon feeding a baby raccoon on our deck.

Raccoons having their dog food dinner on our back patio.

Caught taking a "catnap" after an all-night trip to Fairbanks. We left Seattle at midnight and got back around seven a.m.

We built some condos on the golf course in Miles City; they are the only rentals on the course. They're big, 1,800 square feet. They are like this house; there's an upstairs and a downstairs. You don't have to go downstairs. There's a big rec room, a kitchenette, a big bedroom and a bathroom downstairs, and an open stairway that comes up.

Upstairs you have a bedroom, bath, living room, dining room, kitchen and laundry room, so you don't have to go downstairs. We thought we would spend half our time there and half in Redondo, where we have a condo near Salty's on the top floor. We look right down at the fishing dock they have there. There's a lot of activity there.

So we thought we would spend the summer there and the spring and fall in Miles City, then go south in the winter, and just sell the house.

Our four townhouses on the golf course in Miles City, Montana.

This house is a lot to keep up. But it's nice because it has radiant heat in the slab downstairs, and hot-water heat—baseboard—upstairs.

An architect who lived near us in Gregory Heights said we were going to have to put in two furnaces. A large one wouldn't be that efficient. It would be better to have a furnace for the upstairs and one for the downstairs.

The builder was building ten real expensive homes over in Bellevue. When he looked at this plan he said, "You know, I've got an idea on this heat. I'm putting American Standard instant hot water in all ten of those homes in Bellevue. I got a real good buy; I can add another one. I can put in American Standard hot water."

The furnace is a little bit smaller than a dishwasher. It only has a five-gallon boiler; that's why they call it instant. It heats right up and cools right down very quickly. So he put that in for less money than the two furnaces would have cost. And we've never had a service call on it.

The furnace has two motors; one runs for the circulation up here, and one for the floor downstairs. We can change the temperature of both places. We just keep the basement floor at about seventy degrees. It's nice to walk around without any shoes on.

The kids thought it was great because we didn't finish the downstairs when we built the house. We plaster-boarded everything, but that was all. We put paneling on after the kids grew up. But then they had that warm floor; we didn't put anything on that. Later I put some vinyl on it.

The kids from up the street would walk up to that little school with Shannon and Shawn. On the way home they would all stop here, go downstairs and have a nice warm floor to sit on. We had a TV, a ping-pong table and pool table down there. And there is a nice big fireplace on one end, underneath the upstairs fireplace.

We had some furniture around that, so they could all sit there and watch TV. They all stopped by; there would be half a dozen kids down there after school. They would just call home and say they were visiting Shannon. "What time do you need us home to eat?" they would ask.

Scotty thought it was great because they were all right there.

Snakes and Elephants

There's one thing I can't stress enough: what a fantastic company Pan American was. They bent over backwards, not just with the pilots, but with *all* the personnel. In those days, there were always first-class seats open—because those first-class seats were expensive, to go international. But whenever we traveled, we always rode first-class, and they charged us *nothing*.

I took the kids all the way around the world; we spent a whole month traveling First Class. We had the same four first-class seats the whole way. Pan Am on traffic somehow listed it that we were on vacation, and they wanted these four seats.

I wanted to take the kids when I wasn't flying, because I wanted to show them the countries. During spring vacation they had two weeks off. I called the principal and said, "Can we have another couple of weeks if I take the kids around the world?"

"Oh, boy," he said. "If you've got room for another kid, I'll go with ya."

I had my vacation, so we did. Before that, we always went to Honolulu for spring vacation. But by that time there were several airlines competing, so the fare went down, and Honolulu seats would all sell out. So then we would go to London for the week. Then to Paris for the week. Then to Rome for the week—on different spring vacations.

Well, on this one we had the whole week. We skipped London, Paris and Rome, because we had spent a week in those places. So we went to Beirut, Lebanon and to Israel, and then to Karachi, Pakistan, New Delhi, India, Bangkok, Thailand, Hong Kong, Tokyo, Honolulu and home.

And do you know that of all those stops, the kids liked New Delhi, India the best.

The Sikh tribes are in northern India. They are part of India; but they don't admit it, and neither do the Indians. So they have had a lot of wars up there. But the Indians have never defeated these Sikh; they're tough.

A lot of those Sikhs have their own cabs. And, of course, we laid over on our around-the-world regular trip; I laid over there once a month. So any time I wanted to go somewhere, I would go down to the desk and the gal at the desk would get me a Sikh driver.

The kids and I wanted to go up and see the Taj Mahal. So I

asked the gal at the desk—we had this good Sikh driver, we called him Billy; I don't know what his real name was—"Is Big Bill the Sikh gonna be available tomorrow? I'd sure like to have him take us up to the Taj."

"Well, let me see," she said. "I'll call him—yes, he's available tomorrow."

"Can he pick us up here in the morning?" I asked.

"Sure."

"Have him bring just a normal-sized car." I think he had a Ford. "There's going to be four of us."

Big Bill really showed us a good trip up there. It's over a hundred miles to the Taj Mahal.

The little Indian kids are afraid of the Sikhs, too. Whenever you stop, these little Indian kids come—they're little beggars, you know—and it's sad; it really is. And when that Sikh driver got out, they all disappeared.

On the way up there, Big Bill said, "I know a fellow who trains elephants. We can get an elephant ride there." So he veered us off a little bit and went in. And this fellow sold elephant rides, so both kids got to ride the elephant. The kids were teenagers at the time.

Then he took us off on another little jaunt where this fellow was training and playing with cobras—the big snakes. He took quite a long time to get up to the Taj. He took some side roads.

Finally, we got to the Taj Mahal. You have to take your shoes off to go in the Taj. Of course, the Sikh driver went in the Taj with us, and we all took our shoes off. Then all these little kids came, because they want to take our shoes. But as soon as they saw that Sikh driver, they disappeared.

We hired Big Bill the next day to take us down into Old Delhi. Right at the edge of Old Delhi, New Delhi is a suburb. It's grown up and it's first-class out there. But Old Delhi offered the kids a chance to see the "real" India. There were dead people lying in the gutters. And smelly down there. It was sure something else, but it really opened my kids' eyes.

Big Bill went with us to Old Delhi. Of course, all the Indians recognized that Sikh turban, and they all steered clear and didn't bother us any. But it's a different world.

Anyway, at the end of our around-the-world trip, I asked Shawn and Shannon what they enjoyed the most. "New Delhi," they said—because of the snakes and elephants.

Family Ties

Our son, Shawn, was a real fisherman. He would sit out there on the rocks all afternoon. If there weren't any salmon running, he would fish on the bottom and come in with some flatfish.

We had a little fishing boat that we used here. Shawn and his buddy would go out. If Scotty needed them to come in, she would go out and wave a dish cloth. Then Shawn wanted a sailboat. When Shawn got older, we bought a new Hobie Cat for a couple thousand dollars. We kept that boat here in the back yard. We would take it down right in front of the house and put it in.

Shawn and his buddy Jim would sail it over to Vashon for lunch. They would go across the Sound with one pontoon in the air, and one of the guys sitting on it. Those Hobie Cats are a kick; it doesn't take much wind to get one pontoon right up in the air, and they'll go by a lot of motorboats. They really go.

They sailed it a lot. Scotty didn't like it. It was too tippy, so she wouldn't sail it. Shawn really got a lot of use out of it, though. Shannon didn't take to the boats much. She just liked to sun bathe and swim. She's a good swimmer.

Hobie Cats are easy to right if they upset. We bought it down at Lake Union, and a good friend of Shawn's lived on Lake Burien. His dad was a dentist. They could pull the boat right up on the lawn.

For the first year, we put it in the water down at Lake Union, went all the way through the locks and came up to Three Tree Point. Then we picked it up and got it up to Lake Burien, and left it there for the year. That way they could go out every day, upset it in the lake and turn it right back up.

Both the kids are good swimmers. An apartment complex near here had a swimming pool. During the summer you could buy a season ticket for it. There were some real nice young gals there who were teaching. Shawn and Shannon were about five or six years old when we got them swimming up there.

They closed the Burien Gardens pool, but Rainier Golf Course had a nice pool. They will sell you just a recreational membership, because I've never golfed. And we used that for about four summers. They had a hamburger stand right there, so the kids would always want to go over there for lunch.

They usually had some college kids that were teachers, and they were good.

Growing up, Shawn gave us a scare a time or two. Shawn and his friend Jim, who lived up the street, built a tree house in a big tree that they eventually had to cut down because it was rotten.

Jim was putting down the floor, and Shawn thought that it was nailed down. He stepped on a board; it was on the high side. He fell down the bank, landed in the bushes and broke his arm. He went to school with his arm in a cast, and everybody signed it.

Two or three weeks later, on a Friday, Shawn had the cast taken off. Then on a Saturday—there were a lot of vacant lots up here—he and Jim made a bicycle jump. They'd been watching daredevil Evel Knievel.

So they made a jump up there, and the bike got away from Shawn and he augured in. He was protecting the arm that he had just gotten out of the cast the day before. He put the other arm out and broke it.

I was out on a trip. Scotty had to take him to the doctor to put a cast on the other arm. When he went to school on Monday, the teacher looked at him and said, "I thought that cast was on your *other* arm."

"There was one on it," Shawn said, "but I broke this one yesterday."

My kids are just great. Shannon comes in and spends every Sunday with me, takes me grocery shopping and whatnot. And Shawn has spent every night here since I broke my hip. He's got a real nice condo right around the corner. It's got a view like we have. It's not quite as expensive, but it's nice. He'll go out to his karate class or to his dancing class or something.

Often he'll call and say, "Have you eaten?" If I haven't, he'll stop and bring me dinner. If he doesn't call me, I'll fix something here. He's been here every night, and he gets up early in the morning and goes down to work at the Seattle Water Department.

He's a respiratory therapist. He went through school; has a certificate. He's an outdoorsman. He climbs mountains, skis and does judo and karate. Scotty finally got him started dancing. He goes to a dance class once in a while.

Shannon just turned fifty on her last birthday, and Shawn will be forty-nine on his next one. They're just a year apart, and they're great kids.

Shannon has two boys. Neither of them knew what they wanted to do. So I said, "Well, go to Highline Community College—that's where Shannon and Shawn both went their first two years—until you decide. Because you're not going to one of these expensive colleges until you've made up your mind.

We were able to put our grandkids through college. I didn't have much stock except Paccar. Most people didn't even know what Paccar was. They were the largest builder of refrigerated railroad cars in the world. During World War II, they were building tanks and trucks.

My oldest grandson—Jesse—he's a big guy. His baby is less than a year old. My great-granddaughter, she's a doll. She's something else; she is just a kick. She has a big smile, and I've never heard her cry. She doesn't like baby food, and she's as healthy as she can be. And she's a doer. She's trying to talk: "Mama . . . Daddy."

She's interested in my hair, because she doesn't have any. She gets a kick out of all that woolly hair I've got. She'll reach and laugh at me, I'll go over and she'll muss up my hair. Every time I stick my head around the corner, she laughs.

Now she is trying to walk, but she has to hang on to something to stand. She's pretty wobbly. She crawls, but she uses her feet instead of her knees. Her rear end is up in the air, and she just goes.

So Jesse went to Highline Community College for two years. He had no idea what he wanted to do, other than he thought it would be a good idea to be a chef. He always loved to cook. He's done a lot of cooking for his mom.

There was an ad about this new chef's academy—a nice, big, two-story building down at Southcenter. It's a one-, two-, three- or four-year college. If you don't have any college, you can start right in there and get your chef's training along with your college. They've got state-of-the-art equipment there, and they really put out a top chef.

"That's what I'd like," he said. So he enrolled, took the one-year course and graduated this year. He got a job right away. He's a chef at a restaurant in Auburn. He's doing well. He has us down every once in a while. He knows that I like corned beef. He finds a real good piece of corned beef and fixes a nice dinner for us; he cooks it up.

Junior's just starting college now. He's not sure what he wants to do. He says he wants to be a coach to a wrestler. Imagine that! I said, "Well, I think most of those wrestling coaches are wrestlers themselves. You're not big enough to get thrown around like that." But he thought that would be a really good occupation—being a wrestling promoter. So I don't have a clue what he's going to do.

His girl, all through high school, has been a lifeguard at the big pool in Federal Way. Real nice gal.

We had this great big, hundred-pound, black-and-white collie named Lady. Shannon picked her out of a batch of pups that a woman had raised; they were registered collies. They were long-haired collies. Lady was woolly; she had long hair. Shannon picked her out because she was the only black-and-white one in the whole batch. She was just a little thing, a couple of months old. That was Shannon's dog, but she liked everybody.

She was a doll, but she was big. She knew when school was out, and if she happened to be sleeping, and the kids walked by, she often ran out and lay on the end of the driveway. If there were any school kids going by, she would bark, and they would have to come up and pet her.

She was my buddy, because I gave her chocolate drops. She was something. She would lie out there on the end of the deck so that she could see out on the road; she could see the water and she could look out on the road. She was beyond the window, and she couldn't see me in here.

In the evening, Scotty kept her Hershey's cooking drops in the bottom drawer. I could slide that drawer open so quietly that it never made a sound. I could get those chocolate chips out and not make a sound. But as soon as I got them out and set them up on the counter, I would look and she would be standing at the door, wagging her tail. She knew every time.

Chocolate isn't good for dogs. But I would give her about half a dozen, spread out on the floor so she would have to pick them up. That was fine; she would go back out. But boy she was right there for those chocolate chips.

Lady was kind of the neighbor's dog. We had a lot of snow one time. We had a toboggan and a sled that I would always get out for Shannon and Shawn. The rest of the kids in the neighborhood would come down to get them. "Is it okay if we take Lady with us?" Well Lady was getting older and she was heavy, but she would go up the road with them.

Usually they would bring her back in about an hour. "Lady got tired," they would say. She wouldn't get out of the road; she would just lie there. So we put her on the toboggan and she would be out here lying on the toboggan. They had pulled her back down, so I would get out and help her. She would come back in the house, having had enough sledding with the kids.

Lady lived to be fourteen; that's old for a big dog.

Shannon and our two collies.

Shannon getting horseback riding lessons in Montana.

Fish caught by Shawn and me on one of our trips
to Westport, Washington.

Happy Landing

The Clipper Pioneers, a group of former Pan Am pilots, have a get-together every fall. Three times in a row we had cruises. Scotty and I went on all the cruises, because we had never been on a cruise until we went with Pan Am.

We went to Mexico. We got on at San Diego and went down to Mexico and back. Spent a week. They cruised during the night, and then went in to all the different spots. We went straight down to the tip, then made the stops on the way back. It was a ten-day affair.

We also took a trip where we flew to New York and spent one day touring New York City. Then they got us on a ship, and we went up the New England coast and up the St. Lawrence River, all the way to the end of it, in Canada.

One river flowing into the St. Lawrence was large enough that a big cruise ship could go up there. Whales raced along the sides of our ship, eight or ten on both sides. The whales would want to stay ahead of the boat. The skippers sped up and the whales would slow down. It was a great cruise.

I get the Clipper Pioneer magazine every month. The pilots put it out themselves. I'm lucky, too, to have Hap and Donna Holdtrip, who keep a lot of Pan Am information. They've been taking care of the luncheon we have every other month for all the Pan Am people who are in the area. They get a bulletin out to them about two weeks in advance with the date and where it is, and make the arrangements for it. They do it all.

But I've never strayed too far from my Montana roots. Over the years we had three light planes—a Luscombe Silvaire, Culver Cadet and Air Coupe, all two-seaters—that Scotty and I flew back to Montana several times a year. It took us three hours to get to Missoula, where we would gas up before going on another three hours to Miles City. Six hours in the air was certainly better than two days in the car.

Scotty never did get to like the little airplanes, even when she was flying them. She would ask me a dozen times each trip when we were over the mountains: Where would we land if the engine quit? That was a good question.

The Culver Cadet, for example, was fast, but it could be tricky. Private pilots had a lot of trouble with it because it had retractable gear. It was a mechanical gear; you cranked it up. If you tried to raise the gear too soon after you took off when you were climbing out—it just had a little wheel below, and you would unlatch it—you could lose control. You could see the guys were cranking up the gear because they would be swerving and diving.

Scotty and I with our Air Coupe in Miles City with Mark and
Keith Trafton, our nephews.

Cliff Boutelle (left) and I flew out to Doug Randall's place—a nice
ranch near Broadus, Montana with the Powder River running
through it—and landed in his hay field. Doug's wife is in the
picture. The airplane is a Luscombe. It had a cruise prop and a
large engine, so it cruised at 150 mph. Scotty and I flew it from
Seattle to Miles City several times a year.

Our Culver Cadet that we flew from Seattle to Miles City on summer trips.

Twin-engine Cessna "Bamboo Bomber" owned by a pilot friend, Keith Petrich. I used it to get friends twin-engine ratings.

On our way back to Miles City, where Scotty and I went about six times a year, we quite often would drive to Missoula and spend the night. Once in a while we would drive straight through to Miles City. We would go down and eat in the restaurant in the hotel by the river in Missoula. And every time, we saw three or four people that we knew. The whole state of Montana is big, but it's like a little town. It hasn't changed. There really isn't much industry there except cattle; it's ranching country.

I think Scotty and I would have enjoyed living in Miles City if all of our friends hadn't died off, because people are the most important. I knew everybody in the east end of the state.

I'm on the "Wall of Fame" in Miles City at the Range Riders Museum. They have a large hall and stage, which they also use for a big dining room. All around the wall are eight-by-ten pictures, about four high. You have to have a brand in order to be up there, just a cattle mark. My folks are there; Scotty's folks are there, too.

The manager of the Range Riders Museum is a good friend of mine. He was with Scotty in school. His dad was one of the oldest ranchers in Miles City. He worked with his dad and his sister following rodeo roping. He did pretty well in the summertime. He stayed right there out on his dad's ranch. His dad retired, and spent half his time at my dad's mill, sitting up there in one of those easy chairs, watching the old ranchers come in. Those old ranchers were a bunch of nice people.

The museum wasn't really doing anything, so finally somebody talked Bob into coming in off the ranch and running it. He has really done a great job—and he's still there.

I know so many of those ranchers, because when my dad quit ranching in Ismay, he bought those twin elevators and a feed mill in Miles City. All of the ranchers came in there. Dad had a fairly good-sized office with some old leather chairs. The retired ranchers had moved to town and that was their library. And they were *always* up there.

We had dinner at the Range Riders Museum. They had a whole beef barbecue, no charge for the dinner. The gals made desserts. But I don't think I had one bite of the meal that was hot. As I've said, when I flew for George Askin, the well driller, we would land out in the field right where he was drilling. While he was taking care of the problem or tending to business, pickups full of kids would arrive.

So I took all of those kids up and flew them over their ranch so they could see it from the air. That's why my food got cold at the dinner. Every time I went to take a bite, somebody would smack me on the back and say, "Jack, do you remember that first airplane ride you gave me?"

Of course, I didn't have a clue who they were. But it was a real nice afternoon and evening. Just so many friendly people there.

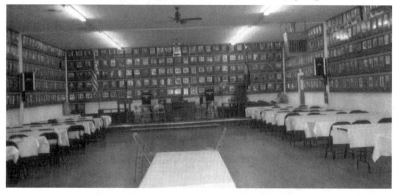

The Wall of Fame at the Range Riders Museum in Miles City, Montana.

My dad, John "JC" Burke, on the Wall of Fame in the
Range Riders Museum.

Scotty and I on the Range Riders Museum Wall of Fame.

I'm eighty-eight, but I don't feel like it at all. I'm not going to quit flying. I don't fly much here in the Seattle area, just because there's so much traffic. In the summer of 2009 I even took up a new kind of flying: sailplanes. Brent Stillings, the son of a friend who worked at Boeing, gave me lessons, riding the updrafts above the ridge of hills east of Arlington, Washington.

Brent was working on his instructor's rating, and I lucked out being his student. Flying sailplanes is a kick. The only sound is the rush of the wind and the whistle of the air as it goes by. Sailplanes are a big improvement over conventional gliders. They are light but strong, and have more wing surface. You can do loops and dives, and stay aloft for hours at a time. Some sailplanes have even gone almost across the entire U.S.

Unfortunately, Brent passed away from cancer during the past year. He was a member of the Boeing Airplane Club, and stayed in good humor until the end. I'm sure going to miss him.

I have friends in Montana who are always waiting for me to come back, especially to give them a little instrument training, instrument dual. They don't have an instrument instructor in Miles City. They always let me use the airplane any time I want. I never charge anybody for it.

Rural Montana hasn't changed much. Charles Redman, my friend with whom I used to spend a lot of time, still has his family's ranch. Their two sons-in-law run it for them. They just moved into Miles City a few years ago; bought a little house and got off the ranch. So they were out there a long time on that ranch. Charles is the same age that I am. Sadly, Charles' wife, Kate, passed away in 2009.

Charles and Kate Redman, 1994. I spent many fun days with Charles, teaching everything on their ranch to fly—especially his mother's geese. We thought the geese liked it, and were sure the dog enjoyed helping us get them into the air.

There's a restaurant called the Airport Inn that looks right down the valley at Miles City. It sits high above Miles City on the north side. It's about two hundred feet above the valley; you can look down and see the Yellowstone River, and the whole valley.

I gave the owner of the restaurant, Tom Pettigrew, flying lessons. There is an Air Coupe mounted above his restaurant. We used to go fishing all the time. There were about four of us who would go. We caught trout, or pike, and brought them back to the Airport Inn, where the chef fixed us a dinner of nice, fresh fish.

The owner's wife, Earlene, is still there every day, and his daughter and son-in-law run the Airport Inn. All the way around on the inside are pictures of airplanes, including one of the 747.

Air Coupe mounted above the Airport Inn in Miles City. I gave
the owner, Tom Pettigrew, a fishing buddy of mine, flying lessons.

So many people still call me Jackie. I was never called that in
school; I was always just Jack. But when I got to flying, fourteen
years old—and these other guys were forty or fifty—they all called
me Jackie. Then when I came with Pan Am, they all called me
Jackie. Johnnie Amundsen's two sons—one flew 747s for TWA and
the other is a minister—they call me Jackie.

I was talking to Shawn the other night. He was wondering how
much flight time I had. I said, "You know, Shawn, I don't know. My
original log books were burned up in the fire at the hangar. And I
started some log books, but lots of times I didn't have them with me
when I was working with my friends.

"I gave a lot of duals for all those years, and I never charged
them a dime—because I know that that was all I had to pay for
when I was flying. I was loading and unloading forty-ton box cars
over at my dad's mill in order to pay for flight instructors."

I hope you have enjoyed some of my flying stories as much as
I enjoyed the flying. Any time I was asked what I did for a living, I

had to tell them I have never had a real job; I got paid for my hobby. Pan Am was always fantastic to work for. It never seemed like a large company, with its four divisions, different domiciles and even a crew base in London.

Also, as I've said, Pan Am always bought a lot of new airplanes like the 707 and 747. I got to fly the 747 my last ten years with Pan Am, and got to instruct on both of them. The instructing was fun because of the unusual pilots Pan Am hired. I had quite a few of the Blue Angels pilots that came with Pan Am when they got out of the navy.

Such a group of sharp gentlemen they were. They were all excellent pilots; but, much more than that, I am sure the navy picked them because of their personalities and as ambassadors for the navy.

It's sure nice when you can look back over your life and not really see anything that you would do differently. I had a little trouble agreeing to go to college with my dad, but he was such a gentle, quiet talker; very convincing.

Grandpa Burke fishing off our sailboat in Lake Washington.
He liked to troll while we sailed.

"Full circle": The airplanes I flew with Pan Am from 1942 until
my retirement in 1982, on the wall of my office. Military leave
during WWII: flew Navy R4D in Aleutians; Pan Am military
contract, Korean War DC-4 & Vietnam War 707; Fairchild
Pilgrim, Alaska 1942 & 1943; Lockheed-10 Electra, Alaska 1943;
Boeing 314 "Flying Boat," New York-to-London, 1944; Lockheed
Loadstar, Alaska 1946; Douglas DC-3, Alaska 1947;

Douglas DC-4, Alaska 1950; Douglas DC-6, Alaska & Honolulu;
Boeing 707 cockpit with Dalmatian crew; Douglas DC-4
(first four-engine passenger flight to Fairbanks); Boeing 377
Stratocruiser, Seattle-Alaska-Honolulu; Douglas DC-7C, Seattle-
Alaska-Honolulu and around-the-world flights; Boeing 747 &
747 SP on ramps at Everett, WA and Sydney, Australia; Piper J3,
coyote pelts shot in Southeast Montana.

When I started flying, there was no place where you could really learn anything about it. The colleges didn't have any courses; there was nothing. Nobody was hiring; there were no pilot jobs.

I was discouraged in my early years because it seemed that I was always too young for most openings and age limits, but it turned out to be in my favor when the aviation industry began to boom during World War Two and after the war.

I look back over my seventy-five years of flying and always have the same thoughts: how lucky I was to be born during the most wonderful fifty years of aviation development. My first Pan Am airplane was a single-engine that didn't weigh much and carried eight passengers at about 90 mph. My last ten years I flew a Boeing 747 that carried 500 passengers at 600 mph, had a takeoff weight of a million pounds and could fly nonstop from Los Angeles to Sydney, Australia.

The four engines were 50,000 horsepower each, a total of 200,000 horsepower. When I advanced those four throttles I always thought about my first airplane, an Aeronca C-3 with a three-cylinder, 36-horsepower engine.

You just can't believe the 747 could be so advanced and complicated as it is, and still so dependable and easy to fly. It's also hard to believe the great changes and improvements in the aviation industry that took place in about 35 years. I doubt we'll see changes like those in aviation in the next forty years.

It sure did work out. And there again, it was all luck. If World War Two hadn't come along, aviation never would have started to grow the way it did. There they were, flying single-engine, eight-passenger airplanes—United and Northwest. The industry hadn't changed any since World War I.

So that's how we were flying in the bush up there in Alaska. When we got the DC-3s, that was a big airplane, two engines. Then we got the DC-4. It was bigger, with four engines, but it still wasn't pressurized. It wasn't until we got the DC-6 that you could cruise at 25,000 feet, above the ice and mountains.

For any of you that are a little nervous when you fly, I can honestly tell you that the most dangerous part of your trip is the drive to the airport. This was not true when I started flying. They had no instruments, radios, radar, accurate weather reporting or dependable engines.

It's been a great life, and I wouldn't change a thing. I bid those round-the-world trips because I really enjoyed the flying, going to all the different countries. But every time I came home to the Pacific Northwest, I thanked my lucky stars that I had this to come home to.

I hadn't seen anyplace on those round-the-worlds that I would want to be. It seemed to me like they were deteriorating all the time; and, as time went on, they definitely did. I was sure happy to get back in the good old USA.

I did have one rough landing, however. I fell and broke the ball right off the top of my hip bone on August 7, 2009—my 87th birthday. I just fell against one of these big rocks out here, turning the water off in the pouring down rain. I learned enough in my three-plus years of med school to know that I couldn't move, and I was not going to move.

So I laid right there in that rain for an hour until Shawn came home. I told him, "Shawn, I broke my hip and my ankle, so we want to make sure that we get an aid car here, along with a regular ambulance."

So they did. They came and they fastened a brace on it. I don't remember getting settled in the hospital at all. All I wanted to know was if Dr. Barronian was there. I wanted to have him, because he worked on my ankle ten years earlier. They said that he was out of town, but his partner was there.

I never met the doctor. They kept me doped for three days. Finally this fellow came in and said, "I'm Dr. Clark. Boy, when you do it, you sure do a nice job. That ball was broken off just as if I'd sawn it off myself. So I pinned it back on."

It was very unusual. Usually it's more mangled. But the end of that bone did chew up the muscle pretty badly. That's what's taking the time to heal. But I had never been in the hospital before.

They kept me there for a week in the big hospital. They have a rehab hospital close by, and it was excellent. Since they built all those new buildings and have all that new equipment, they have Swedish in there with them.

I still have 20-20 vision in one eye, but I have some macular degeneration in the other. Until recently, they haven't been able to do much for macular degeneration. Some of those little veins rupture and spill over into your eye.

After I noticed a black spot in one eye, I went right in to see the eye doctor. All he does is the back of the eye: the macula, where all the blood vessels and nerves are. A little vein was leaking into my eye. He said, "I can fix that one real quick." So he put me in the other room where he had a little laser.

He said that it wouldn't scar, except for that one spot. And he stopped it; it didn't grow any more. I went over every week for a couple of months. He wanted to make sure there wasn't something else breaking loose in there. Luckily, the black spot has thinned out; it has dissipated, so that I can actually see through all but just the very center of it. The doctor said he had never seen anything improve like this.

So that black spot is getting thinner all the time. It has been several years, but it has taken that long. My vision in the other eye stays 20-20, so I don't have any trouble passing my flight check.

All in all, we've had a good life. I've been lucky; just awful lucky—in everything I've done. I started flying when I was fourteen years old, and my mind was made up to keep flying, if at all possible. I have now been flying for more than 74 years, and am still flying at 88, and plan to continue.

My good friend Ralph Savory, our Chief Pilot for Pan Am for many years, has always been my inspiration and goal to shoot for. He turned 100 years old in October, 2009 and renewed his California driver's license for another five years. I hope to do the same, and keep my pilot's license current also.

Writing this book—I wasn't interested at all. But Scotty and the kids kept bugging me and bugging me. My son and daughter have asked me for a long time to write my memoirs.

My relatives have been encouraging me to write my 'life story' for fifty years. And I would say, "Aw, nobody wants to hear those stories. So many pilots have written books that just brag about themselves, you know. I don't need one of those."

I hope you have found something to enjoy in the book. I never planned to tell about my seventy-five years of flying, but three good friends talked me into it by promising that I would not have to do any writing, just tell my story to their tape recorders.

I have a very good friend, Ian Briscoe, my accountant and financial advisor, who enjoys my stories at lunch. He was the main catalyst for this book. Ian has a good friend, Jerry Robinson, publisher of the Highline Times, who tells us we should do this so the grandsons will know what grandpa really did when all he says is that he never had a job—just got paid for his hobbies. That is still how I honestly feel.

I also would like to thank correspondent Charlie Ganong for converting my stories and photographs into the book you are holding in your hands. I sure appreciate the work, expertise and encouragement that these three provided. I know my family is happy that they finally got what they have been asking me for for so many years.

As I've said, the only flying book I ever really enjoyed was *God Is My Co-Pilot*. And I sure used Him a lot. That was a good book, and it makes a lot of sense. Because there are times that you get caught in stuff that you have no control over.

It's been a great life. It is true: I've never had a job; I felt I was getting paid for my hobby. And it was just so much fun because I was able to fly those airplanes. I never scratched a plane—and I hunted coyotes.

ACKNOWLEDGEMENTS

THE author is grateful to the following people and organizations for their help in creating this book:

Montana historian Mary Haughian and her book, *Home on the Range—Recipes and Stories from Montana*, 1981, for information and images of Scotty's mother, Nonie Trafton, providing "meals on wheels" to the Milwaukee Railroad crews.

Laura Heller and the staff of the Dickinson Research Center, National Cowboy and Western Museum, Oklahoma City, for their assistance in locating and using images of rodeo legend Bob Askin.

Pat Burke Gudmundson, Gene Etchart and Orval Markle, whose 1998 book, *A Flying Start into the Big Sky*, has greatly helped preserve the history and spirit—and rekindle the memories—of the "early days" of flying in Montana.

The Foynes Flying Boat Museum in Ireland, for preserving the heritage of this remarkable airplane with a full-scale replica, and for providing the images of the 314 used in this book.

The Boeing Company, for building airplanes as majestic and elegant as the 314 flying boats, as rugged and durable as the 707, and as sleek and sophisticated as the 747. They all were a pleasure to fly.

John Little, Amy Heidrick and the staff of the Boeing Museum of Flight for their help locating and using the images of Charles Lindbergh, Tex Johnston and the Boeing 314 Flying Boats, and for other timely research assistance and suggestions.

The folks at Selfpublishing, Inc., whose patience, expertise and commitment to excellence helped propel *A Life Aloft* from the drafting table and drawing board to an "airworthy" finished product, and a "safe and happy landing" in the hands of the readers.

The Range Riders Museum in Miles City, Montana for helping to preserve and honor the memories of those who created the world, values and way of life which nurtured my youth, and which remain with me to this day.

Hap and Donna Holdtrop, for patiently and promptly answering all of my questions related to Pan Am's early routes and planes in Alaska, and for coordinating and organizing all of the local Pan Am reunions and gatherings.

Finally, Pan American Airlines and the Pan Am Historical Society, for the use of several photos and other materials, and for maintaining the archives, displays and forums needed to perpetuate the memories and legacy of the great Clipper ships, those who sailed them across the skies, and the millions of lives around the world that were enriched by this great company.